"How could I have believed your lies?"

"I did not lie to you, except—"

"How could I have lain with you? How could I have loved you?" The tears Catlyn had held at bay slid down her cheeks.

Ross grabbed hold of her shoulders. "We nearly burned down the night with our loving. You cannot think that was a lie."

Her eyes bright with loathing, her voice cold, she said, "I think you are a skilled lover and an even more skilled manipulator of people. You used me to try to gain control of Kennecraig."

Ross groaned. "If you would only let me tell you the whole story, I—"

"Oh, you are very good at that... ̲ ̲ ̲ ̲ ̲ ̲ ̲ ̲ ̲nd things to suit you." She stepp̲ ̲ ̲ ̲ ̲ ̲ ̲ ̲ ̲o. "But now I am wise to yo̲ ̲ ̲ ̲ ̲ ̲ ̲ ̲ ̲not succeed."

Dear Reader,

Heroes come in many forms, as this month's books prove—from the roguish knight and the wealthy marquess to the potent gunslinger and the handsome cowboy.

The roguish knight, Ross Lion Sutherland, appears in *Taming the Lion,* a new medieval novel by Suzanne Barclay. Critics have described this award-winning author in many ways, including "a great superstar," "a magician with words" and "one of the best authors today in historical romance!" In this continuation of THE SUTHERLAND SERIES, Ross sets aside his honor to steal a clan's secret for whiskey-making, only to fall in love with the clan's lovely leader.

Golden Heart winner Julia Justiss brings us Nicholas Stanhope, the devastatingly handsome Marquess of Englemere who marries a friend in trouble and finds a profound love in *The Wedding Gamble.* And you *must* meet Sheriff Delaney, the smooth but kindhearted ex-gunslinger who inherits a house—and a beautiful young widow—in *The Marriage Knot.*

Rounding out the month is Will Brockett, the magnetically charming wrangler who uncharacteristically finds his soul mate in tomboy Paulie Johnson in *A Cowboy's Heart* by Liz Ireland. Don't miss it!

Whatever your tastes in reading, you'll be sure to find a romantic journey back to the past between the covers of a Harlequin Historicals® novel.

Sincerely,

Tracy Farrell
Senior Editor

Please address questions and book requests to:
Harlequin Reader Service
U.S.: 3010 Walden Ave., P.O. Box 1325, Buffalo, NY 14269
Canadian: P.O. Box 609, Fort Erie, Ont. L2A 5X3

Suzanne Barclay

Taming the Lion

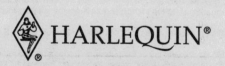

HARLEQUIN®

TORONTO • NEW YORK • LONDON
AMSTERDAM • PARIS • SYDNEY • HAMBURG
STOCKHOLM • ATHENS • TOKYO • MILAN • MADRID
PRAGUE • WARSAW • BUDAPEST • AUCKLAND

ISBN 0-373-29063-2

TAMING THE LION

Copyright © 1999 by Carol Suzanne Backus

This edition published by arrangement with Harlequin Books S.A.

® and TM are trademarks of the publisher. Trademarks indicated with
® are registered in the United States Patent and Trademark Office, the
Canadian Trade Marks Office and in other countries.

Look us up on-line at: http://www.romance.net

Printed in U.S.A.

Books by Suzanne Barclay

Harlequin Historicals

*_Knight Dreams_ #141
*_Knight's Lady_ #162
*_Knight's Honor_ #184
†_Lion's Heart_ #252
†_Lion of the North_ #272
†_Lion's Legacy_ #304
*_Knight's Ransom_ #335
*_Knights Divided_ #359
*_Knight's Rebellion_ #391
†_Lion's Lady_ #411
†_Pride of Lions_ #443
†_Taming the Lion_ #463

* The Sommerville Brothers
† The Sutherland Series

SUZANNE BARCLAY

considers herself sublimely lucky to be writing historical romances. What other career would allow her to watch old Errol Flynn movies and call it research? Or daydream and call it work?

On those rare moments when she can tear herself away from the stories she is creating, she enjoys walking in the woods with her two dogs, Max and Duffy, whipping up exotic meals for her husband of twenty-three years and pawing through the local antique marts for special pieces to decorate her office/study.

Suzanne freely admits that she has trouble keeping track of all the Sutherlands and Carmichaels who people her stories, and has prepared an updated family tree detailing the various characters, their marriages and their children. To receive a copy, send a large SASE to: Suzanne Barclay, P.O. Box 92054, Rochester, NY 14692.

Prologue

Stirling, Scotland
August 10, 1407

Hakon Fergusson paused in the doorway of the Running Fox. Squinting against the pall of smoke from the torches rimming the long room, he surveyed the establishment with a critical eye.

The tavern appeared to be a cut above the others he had visited tonight. The benches and tables sat in orderly rows, scarred from use but lacking the layers of filth tolerated by drunken patrons and careless owners. The serving wenches who moved through the crowded room dispensing food and drink were comely, their gowns snug but not slatternly.

Lastly Hakon studied the customers themselves. Though it was just past nine on a Saturday night and every table was occupied, it was a remarkably orderly crowd. At the nearest table, four men amiably argued the merits of chain mail over boiled leather vests. Six others sat before the empty hearth, their heads bent over a game board. Elsewhere, men drank and laughed and talked in civil tones. Torchlight winked on golden jewelry and shimmered on garments of silk and velvet.

Clearly these were men who appreciated the best. And would be willing to pay for it.

"This is the place," Hakon murmured to the man behind him.

"'Bout time." Seamus shifted the whiskey keg on his shoulder. "This damn thing's heavy. Don't see why we couldn't have sold it at the first inn."

"We can get more here." Hakon needed every coin he could lay his hands on if his plans were to succeed.

Four months ago, he had received the pleasant news that his uncle and two cousins had died after eating tainted meat at a truce day feast hosted by the church, leaving him heir to a Highland estate. Hakon thought it a sad end for a Fergusson. All the male members of his Border branch of the clan—and a few of the women besides—had died with swords in their hands or dangling at the end of the hangman's rope.

Still the idea of having his own tower, even if it meant leaving the rough and ready Borders he loved, had appealed. Especially since at the time, the Border Warden had Hakon high on his list of men to be caught and hanged. So Hakon had gathered his band of hardened fighters, thumbed his nose at Lord Hunter Carmichael and headed north.

To say the inheritance was a disappointment was a vast understatement. Dun-Dubh consisted of one broken-down keep, a few acres of stony ground and two hundred hungry mouths. Hakon had been all for selling off what he could: his relatives' clothes, furniture and the like, abandoning the two hundred unwanted burdens and taking his men back to the Borders. He'd changed his mind when he'd learned that the neighboring Boyds possessed a prosperous distillery.

Unfortunately, Thomas Boyd had proved to be more tenacious and far cannier at holding on to what was his than any other victim Hakon had tried to best. Months of planning and scheming it had taken him to get this far. With any luck, he'd come away from the Running Fox with the wherewithal to win.

"Well, let us see how much we can get for the Boyds' whiskey." Hakon pasted on a genial smile and entered the tavern. Curbing his usual swagger, he walked with the cautious air of a merchant offering wares to a new client.

He approached the long wooden serving bar and hailed the man behind it. "Would you be Brann of the Side?" His tone was respectful but not groveling.

"Aye. Who's asking?" Brann's fleshy face folded into a series of frowns as he looked Hakon over. He had a barrel chest, thick arms and the sharp eyes of a tradesman.

"Robert Dunbar." The lie came easily to a man who often found his own name too infamous. "I heard ye have the finest tavern in Stirling."

"That it is." Brann's chest puffed out.

"Oh, I could not agree more." Hakon looked about the room and sang its praises. Chuckling to himself, he watched Brann relax, completely taken in by the act. Da would be proud of him, Hakon thought. The thieving old bastard who had sired him had always said Hakon's looks were his greatest weapon. He was tall and blond with pleasing features and brown eyes he had trained to hide his thoughts.

"This yer first visit to town?" Brann asked.

He took them for bumpkins. That made Hakon smile. Before setting out tonight, he'd taken pains with his appearance, choosing a blue tunic and black hose that had belonged to his dead uncle *because* they were a trifle small and patched at the knees and elbows. They were the garments of a poor man who prided himself on neatness. In them, he looked sober and honest. Just the sort of man other men trusted. "Aye, first time."

"Well, ye'll find that taverns like this are a bit, er, more expensive than the ones down under the hill."

What grated on Hakon was the knowledge that his uncle's mean castoffs were better than his own few garments. Looking about at the finely clad nobles, he vowed that when the Boyds' distillery was his, he'd buy a dozen velvet tunics.

"What'll it be? Ale? Wine?" Brann asked.

"Actually, I've something here I'd like you to try." Hakon motioned Seamus forward, took the keg and set it on the bar.

Brann eyed it as he might a pile of manure. "I've got my own sources for ale and—"

"Whiskey."

"That, too," Brann growled. "My customers are particular."

Which was exactly why Hakon had chosen this place. Particular people paid more. "So am I. What I offer is of the highest quality. The finest whiskey in all Scotland."

"They all say that." But Brann licked his lips and glanced at the keg again.

"Would you like to taste it?"

Brann shrugged. "I dunno."

"Perhaps your customers would sample it, as well." Hakon smiled genially, hiding his annoyance and impatience. In order for his plans to succeed, he needed money for arms and bribes.

"How much will it cost me?" Brann asked.

"Nothing for a taste. If your customers like the whiskey and want more, I've ten more kegs I will sell you."

"Ten is not many."

It was all Thomas Boyd had with him at the time he'd been unlucky enough to wander into Hakon's ambush. "I've more at home." Or rather, the Boyds did. All Hakon had to do was figure out how to wrest it from them. "If we reach an agreeable price, I can send ye regular shipments."

"Seems fair enough."

Hakon smiled. He always seemed fair. And open. And honest. The guise had lured more than one victim into his web.

"If yer man'll tap the keg," Brann said.

Hakon glanced at Seamus. The wiry little man had ridden with his father. He was adept at many things—spying, tracking, thieving and slitting the occasional throat—but the only way he'd ever broached a keg was with the edge of an ax. "It's yer tavern, Master Brann. We'll leave that to ye."

Brann nodded, pulled a small metal hook from beneath the bar and expertly drew the bung. Keeping one eye on them, he bent and sniffed suspiciously. He straightened so quickly it was comical, his eyes wide with astonishment and new respect.

"Well?" Hakon asked.

"It smells right promising. The subtle blend of smoke and fire." Fumbling in his haste, Brann poured a measure into a wooden cup, lifted it and breathed deep. "Ah." Reverently he sipped. His eyes closed. His head tipped back to let the liquid run down his throat. He sighed again.

Got him, Hakon thought, winking at Seamus.

Master Brann slowly lowered the cup and opened his eyes. "It is, er, not too bad," he murmured, obviously a man used to bargaining. "Ye did say my customers could try a measure?"

Hakon nodded. "Just a sip, mind."

While Brann called for cups and fussed over the keg, Hakon and Seamus moved away from the bar and leaned against the wall.

"A Fergusson giving something away?" Seamus shook his head. "Yer da's likely spinning in his grave."

"Nay, he'd understand. Master Brann will pay twice what we ask if his customers are clamoring for the stuff."

Seamus grunted and crossed his arms over his narrow chest. "So we sell the lot for a tidy profit, then what?"

"We bribe someone inside Kennecraig to tell us if Thomas spoke true about having black powder kegs tied to his stills." Ready to be set off if Hakon attacked the keep.

"He was lying. What fool would blow up his whole tower to stop us from getting it?"

"A desperate one." Last month, Thomas Boyd had died a horrible death rather than surrender Kennecraig to Hakon.

"And the Boyds will be even more cautious now their laird's gone." Hakon was certain they blamed him, even though he had gone to considerable lengths to make Thomas's murder look accidental so as to not rouse their suspicions. "Damn, I wish Guthrie had controlled himself. Thomas was worth more alive than dead."

"Yer lad's got his grandsire's taste for killing, that's sure," Seamus said with a hint of awe.

"Killing Thomas was damned inconvenient. With him as a hostage, we'd have gotten inside Kennecraig slick as ye please."

"Aye, but we'll win. They've got a lass leading them now."

Hakon grunted. Catlyn of Kennecraig might be only a lass, but she had thus far proved to be no weak-willed miss. When Hakon had ridden over to offer sympathy and protection for her now leaderless clan, the little witch had stood atop her walls and denounced him as a murderer. She had loudly rejected Guthrie as a potential husband, though how she had chanced to hear about the maid he had carved up in Doune Town, was a mystery. She had ended her tirade by threatening to blow up the stills Hakon coveted if he tried to attack the keep.

"Damn." Hakon spit on the floor. "Who'd think a Fergusson could be kept at bay by a lass and a clan of distillers."

"Our time will come. Ye'll think of something. Some plan."

"Aye, but what? Catlyn Boyd'll not let a Fergusson within a mile of her gates. And I do mean to have those stills." Just thinking of the piles of gold they'd bring made his palms itch.

The door to the tavern opened, and a group of men spilled in, bringing fresh damp air and cheery laughter.

Hakon's lip curled. They were just the sort he despised. Young, handsome and well dressed. Sprigs off some noble bough, wearing their arrogance as naturally as their velvets and silks.

"Dod!" Seamus exclaimed.

"What is it?"

"I recognized one of them. The tall one with the black hair and the pretty face."

Hakon picked him out of the jovial crowd. Taller than the rest, with impossibly broad shoulders, his glossy black hair swept back from a face too perfect to be believed. Apparently the maids thought so, too, for they fell all over themselves making the man and his companions welcome.

"Who is he?"

"Ross Lion Sutherland."

"Hunter Carmichael's nephew?" Hakon hissed.

"Aye. Young Ross is not a man ye'd forget. I saw him from a distance at Keastwicke when I went to claim yer da's body."

Hakon stiffened, hatred curdling low in his belly. Hunter had not killed Aedh Fergusson, but he had led the retaliatory raid that had ended in Aedh's death. And the Warden had been a thorn in Clan Fergusson's side from the day he'd taken the post. Righteous bastard, always ranting on about peace on the Borders. Thanks to his patrols, it became nigh impossible for a man to conduct a successful raid or lift a head of cattle. Why, Hunter and his ilk had practically starved the Fergussons to death.

Through narrowed eyes, Hakon watched as a trio of chattering maids led the newcomers to a table at the far side of the room. His hatred congealed as he studied Ross Sutherland's handsome, laughing face. There he sat like a bloody king, ordering food and drink, patting the maids on the cheek and pressing coins into their palms.

"It would be a pleasure to bring that lordling down," Hakon murmured.

"Want I should kill him?" Seamus fingered his dirk.

Hakon shook his head slowly. Unlike his father and his son, Hakon had never found death a satisfactory form of punishment. Death was too final. But if someone who had wronged you could be made to suffer…

Ah, that was the best form of revenge.

"Well, he's got a way with the lassies, that's sure." Seamus grinned wistfully. "There's not a one of them wouldn't sell her soul to end up in his bed tonight. Providing he stays sober enough to satisfy her. Looks like he's taken a fancy to our whiskey and is trying to buy—"

"Master Robert." Brann bustled up, his face alight with greed. "Lord Ross would like to buy a keg. A whole keg. He and his men have been coming in here for a week, and he always pays in coin. If we can fix a price…"

"I am sure we can." Hakon looked at Ross and nodded.

Lord Ross wore the easy smile and slightly bored expression of a man well used to getting whatever he wanted. A man who likely indulged in the usual vices: women, drink, gaming.

Vices were something Hakon understood, and used.

Excitement stirred in Hakon's blood, and an idea began to take shape in his fertile mind. A plan that would use Ross Sutherland's looks to good advantage and make him suffer into the bargain. "Donald, fetch the rest of the kegs."

"Donald?" Seamus blinked, the recalled that he was Donald Dunbar while they were in Stirling. "Oh, aye." He scurried out of the tavern, grinning like a fool.

Hakon had a plan! And it was bound to succeed, because Hakon was a deucedly clever bastard. Ask anyone who had ever run afoul of one of Hakon's schemes.

Chapter One

Kennecraig Keep, Scotland
August 17, 1407

Thunder rumbled across the broad-shouldered Grampian Mountains and down the narrow cleft that was Finglas Glen. As it collided with the walls of the keep set on the lip of the glen, the low, ominous roll accented the drama unfolding in the chamber beneath the keep.

The tasting of the *uisge beatha.*

The water of life.

The life's blood of Clan Boyd.

Clad in a gown of virgin white wool, her honey-colored hair falling free to her waist, Catlyn Boyd stepped into the high-ceilinged room. This was the moment she had trained for nearly all her life. Her palms were slick from nerves, but the anticipation she should have felt was clouded by sorrow.

"Papa," she whispered. "You were taken from us too soon." Sweet Mary, how she missed him, the patience with which he'd answered her hundreds of questions over the years, the wisdom he had unstintingly shared with her, the courage he'd shown in insisting she be named heir after her brother died.

"I need you, Papa, now more than ever."

Silently she scanned the room, gathering what strength she could from the familiar. It was not a large chamber, measuring twenty feet by twenty, but rich in history. On the walls hung the tapestries woven by her mother, her grandmother and so on back for six generations. Two stone columns supported the vaulted ceiling from which hung an iron wheel set with a dozen tallow candles. The light gleamed softly on the only piece of furniture, an oaken table nigh as old as the keep. In its center sat an heirloom of even greater age. The chalice.

The tiny scallop shells on the base were white and worn smooth from use. The bowl formed of rock crystal was so clear the torchlight passed right through the dark amber liquid in it. Centuries ago, a restless ancestor, Henri of the Boyd, had returned from trading in the Mediterranean with the chalice and the recipe for distilling spirits from grain. Each succeeding generation of Boyds had improved upon the original.

Family pride and a sense of destiny filled her as her eyes moved from the chalice to the kinsmen assembled in the golden circle of light. Each man was here because tradition dictated it, and because he had a stake in the whiskey's making. Roland the brew master's narrow face was tight with anxiety. If the whiskey was found lacking, he could lose the position held by his father and his father before that. His son and apprentice, Wesley, grinned at her with the confidence of youth. Gordie the cooper stared at the small keg on the floor beside the table, grateful, no doubt, to see it did not leak.

Lastly Catlyn looked at Adair, the craggy-faced captain who was mentor to her as he'd been friend to her father.

Oh, Papa. Pain squeezed tight in her chest. Even after a month, it was hard to accept the fact that he was gone, the bluff, generous man who had guided her steps as a babe and taught her the craft when fate decreed she would succeed him.

"'Tis time, lass," Adair said gently. In his level brown eyes she saw grief held at bay by the prod of duty.

Catlyn nodded, took a steadying breath and moved to the table. Without hesitation, she lifted the chalice and let the pungent fumes waft up her nose. Strong and so sharp they nearly stole her breath. Just as it should be for whiskey that was only a year old. She had been bred and raised for this, educated in the ways of marrying barley mash and fire while other lasses learned needlework and housework.

It was time to put theory into practice.

The cool liquid burned in her mouth. She tilted her head, let it slide achingly down her throat to set her belly afire. The heat lingered on her tongue then receded. In its wake subtle nuances tickled the back of her pallet. Earth and smoke and fire. Intriguing, but it was the underlying hint of sweetness that soothed away the sting and demanded to be sampled again.

"How can ye tell if it's fit?" demanded Roland, scowling.

Catlyn jerked, swallowed a second sip too quickly and choked, something she had not done since she'd had her first taste at age five or so.

"That strong, is it?" Adair plucked the cup from her hand and clapped her on the back.

"Whiskey's a man's drink," grumbled Roland. "Laird Thomas should have left one of us in charge of the stills."

The implication that she was not fit to succeed her father dried Catlyn's tears and brought her chin up. "I worked by Papa's side from the time I could walk."

"Watching and doing's two different things." Old Roland filled a plain horn cup and drank. The others, even Catlyn, held their breath. "It'll do," he growled.

Wesley let out a whoop and grabbed up a cup of his own. He filled and drained it, then sucked in air. "Dod," he wheezed, eyes round and wet. "It fair steals yer breath, it does."

"Just as it should." Roland took the cup. "And ye'll be showing more respect for my brew, not swilling it like a drunken sailor in a dockside alehouse."

"Aye, Da."

"Best in several years, I'd say." Adair took another sip, rolled it on his tongue, then swallowed.

"And why not? Laird Thomas knew what he was about. Had the touch, he did. And experience." Roland looked down his hooked nose at Catlyn, clearly hinting she lacked both.

"I know I am young," Catlyn said, her gaze meeting each man's in turn. "But Papa said I had the nose and pallet."

"Ye'll need more than that if ye're to keep Hakon Fergusson from taking everything we've got," Roland said darkly.

Adair glared at the brew master. "Kennecraig has never been taken, and it won't be while I've breath in my body."

"Brave words. Laird Thomas said much the same when Hakon came sniffing around. Look where he is," Roland muttered.

"Dead," Wesley whispered.

Catlyn shivered, fighting sorrow and fear. "We have Hakon over a barrel. He cannot attack for fear we will destroy the distillery and the whiskey he covets."

"He's stymied for the moment," Roland allowed. "But—"

"Papa said he was the sort of bully who expects his victims to roll over and give him what he wants. When he sees he cannot best us, he will go off in search of easier prey."

Roland grunted. "Well, last year's whiskey is ready for the kegs and the four-year-old is ready for market. But how will we get it there with Hakon lurking about like an evil spider?"

"That is my worry," said Adair. "If we had the coin, I would hire mercenaries to guard the shipment."

"We are over a barrel of our own. Till we sell some of the Finglas, we've no money. Not even for food, and God knows if we do not get supplies soon, we will all starve and save Hakon the trouble of attacking the keep." Roland looked almost pleased.

Did he want her to fail so badly he wished them all ill? Catlyn wondered. The weight on her shoulders felt even heavier, yet she dared not show any weakness. "I will find a way to—"

A knock sounded at the door. For a stunned instant, they all looked at one another. It must be something important to interrupt the sacred ceremony.

Adair scowled, then went to open it a crack, revealing Eoin's handsome face. "I told you that you were not welcome here," Adair growled.

Catlyn's former betrothed lifted his chin. "There's a party of men at the gate seeking shelter from the storm."

"Fergussons," Roland whispered. The word echoed ominously off the stone walls.

"Nay," Eoin said quickly. "They are travelers. I think—"

"No one cares what you think," Adair snapped.

Catlyn laid a hand on her captain's arm. He could not forgive Eoin for supposedly breaking her heart, but this bickering divided them when they most needed to pull together. "Thank you for bringing word, Eoin. I'll come see for myself."

Up the steps from the distillery she went, down the dimly lit corridor and out into the courtyard. The wind tugged at her skirts and whipped her hair about, carrying with it the damp promise of rain. Overhead, thunder rumbled and lightning raked through a sea of bilious gray clouds.

"Best hurry before you get wet," Eoin advised. He trotted along beside her like a faithful hound.

Nay, not faithful. He had betrayed her with the woman

who had once been her dearest friend. Despite her best efforts, Catlyn could neither forgive nor forget their treachery. Dora had accepted this and stayed out of Catlyn's way as much as possible. Perversely, Eoin seemed determined to win her back.

"Careful, the steps are steep." He reached to help her up the stairs of the guardhouse.

Catlyn neatly avoided his grasp. "I have been climbing them all my life," she said through clenched teeth. Clinging to the wall with one hand, she battled through the wind to the top of the tower. Looking down, she spied a group of men huddled in the lee of the gate. "Oh, dear, we must do something."

"We cannot let them in," Adair said.

"I know, but Papa is doubtless spinning in his grave to see us turn travelers away in such weather."

"If we let them in and they prove to be Fergussons, we'll be moldering in *our* graves," Adair reminded her.

At her other side, Eoin snorted. "What Fergusson ever dressed so fine? That's chain mail they're wearing under their cloaks, and the leader has full armor."

"They are mercenaries, then," said Adair.

"Hakon couldn't afford to buy one man, much less—"

"He could if he pledged to pay them after he'd gotten his hands on our distillery," Adair growled.

Eoin stuck his handsome face into Adair's weathered one. "Lot you know, old man. Mercenaries want coin, not promises."

"Hush, the both of you. I cannot think what to do with you ripping at each other." Catlyn returned her gaze to the man who had hailed them moments ago. Ross Sutherland was the name he had given Eoin when he sought shelter for his band. He claimed they were travelers lost on their way to Inverness.

In defiance of the biting wind, Ross Sutherland sat straight in the saddle, controlling his restive mount with ease. His face was raised expectantly toward the gatehouse window where Catlyn stood, but there was nothing of the supplicant in his pose. Arrogant, he was, from the tilt of his head to the stubborn set of his square jaw. The rest of his face was hidden in the shadows cast by his visor, but she knew his eyes would be as dark and imperious as his bearing.

"Not Fergussons," Eoin said. "I say we send someone down to look them over closely and—"

"You get no say," Adair snapped.

Eoin flushed. His eyes—the big brown ones that had looked so sincere all the while he lied about giving her a lifetime of love and devotion—slid to Catlyn. "The decision is yours."

She resisted the urge to slump beneath this latest burden. "We cannot afford to let them inside. If they were fewer." Five and twenty, she'd counted. True there were one hundred men of fighting age under her roof, but...

"I know it pains your tender heart to leave them to the elements." Eoin laid a hand on her arm. "Let me go down and speak with them, see if I can learn their intent."

Catlyn extracted her arm from his grasp. Once his touch had made her blood warm with possibilities. That was before she had learned Eoin had been warming Dora's bed all the while he'd been courting her. "'Tis a kindly offer, but if they captured you—"

"Good riddance," Adair grumbled. He'd been all for tossing Eoin out for breaking Catlyn's heart.

Catlyn scowled at her captain. "If they took Eoin, we'd be forced to bargain with them." Pleasant as it was to think of life without Eoin trailing after her.

"Hello the keep!" shouted Ross Sutherland.

Catlyn whipped back to the window and opened her mouth.

"We cannot let you in," Adair leaned out and bellowed.

"Not very Christian of you."

"A man's gotta look to his own."

"We mean you no harm."

"The world is full of liars." Adair glanced at Eoin.

A rumble of thunder cut off Sutherland's reply. A few fat raindrops began to fall from the darkening sky.

Catlyn flinched. "A moment, sir knight," she called down, ignoring Adair's grunt of disapproval.

Ross Sutherland's mouth swept up in a smile, his teeth a slash of white in the gloom. "My thanks for your intervention, my lady. It is getting right wet."

"Oh, we cannot let you inside, but if you'll wait a moment, I'll have food and blankets lowered to you."

The smile became an angry slash. "We've blankets aplenty. Yours would no doubt soak through as quickly as ours. What we need is a roof over our heads ere this storm breaks loose."

Catlyn glanced at Adair and sighed. "I—I am sorry, Sir Ross, but we cannot." Pride made her add, "Please do not think us uncharitable, but we've a powerful enemy hereabouts and dare not take the chance that you are allied with them."

"So be it." Ross Sutherland obviously had his pride, too, for he wheeled his great horse and started down the narrow road to the plateau below.

Kennecraig Tower sat on the edge of a deep cleft in the mountain, stark and nearly unassailable. The only access to it was up this trail. Archers on the walls could send a withering stream of arrows or even hot pitch down on the attackers who must move single file up the trail. Every Boyd knew that Kennecraig could not be taken, except by treachery.

Reason enough to turn the Sutherlands away, Catlyn thought. Still she hated doing it. Cupping her hand to her mouth, she called out, "There's a thick stand of pines along river." She expected no reply and got none, but she watched them anyway.

When they reached the plateau, the troop stopped abruptly. The reason came clear, for a horde of men suddenly stepped out from behind the huge boulders rimming the plateau.

Catlyn gasped, recognizing their dark plaid with its distinctive threads of red and white. "Fergussons!" And in the fore was Hakon, of the sparse figure and long blond hair.

"Hakon's leading them." Eoin scowled. "What are they doing this close to Kennecraig?"

"They must have been waiting to attack us," said Adair. "If these Sutherlands had not spotted them—"

"Sweet Mary. You don't think Hakon will harm them."

"I do not know."

"But these men have done nothing to Hakon." Catlyn held her breath and watched the drama unfold in the gathering gloom. She saw Ross Sutherland gesture toward Kennecraig, the wind whipping his cloak back from wide shoulders as he explained their predicament. "Maybe Hakon will take the travelers back to Dun-Dubh and give them shelter."

No sooner had the words left her mouth than Hakon drew his sword. The Boyds' gasps of horror were drowned out by a sharp clap of thunder. Lightning flashed across the sky. In the spats of dark and light, the battle was joined. The Sutherlands fought valiantly, but the Fergussons were pressing them back. When the first Sutherland fell, Catlyn made her decision.

"Adair! We must do something," she cried.

"Aye. Archers to the wall!" Wheeling, Adair ran down the tower steps with a swiftness that belied his forty years. Eoin and Catlyn scrambled after him.

"What are you going to do?" she demanded, grabbing Adair's arm at the base of the steps.

"Get the Sutherlands inside if I can."

"You won't have to go out there, will you?" A hundred fears crowded her mind. Concern for her kinsmen's welfare. Terror that the Fergussons would somehow sneak inside Kennecraig.

"Aye." Already the creak of chains and gears accompanied the winching up of the portcullis whose iron bars shielded the gate. "But the archers'll cover us and see no Fergusson gets up the road. Stay inside, mind," he admonished, patting her cheek. "You'd best be ready with bandages and the like."

He was gone before Catlyn could protest. As she turned away from the gate, she nearly fell over a knot of household servants. They clung together, whimpering and shivering. Before Hakon Fergusson entered their lives, the folk of Kennecraig had not known fear or violence.

"Is it true?" asked Ulma. "Is it Hakon?" Her maid's normally ruddy face was white, her merry blue eyes stark.

"It is." Her parents had taught her that the truth, even a terrible truth, was better than a lie. "But his plans were foiled by the Sutherlands. Some of them have been wounded," she continued briskly. "We must make preparations to tend them."

"What shall we do?" a frightened voice cried.

"Dora will know what needs…" Catlyn stopped. Dora was no longer housekeeper here. Catlyn had little training in such matters. Between them, Dora and Catlyn's mother had run the keep, but Catlyn had dismissed Dora when she'd found her with Eoin, and Lady Jeannie had not been herself since Thomas died.

"Maybe we should tell Old Freda to ready her medicine chest," Ulma said gently.

"Of course." Catlyn nearly kissed the old woman. "Freda will know what should be done. Go along, all of you, and help her gather what is necessary."

Feeling grossly inadequate, Catlyn raced back up into the gatehouse. Buried beneath the grief of her father's loss and the weight of her new responsibilities, she had given little thought to who was running the keep. Tomorrow she must remedy that.

From the window, she watched Adair and a score of Boyds trot down the path. It had begun to rain in earnest now. Their weapons—swords, spears and a few fearsome Lochaber axes—shimmered in the cascading lightning. For a moment, she feared Adair planned to take her men into battle against the Fergussons, but halfway to the plateau, he halted.

"To me, Sutherlands!" Adair cried.

The battle seemed to stop as Fergussons and Sutherlands turned and looked up the mountain.

"Retreat!" Adair screamed. "Come within! We offer succor!" To punctuate the offer, he hurled a spear at the nearest Fergusson, catching the gaping man full in the chest. As he toppled off his horse, the gruesome tableau scattered.

Hakon Fergusson roared something coarse and pithy.

The Sutherlands wheeled and spurred back up the hill.

The Fergussons raced after them, swords aloft.

"Archers!" Catlyn screamed, turning to the men pressed shoulder to shoulder on the walls.

The night sky filled with arrows. Metal tips glistening against the lightning-raked sky, they arched high then fell just behind the retreating Sutherlands.

Catlyn grinned as she watched the Fergussons halt, their mouths wide with rage. Their mounts danced in agitated confusion, hooves perilously close to the edge of the ravine. "Again! Another volley," she shouted.

The second flight of arrows kept the Fergussons at bay while the Sutherlands clattered through the gate, with the Boyds streaking in just after them.

Catlyn hurried down the steps and into the courtyard looking for Adair so she might congratulate him. All was chaos: servants darting to and fro like fish in a barrel, horses pawing and shivering with latent excitement, men shouting triumphantly and clapping one another on the back.

One voice rose above the others.

Catlyn whirled around just as a man swung down from an enormous black stallion. She instantly recognized Ross Sutherland by his size and commanding air.

"God damn!" He tore off his helmet and flung it on the ground. "Ambushed. Of all the heathen deeds." Rain slicked inky hair back from a tanned face too rugged to be called handsome. Arresting, more like. Even dripping wet, he exuded strength and power, like some dark, raging beast. A wolf. Nay, a dragon.

Catlyn gaped in astonishment. She had never seen anyone remotely like this large, fierce-looking warrior. Around her, all activity ceased.

"Don't stand about like you've been struck dumb," the knight growled, voice sharp as thunder. "Gordie, go up on the wall and make certain the ambushing bastards are gone. Lang Gil, see to the horses. Nigel, take stock of our wounded."

His men scrambled to obey. The Boyds hung back. Huddled together in anxious knots, they eyed the knight as they might some strange and fearsome beast.

We never should have let him in, Catlyn thought. Out of habit, she looked for Adair. He stood a few paces away, his hand on the hilt of his sword, his worried gaze on Sir Ross.

"Who is in charge here? Who ordered the gate opened to us?" Ross Sutherland raked the crowd with narrowed eyes.

Catlyn, who had always met trouble head-on, fought an unaccustomed urge to flee.

"I am captain here." Adair stepped forward.

"Ah." Ross crossed to them in two long, determined strides. "I am indebted to you." His eyes flicked to Catlyn, then widened. "You were in the gatehouse." She'd been wrong about his eyes. They were not dark at all, but a clear, pale blue. In the flickering torchlight, he appeared even more formidable than he had in the shadows. His face was lean and rugged. His wide shoulders and broad chest strained the seams of his chain mail.

Dark, powerful and uncomfortably large.

A shiver worked its way down Catlyn's spine. Fear, she

thought. Nay, not fear, not exactly. There was an untamed quality about this knight that made her feel skittish, she who had worked alongside men all her life. "I—I am Catlyn Boyd, lady of Kennecraig," she stammered, shaky and unsettled.

"Indeed?" His unusual eyes widened and skimmed her from head to toe. Something flared in them. Something that could have been triumph or smugness or a trick of the light. "Well, I am grateful to you for letting us inside, Lady Catlyn." He purred her name, then smiled, a slow, dazzling grin that transformed his face from arresting to sinfully handsome.

Catlyn stared at him, her tongue stuck to the roof of her mouth, her mind empty.

Adair cleared his throat. "We'd best be getting inside. The rain grows worse. I'll see to your men and horses."

"I would appreciate that." Ross looked away from Catlyn, but still she found speech impossible.

"Dry clothes, hot food and the care of your wounded is the least we owe you," said Adair. "Had you not discovered him lurking at our gates, Hakon might well have attacked us the next time we ventured from our keep."

"Hakon?" The knight scowled.

"Hakon Fergusson. That is the name of the fiend who so foully ambushed you."

"Is it?" Ross Sutherland glared at the gate once more. "Fiend is an apt description. I begin to see he is more ruthless than I'd supposed." He turned away and gave orders for his men to disarm.

Catlyn started for the keep, feeling gauche and damp and a little dazed.

Ross stomped across the muddy courtyard in the wake of his reluctant hosts. So, Robert Dunbar had lied about his name. Hakon Fergusson. That name set off a distant bell in Ross's head, but his mind was so full it scarcely made a dent.

Instead, he cursed the Fates that had brought him here. And he cursed Lady Catlyn for looking younger and more beautiful than he had expected. In her pure white dress, her honey-colored hair flowing loose about her shoulders, she looked exactly right for the part she must play. The virgin sacrifice. The innocent victim of Robert Dunbar's fiendish plot.

Nay, Hakon Fergusson.

Furious with himself, but mostly with Hakon for forcing him into this, Ross glanced over his shoulder and picked out a narrow, crafty face among the familiar ones of his men.

Donald Dunbar grinned smugly. If that was his name.

Ross cursed and dropped back to walk beside the wiry man sent along, ostensibly to guide them to Kennecraig. "Are you a Fergusson, too?" he hissed.

"Aye, Seamus Fergusson's the name, but it'd doubtless be safer if ye continued to call me Donald."

What Ross wanted to do was strangle the man. "Did you know your master planned to attack us?"

"Well…" Seamus shrugged. "He said he might have to do something if yer good looks and glib tongue weren't enough to talk us inside."

"Two of my men were wounded," Ross growled.

"And a dozen Fergussons, as well."

"Serves them right. Of all the foul—"

"Got us into the keep, didn't it?"

Ross looked ahead to the litter bearing the still, bloody form of his young squire and his hatred of Hakon intensified. "Your master promised me there'd be no bloodshed."

"Aye, well, yer men are not like to die from their hurts. And *himself* is that determined to have the Boyds' fine whiskey-making secrets for himself. By the looks of things, he did well in choosing ye for the task of getting it." Seamus chuckled. "Young Catlyn was fair struck dumb by that pretty face of yers. Should be child's play for ye to pry what we need from her."

"I will get what *he* wants." Ross had no other choice. The safety of his clan was at stake. "But I will do it my way." He glared at Seamus. "And there's to be no more bloodshed."

"Like my master, I will do what is needful to win," Seamus whispered as they crested the steps and entered the keep. "He said as how I was to watch ye close like. At the first sign ye're failing, I'm to take matters into my own hands."

Chapter Two

Catlyn sat in her accustomed place beside Adair at the supper table. Her hands clenched tight in her lap, her cheeks still burning with humiliation.

She had acted like a fool earlier in the courtyard, staring at Sir Ross like a green lass. You would think she had never seen a handsome man before.

Catlyn shifted on the bench, cursing the impulse that had led her to don these trappings of a fine lady. The pins holding her cornet of braids pressed into her head, making it ache. The high-necked woolen gown itched. She had wanted to appear mature and assured when she encountered the knight again. Instead, she felt foolish, like a child dressed up in her mother's clothes.

Around her, the folk of Clan Boyd talked and sipped ale while they waited for the Sutherlands to arrive. They did not gossip or engage in idle chatter. Uppermost in everyone's mind was the all-important whiskey. Roland and Wesley argued the merits of triple distilling. Eoin, Rabbie and Cinaed, chief crofter, went over the plans for bringing in the barley.

Catlyn chafed to be away from here. "'Tis obvious they are not coming," she said to Adair. "I will take a bowl of stew and go down to my counting room."

Adair laid a restraining hand on her arm. "Patience, lass.

I am sure they will be along directly. It takes time to get men and horses settled into a new place.''

"There is no reason why I must be here to greet them,'' she grumbled. "They are not guests, only wayfarers.''

"Hmm.'' His sharp eyes roved over her feast-day clothes.

Catlyn lifted her chin. "I did not lace myself into this uncomfortable gown out of vanity, but to show these warriors what sort of lady holds sway here.'' *And to prove something to Sir Ross,* whispered a traitorous voice. She tamped it down.

"I know it is not your way to preen for a man. Has one of these Sutherlands caught your fancy?'' His eyes twinkled. "Sir Ross seemed to stare at you quite boldly.''

"Him.'' Catlyn snorted. "I'd say he is the sort who stares at every lass that way, hoping he can coax her into his bed. Well, we will have none of that while he is here.''

"Quite right.'' Adair frowned. "Still it is time and past you found a man to wed.''

"I know my duty,'' she replied stiffly. She would need an heir, a child of her blood to be the guardian of the family legacy. But after Eoin's betrayal, she could not imagine trusting any man enough to wed with him, to make him privy not only to her clan's business but to her person. Her heart.

"Perhaps when we go to the Doune Fair to sell the Finglas Water you will meet someone who'll take your fancy.''

"I have already met them all, and none will do.''

"Gillegorm MacAdam is a fine, upstanding lad.''

"He has buckteeth, clammy hands and not a lick of sense between those two great ears of his.''

"Aye, well, you won't look at any of the handsome ones.''

Catlyn ground her teeth in exasperation. "Just because I will not wed a pretty, faithless rogue does not mean I want an ugly husband. Would you have my bairns look like Gillegorm?''

"Nay." Adair chuckled. "I just want you to be happy."

"I am. I have my work, my friends, my kin." And hopes that one day her mother would come to her senses. "What need I with some troublesome male?" She pursed her lips. "Speaking of which, how long must we let the knights stay?"

"A day or two. Till the storm passes and their wounded are on the mend."

"Good. I do not like having strangers in the keep. I know I asked to have them brought inside," she added before Adair could. "But I..." *I did not know how oddly Sir Ross would affect me.* His darkly handsome face, the barely leashed power in his unusual eyes, played havoc with her senses.

"I've got men watching them, if it makes you feel easier."

It did not. Deep inside, she knew she would not be comfortable till he was gone. "You do not trust them, either?"

"These days we must be on guard against everyone. But they've been orderly thus far and given me no cause for alarm."

Catlyn wished she could say the same. Remembering the way Sir Ross had looked in the courtyard, his eyes changing from anger to appreciation as they moved over her, made her heart trip. She steadied it with the iron will that had gotten her through so many trials. "I suppose we owe them a few nights' lodging for saving us from Hakon."

"Aye, that they did." Adair took a swallow of ale. "They are skilled fighters, that's sure. You should have seen Sir Ross handle that claymore of his." He shook his head in wonder. "And he sets high standards for his men."

"How can you tell that?"

"Little things. One man was cut down while guarding Sir Ross's back. The knight delayed his retreat, put himself in danger, to rescue the fallen man. Carried him in over his saddlebow, he did. And, too, each of the Sutherlands saw to the comfort of his mount before settling in himself. They washed their weapons and themselves ere they accepted our invite to dine. They've demanded nothing and expressed gratitude for what we have given them.''

Catlyn nodded, recalling the arrangements Adair had made. Sir Ross and Sir Mathew were lodged in her solar, it being the only suitable chamber. The others were sleeping in the barracks. Old Freda had seen to their wounds. The smithy would mend the dents in their weapons and shields.

Catlyn was astute enough to realize that these ''little things'' spoke volumes about a man's character. ''I suppose you think me foolish for being wary of them.''

''Not at all.'' Adair patted her hand with his callused paw. ''You are unused to such warlike men.'' He sighed. ''But we could use such a troop of experienced swordsmen just now.''

''Surely you are not suggesting we hire them.'' Saints above, if a few moments in Sir Ross's company tied her belly in knots, how would she survive having him around for days? Weeks?

Instead of a quick denial, Adair heaved another sigh. ''Even if we had the coin to pay them, I'd be remiss in my duties if I suggested we take on men whose mettle we do not know.''

Relief coursed through her veins. ''My thoughts exactly.'' The sooner Sir Ross left, the better.

''The Sutherlands are come,'' someone called above the chatter in the crowded room. Instantly a cheer went up.

Catlyn whipped her head around, eyes narrowing against the thin pall of smoke hanging on the damp air.

Ross Sutherland stood on the threshold, his head high, inky hair blending with the stark tunic he wore over close-fitting black hose. He inclined his head in acknowledgment of her clansmen's gratitude, like a prince accepting his due.

The fine hair on Catlyn's nape prickled. She did not like him. He was too assured, too haughty by half.

''I'll say one thing, this knight has the look of a man

who lets nothing stand in the way of what he wants,'' Adair muttered.

"Aye,'' Catlyn said weakly. He was a force to be reckoned with. At that moment, Sir Ross's eyes pounced on her. There was no other way to describe the manner in which his gaze latched onto hers. The rest of the room faded into nothingness. She wanted to look away but couldn't, held prisoner by the searing focus of his attention. Such power. Such intensity.

"Catlyn.'' Adair poked her in the ribs.

She jerked her head around. "What?''

"You should stand and bid them welcome.''

She wanted to run. Years of adherence to duty propelled her to her feet. "Come, join us in a simple meal, good sirs.'' She was grateful her words did not knock together like her knees.

"Thank you, my lady.'' Ross Sutherland's deep voice echoed like thunder off the ancient stone walls. His gaze still full on her face, he entered the hall. His big body moved with fluid grace as he strode between the rows of tables. Behind him trailed his men, their faces freshly scrubbed, their chain mail replaced by dark hose and tunics.

"Sir Ross seems keen to reach you,'' Adair murmured.

"I am sure you are mistaken.'' But a thrill raced down Catlyn's spine as he drew nearer. His eyes shone with determination, glinting like silver in the torchlight. For some reason, her blood heated.

"See what you can find out about him,'' Adair whispered.

"Wh-what?'' Then his meaning sank in. "I cannot.''

"The more we know of him, the better we'll both feel.''

"But...but I have no skill at talking with men.''

"You talk with men all the day.''

Not men like this. "That is work, this is...'' Impossible. She could not even look at him without having her tongue knot.

"I'll seat his men elsewhere. So as you can be alone.''

"Nay, I—"

"Just ask him a few questions. Men are ever eager to boast of their exploits."

"Wait!" she cried softly, but already Adair had left her and was moving to intercept the line of men. With sinking heart, she watched her friend, the man sworn to protect her, divert the Sutherlands to other nearby tables and leave her in danger.

"My lady." Ross Sutherland stopped a few paces away and inclined his head. "I apologize for our lateness. It took us some time to get settled and make ourselves presentable."

Presentable? He was that and more. Tall, perfectly proportioned and so fair of face it was sinful. The finely woven tunic and hose he wore, so different from the loose saffron sherts and plaids worn by her clansman, showed off his broad chest and muscular legs. Every woman in the hall, even those who were happily married, watched him with ill-disguised hunger. The only flaw Catlyn could find was the smugness in his gaze. He knew what a fine specimen he was and doubtless used his looks to ensnare hapless females.

Just like Eoin.

The comparison struck Catlyn hard, wrenching the blinders from her eyes. This knight was no larger-than-life being, but a conceited oaf who thought to charm his way into her bed. Disgust flooded her. She welcomed it as an antidote to her earlier fascination with him. "Do not trouble yourself over it, sir," she said coolly. "We do not stand on ceremony here, and the meal is a simple one. We were not expecting, er, guests."

"Nor were we expecting such a rowdy welcome." His grin hinted at a wry sense of humor. Worse, it made him look as guileless as a lad. "Again, my thanks for taking us in."

"And ours to you for foiling the Fergusson's plans to attack Kennecraig."

"Hmm." He winced slightly and shifted his weight.

"Oh, how thoughtless of me to keep you standing here." Catlyn plopped down onto her bench and motioned for him to take the one across from her. Better than to have him sit beside her, she reasoned, signaling the maids to serve them.

"Allow me, my lady." Sir Ross courteously spooned stew into her bowl, then presented it with a flourish so grand it might have been fillet of beef he was offering.

"Thank you." Catlyn brought a spoonful of stew to her lips and found it as hot as her temper. His every charming word, his every seductive glance infuriated her.

"May I say how lovely you look this evening?"

Catlyn groaned. Next he would be composing verses that compared her hair to honey and her eyes to autumn leaves. "Thank you, sir," she mumbled through clenched teeth.

Shy, Ross thought as he stared at the top of Lady Catlyn's head. If she bent any closer to her bowl, she'd have her nose in the mutton stew. He found her shyness as endearing as the pains she had taken with her appearance. Gone was the ethereal maiden from the courtyard. In her place sat a lovely woman, as regal in bearing as any he'd met at court. And yet, he'd seen the vulnerability in her eyes and her awareness of him as a man. He must play on both, God help him, if he was to redeem the note he had signed last week.

Dieu, was it only a week ago he'd been sitting in the Running Fox, enjoying a victory celebration with his men? And then, the man calling himself Robert Dunbar had slithered into his life like the serpent into the Garden of Eden, offering whiskey whose smoothness hid its deadly effect.

"The smoothest in the Highlands," Hakon had boasted.

Oh, it had gone down smooth, all right. And exploded like fire in his head. Ross, unused to strong liquor for he liked to keep his wits clear, had only the vaguest recollection of his men drifting off to bed. The pack of cards Robert had produced was an even dimmer memory. Next morning, through a haze of misery and stale whiskey fumes, Ross had recognized his signature on the note pledging Stratheas Keep in exchange for his debts.

One night—one damned night—it had taken Ross to gamble away the keep that had been in his mother's family for generations. And the only way he could get it back was to steal from these people who had rescued him from ambush.

Why had Hakon lied about his name? How had he known that the Boyds would offer sanctuary to the Sutherlands?

Ross sighed and studied the folk he'd come to rob. He'd expected living conditions as wild and desolate as these stark mountains, yet found order and civility. The ancient walls had been brightened by a coat of whitewash. Woven tapestries lent color and warmth to the long, crowded room. More banners hung from the vaulted ceiling two stories above the rush-strewn floor. The well-run hall, the thread of camaraderie made Ross's gut twist with remorse. Kennecraig and the Boyds reminded him of Edin Valley, the home he had turned his back on a year ago. The home and the clan he had betrayed as despicably as he was about to betray the Boyds.

The key to redeeming his pledge was this shy, gentle lass who, according to Hakon, was heir to the family's whiskey recipe. However much he disliked it, Ross would pry from her the secret Hakon demanded in exchange for Ross's note.

Poor little bird, Ross thought, gazing at the top of her head. He guessed Catlyn was a simple lass, not used to dealing with men, while he not only possessed a quick and highly educated mind, he had over a dozen years' experience with the lasses. From the time his voice had changed, women had been chasing after him. Not that he minded. He found them delightful creatures, full of soft promise and earthy mystery. He enjoyed exploring the differences that made each woman unique. It pleased him to give pleasure, in and out of bed, to share a meal, a song or a quiet moment watching the sunrise. It hurt him immeasurable that he must lie, cheat and steal from this compassionate young thing. But he would do whatever he had to to gain the information he needed.

With a heavy heart, Ross began his campaign. "The food is very good," he murmured. Indeed, it was, mutton stew, barley bread and cheese washed down with ale.

"Cook does his best, but the time just before harvest is always lean and monotonous," said the lady, her head still down.

Again Ross thought of Edin Valley, the hills lush with grain ready to cut, the sheep fattened by summer grazing. There, too, the harvest was only a few weeks away. If he did not succeed here, Hakon would be reaping the benefits of the Sutherlands' hard work. Or trying to. Though Ross had pledged his estate to Hakon, his sire and clansmen would not give up an inch of Edin Valley without a bloody fight.

And that blood would be on his head.

Ross gritted his teeth. "The harvest fast approaches."

"Aye."

"What crops do you raise so far north?"

She raised her head, spearing him with surprisingly intelligent hazel eyes. "Why do you ask when you cannot care?"

Ross blinked, startled as much by her candor as her vehemence. "I was but making conversation."

"To what purpose?"

Betrayal. Thievery. "I would know you better."

"Why, when you will be leaving in a day or so?"

So the Boyds were anxious to be rid of him. Perhaps they were not as trusting as he had supposed. Which meant the Boyds who had trailed after him had not only been helping him settle in but watching him. Inconvenient, that. It would make it more difficult for him to locate the stills and make a drawing of the equipment. "It is a thing people do. A courtesy."

"Something you use on the ladies at court in Edinburgh?"

"What makes you think I've been to court?"

"You speak French."

Ross recalled the orders he had bawled at his men when they'd arrived, and vowed to watch himself. "You must speak it, too."

"One does not have to speak a language to recognize it."

"True." Ross inclined his head, surprised anew by her facile mind. And sharp tongue. "You are wroth with me?"

"Is there a reason I should be?"

Oh, aye. "I can think of none."

"Then I cannot possibly be angry with you." She shut him out again by lowering her head.

Damn and blast, he'd coaxed women into his bed with less effort than this. Puzzled by her coolness, especially after the way she had acted in the courtyard, he took another bite of stew and looked about.

Dressed in dark wool adorned by nary a gold chain or a sparkling gem, the Boyds had made his own troop welcome. For a clan supposedly in possession of the perfect recipe for whiskey, they drank little. Indeed, their manner was as subdued as their clothing. He wondered at that, for Ross was a man who liked people, male and female. The subtle nuances that made one person different from another fascinated him. It was part of his charm, claimed his mother. "People sense that you are genuinely interested in them, and so they confide in you."

Apparently that charm was lost on Lady Catlyn. A pity, for he found her more and more appealing. While he had been changing into dry clothes, she had exchanged her white gown for a simple one of dark green wool. The color was a perfect foil for her pale skin and honey hair. She wore it up, but a few tendrils had worked loose to froth around her face. He had an unaccountable urge to demolish that braid and bury his hands in her hair, a nearly uncontrollable need to kiss the starch from the prim pink mouth that spoke to him so coolly and disapprovingly.

Did she dislike all men? Or did she sense that his interest in her was dangerous? Either way, winning her trust would be a challenge. One he might have relished had the stakes not been so high. "Did you create the lovely wall hangings?"

"Nay, they are my mother's work."

He heard the pain in her voice and dropped his own tone to a sympathetic murmur. "Is she gone?"

"Nay."

Ross groaned. What would it take to break through that shell of hers?

"My lady?" A young serving maid stood beside their table, a flagon and cups in hand. "Adair thought ye might like a dram of whiskey to warm yer bones."

"None for me," Ross said quickly.

Lady Catlyn raised her head. "You do not care for whiskey?"

"Nay."

"We distill this ourselves." A vengeful light danced in her eyes. "It would please me if you tasted it."

Witch. "How could I refuse?" Ross forced himself to take the cup the maid held out. But as he raised the cup to his lips, the sharp, smoky fumes filled his senses. Damn, he knew that smell. His head thumped. His belly rolled, threatening to rebel if he took even one sip.

It was the very same liquor that had done him in. Ross knew in a heartbeat that the whiskey Hakon had served him that fateful eve had come from this stock.

What dreadful irony.

What a test of his internal fortitude.

Could he get it down without losing his supper?

Conscious of Lady Catlyn's gaze, Ross took a tiny sip. He swallowed it three times before his belly grudgingly kept it.

"You do not like the Finglas?" Catlyn asked incredulously.

"Strong." Ross wheezed, keeping his teeth closed just in case his stomach rose again.

"Whiskey is supposed to be strong. Most men like it." Her eyes measured him and obviously found him lacking.

"I am sure." He had liked this whiskey too much. And that unaccustomed lapse now threatened everything he held dear. Ross swallowed again, determined to brazen this out. "Is there a difference?" he asked. It was too much to hope she'd just spill the information he had come to steal. But then, women, even one as canny as this one, were flighty.

"Of course there is. Anyone with a nose can tell that." She looked down her nose at him. "If you like, tomorrow I can arrange for you to taste a few cups from different years."

Cups? Dod, he'd never keep down even one cup. "I doubt I'd notice the difference, but I would like to see how it is made."

Her gaze turned frosty. "I am afraid that is not possible."

"Why?" Did she suspect something?

"This is a busy time of year. You would be underfoot."

"I am quick on my feet and good at staying out of the way."

"The better to avoid those you cuckold?"

"What?" Ross exclaimed, though her meaning and her contempt could not have been plainer. "My lady, I assure you that I never dally with married women." Not knowingly, at any rate.

"It is of no interest to me." She turned away and spoke to an old man at the next table. "Roland, what say we make an early start on the morrow to make up for the time lost today?"

"Aye." Roland's tone was curt. His dark eyes glowered at her from either side of his hooked red nose. "In fact, I've a mind to get at it tonight."

"Nay. 'Tis late, and we've had a busy day. We'll be all the fresher for a good night's sleep."

"We'll start at dawn, then." Roland heaved his bulk off the bench. "Come along, lads. We'd best turn in."

The Boyds, with the exception of those sitting with Ross's men, rose from their seats and drifted toward the door in an orderly procession. Those who passed close by wished Catlyn good sleep. The warmth of her smiles as she bid them sleep well were a revelation to Ross. If she was not cold and caustic by nature, why had she taken such a dislike to him? It was lowering. It was infuriating. Worst of all, it endangered his mission.

By force of will, Ross kept a bland mask in place. "If we could help with your work, we'd be happy to."

Catlyn glared at him. "There is no need."

"Oh, but I disagree." Ross gave her his most winning smile, his temper fraying further when it made no dent in her scowl. "You saved our lives, and we'd like to repay you."

"We neither require your help nor want it." Her chin was high, her tone that of a queen to a lowly knave.

Never in his life had he been treated so by a woman. "My lady, there must be something I can do to express my thanks."

"Aye, there is. You can leave on the morrow."

Leave? Without the whiskey recipe? Impossible. "Do you not think you owe my wounded men a few days in which to heal?"

Her expression softened. "I suppose." Very grudgingly. "I will consult with Freda tomorrow and see how long she thinks you need stay." With that, she turned away.

Ross caught her wrist. The flesh was warm and surprisingly firm. The beat of her pulse against his palm sent a ripple through his lower belly. "My thanks for your hospitality, Lady Catlyn." He said the words through his teeth, barely holding on to civility. "On the morrow, when you are rested—and mayhap more congenial—let us see if we cannot find some way in which I might repay you.'' He gave her a slow, burning smile, the one that never failed to melt opposition.

Beneath his hand, her pulse skittered, but her skin remained cool. ''I will be busy—'' she loosened his grip, one finger at a time ''—for the foreseeable future. I wish you good journey to Inverness.''

''But...'' Ross moved to block her retreat.

A yellow-haired man pushed in between them. He was large, muscular and handsome, despite angry brown eyes and a pugnacious expression. ''Do not touch her,'' this newcomer growled at Ross.

''I can take care of myself, Eoin.'' The lady looked even more displeased with her champion than she was with Ross.

''He is bothering you,'' Eoin grumbled.

Lady Catlyn sighed. ''You are both annoying me.''

''Let me escort you to your room.'' Eoin reached for her arm.

Catlyn avoided his grasp. ''Stay and keep Sir Ross company.''

''But Catlyn,'' Eoin whined. ''I should go with you.''

''My lady,'' Ross protested. ''I thought we might talk.''

''Talk with Eoin.'' Eyes glittering with mockery, she glanced at each of them in turn. ''I think you have much in common.'' Lifting her skirt, she moved away.

Ross watched her leave, thinking that the queen had never made as regal an exit. But with her went his only hope of recovering his family property.

''Leave her alone,'' Eoin growled. His face flushed with hostility, he stalked off in the lady's wake.

''Plans going awry?'' Mathew Sutherland, Ross's cousin and second in command, strolled over to join him.

''For some reason, the lady has taken a dislike of me.''

''Inconvenient.''

''Damnably so.''

''What will you do?'' Mathew whispered.

Leave at first light. But he could not. Ross clenched his

teeth. "I will just have to find a way to charm the lady into revealing her secrets."

"That should not be difficult for a man with your skill at wooing the lasses." Mathew winked lewdly.

"This one is made of ice." It rankled to chase after a woman who obviously disliked him. Yet her rudeness made him feel less guilty about what he must do. "Were you able to learn anything from the Boyds you dined with?"

"Just that they seem to be simple, hardworking folk who think of little else besides their whiskey making. Adair did ask several sharp questions of us."

Ross grunted. "I marked him for a canny man. Our lads?"

"Have quick wits and careful tongues."

That they did, for they had been trained in the fine art of thief-catching by Ross's uncle, Hunter Carmichael, Warden of the Scottish Middle March. "This is not so different from other tasks we've performed for Uncle Hunter. We need information before we can decide how best to get what we came for. Have the lads find out where the stills are located, who has access to them and, if possible, where their records are kept."

Mathew nodded. "I will see to it immediately."

"I trust you had enough to eat," Adair said as he joined them. "This is a busy season for us," added the older man. "We retire early and, much as I dislike forcing guests to do the same, I must ask you to seek your beds." Behind the grizzled warrior stood a quartet of beefy Boyds.

"Guards?" Ross exclaimed.

"Aye." Adair's level gaze offered no apology. "We are pleased to offer you shelter, but you are strangers to us."

"Are we to be locked up like prisoners?" Ross demanded.

"Only if you will not follow a few rules."

"Such as?"

"Keep to your rooms, the great hall or the courtyard and do not attempt to evade those set to watch you."

The rules were reasonable. No more than he'd have insisted upon himself if the situation were reversed. Ross was in no mood to be reasonable. And guards would make it difficult for his men to move about freely. But arguing would only raise more suspicions. "We agree," Ross grumbled. "But tell me this. Was it your lady who ordered that we be watched?"

"Nay. I have charge of such things. Why do you ask?"

"She does not like me."

"Oh." One of Adair's gray brows rose. "Why is that?"

"I did not insult her, if that is your meaning. Quite the contrary. The more charming my manner, the colder hers grew."

"And why would you be wanting to charm our Catlyn?"

Ross blinked. "Because...because I owe her a debt."

"A debt, is it?" A grin tugged at the corners of Adair's lined mouth, and a knowing gleam entered his dark eyes. "Well, since we're owing you a debt as well—for thwarting Hakon's plans—I'll be telling you the lass is not much one for charm."

"What do you mean by that?"

Adair's grin spread to lighten his weathered face. "If you are around long enough, you may just find that out." He winked at Mathew. "And now, lads, I'll bid you goodnight. We've put the pair of you in Catlyn's solar, it being the only chamber that's not occupied. I'm told the maids took up sleeping pallets, blankets and such. If you need anything, just ask."

Anything but freedom. Still Ross could not fault their caution. Nodding, he followed the pair of guards up two flights of narrow, winding stairs, conscious of Mathew's suppressed tension. His cousin was canny enough to hold his tongue till the door to their borrowed chamber had shut behind them.

"By the rod!" Mathew exclaimed. "Do you think they plan to keep us prisoners here? Murder us in our—"

"Shh." Ross drew Mathew across the long, spacious

room to the window. "If they meant to harm us, they'd have taken our weapons. Their wariness is reasonable, if damned inconvenient."

Mathew's tense shoulders relaxed. "What now?"

"We find the stills," Ross said softly.

"Oh, and how will we get out of here?"

"Climb, I hope." Ross unbarred the double shutters covering the window and eased open one side. Cool, damp air swirled in as he leaned out. "Ah, only three stories to the ground."

"Only," Mathew gasped.

"Aye, and there's a wee ledge just below."

"You cannot be thinking of walking *that!*" he whispered.

Ross just grinned. He had always had a penchant for climbing, whether it was a tree to filch apples or down a cliff side after falcon chicks to train for hunting.

"Idiot."

"I just don't have your fear of heights."

"Respect. I respect the fact that birds fly and men were meant to keep their two feet on the ground."

"I will be careful." His mind made up, Ross turned and surveyed the room.

Like everything at Kennecraig, it was neat and clean if sparsely furnished. An attempt had been made to make them comfortable. At one end, a large table held a trio of pitchers, cups and a bowl for washing. Surprisingly, there were also stacks of books and what looked like writing materials. Did Lady Catlyn read, or were these her father's?

There was no bed, of course, but the promised sleeping pallets had been laid out before the hearth at the other end, where a small fire crackled. Blankets and pillows lay nearby, along with their saddle packs.

Ross made for his pouch, pawed through it and found the thin coil of rope at the bottom. "It pays to be prepared." Grinning, he straightened and looped the rope around his torso.

''And what am I to do while you are off risking your fool neck?'' Mathew whispered fiercely.

Ross scanned the chamber again as he had so many others in his career as a thief-taker. ''Conduct a thorough search.'' He pointed to the two large tapestries that brightened the long walls. ''Look behind the hangings for hidden passageways or safe-holes. It is doubtless too much to hope that she has left this recipe laying about, but examine the books and papers on yon table.'' He frowned, surprised to find little evidence the lady spent time on the traditional female pursuits—no needlework frame, no mending basket.

But then, Catlyn Boyd was a most unusual lady. One he wished he had met under different circumstances. If he was to steal her secrets, he must know her better.

Chapter Three

Catlyn found herself standing before the double doors to the distillery with no memory of how she'd gotten there after fleeing the great hall. There was no other word for the way in which she had run from the hall, from Ross Sutherland's touch. Even now her wrist still prickled where his callused hands had encircled it. And her heart beat much too swiftly.

The man was a menace to womankind. And it was a blow to her pride to find she was not as immune to him as she should be. Awash with shame, she leaned her forehead against the door, drawing strength from steel-banded oak.

There were too many people counting on her, too many decisions to be made without cluttering her head with silly thoughts of Ross Sutherland. It was just that he was handsome. And strong. Curiously his size and warrior skills appealed to her even more than his poet's face. Part of her wanted to acquiesce to Adair's suggestion and hire the knight.

Oh, and would that not be the most foolish thing she had ever done.

Agitated, Catlyn pulled open the right-hand door and stepped into the distillery's anteroom. Immediately, the familiar scent of the Finglas wrapped itself around her. To her, this was the heart of Kennecraig, the center of her world for as long as she could remember. She knew and loved every inch ·of this ancient tower, from the keg maker's workshop on the floor above to the cellars beneath housing the mash tuns and stills. On this main floor were the settling rooms and her workroom. Her province, her responsibility.

Catlyn sighed. Small wonder she craved a champion. Even before Hakon had come into their lives, her days had been hectic and full. Now, as she passed through the entryway and into the maze of dimly lit rooms beyond, she felt weighed down by all that must be done. Always before there had been others to share the burden, but her father was gone, her mother as good as.

Oh, Roland and his men would perform the manual tasks associated with each phase of the whiskey making, but it was up to her to record these steps in the journals. It was up to her to decide if the Finglas from four years ago was up to Boyd standards and how much of it should be sold, how much kept by for her father's pet project.

Tucked away in a darkened corner of the still rooms were kegs from as far back as ten years ago. Thomas had reasoned that whiskey became smoother and more drinkable every year. At ten years, he felt it had reached its peak. If he had been able to, he would not have sold a drop of the Finglas till it was ten years old. But in order to provide for his clan, he'd been forced to sell most of each year's production.

This year, he had intended to offer the ten-year-old Finglas to a few discriminating customers in Edinburgh. Among them, the king.

Now it was up to Catlyn to make her father's dream reality. But was she strong enough to do it? Would the nobles deal with a Highland distiller who was also a woman?

Frowning, she wandered into the settling room. It was twice the size of the great hall, the ceilings one and a half stories above the stone floor. During the day, air and light filtered in through narrow openings at the rafter line. By night, only a single lantern, such as the type used on ships, was left burning in a center table, for flame and liquor were an explosive mix.

Row after row of shelves filled the room, so it resembled a maze. They were lined with single rows of whiskey kegs. Each keg bore a label with a date and batch number inscribed in Catlyn's precise hand. The numbers were recorded in her ledger books, and from them she could tell what barley fields had been used in the distilling, how many times the liquor had been run through the stills and, of course, how old it was. The chimneys that vented away the smoke from those stills ran up through the middle of the room and thence through the second-story cooperage.

Bypassing the shelves, Catlyn took the lantern from the table and continued on to her counting room. The door was always locked unless she was inside, not out of fear someone would steal the records but because it had been done so from the beginning and the Boyds were great ones for tradition.

She took the key from the pouch at her waist, unlocked the door and stepped inside. Immediately she felt her remaining anxiety melt away. Small and cozy, with a fireplace to keep the damp at bay, the chamber had served the lords of Kennecraig as a record room for generations. Ever since her great-great-grandfather had added this building to house the distillery.

The shelves lining two of the walls of the record room were crammed with the leather-bound ledgers and crumbling parchment rolls that chronicled every step of the distilling process for each year going back six generations. Some were written in Latin, others in French.

As a child, Catlyn had sat on the floor and fashioned dolls from wood curls while her brother, Thom, studied the languages and ciphering essential to every lord of Kennecraig. She'd been far more interested in his lessons than the silly dolls, which was fortunate. When Thom had died at age fifteen, Catlyn had assumed the heir's role. There had been grumblings among some of the men, but her father had stood firm. "The lass has my head for details and her grandsire's nose for the brew."

That she'd stepped in to fill her papa's role far too early saddened her. Yet she loved this craft. Every step held its own fascination. The earthy pleasure of visiting the fields and assessing the barley, of judging when the grain was at its peak and ready to be married to the purest burn water. The careful mixing of barley and water, in just the right portions, appealed to her sense of order. But nothing equaled the thrill she felt when the first drop of liquor fell from the coil of hammered steel tubing.

A grating sound from the main room had her spinning in the doorway.

"Who is there?" she called, raising the lantern. Its pale golden light bounced off the nearest kegs but was swallowed up by the darkness beyond. A shiver worked its way down her spine. She had never been afraid to come here, even at night and alone, but that was before Hakon had come to the mountains.

She thought about the barrels of black powder sitting next to the stills in the cellars. Her father's desperate scheme to keep Hakon from attacking them. Thus far it had worked, but what if one of his men sneaked into Kennecraig and moved the barrels away? It would take time and many strong men.

Like the Sutherlands.

She swayed for a moment, terrified. Then she remembered the injuries Hakon had inflicted on the Sutherlands. Nay, Ross was not a danger to them. At least not that way. And the doors to the cellars were kept locked except when Roland and his men were working there.

Still it might be wise to post guards here until the Sutherlands were gone.

Catlyn felt a bit better till she glanced at the papers piled on her worktable. She should spend an hour or two on them, but her eyes were gritty, her nerves frayed. And she had one more duty to perform before she retired. Resolving to be down here at first light, she shut the door and locked it.

Ross crouched down behind one of the keg-laden shelves and watched Catlyn walk past, confident the shadows would hide him. Still he did not let go the breath he had been holding till he heard the door clang shut.

"*Dieu*, that was close," he whispered into the gloom. He had found what appeared to be the distillery by following his nose. Surprised there were no guards outside, he had cautiously opened one side of the door and eased inside. The stench of whiskey had made his eyes sting and his belly roll. He'd ignored both.

Used to sneaking about in darkened places, he had slipped into the cavernous room and started his search for the stills themselves. Only a small amount of pale light came in from some openings high above. A locked set of double doors just off the entryway looked promising, but he had moved on, down row after row of kegs. The neatness impressed him. He rapped his knuckles gently on a few and judged them to be full. Full of whiskey. If Hakon knew the Boyds had so much on hand, he'd have worked harder to get inside and steal it.

Then he had seen the light spilling from a chamber cut into the wall. It drew him, but before he could get close enough to see what was inside, an incautious step betrayed his presence.

Ross looked toward the door, then back to the one Catlyn had so carefully locked before leaving. Possibly it led to the stills, or to a room where the accounts were kept. Orderly as everything was, he did not doubt that the Boyds had a scribe who kept a record of how much whiskey was produced and sold. Tempted as he was to see if the lock would yield to the tip of his dirk, the time was not right.

Keeping to the shadows, Ross retraced his steps down

the long corridor, out the back door and around the side of the tower. Up the rope he'd left and onto the ledge.

Tomorrow night he'd come prepared, with parchment and charcoal to sketch the stills.

Catlyn paused outside the chamber that had been her parents', dreading what she'd find when she entered.

On the day Adair brought her father's body back to Kennecraig, Catlyn had also lost her mother. Jeannie Boyd had taken one look at her departed husband and faded into a stupor from which she had yet to emerge. The pain of watching her mother retreat further and further into herself was almost more than Catlyn could bear.

She bowed her head, her heart aching. She would give all she owned, aye, even the precious stills, to have her mother whole again. "Please, please let me find her better."

Bracing herself for disappointment, Catlyn knocked softly. She did not expect an answer. Even before her husband's death, Jeannie Boyd had been considered a bit fey. She would immerse herself so thoroughly in the scenes she created with needle and thread, that she paid scant attention to the real world around her. Now her mind seemed to have permanently retreated into one of those imaginary worlds. A better world, where her husband was not dead, just away.

Catlyn pushed open the door and immediately spied her mother sitting cross-legged on the floor beside her husband's clothes chest. It was empty now, every garment Thomas had possessed arrayed around Lady Jeannie in neat piles.

"Mama, how nice to see you up." Hope buoyed Catlyn's steps as she crossed the room. Could it be her mother had regained her senses and was finally setting Papa's things to rights?

Jeannie raised her head, her once glorious mane of chestnut hair dull, her eyes red rimmed. "Thomas is due back any day, and I cannot find his best plaid."

Catlyn's knees went weak, and she sank down beside her mother. They had buried her father in his bloodied tartan. "He may not need it with the weather so warm," she said gently.

"He counts on me to keep it in good repair. He teases me sometimes…says 'tis the only practical thing I do. And now… I—I can't understand where it's got to." She picked up a saffron shirt and shook it, as though expecting the eight-foot length of plaid to fall from it onto her lap.

"It will turn up." Catlyn captured her mother's fluttering hands, found them icy cold and painfully thin. She chafed them between her own hands. "Let me put you to bed, Mama."

"I cannot sleep till I've found the plaid." She freed her hands and went back to shifting through the clothes.

Catlyn watched through a veil of tears. It seemed her mother was wasting away before her eyes, her plump body gaunt, her once golden skin pale from hours indoors. "Tomorrow we will take a walk on the battlements. The fresh air would do you good, Mama. You have not been outside since…" Catlyn choked on a sob. "It's been so long since you've been out."

"I will not leave this room till I have his plaid." Frowning, Jeannie picked up a pair of worn woolen hose. "These are Thomas's favorites. I know he'll be surprised I've mended them so the hole barely shows, but he'll be most displeased if I cannot find the plaid."

The door to the chamber opened.

Catlyn turned toward it, her already low spirits plummeting when she saw Dora standing awkwardly in the doorway, a covered tray in her hands. It was surely the cruelest of ironies that the one woman upon whom her mother depended was Eoin's mistress.

"Oh, Dora," Jeannie exclaimed. "I'm so glad you're back. You've got to help me find Thomas's plaid."

"Aye, my lady." Blue eyes downcast, Dora sidled into the room and set her burden on the table. She was slender, blond and so radiantly beautiful that men, even those who'd known her all her life, stared when she passed by.

Small wonder Eoin had been tempted to dally with her while courting the plain wren of a woman who was heir to the distilleries, Catlyn thought. Even her mother preferred Dora's company. Where Catlyn attempted to coax her mother back into this world, Dora seemed to slip readily into Jeannie's.

"It may be that one of the maids took the plaid to wash," Dora said. "Tomorrow we'll go down and look about."

"Let us go now." Jeannie got awkwardly to her feet.

Dora swiftly put a hand under her elbow, steadying her. "Oh, nay, my lady. 'Tis night, now, and the maids will be asleep. You should be abed, too."

"I am not sleepy," Jeannie protested.

"Come sit by the hearth, then," Dora coaxed. "I've brought up a cup of warm milk."

"All right. But at first light, we must go down and search. Search everywhere." Jeannie dutifully walked to her chair.

Dora glanced quickly, apologetically, at Catlyn. "I know 'tis a futile errand," she whispered. "But the fresh air and a wee bit of exercise might do my lady good."

"Aye." Catlyn jumped up and crossed to her mother. She should be glad her mother had someone in whom she could confide and trust, but instead, she was jealous of Dora. Again. "I will ready Mama for bed, Dora. Eoin is doubtless waiting for you."

"Nay, that is over. He…he is wroth with me." Her hand absently fluttered over a bruise at her temple.

"Did he do that?" Catlyn exclaimed.

"Nay." Dora shook her head so violently her long blond braids flew back, revealing another dark mark below her ear.

"Dora." Horrified, Catlyn went to her, took her gently by the shoulders. "Tell me true if Eoin has beaten you."

"Nay, at least I do not think it was him."

"Tell me what happened," Catlyn demanded.

"Accidents. A stone flying out of the darkness."

"Oh, Dora, I had no idea."

Dora turned her head aside. "Please let it go. It is right that I be punished. I should not have let him kiss me knowing he was promised to you, but I have been so lonely since Alan died. One minute Eoin and I were speaking of the past, the next…" A single tear trickled down her cheek.

Catlyn's eyes filled with tears. "It is not your fault. It is Eoin's, taking advantage of your grief."

Dora raised her head, looking Catlyn in the eye for the first time since Catlyn had found them together. "I swear it was the first time, and it went no further than a few kisses."

Catlyn believed that as surely as she now believed that she had not really loved Eoin. She had agreed to wed him out of duty and respect for her father's wishes. "Thank you for telling me," she said. "Now tell me who threw these rocks at you."

"Someone who wishes me punished."

"I will put a guard on you and alert Adair to watch."

"Nay." Dora grasped Catlyn's hand. "It would only make matters worse if they thought I had complained."

"Very well, I will say nothing." Directly, but she meant to spread the word that she would not tolerate such behavior.

"I am sorry I ruined things for you."

Catlyn smiled faintly, her heart lighter than it had been in weeks. "Dora, I begin to think you did me a very great favor. For all he was my father's foster son and lived here ten years, I realize I did not truly know Eoin. He has revealed his true nature, the charming, self-serving rogue. Had we wed, he would likely have pursued other women." She chuckled. "And I would have been forced to cut out his cheating heart."

Dora managed a watery smile. "Thank you for not turn-

ing me out. You are truly the most generous of women."
She grabbed Catlyn's hands and kissed them.

Embarrassed, Catlyn freed her hands and patted Dora
awkwardly on the shoulder. "You have amply repaid me
by caring for Mama." She looked over at her mother, who
stared into the empty hearth as though it contained the secret of life.

"She will regain her senses," Dora murmured.

"I pray you are right." Catlyn walked over and hunkered
down at her mother's knee. "Mama, shall I read you a
story?"

Her mother glanced at her and smiled brightly. "I think
that's why my Thom has stayed away so long," she said.
"Because he knows the plaid's not mended. He'll not come
back to me till I've found it and set it to rights."

"Aye, Mama," Catlyn said softly. Her heart aching, she
stood and walked toward the door.

"We must be up and looking at first light," Jeannie said.

Dora's reply was lost in the closing of the door, but
doubtless it was something soothing.

Catlyn stood outside the room, shaking, her emotions a
shambles. After a moment, she found the strength to move
down the hall to her own chamber.

Why? Why had these things happened to her clan?

Father Griogair, the priest who had come over from the
town of Doune to bury her father, said that God visited
such hardships as these on folk as a penance for past ill
deeds. If so, she was paying a very high price for having
teased her brother when he was alive and tormented their
tutor with her endless questions. Of course, if Eoin was to
be believed, she also suffered from the sins of being cold,
inflexible and indifferent to a man's natural need for a mistress.

Did Ross Sutherland have a mistress?

Without a doubt. He was a rogue, the sort of handsome
rascal who thought all women worshiped him. It would be
folly to have him here, luring her maidservants into trysts

in darkened corners. Oh, and he'd be good at that, Catlyn thought, shivering as she recalled what it was like to be the focus of his searing blue eyes.

He made a woman, even one as cautious as herself, feel as though she were the most important creature on earth. It was all a lie, of course, an act. But she would not have him here, breaking hearts.

Through the slits between the window shutters, Ross watched Catlyn make her exit. How lonely and sad she looked, he thought, her shoulders bowed, her steps slow.

He transferred his gaze to Catlyn's mother. Clearly the death of her husband had unhinged Lady Jeannie's mind. His heart contracted in an unwelcome spurt of sympathy. He tried to push it away, reminding himself he could not afford to feel anything for the lass he'd come to rob. But his own mother was dear to him, though Lady Laurel probably did not realize how much he loved her. He had disappointed both his parents with his refusal to settle down and accept the responsibilities for the estates he'd one day inherit.

The land he had lost in that drunken wager.

Just let him get back that damned note from Hakon, Ross vowed, and he would spend the rest of his life proving he was worthy of his parents' love.

"Come to bed, my lady," murmured the maid.

Ross watched the stunningly beautiful Dora help Lady Jeannie to her feet. It was not surprising that Eoin had trysted with the maid. Doubtless he preferred her warmth to Lady Catlyn's haughty coldness. And yet, the lady had displayed an unexpected compassion in dealing with the girl. Another piece of the puzzle that was Lady Catlyn, the puzzle he must solve if he hoped to regain his property.

Ross turned away. Stepping carefully, he moved past the window, placing his feet with great care on the narrow ledge that ran around the tower. The stone was rain slickened beneath his boots, making the adventure a bit more dangerous than he'd expected, but well worth the risk. Not only had he discovered the location of the distillery, but the scene between Lady Catlyn and Dora had provided him with important information.

Considering what he'd learned, Ross inched past the last barred window. He had no more than cleared it than the shutters were abruptly thrown open. A curse hissed between his teeth as he flattened himself against the wet stone wall of the tower.

A pair of slender hands appeared on the sill. Someone sighed, the sound filled with longing. "The air smells so fresh after a rain," murmured Catlyn Boyd.

Ross shrank back, praying she did not lean out.

"Ye'll catch the ague breathing in that dampness," grumbled a rough female voice.

"I'm used to it, Ulma. Besides, I must ride out tomorrow to see if the storm flattened the barley."

"There's no need for ye to muck about in the muddy fields. 'Tis Eoin's job to manage the crops."

"So it is, but Papa always checked such things himself. I also need to record the amount of rainfall in the gauge and measure the height of the crops for the book."

The book? Ross's ears pricked up. Did this book also contain the recipe Hakon sought?

Ulma sniffed. "Ye do too much, lass."

"I do no more than what is required. It just takes me longer because I am new at doing some things." She sighed again. "These days I need to be two people."

"Well, if Eoin had not proved such a deceitful rascal, ye'd have a husband to bear part of the burden. Ye should have turned that...that bastard out the very night ye found him and—"

"Oh, I wanted to," Catlyn said fiercely. "And Papa would have exiled him, no matter that Eoin was his foster son." Her voice grew softer. "But once I was over the initial shock, I realized how important Eoin was to the clan, and knew we could not dispense with him to ease my pride.''

''Ye think too much of others and not enough of yerself.''

Ross heartily agreed. How many women would have put their clan's needs above pride? Or revenge?

''Such is the way of things when you are laird, or so Papa always told Mama when she chided him for overworking.''

''True as that may be, ye'll be fit for nothing if ye don't get more rest,'' muttered the maid. ''So it's off to bed with ye.'' Work-worn hands drew Lady Catlyn inside and closed the shutters. Their voices were muffled as they moved farther into the room.

For one instant, Ross was tempted to creep over and peek between the wooden slats. Not to listen, but to look, to see if the lady's body was as enticing unclothed as he suspected.

Wretch.

He slunk to the corner of the building, carefully worked his way around it and down the narrow end of the tower to the other long side. Midway along the wall was the window he had crawled out of a dangerous hour ago. It was still open, though no light glowed from within.

''Mathew?'' Ross whispered.

''Dieu.'' His cousin appeared in the opening. He reached out, steadying Ross, guiding him over the sill. ''I thought you'd either been caught or fallen.''

''Neither, thank God.'' Ross leaned gratefully against the inner wall for a moment. ''Though the ledge was narrower and a bit more slippery than I'd expected.''

''You and your foolish risk-taking will be the death of me, yet,'' Mathew whispered as he lit a candle.

Ross closed his eyes against the flare of light. ''You were safe in here.''

''Oh, aye, but my heart's been racing fit to burst since

you crawled out there." Mathew pressed a cup into Ross's hand.

Ross sniffed suspiciously. Ale. He drank deep of the cool liquid then looked toward the door. "Our friends?"

"One's sitting with his back to our door. The other leans against the wall across the way. Did you find the stills?"

"Possibly." Keeping his voice low, Ross told his cousin about the orderly storage rooms and the two locked doors.

"Lady Catlyn was there by herself?"

"Aye." It had disturbed him to see her alone like that. What if he had been Seamus? "Clearly she takes her duties seriously." Ross was uneasy with his changing image of her.

"What is wrong?"

"Nothing, I... oh, hell," Ross muttered. "I never could keep anything from you." Reluctant, but not sure why, he told Mathew of the conversations he had overheard. "Personally, I do not think he stands a chance of winning back Lady Catlyn." He hesitated, then added, "I am surprised she did not turn Dora out over this. She is more generous and softhearted than I had supposed."

"You cannot afford to admire her," Mathew warned.

"I do not," Ross grumbled. "I was but going over what I learned, deciding how I could use it to gain my ends."

Mathew grunted but looked unconvinced. "You have that gleam in your eyes, the one you get when you've spotted a lass you consider worthy of chasing."

"This is not that kind of *chase*," Ross grumbled. "Hakon said that she alone possessed the secret of the whiskey making. To get it, I must win her trust. I see now that I used the wrong strategy. She rebuffed my attempts to charm her because she has ample reason to distrust such shallow flattery." A welcome change from the women he'd met at court, who not only lapped up praise like cats did cream, but became petulant if a man did not wax poetic over their beauty. Bah, he could not dwell on that. "She even said that Eoin and I were much alike."

"How does this aid our cause?"

"On the morrow, Catlyn will meet a different Ross Sutherland. One who does not utter meaningless phrases, but who…" Ross scowled. "What should I say to win her over?"

Mathew shrugged, a grin lurking around his lips. "You are the master in this field, not I. But offhand, I'd say that the lady Catlyn is not like any other lass you've wooed."

"I am not wooing her, I am here to…to…"

"Betray her?" Mathew whispered.

Aye. And therein lay the problem.

Chapter Four

Dawn came slowly, pale fingers of light stealing over the jagged mountain peaks and in through the window in Catlyn's narrow bedchamber. She greeted the sight with a sigh of relief and climbed from bed.

Sleep had been long in coming last night and filled with dreams when it did. Dreams of a magnificent black-haired man with eyes of sizzling blue.

Ross Lion Sutherland.

Groaning, Catlyn dragged herself across the chilly room, washed her face, braided her hair and pulled on a faded brown gown. She tried to keep her mind on the tasks ahead of her today, but it kept drifting back to the strange dreams.

She and Ross had been walking through a field of golden barley. Her field. She should have been busy seeing to the harvest; she had preferred being with him. He laughed, and her heart felt lighter than it had in months. He held out his hand, and she wanted to take it. To follow where he led, even though it meant leaving Kennecraig.

Catlyn shivered and chafed the gooseflesh from her arms. It was a dream, nothing more. She would never leave Kennecraig. That she had vowed on her father's soul.

She threw a light cape over her arm, for the cellars were cold, even in summer, and hurried into the dim corridor. Habit slowed her steps outside her mother's door. Hoping her mother had slept better than she had, Catlyn headed for the great hall.

"Lady Catlyn!" The deep voice of the man she had hoped to avoid echoed down the corridor from behind her.

Run, urged her instinct for survival. Pride stayed her steps. She stopped, braced herself and looked over her shoulder.

He advanced toward her through the gloom, his movements quick and lithe, his smile a white slash in his tanned face.

"Were you lying in wait for me?" she asked sharply. Eoin had taken to doing that till Adair threatened to turn him out.

"Nay." He halted close to her, so close the tips of his boots nudged the hem of her skirt.

Catlyn fought the urge to run. "I thought you were, er—"

"Confined to my room, or rather, your solar?" He grinned, something he did often. "Adair said we might be about the keep."

"Oh." She fumbled for words. "Why are you are up so early?"

"It is my custom, but today I was up before the sun, anxious to check on my wounded men."

"Ah. How fare they?"

"Well enough. One of the men-at-arms took an arrow to the arm, but is already up and about. My squire…" He sighed.

"The lad? He is worse?"

"A little fevered and restless. I feared he'd tear out the stitches your Freda set in his shoulder, so I came up to fetch this." He held out a dark object. "I should have asked before borrowing it, but I did not realize you would be awake."

Catlyn squinted. "A book?"

"Yours, or at least it and two others were in the solar.

The Green Knight. I thought the tale might entertain Callum.''

"It is in French."

"You already pointed out that I speak it."

"And read it?"

"Not as well as Father Simon would have liked." His smile turned rueful. "As a lad, I was more interested in swordplay and the like, but Mama and Papa insisted we all learn."

"My brother felt the same way about studies," she said.

"You have a brother?"

Into her mind flashed the image of Thom, lying cold and still in a pool of blood. Guilt rose in her throat.

Catlyn shook her head and shoved the memory away. "He died when he was ten and five."

"I feel for you," he said gently.

And Catlyn believed he did. As she stared into his eyes, she fancied she saw her own pain reflected there. "Thank you."

"I have two younger brothers and a sister. Much as they did plague me when we were growing up, I do love them dearly."

"You are fortunate to have a large family."

"Aye." Something shifted in his eyes, a shadow of remorse or a trick of the light? "I did not fully appreciate how much they meant to me until just lately."

"I, too, took my family for granted," her heart contracted, "not realizing how precious they are till they are gone."

"Or threatened." His voice went hard and flat. "When your family is in danger, you will do anything to protect them."

Catlyn nodded, understanding that grim determination. Sharing it. "My father died a month ago while taking a shipment of whiskey to Doune. I know Hakon had a hand in it, though I cannot prove it. As I stood over Papa's grave,

I vowed on his soul that Hakon would not get Kennecraig, too.''

''That is a large undertaking.''

''For a woman?''

''For anyone. From what I saw, he is ruthless and canny.''

''We will survive.''

His eyes locked on hers, and his expression changed. What looked like respect flickered in their azure depths, along with something else. Something strong and earthy.

Catlyn's pulse quickened, and her skin prickled. She could not move, could only stare into those compelling eyes, acutely aware of him on some new level. She inhaled sharply, her senses filled with the unique scent of soap and man. This man. Never before had she felt so small, fragile and wholly female.

''Catlyn,'' he whispered.

Never had her name sounded so beautiful and lush. ''Aye,'' she murmured, her body warming, melting.

''I…'' He lifted a hand, grazing her cheek with the backs of his fingers. ''I am sorry, I—'' He started, dropping his hand as though he'd been burned, shattering the moment.

Catlyn blinked. ''What?''

''I am sorry,'' he said again, eyes flat and shuttered.

For touching her? Confused, Catlyn turned away from him, tripped over her hem and would have fallen had he not grabbed hold of her elbow. Even that slight contact sent a jolt up her arm. She looked at him again and saw her dazed features reflected in his eyes. Or was he as confused as she? ''What is it? What is happening?'' she whispered.

For a long moment, he did not reply, just studied her, as though seeing her for the first time. When he spoke, his voice was low and harsh. ''You are a most unusual lass.''

Catlyn tried not to be hurt. ''Thank you, I think.'' She dredged up a smile and freed her arm. ''If you will excuse me, I have much to do today.'' It astonished her that she had wasted so much time talking to him. It frightened her that she had felt at ease doing it. Turning away, she started down the hall.

He kept pace beside her. "I wonder if I could beg a favor?"

Glancing sidelong at him, she saw the easy smile was back. "I doubt you have ever begged anything from a woman."

He laughed, the sound, deep and infectious. How could a large man manage to look like a lad caught in a false-hood?

Catlyn couldn't help but smile. "What do you want?"

"Hmm." He arched one black brow, teasing. "You should not ask a man that, lass. Gives him all sorts of ideas."

"I am not the sort of woman men get *ideas* about," she said crisply, braced for a flood of false compliments.

"Then you've not met the right sort of man."

"Mmm."

"But as to the boon," he said as they reached the stair-well. "Would you read to Callum? I speak French well enough, but I read so slowly the story would suffer."

"I am far too busy," Catlyn said quickly. Too quickly.

"Are you?"

Catlyn sighed and stopped. Because they'd spoken openly about losing family, she felt she owed him the truth. "I cannot be near the wounded." She looked down at her knotted fingers. "It's the blood." No matter how she fought it, the sight of blood turned her stomach. Even saying the word made her shudder.

"Why? What happened?"

"I cannot speak of it." She gritted her teeth, trying not to remember the horrible way she'd found her brother.

"Callum's wound is completely bandaged."

"It would not matter. I...I would know." She shivered.

"Easy. I am sorry to upset you."

Catlyn nodded. "And I am sorry I cannot do as you ask.

It is my mother's book in any case. I have no time for romances.''

"Indeed?" He cocked his head. "You should find time."

Catlyn shrugged, uncomfortable with the subject. "You must be fond of your squire to worry so."

"It is my fault. Had he not placed himself between me and a Fergusson ax, he'd not have been wounded."

Catlyn gasped. "You were nearly killed?"

"Nay, my armor would have blunted the worst of the blow, but it cut right through—" He cleared his throat. "Suffice to say, he was hurt in my place."

"I see," Catlyn mumbled, shaken to learn he could have been hurt. Last night it would not have mattered so, but something had changed while they stood talking this morning. She had begun to see him not as a shallow rogue, but as a compassionate man who cared for his family, his men and even for her losses. *She* could not afford to care about *him.* "I will pray for Callum's swift recovery." *And your swift departure from my life.* Picking up her skirts, she scampered down the stairs.

Catlyn half feared, half hoped he would follow her. That spark of anticipation worried her. She must find Old Freda and ask when the wounded would be able to ride.

Ross stared after Catlyn till she turned the corner and disappeared from sight. Tempted as he was to go after her, he knew better than to press the slender advantage he'd gained.

It had been worth the hour spent lurking outside her door for the chance to waylay her. And the book had worked as well as he had hoped, giving them a common interest, a base from which to launch his assault on her defenses. They had not crumbled, but there were chinks in them.

The victory left a sour taste in his mouth.

You cannot afford to admire her, Mathew had said last night.

Ross doubted his cousin would be pleased to hear that he not only respected her but lusted after her as well.

There was no other word for the flash of heat that had passed between them as they gazed into each other's eyes. The unexpected quickening sensation had rocked him, mocked him. It was surely the greatest perversity that he should desire the woman he had come to betray.

For one mad moment, Ross considered following Catlyn, telling her why he was really here and...

And what? Throwing himself on her mercy? She had no reason to help him, not when it would mean betraying her clan.

Growling a curse, he slapped the flat of his hand against the stone wall of the stairwell.

He had no choice but to go ahead.

Ross walked quickly to the sickroom on the ground floor, his soul in turmoil. The room was unadorned but clean and comfortable. It touched him that the Boyds had given his injured squire this bit of quiet space. "Sorry I was so long, lad, but I've brought back the book I mentioned."

Callum smiled wanly, his face paler than usual beneath a shock of thick red hair.

"Is something wrong?" Ross hurried to the bed.

"Nay, only..." Callum's eyes strayed to the book. "I'd rather be fighting than hearing about it."

"Ah."

"I thought it was just a ruse to speak with the lady."

"In part it was."

Callum levered himself up on the pillows, wincing slightly. "Did it work? Did you get what we came for?"

"Not yet, but I think she trusts me a bit more." It struck Ross ill that he'd involved this innocent lad in his sordid business. He had considered leaving him at Stirling, but had foolishly thought Callum would be safer with him than fending for himself. "About the battle we fought with the Fergussons..."

"Freda said I would have a scar." Callum beamed. "Not

as big a one as you've got on your leg, but proof I was in battle.''

Ross grunted and strolled over to the bed, shaken by how close he'd come to losing the boy. ''I know you reacted out of instinct, but next time you see a man coming from my blind side, call out to me instead of stepping up to take the blow.'' The gentleness of his tone belied the horror he'd felt when he'd heard Callum scream.

''Mathew says a squire's first duty is to guard his lord's back,'' Callum replied defensively.

''But not with your body.'' Ross laid a hand on Callum's unhurt shoulder. ''I mean to see you knighted.''

''''Tis my fondest dream, too, my lord.''

''Then see you are alive to do so.''

''Aye.'' Callum looked down, but his meekness lasted only a moment. His head came up, his brown eyes dancing again. ''A maid brought me broth while you were gone. I had to let her feed me, but I asked her questions.''

''Oh, Callum.''

''I was clever about it.''

''I am certain you were, but—''

''Brita is her name, and her father is Roland, the head distiller. She helps with preparing the barley mash. She told me that Lady Catlyn keeps records of everything they do in a book.''

''Callum.''

''But this could be what you're looking for,'' the lad cried.

Ross groaned and sat down on the stool beside the bed. ''Aye, it could be, but I do not want you endangering yourself by prying into things.''

''I wanted to help.'' His lip came out. ''Dallas came by to see how I was. He said that he and the other lads are gathering information. I just wanted to help,'' he said again.

''You can help by getting well. But not too quickly.''

''What?''

Ross smiled and ruffled Callum's carrot red hair. ''The

Boyds are a wary lot. The only reason they have let us stay is because you and Ned were hurt. Ned took an arrow to the arm, but he's already up and about. Once you are well enough to ride, they will doubtless send us on our way.''

"Even if we have not found the recipe."

"I can not use that as an excuse, can I?" Ross asked dryly.

"That is true," Callum said seriously.

Ross hid a smile. "But if you were to act weak-like."

"They would have to let us stay," Callum said.

"It will not be easy, lad. You must pretend to sleep a lot and not ask questions. Sick men have not the strength or the will for that."

"I suppose."

"Meantime, I will look for this book you've mentioned."

Callum smiled. "You can count on me, my lord."

"Visiting the patient, Sir Ross?" inquired a dry voice. Freda stood in the gloomy corridor. Old and gnarled as an ancient tree, she leaned heavily on a walking stick and stared at him out of dark, suspicious eyes.

How much had she heard? Ross wondered.

"Freda," Callum whispered. "I'm glad you've come. My shoulder aches something fierce." He had slumped against the pillows, his usually pale skin adding to the deception.

"Oh, dear." The old woman swept into the room, stick thumping out a frantic tattoo as she crossed to the bed. Muttering under her breath, she fussed with the bandage, then laid a hand on his forehead. "Ye don't feel warm."

"Inside I do," Callum said weakly.

Ross rolled his eyes. Is this what he had become, a man who encouraged the honest youths in his care to lie? It little eased his conscience that the safety of his clan was at stake.

"Hmm, well, I dinna suppose it would hurt to dose ye with my sorrel tonic, just to be safe." Freda straightened and looked at Ross. "My lady inquired after the lad a bit ago. I told her he was mending fine and like to be fit for the saddle in a day or so, but if the fever takes him…''

Ross nodded, glad this was only an act. "I would not be able to live with myself if something happened to him," he honestly replied.

"Hmm. Catlyn said ye were fond of this scamp." The healer smiled at Callum, then hobbled to the chest in the corner and began to rummage through it. "Where is that sorrel?"

Callum grinned slyly at Ross.

Ross scowled. "Take care you do not *overdo,* Callum. I leave him in your capable hands, then, Dame Freda."

"Aye." She waved him off with a weathered hand. "Run along but mind ye stay out of trouble. Don't need any more injured men cluttering up the place."

Ross grunted. "I'll be back later, Callum. See you mind Dame Freda." As he stepped into the corridor, a figure materialized from the gloom. Ross's hand fell to his sword.

"Easy." His cousin, Dallas MacLellan, moved into a pale circle of torchlight, his expression taut. He made an excellent spy, for his brown eyes and unremarkable features attracted little attention. Few guessed that beneath that plain exterior dwelt a mind as sharp as flint. "I strolled past the doors you believe lead to the distillery, but a pair of guards now stands watch before them."

Ross cursed softly. "No chance to get inside?"

"None. From a distance, I saw the lady and the old knight, Sir Adair, go in. There were also servants or workmen coming and going. It is possible I might disguise myself as one of them."

"Nay. This is not some town where strangers are commonplace. Everyone here will know each other. We will wait for dark."

"What if they close us in the barracks?"

"I will go myself, as I did last night. I hope that with us locked away, they won't feel the need for guards. What else?"

"The keep is old, the walls in poor repair. A few catapult strikes in the right place, and they'd crumble like dust."

Ross shook his head. "They know the Fergussons are after their whiskey, yet they do little to protect themselves."

"From the talk at the table last eve, I gathered this is the first time anyone has bothered them." Dallas's eyes were troubled. "They lived hand-to-mouth for generations, keeping to themselves, brewing their whiskey. 'Twas Lady Catlyn's father who interested the Edinburgh tavern keepers in the Finglas Water." His voice dropped. "They've hopes they can earn enough to secure their livelihood and their children's future."

Ross exhaled and dragged a hand through his hair. "'Tis a damnable business we're about. If there was a way I could just leave without taking their secret."

"There isn't." Dallas hesitated, then smiled faintly. "But I know you'll find a way to make things right for the Boyds."

If there was a way, Ross could not see it.

"What would you have me do now?"

There is nothing we can do. But Ross found that unacceptable and knew his men would, too. "Are the rest of the lads keeping busy?"

"Aye. Johnnie and six men are in the courtyard, enjoying the air and watching. Gordie's group has the hall. Lang Gil is in the stables, making certain our horses did not suffer any ill effects from the fighting. And Mathew..." Dallas sighed.

"What of Mat?"

"The last I saw him, he was speaking with a lass too beautiful to be real."

"Dora." Ross nodded. "Mat is working, too, believe it or not. That pretty lass is maid to Lady Jeannie."

"Ah. Laird Thomas's widow."

They rounded a corner and came face-to-face with their

scout. "I'd have a word with ye," Seamus muttered. "Alone."

Ross's gut rolled, but he motioned for Dallas to go on.

Seamus glanced surreptitiously around and leaned close. Stinking of stale sweat and sour breath, he whispered, "I know where the stills are."

"As do I."

"Well, well. Ye're cannier than Hakon said ye were."

"If I was, I'd not be here now."

"That's true enough." Seamus grinned, revealing three blackened teeth. "Ye'll go tonight and draw the stills."

"There are guards on the door."

Seamu touched the dirk at this belt. "I'll see to them."

"Nay. No more bloodshed."

"There'll be bloodshed if that's what it takes."

Ross stared into those merciless black eyes, a terrible thought taking shape. "Do you not want to know if I've gotten the recipe from Lady Catlyn?"

"If ye had, ye'd have said so."

"Does this secret recipe even exist?"

"Of course it does. Everyone knows that's what makes the Finglas Water finer than any other whiskey."

"And Hakon wants the recipe and drawings of the Boyds' stills so he can go into competition with them?"

"Aye."

What if Seamus had been sent to move the powder? With that threat removed, Hakon would be free to besiege Kennecraig. Given the state of the defenses, that should not take long. Then Hakon would have Catlyn to give him the recipe, and ready-made equipment and, if he did not kill them in the siege, slaves to work the stills.

Ross saw now that Hakon had lied to him. Perhaps he had thought that Ross would not go along with his foul scheme, even to redeem that cursed note. Hakon did not want to set up his own distillery. He wanted to take over the Boyds'. Ross's blood ran cold as he considered the possibilities. Hakon would have attacked months ago, if not for the black powder reputedly waiting to be exploded if he tried.

Ross's stomach rolled.

"I'd be worried about protecting my own property, if I was ye," Seamus muttered. "A week Hakon gave ye to get what he wants or he'll be taking possession of *your* keep."

Ross stiffened, horrified at the thought of Hakon and his unholy band wreaking havoc in Edin Valley. "I have a week. I'll use it as I see fit. But my bargain was for the whiskey recipe, nothing more. If you try to harm the lady or open the keep to Hakon's men, I'll tell the Boyds who you are."

Seamus's revolting grin spread. "Will ye, Lord High-and-Mighty Sutherland. And how will ye explain yer presence here?"

"I'll tell them the truth."

"And lose yer lands?"

"Better that than be a party to murder."

Seamus hawked and spat onto the floor. "Told Hakon it was a mistake to choose ye."

"Why did he?"

"Because I recognized ye…from Keastwicke on the day I came to pick up Aedh Fergusson's body from yer Uncle Hunter."

Ross groaned. Hakon was a common name on the Borders, still he should have made the connection. "Aedh was Hakon's father?"

"The same. Hakon thought it fitting ye help him with this, since ye're kin to the man who caused the death of his pa."

Ross turned and walked away before he gave in to the urge to wring Seamus's scrawny neck. He was even more disgusted with himself. How could he have been so stupid?

Seamus's coarse laughter followed him down the corridor. By the time Ross reached the great hall, he was seething. He burst into the room, sending the doors crashing

against the walls. Folk the length of the hall froze in place.
All talk ceased. Even his own men gaped at him in astonishment.

Get yourself in hand, cautioned an inner voice. Ross
reined in his temper with difficulty, scanned the room and
spotted Mathew sitting with two women. Dredging up a
smile that likely showed too much tooth, he crossed the
room.

"Mathew, I need to speak with you," Ross said.

"Of course." Mathew rose swiftly, his widened eyes the
only sign of his alarm. "May I present Lady Jeannie and
Dora."

Ross bowed stiffly. Seen up close, Dora was truly breathtaking, but her face held the wariness of one who had
learned beauty brought pain.

"Have you seen my Thomas's plaid?" inquired the lady.
Her eyes were the same unusual hazel as her daughter's,
but they were as blank as the windows of a deserted keep.

"Nay," Ross said gently. "But I have heard of your skill
with a needle, my lady, and wonder if you've time to mend
my best tunic? It's velvet and was made for me by my dear
mama, so I cannot trust its repair to just anyone."

A light shone briefly in the lady's eyes. "I would be
pleased to look at it and see what can be done."

"Excellent." Ross motioned for Dallas to join them.
"Lady Jeannie has agreed to mend the rents in my best
black tunic. Will you go upstairs with her and find it?"

"Of course." Dallas bowed smoothly, betraying no hint
of surprise, asking no questions. He extended his arm to
the lady and escorted her away.

Dora gave Ross a hard look before following her mistress.

"I'd say the maid is no fool," Ross muttered as he sat
down on the bench, his gaze on the exiting trio.

"Nay. She gives lie to the notion that beautiful women
are empty-headed. But she has suffered."

Dora paused in the doorway and looked back at Mathew. A small smile tugged at her lips before she hastened away.

"And I'd say you'd made an impression on her."

Mathew grunted, his jaw tight, his eyes narrowed.

"I like this no better than you do." Ross curled his hands into tight fists. "And things are worse than we thought."

"Worse? What has happened?"

"I've been blind, that is what. I should have guessed from the start that Hakon wanted more than the recipe. He wants it all—the keep, the stills and the secret to making the whiskey."

"*Dieu!* How—?"

"Seamus. Blackmailing me into supposedly stealing this damned recipe was but a ruse to get Seamus inside Kennecraig. That bastard all but admitted it to me moments ago."

"So Seamus can move the black powder away from the stills?"

"Possibly, but it would take time for a lone man to do that. And then there's the risk of discovery. I think Seamus may try to open the gates to Hakon."

"What can we do?"

"Make certain Seamus does not succeed."

"But what of the note Hakon holds? What of Stratheas?"

"Somehow I must find a way to thwart his plans."

Chapter Five

It was nearly noon by the time Catlyn left the still rooms, tired but pleased with the morning's work.

They had finished sampling last year's whiskey with only minimal griping from Roland. He and his men were even now decanting the twenty large tuns of liquor into smaller kegs, which were transferred from the underground still room to the settling room on the ground floor by means of a winch.

One task down, but many more to do. The kegs of whiskey from two and three years ago had to be checked against leakage and the contents sampled to make certain the liquor was aging properly. Lastly and most importantly, the whiskey kegged four years ago had to be readied for market.

Wesley and his crew had begun preparations for this year's whiskey. The tuns would be scrubbed with ash and boiling water to free them of scum that accumulated and set aside to receive this year's batch of liquor gleaned from the time consuming distillation process carried on in the still room.

"It is not necessary for you to ride out and inspect the fields yourself," Adair grumbled as they climbed the stairs.

"Papa always saw to it himself." She braced for him to say something about her being weak and female.

"That was because he had you to carry part of the load.

You'll wear yourself out doing the work of two. Let me bear a share of the burden.''

It was tempting. Her back was tired from hours on her feet, her eyes gritty from lack of sleep. But this year, everything had to be perfect. A tribute to her father. "I'm looking forward to a ride in the fresh air.''

"Stubborn," Adair muttered.

"Only when I am right." Catlyn opened the door and entered the settling room. "I'd like to continue Papa's plans to take a keg of the ten-year-old Finglas to the Doune Fair this year.''

"Ah, the fair." Adair tugged at his right lobe. "I've been thinking we should stay away this year.''

"But the Boyds have always gone." With the first offering of the Finglas Water. "It is tradition. Da said it was how he judged the worth of the whiskey." All the folk in the Grampians made a bit and were consequently the hardest to please.

"What if Hakon attends the fair?''

"It is a truce day. He'd not dare cause trouble. And we need the coin the whiskey will bring to see us through till we can take the rest to market in Edinburgh.''

"That's true enough." Adair frowned. "Cook will need salt for the pigs the lads'll be bringing in from the glen.''

"And wood for new casks.''

"I'd feel safer if we had more men.''

Catlyn stiffened. "Sutherlands, I suppose?''

"Why not? They are experienced fighting men. We could not hope to find better elsewhere. And we know them a bit.''

"I do not want them here.''

"Because you fancy Sir Ross and you do not want to?''

"I do not *fancy* any man, and especially not one who does not like our whiskey." Or trust him.

"Oh, but you're a stubborn lass. Very well." He tweaked her chin as he used to when she was a lass. "We'll say nothing of the matter for now, but you'll be taking extra men with you when you ride out to the crofts.''

''Agreed.'' Catlyn stood on tiptoe to kiss his whiskery cheek, then dashed away before he found more objections. Bypassing the great hall, she put on her cloak and headed through the entryway with its ancient shields. Outside, the sunlight seemed blinding. She shielded her eyes and paused at the top of the stairs.

Eoin and a dozen well-armed Boyds awaited her at the entrance to the stable. Across the courtyard, a handful of Sutherlands practiced with sword and targe. Muscles bulging, they parried and thrust, filling the air with coarse grunts and the sharp ring of steel. As she descended the steps, a burly redheaded Sutherland sidled past her and into the keep.

Eoin hustled over to greet her. ''Good day to you, Catlyn.'' He reached for her arm.

''Hmm.'' She evaded his hand and made for her mare.

He dogged her heels. ''I took the liberty of having Cook pack a wee lunch for us to share in that glen you like so—''

''No time,'' she said briskly. ''We'll eat as we ride.'' She shook off his helping hand and swung into the saddle.

Eoin scowled, his lower lip sticking out like a sullen lad's as he mounted his own beast. ''Catlyn, I think—''

Ross Sutherland exploded out of the keep, charged down the stairs and across the courtyard. He grabbed hold of her horse's bridle before she could back away. ''Where are you going?''

''To…to check on the bar—''

''It is too dangerous.''

''See here.'' Eoin leaped from the saddle and into the fray.

''Keep out of this.'' Ross looked Catlyn straight in the eye, his own blazing with fury. ''Have you forgotten Hakon and what happened yestereve?''

Catlyn's heart beat wildly against her temples. ''He will not burn the barley fields,'' she said. ''He wants us to harvest them and turn them into whiskey, but he will not dare to attack Kennecraig to get it.''

''He would not have to if he takes you hostage.''

''Me!'' Catlyn's anger drained away in a wash of fear.

''You. Even now he could be watching from yon hills, waiting for you to ride out with your puny escort so he can ambush you and make you his prisoner.'' He leaned closer. ''Your clansmen would open these gates quick enough if your life was at stake.''

''Nay,'' Catlyn whispered.

''I'd protect Lady Catlyn with my life,'' cried Eoin.

Ross snorted but kept his gaze on her. ''They'd cut you down like stalks of barley.'' Before she could guess what he intended, Ross grabbed hold of her and snatched her from the saddle.

''Put me down!'' she cried. ''I am going and that's—''

''You are going inside.'' He tucked her under his arm like a sack of laundry and made for the steps.

Adair waited on the bottom one.

''Adair! Do something!'' she cried.

''Is she always this stubborn?'' Ross asked.

''Hmm. Come inside, lass. Eoin can go out to the crofts.''

''Why are you doing this?'' Catlyn demanded, staring into Ross Sutherland's upside-down face.

''Because I do not want to see you hurt. And I do assure you that although Hakon might leave your crops alone, he most surely would seize you if he got half a chance.''

The conviction in his voice cut through Catlyn's objections. ''Very well. If you will put me down, I will go inside.'' When he released her, she walked slowly up the steps, her head high, her shoulders square. It took all her willpower to appear calm and dignified when her insides were roiling like a storm-tossed loch.

He had touched her, held her. And nothing would ever be the same again. She understood that on some deep, primitive level that frightened her nearly as much as Hakon's threats. What she did not know was how to deal with it. Or Ross Sutherland.

From the crest of the opposing mountain, Hakon watched the little cavalcade ride away from Kennecraig. "Ye've got the sharpest eyes, son, do ye see Catlyn Boyd among them?"

Godless Guthrie Fergusson shielded his eyes and squinted. "Nay, not that I can tell from this distance."

"What of Seamus?"

"How could I be picking that wee gorm out of the crowd?" Guthrie muttered. "I say we just attack them."

"We need the lass alive."

"Fine." Guthrie's hand inched toward the ax on his belt. "We'll spare her and kill the rest."

Hakon sighed. Guthrie was so like his grandsire. Something inside him seemed to crave the fighting, the bloodletting. Even as a lad, Guthrie had liked killing things. This penchant for violence had proved useful in their line of work. Tales of Guthrie's appetite for torture worked like magic in loosening the purse strings of would-be victims. But the lad was too impulsive by half. "We let them pass."

"We've not had a decent skirmish since we left the Borders," Guthrie grumbled. "Fair makes a man itchy, it does."

"'Twas your itchy hands on Thomas Boyd's neck that ended his life ere we could use him to get inside Kennecraig."

Guthrie sniffed. "I was just trying to make him plead."

"I know, son, and I hate to deprive ye of yer pleasures, but this is important. Once we get control of Kennecraig, we'll live like lords. We'll have a grand fortress, coin for food, clothes. All the whiskey we can drink."

"And women." A feral grin slid over Guthrie's swarthy face. "Ye said I could have the women."

"Aye." Hakon shrugged off a shiver of distaste. "If

we're to succeed, we cannot tip our hand to the Boyds till after Seamus has found a way to get us inside the keep.''

"I'd like to see the mighty Ross Lion's face when he realizes how ye tricked him, Da.'' Guthrie cocked his head. "Can we hold him for ransom, do ye think?''

"An excellent idea. One I'd not thought of,'' Hakon lied. He wanted to encourage the lad to use his mind. "Tail them, then.''

Catlyn was too upset, and too embarrassed, to go down for supper. Instead, she requested a tray be sent up for her to share with her mother. She entered the master chamber ahead of Dora and found her mama bent over a bit of mending.

"Set the food on the table, will you, Dora?'' Catlyn walked over to her mother. "What are you working on?''

"Sir Ross's tunic.''

Catlyn stopped and eyed the black velvet with loathing. "Why ever are you sewing for him?''

"Because he asked me to.'' Her needle moved in and out, taking nearly invisible stitches. "His mother made this for him, you see, and he'd not trust another to mend it.''

Catlyn looked at Dora.

"He did ask her to mend it, my lady.'' *My lady.*

"Dora, I thought we'd agreed to put the past behind us.'' She held up a hand to stay Dora's apology. "We have been friends since birth.'' Which had made the betrayal all the more painful. "Just now, I need my friends...all my friends.''

"Oh, Catlyn.'' Dora's eyes teared. "You are so good.''

"Not according to Sir Ross.''

"Do you think Thomas sent Sir Ross here to protect us from the Fergussons?'' Lady Jeannie asked.

Catlyn exchanged shocked glances with Dora. Was her mother more aware of things than they'd supposed? "Mama, I—''

"I like him.'' Lady Jeannie looked directly at her for the

first time in months. "He has kindly eyes and the widest shoulders I've ever seen. A lass would feel safe with him." She looked down at her work again. "But he must take better care of his garments." She poked a finger through a long slash. "From the looks of this, Sir Ross must have been clawed by a bear."

"A bear?" Catlyn said weakly.

"I think those cuts were made on purpose," Dora whispered. "Your mother was terribly upset about not finding the laird's plaid. Sir Ross overheard and approached with a tale about a ruined tunic. Lady Jeannie agreed at once to mend it. Sir Ross's man was a long time fetching it, and when he appeared… well, you can see for yourself what a state it is in."

"He cut the tunic on purpose?" Catlyn exclaimed. "Oh, but he is an arrogant, high-handed meddler."

"I thought him kind," Dora muttered. "And perceptive."

Catlyn sniffed and turned away from her friend's probing stare. "Let us eat."

They coaxed Lady Jeannie away from her mending, and the three of them ate boiled mutton and oatcakes in companionable silence. Things were not as they had been, but at least the tension between Dora and Catlyn was less.

"I will be glad when harvest time comes," Catlyn said as she forced down the last bit of stringy meat.

"So Sir Mathew said also at dinner this noon."

"You were talking with one of *them?*"

Dora blushed and dipped her head. "He is very nice."

Catlyn could imagine why. Doubtless the lecher had looked at Dora's face, listened to the gossip and assumed she would be easy pickings. "Dora, men can be—"

Dora's head snapped up. "I know they can be deceiving, but this Sir Mathew is different. He did not tell me I was beautiful. He spoke of his home and crops and such."

"Oh." Warily.

"They grew up in a place called Edin Valley, which is as peaceful and pretty as its name."

"They?"

"Most of the men in their band were born there, Sir Ross included. He is Mathew's cousin and lord of a large keep inherited from his mother's family. Stratheas Tower is—"

"I do not wish to hear more." Catlyn stood. "I—I am glad we had this time together, but I must work on the ledgers tonight."

Dora followed her to the door. "I do not like the idea of you working in the cellars alone."

"Wee worrier," Catlyn teased, a nickname from happier days that drew a smile from Dora. "But in this, Adair agrees with you. He has ordered a guard posted outside the distillery and another to sit about outside the counting room while I work."

"Good. You'll be safe, then." Dora smiled faintly. "I— I am glad we have smoothed things. I missed you."

"And I, you."

"I don't like the idea of you looking for the stills," Mathew grumbled. "Suppose you are discovered?"

"I won't be." Ross would be going across the roof and into the window of the cooperage on the second floor of the distillery, which Dora had showed to Mathew this noon while they walked in the courtyard. "Thanks to your Dora."

Mathew scowled.

"I do not like it, either, my friend. But needs must. I've got to find out if the powder really is there, and make certain that Seamus cannot move it." Dallas would be making certain Seamus did not leave the barracks at night, and during the day there were folk about.

"Seamus strikes me as the sort of sly creature who can slip through cracks," Mathew grumbled.

"You worry too much." Ross stepped out into the night.

* * *

A noise jerked Catlyn's attention from her records. As she lifted her head, pain shot down her neck. Groaning, she massaged her nape with one hand and scanned the room.

Catlyn heard the noise again, a furtive scratching that seemed to come from the settling room. Had a rat somehow evaded the army of cats brought in to keep the vermin from the barley?

Frowning, she stood and walked to the open doorway. A shiver moved down her spine as she scanned the cavernous chamber. It was dark save for a golden pool cast by a candle in the ship's lantern on the tasting table. At the moment, she wished the walls were rimmed with torches so she might see what—if anything—lurked between the neat rows of kegs.

And where was her guardsman?

"Harry?" she called softly.

The silence grew, pressing in on her ears.

"Harry?" she called, louder this time.

"Here." His voice came from the next room. A single candle burned in there, too, its pale golden light spilling through the doorway and a few feet into the settling room.

Catlyn headed for the light. "Is it rats again, Harry? I thought I heard one in the settling room, as well. We'll have to see about more cats, for the problem will only worsen when we bring in the grain." She was thinking about the harvest, the dozens of details to oversee, as she stepped over the threshold.

"Harry?"

"Here." His voice came from the nearest storage shelves. The shadows were so thick she could not see him.

She took two steps toward him, tripped over something on the floor and landed hard on her knees. "Ouch!" Palms and knees smarting, she looked over her shoulder to see what had felled her, and straight into Harry's face. "Harry?" she gasped.

He lay on his back, unmoving, eyes closed. Blood trickled from his mouth, a black smear in the half-light.

"Harry!" Ignoring the sting in her knees, she crawled to him. "Harry, what happened? Did you fall?" She shook his arm. It was leaden, unresponsive. Dread coiled tight in her belly. "Ha—"

"He cannot hear you," whispered a coarse voice.

Catlyn twisted around and looked up.

A figure towered above her, a menacing shape backlit by the lantern on the table.

"Sir Ross?" It was her first thought, that once again a man to whom she was drawn had betrayed her.

The man laughed, a harsh, mirthless sound that raised the hair on her nape. "Nay, but I'll tell him ye were asking after him. Fancy him, do ye." He chuckled again.

"Who are you?" She started to rise.

He grabbed her shoulders and pushed her back down. "Stay. I like having a lass at my feet." His fingers dug into her flesh.

"What do you want?" Her mind raced. He must be one of Ross's men. Had he come down here looking for whiskey, been discovered by Harry and attacked her clansman? It seemed likely. And now that she had seen him here— her gut tightened with dread—would his thoughts turn from drink to rape? "Is it whiskey you want?" she asked faintly.

"Aye. I want to know how it's done."

"Done? How what is done?"

"How ye make the whiskey."

Catlyn blinked. "Why would you care?"

"I don't." He dragged her to her feet, turning slightly so the light played over his features. They were sharp, like a weasel's, his eyes narrow, glittering slits. "But Hakon does."

"Hakon." Catlyn's mouth dropped open. "You...you are—"

"A Fergusson." He grinned, revealing a trio of black-ened teeth. "Seamus Fergusson."

"How did you get in?"

"Trickery," he said proudly. "Now." His hand tight-

ened on her, making her bones grind. Her gasp of pain
made him chuckle. "That's nothing to what ye'll feel if ye
don't do as I say."

"Wh-what do you—"

Seamus shook her so sharply her head snapped back.
"Ye know. I want the secret." He pushed his face into
hers, suffocating her with his rancid breath. "Ye're going
to give me the book it's writ in."

"It isn't in a book." Not a single one, that is. Hysterical
laughter bubbled as she thought of Seamus trying to make
his escape weighed down by centuries of Boyd records.

"That's a lie. We know it's writ down, same as we know
that ye're the only one who knows where it is."

"I don't kn—"

"Ye do." He slapped her.

Pain exploded in Catlyn's cheek. Tears filled her eyes,
blurring Seamus's evil face, but his intentions were clear.
He meant to hurt her till she gave him what he wanted.
Sweet Mary, give me strength, she prayed. But she feared
she'd not long withstand his torture. Everything inside her
rose up in revolt. She could not let him win. Somehow she
had to get away. "A-all right," she whispered, the quaver
in her voice unfeigned. "I will show you where it is."

Seamus grunted. His grip on her shoulders eased. "If ye
play me false, I'll carve ye up so's even yer own mother
won't recognize ye."

Catlyn nodded, keeping her body limp and unresisting
as he shoved her toward the door. He had only one hand
on her now, resting on her shoulder. Out of the corner of
her eye, she saw the blunt, dirty fingers against her brown
gown. So near all she had to do was turn her head...and
bite.

"Argh!" Seamus screamed, and released her.

Catlyn took off running, the metallic taste of his vile
blood in her mouth, his curses filling her ears.

A scream stopped Ross in the middle of the settling
room. His first thought was that he'd been discovered.

Dropping into a crouch, he drew his dirk and braced for an attack.

Nothing stirred near him, but from somewhere in the gloomy rooms beyond, came the sounds of running footsteps. An instant later, they were drowned out by a string of vile curses.

What was going on?

Ross straightened, torn between leaving and investigating.

A second scream, a woman's this time, decided the matter.

Ross started forward. Faint light from the center of the room showed him the path through a maze of kegs stacked chest high. As he approached the table, a woman burst from the doorway at the other end of the room, her face white, a long, pale braid flying behind her. Just as she was swallowed up by the gloom, a man charged after her. He stopped in the doorway, his head swinging back and forth like a hunting hound's.

Ross stopped, too, and retreated into the shadows. What was going on? A lover's spat? Or something more sinister? Should he betray his presence here, or leave? Over the rasp of his own breathing, he heart furtive movements to his right.

The other man must have heard them, too, for he charged into the darkness. ''I've got ye now,'' he called out.

Seamus.

The woman screamed again just as Ross moved from hiding. The sight that greeted him halted him.

Seamus had Lady Catlyn backed up against the far wall, one hand knotted in her hair, the other pressing a blade to her throat. ''So, thought ye'd get away, did ye?''

Even in the dim light, Ross could see the fear in her bleached features and read the hopelessness in her eyes.

''Please, I—''

''Shut up.'' Seamus wrenched her head back even further, exposing the slim column of her throat to his blade. "Never doubt ye'll tell me everything ye know," he said. "And then we'll open the gates for Hakon."

Her whimper, the sheer look of terror in her gaze, cut through Ross. He stepped from the shadows, ready to order Seamus away from her and to hell with what he owed Hakon. Before he could challenge the bastard, Seamus spoke again.

"I warned ye I'd cut ye up if ye defied me." Seamus raised the tip of his blade to the pristine curve of her cheek, chuckling when she cried out and tried to move away.

Seamus was going to torture Catlyn till he had her secrets, then he would kill her. Ross knew it as surely as he did that no words he could utter would stay Seamus's hand. Only one thing would. Lifting his own dirk, he sent it flying.

Seamus jerked as the blade buried itself in his back. He half turned, his eyes widening. He opened his mouth, but the only sound that emerged was a faint gasp. Then his knees buckled and he slid to the floor at Lady Catlyn's feet.

"Oh, my God," Catlyn whispered.

Ross leaped forward in time to catch her before she joined her attacker on the floor. "It is all right." He swept her into his arms and held her tight, his breathing as unsettled as hers.

"He…he…" Her teeth chattered so she could not go on.

"Shh. It is over. He cannot harm you now." Ross glanced down at the wretch just to make sure Seamus was not moving.

"Catlyn! Catlyn!" Adair bounded into the room, a pack of Boyds at his back. "Damn you, put her down!" he shouted, setting the edge of his sword to Ross's throat.

"Adair, wait." Catlyn put a hand up to stay his sword. "It is not what you think. Sir Ross saved my life. If he had not come…" She shivered again.

"What happened?" Adair demanded, his gaze darting

between the two of them, then down to Seamus. "Who is this?"

Ross instinctively clasped Catlyn a little closer, sensing she was a hairbreadth away from falling apart. "We will speak of it later. Let me carry you up to your women," he said gently, looking down at the pale woman who lay so trusting in his arms. He knew he did not deserve the gratitude that shone beneath the latent fear in her eyes. "There is a scratch on your neck. It does not look deep, but it will want tending."

She nodded. "Thank you. If you had not come—"

"Do not think of it." Ross started for the door. "You are safe and unharmed save for that scratch."

"I owe you my life."

Feeling lower than he ever had, Ross started for the door. "I am glad I could help."

She was silent except for murmured directions to her chamber, and so light in his arms. Yet the trip down the long, dimly lit corridors and up the steps to the second floor was the longest in his life.

Chapter Six

Ross came away from the wall as the door to Catlyn's chamber opened and Adair emerged. "How is she?"

"She's had a bad fright, but the wound's only a scratch."

"She fainted."

"Likely the sight of the blood. Hasn't been able to stomach it since she found wee Thommie." He pulled the door closed. "If you're up to it, I've a few questions."

Ross nodded. He'd been expecting them, but he was surprised when Adair led him up to the battlements. The air was fresh and warm, the sky filled with stars. Ross concentrated on what he would say. The truth…as far as he could. That was always best, for no matter how skilled a man was at telling a lie, it often came back to bite him.

Adair crossed to the parapet and leaned against the chest-high wall, gazing out over the dark landscape. "The man you killed…do you know who he was?"

"Donald Dunbar, the scout I hired in Stirling to guide us through the mountains to Inverness." Hakon had insisted his man go with them. To show him the way to make certain he got the job done. Or so Ross had stupidly thought.

"Did he suggest you come to Kennecraig?"

Ross pretended to consider that. "When the storm threatened to break, he did suggest we might find shelter here."

"Ah. The weather has been unsettled of late, but if it

had not stormed, he would doubtless have used some other ruse—a lame horse, whatever—to get inside.''

"You mean Donald planned this?'' Ross asked. "Why?''

"Because his name is Seamus Fergusson. He told Catlyn so.''

"Fergusson. Is that not the name of your enemy? The ones who ambushed us outside your walls?''

"Aye, and the very same bastard who wants our distillery. This Seamus was not with Hakon the few sorry times our paths crossed. Which was doubtless why he was chosen for this task. But he's cut from the same vile cloth as Hakon and Guthrie. His mission was to capture Catlyn and force our surrender.''

"I heard him.'' Ross's voice held all the fear, all the revulsion he'd felt when he'd seen Catlyn in Seamus's grip. At his mercy. "When she refused to cooperate, he threatened to cut her and go on carving till she surrendered.''

"Dod.'' Adair's fist tightened till his knuckles turned white. "Thank the good Lord you were there.''

"It is thanks to your trust in me. Had there been guards outside my door as there were last night, I'd not have been out and about looking for the garderobe,'' Ross said, careful to keep his eyes on Adair's. The guards had, indeed, been removed, but fearing a trick, Ross had gone over the roof.

"I realized I had gotten turned around and was retracing my steps when I heard a cry. I saw a lady dash from a room at the far end of that first chamber. A man followed her. At first, I thought I had chanced on a midnight tryst. I was about to leave them to their games when the woman screamed again. She did not sound like a willing partner, so I went to intervene. As I stepped closer, I recognized their voices, heard his threats and assumed Donald, er, Seamus was bent on raping the lady.''

Adair nodded. "His back was to you. Why did you not just step up behind him and disarm him?''

"He had his blade to her throat. If I made my presence known, Seamus could have used her to force me to disarm. Then we would both have been at his mercy." It was the truth, and Ross's voice rang with the fear he'd felt. "As I hesitated, trying to decide on the best course to free her, the bastard began to speak of secrets and of the pain he'd inflict to get them. I knew, then, that he would take great pleasure in hurting her. And killing her. I could see no other way to save her."

"Aye." Adair shook his head, his face gray. "He'd already killed once. The young guardsman I'd left with Catlyn."

"If only I'd come sooner."

"You could not have known. I'm just grateful that you arrived in time to save our Catlyn."

"As am I." Catlyn's injury and the guardsman's death weighed on his conscience. Damn Fergusson's soul. And his own.

Adair sighed. "Kennecraig has been our home for centuries. Unassailable, it seemed. Never thought I'd see the day when a Boyd was not safe within its walls." He dragged an unsteady hand over his face. "I've been a blind fool to think Hakon would just leave us alone."

"'Tis a common failing of peace-loving people. Edin Valley, the home of my mother's clan, is guarded by steep mountains. The MacLellans felt safe behind them till a band of greedy, vicious men found a way in."

Adair turned to him. "How did her people prevail?"

"Fortunately my grandsire had the wisdom to hire a mercenary before it was too late." He smiled. "A clever warrior who not only vanquished the enemy, but wed Duncan MacLellan's granddaughter and now leads the clan."

"Your father?"

"Aye. Kieran Sutherland, Laird of Edin Valley now, but at one time a warrior without equal, strong, resourceful—"

"And honorable, I'd guess." Adair's gaze held a respect Ross did not deserve. "For he raised a fine, stalwart lad."

"I am not half the man I should be," Ross muttered.

"Your modesty is misplaced. I've watched the way you comport yourself, and I've watched your men. My da always said you could tell much about a leader by the mettle of his men. Despite their rough appearance and fighting skills, yours are sober, hardworking and respectful."

"They are good lads." He was the one lacking in wits.

"Which is why I would like to hire you and them."

"What?"

"'Tis obvious we are no match for Hakon. In fact, when I saw how well your men fought against the Fergussons, it occurred to me that we might hire you. Catlyn was, er…"

"Opposed to the idea?" Ross asked dryly.

"She is distrustful of strangers after what happened to her father," Adair said gruffly.

"A wise lass." Ross suspected she was more wary of the unexpected attraction that flared between them. He knew he was.

"But this latest scheme forces our hand. Hakon is more ruthless and more determined than I'd guessed." Adair fingered the stubble on his chin. "The only reason he has not attacked Kennecraig is that Laird Thomas told him he had black powder kegs alongside the stills and he'd blow the whole thing up if Hakon approached the gates."

"Effective, if drastic. Is it true?"

"Aye." Adair sighed deeply. "It was one of the last things Laird Thom did before he died. He believed that if he made taking Kennecraig seem impossible, Hakon would find other prey. A week later, we found Thom and his guard dead at the bottom of a glen. He'd gone into Doune to sell some of our whiskey and apparently went over the cliff in a storm."

Laird Thom had never made it to Doune. Of that, Ross was certain. Hakon must have waylaid him and taken the whiskey. Why had he not used Thom to force Kennecraig's surrender?

"When he heard of her father's passing, Hakon came

calling with an offer of marriage. To his son. Godless Guthrie.'' Adair made a growling sound in his throat. ''Rumor has it he's called that because he sacked and burned a nunnery.''

That had been but one in a long string of heinous crimes dating back to Guthrie's youth. Ross's Uncle Hunter said the entire Border breathed a sigh of relief when Hakon, his son and their band of thugs left for the far-off Highlands. What ill fate had crossed his path with theirs? Ross wondered.

''She refused, of course. But I see now Hakon is not giving up.'' Adair's shoulders sagged. The gloom emphasized the circles under his eyes and the despair in them. ''We need help.''

''I agree, but I am not the man to—''

''Oh, I'm sure you've got an important task waiting you in Inverness, one that'll likely pay you more than we can. And there's no reason you should feel obliged because we gave you shelter after the ambush.'' He cocked one brow. ''Though I suppose you are a might piqued at him over that yourself.''

Ross chuckled. ''You would do well at court with that sharp mind and clever tongue.''

''I've got my hands full here. Well?''

''I do not know what I could do.''

''Protect us till we can get our large shipment of whiskey to Edinburgh. Then we will have funds to hire more men. Or to keep you on if you've a mind to,'' he added hopefully.

It was the excuse he needed to remain at Kennecraig, but Ross hesitated, hating what he must do. ''All right.''

''Excellent.'' Adair clapped him on the shoulder. ''On the morrow, you can inspect Kennecraig, tell us what needs doing to shore up the defenses.''

''Your men will need training in arms.''

''Assuredly. Whatever you think best, we'll do.'' Adair's weathered face glowed in the half-light. ''Well, I'm for bed.'' He turned toward the stairwell, his arm still slung over Ross's shoulders. ''I fancy I'll sleep better tonight than I have since my lord's death.''

Ross doubted he'd sleep at all. He trudged back to the solar, not surprised to find Mathew waiting for him. The whole keep had been roused by the aftermath of the attack. Adair's bellowed orders had sent guardsmen rushing about to check for other intruders.

''How is she?'' Mathew asked.

''Shaken, but not badly hurt.'' Ross crossed to the table, filled a cup and took a huge swallow. It was not ale. Whiskey burned its way down his throat. He gasped for breath, but his belly had obviously forgiven his past excesses and accepted the liquid fire. His own soul was not as forgiving.

''They questioned you?''

Ross nodded, took a more cautious sip and glanced at his cousin over the rim of the cup.

''What is it?''

''We have been hired to protect the Boyds from Hakon.''

''What?'' A string of curses followed, most having to do with the state of Ross's mind. ''How the hell are we going to do that and get back the note for Stratheas Tower?''

''I am not sure…yet. But I will find a way. Now that I know who Hakon is and what his real purpose is, do you think I can just leave these people to his mercy?''

''I smell trouble,'' Mathew said morosely.

Despite a night spent fleeing Seamus Fergusson in her dreams, Catlyn awoke at first light.

For a moment, she lay still, staring up at the needlework on the underside of the canopy. Her mother had designed the scene and stitched much of it herself five years ago. It depicted Finglas Glen in full summer, the trees lush with fruit, the barley fields shimmering in the distance like a sea of gold. The peace and beauty threatened now by Hakon.

Shivering, Catlyn sat up and tossed the covers aside. Her bruised muscles protested as she dragged herself from bed.

Reminders of last night's horror, of the tremendous debt she owed Ross. If he had not arrived when he did, she might be dead or, worse, Hakon's hostage. And the rest of the clansmen, too.

Catlyn crossed the bare wooden floor, chilled despite the summer heat that had finally warmed the old stone room. By rote, she washed her face and cleansed her teeth with salt before pulling on a plain brown work gown. But her mind would not stay on the day's tasks. It kept straying to that moment when she'd looked over Seamus's shoulder and seen Ross.

Clad in black, his body had blended with the shadows, nearly invisible, so his face had seemed to float suspended. At first she'd thought it a figment born of fear and desperation. Then their eyes had met and she'd read in his such fury, such strength of purpose she'd known it was no dream.

Rescue had come swiftly, hurtling out of the darkness, a flash of shiny steel, biting deep into Seamus's back.

Catlyn gasped and turned away from the washstand, not wanting to relive that terrible moment. No matter he'd been her enemy, bent on hurting her, his death disturbed her.

She thought instead of Ross. Would he be up and about so early, her rescuer? Or sleeping in her solar down the hall? She had yet to thank him properly. What did she say to the man who muddled her mind and made her tongue tangle?

Thank you for my life? Thank you for saving all I hold dear? Thank you for not holding against me all the terrible things I shouted at you in the afternoon.

Catlyn groaned. Maybe she'd just pen him a note and hide in her counting room till he left. Her usually nimble fingers shook as they divided her hair and plaited it into a single braid. She tied the end with a bit of leather and hurried from the room, intent on breaking her fast and getting back to the records she had not finished last night.

Early as it was, the great hall was filled with folk breaking their fast on ale and oatcakes. Catlyn got two steps into the room before she was spotted.

"It's our Catlyn!" someone shouted. The rest of her kinsmen took up the chant, shouting her name, some weeping, some giving thanks to God as they converged on her. Their outpouring of love brought tears to her eyes.

"I am fine, really," she insisted, swaying a little.

"Idiots! What are you doing to her?" Eoin pushed his way through the crowd and swept her up in his arms. "I will get you out of here," he crooned.

Last night, she had welcomed the haven of Ross's embrace. It felt strange to be held by another man. "Please put me down," she said before Eoin had gone two steps.

"You need your rest."

"I just slept the night away." She pushed at his chest. "And I have a wee scratch on my neck, not a broken leg. Down."

"Very well." Expression sullen, he set her on her feet. "But you need to sit." He kept an arm around her waist and herded her to her usual table.

Catlyn sat, groaning inwardly when Eoin plopped down onto the bench beside her.

"I have been frantic with worry for you. I tried to see you last eve, but Freda said you were sleeping and turned me away."

"She gave me one of her potions. But I thank you for your concern." Catlyn stared at the steaming meat pie the maid set before her along with a cup of ale. "What is all this?"

"Cook stayed up all night baking that special for ye. Said ye'd be needing to build up yer blood."

Blood. Yuck. "Th-thank you. And thank Cook for me. I will take it with me to eat later." Providing she could swallow it. Feeling queasy, Catlyn stood to leave.

Eoin tugged her back down. "I need to speak with you."

"About the barley?" she asked hopefully.

"Nay."

"You did inspect the fields yesterday."

"Aye. Without incident, I might add," he sneered. "I think that knight just wanted to embarrass you before your kin."

"Well, he got considerable help from me."

"He had no right to tell you what to do."

"I agreed at the time." Loudly and foolishly. "But after last night…"

"What was he doing wandering about?"

"Saving me," she dryly replied.

"Humph. The knight claims he did not know his scout was Seamus Fergusson, but if you ask me, he is lying."

"To what purpose?"

Eoin threw up his hands. "How should I know?"

"Exactly."

Eoin scowled, clearly not certain what she meant. Another sign they'd not have been compatible. "Well, I will not feel easy till the Sutherlands are gone."

Nor would she, but her reasons were doubtless much different from Eoin's.

"Catlyn." He reached along the table to capture her free hand. "I cannot stand this tension between us. How can I convince you that I am sorry about Dora."

She extricated her hand and put it in her lap. "I believe you. Now let us put the whole thing behind us."

"I cannot. I love you still."

As a brother, maybe. As an heiress, certainly. But as a lover? Their courtship had been a tepid thing, a few chaste kisses that had left her wondering what all the fuss was about. "Please, Eoin, let us speak of it no more."

"Ross! Ross!" The name swept through the hall.

Catlyn gasped and turned toward the door.

Ross Sutherland filled the opening, acknowledging the cheers of her people with a red face and lopsided grin.

Catlyn had wondered how she'd feel when she saw him again. Nothing prepared her for the surge of emotion that filled her as he gazed over the mob and their eyes met. Her heart did a slow roll in her chest, then beat wildly against her ribs as he walked slowly, inexorably toward her.

"My lady." Ross nodded in greeting. His eyes flicked to her throat and narrowed. "How fare you?"

"Alive. And glad of it."

"As am I." He smiled. "May I join you?"

"Nay," Eoin growled. "Can you not see we are busy?"

Catlyn looked from Eoin's furious face to Ross's controlled one. "I would speak with Sir Ross in private, Eoin."

"But…"

"Bad enough I must apologize for my behavior yesterday. I will not do it with an audience."

Eoin glared at Ross. "I will be watching you." He whirled and retreated to a nearby table to glower.

"I do not think he likes me," said Ross.

"It was once understood we would wed."

"Indeed?" Ross raised one brow.

"You are likely wondering why we did not." Flustered, she tossed her head. "It is a private matter."

"I am certain you had good reason for not wedding him."

"What makes you think it was my decision?"

"He wants to win you back."

"Aye." Catlyn sighed. "He refuses to see it is over between us. He betrayed me, you see, and I could never trust him again."

"Trust is very important." His expression was bleak, as though he recalled a betrayal in his past. "May I sit?"

"Aye. Of course." She sat down. He stepped over the bench and sat across. Dimly she was aware that the hum of conversation had resumed around them. A maid bustled up with ale for Ross. She waited till the lass had gone, then embarked on the speech she'd practiced. "I thank you for what you did last night. If not for your timely arrival…" She shivered.

"I am glad I could be of service but furious that he came

here with me.'' He told her about hiring the scout and being duped into seeking shelter at Kennecraig.

Catlyn listened, nodded. ''I forgive you readily, and hope you'll accept my apology for yesterday afternoon. I acted so—''

''It is I who owe you an explanation. As my men will tell you, I am not always rational when it comes to the safety of those I care about. I was worried and spoke harshly.''

His speech made Catlyn's cheeks warm. ''I am told I'm a bit irrational about having my own way.''

''Hardheaded, Adair did call you.'' Ross grinned.

Catlyn felt her own smile slip. ''I prefer to think I am determined to do what is right for my clan.''

''The problem is knowing what is right, is it not?''

''I have the experience of my ancestors to call upon.''

''Ah, but times change. The wise leader recognizes this and makes adjustments.''

''You are saying I am not a wise leader?''

''Not at all, only—''

''Only I am a woman.'' Her temper flared. ''You think because of that I am not fit to lead.''

''You put words in my mouth.''

''Or pluck them from your heart.''

''Nay, I was going to say that you are new to this business of war. As are most of your clansmen. Even Adair.''

Catlyn scowled at him. ''You are quick with your wits and your tongue, sir knight.''

''And with my sword, which is why Adair has hired me to protect Kennecraig from—''

''What!'' Catlyn's cry turned heads the length of the hall and had Eoin rising from his seat. She motioned him back and stared aghast at Ross. ''That's impossible. Adair would not hire you without my say-so.''

''He was concerned about what happened last night.''

So was she. Catlyn's mind warred with her heart. The logical side of her knew they needed a champion, but some primitive instinct warned this man was a danger. To her. It was not only his looks that attracted her, but his strength, the aura of barely leashed power. She could not be near him without feeling that drugging heat wash through her, drawing her to him, even against her will, like metal filings to a magnet.

Catlyn curled her hands into fists and tamped down the traitorous longing. A quick tumble with a handsome man was a pleasure she could ill afford. She had a responsibility to wed and bear an heir, and she had pride in her own worth. "Adair should have consulted me," she said in her most lofty manner.

"Perhaps, but that is not the reason you fear me."

"Me, afraid of you?" She laughed, the sound as brittle as her fraying nerves.

The expression in his eyes changed, heating. "I think we are both a little afraid of this attraction between us."

"I do not know what you mean." Catlyn tried to look away, but the sensual promise blazing in his gaze held her captive.

"Ah, there you are." Adair materialized at her elbow, braking the spell.

Catlyn started, almost glad to find a focus for her anger and uncertainty. "Adair, have you hired Sir Ross?"

Her mentor's smile faded. "I should have waited."

"Aye, you should have." She rose, certain that if she stayed, she'd make a fool of herself, again. "I will be in my counting room." She gathered her pride and exited the hall, hoping it did not look like she was running away.

Eoin leaped up to follow Catlyn, but Roland grabbed his arm and tugged him back down.

"Take it from a man who's had three wives," Roland said. "If ye don't give her a few moments to calm down, she'll be flaying ye with the sharp side of her tongue."

"Catlyn never loses her temper." But Eoin noted her stiff spine and squared shoulders.

"Well, something's got her astir." Roland popped the last of the oatcake into this mouth.

"She got angry when Sir Ross said as how Adair had hired him to protect us from Hakon," Wesley said.

"How do you know that?" Eoin asked sharply.

Wesley grinned, his broad face glowing. "I can tell what folks are saying by watching their mouths move."

"Did I not tell ye that was rude and tell ye not to do it?" Roland grumbled, glaring at his son.

"Aye." Wesley shrugged. "But it's boring standing about all day scrubbing casks and—"

"Boring!" Roland exclaimed. "Here ye've got a chance to become the next master of the stills, and ye're bored."

"Every day's the same. Turn the kegs. Check the kegs."

"It's doing it the same that makes the Finglas the best."

"What else did Catlyn and Sir Ross say?" Eoin asked, as bored with the familiar argument as Wesley was with his work.

Wesley glanced sidelong at his father, then mumbled, "Oh, something about being afraid."

"Of course she's afraid," Eoin said. "She was nearly killed last night by that Fergusson."

"A Fergusson who came into Kennecraig with the Sutherlands," Wesley said darkly.

Roland grunted. "Laird Thomas didn't hold with having strangers inside the keep."

"Now Adair has hired him, Ross will not be a stranger. He'll live here, and likely have the ruling of us," Wesley said.

"He'll have no say in the distillery," Roland grumbled. "Bad enough we've got a lass trying to give orders." He glanced at Eoin. "There's some of us who think ye should wed the lass, as Laird Thomas wanted."

"She is wroth with me."

"Women are always wroth with a man about something," muttered Roland. "I say ye'd best wed her will she, nill she, for I dinna like the way yon knight is sniffing about her.''

Eoin looked over just as Ross disappeared through the door and turned to the right. Was he following Catlyn? Trying to stake a claim? "I will not let that happen."

Chapter Seven

Ross caught up with Catlyn just before she entered the distillery. "My lady, a moment, if I might."

She stopped but did not turn. Light from the torch beside the door glinted on her golden head, proud and unbowed. "I do not want to speak with you."

"I understand why you are wroth with Adair and me, but—"

"Nay, you do not." She swung around to face him. The vulnerability in her eyes made him regret having told Adair he would handle this. "You have never been backed into a corner, forced to do something you do not want to do."

Oh, how wrong she was. But Ross had no time to dwell on his past mistakes. If they were to thwart Hakon's schemes, they must first come to grips with the desire they could not afford to indulge. He dragged a hand through his hair, groping for the right words to ease the tension. "I constantly err where you are concerned. The only excuse I can offer is that you unsettle me."

"*I* unsettle *you?*"

Her disbelief made him smile. "You fascinate me, Lady Catlyn, and have from the moment I first saw you, on the battlements, in your virgin white gown, your hair loose and wild, directing the archers as they covered our retreat. To put it bluntly, I desire you more than any lass I've yet met."

Her mouth opened. Her eyes widened, shock mingling with something dark and earthy. "You go too far," she whispered.

Not as far as he would like to go. "You value the truth."

"Aye, but what you say is…is not true."

"It is. We are interested in each other, no matter that such an association would be impossible." Bad enough he must steal from her to regain his estates, he could not compound the crime by seducing her. "But we are both logical people who think before we act. It seemed reasonable to me that if we spoke plainly of this attraction between us we could put it aside and get on with the business at hand."

"It did?" she asked weakly, her expression still dazed.

"Aye. Your clan needs help in keeping Hakon at bay and getting your whiskey to market. My men and I have the skills to aid you, but we will not work well together, you and I, if we are constantly at odds over this itch we cannot scratch."

His crude speech made her blink, but it also set her back up, as he'd intended. Eyes flashing, she replied, "It is indeed as unwelcome as an infestation of fleas, but I can safely say I will not succumb to it, sir."

"And neither will I." Not if it kills me. "Let us begin with a tour of the keep so I may see what you have in the way of supplies and judge what is needful to reinforce your defenses."

"Adair can—"

"Nay." Judging from his own observations and those of his men, life at Kennecraig had unraveled since the laird's death. With Thomas gone, Lady Jeannie incapacitated and Dora removed from her post as housekeeper, there was no one to run the keep. The tradition-bound Boyds would not turn to Catlyn, for her province was the distillery. It was time someone opened the lady's eyes to these problems. "As you pointed out earlier, some folk question your leadership because you are female," Ross said carefully. "You must make them see that you are in charge here."

He was right, Catlyn thought and hated him the more for it. She welcomed the anger as an antidote to softer emotions. "But the only thing I know is the distillery. Adair saw to our defense, even when..." When Papa was alive. "Even before. Mama managed the household with Dora's help."

"A good leader is passing familiar with everything that goes on inside his...or her...domain."

"All right," she said reluctantly.

"We can speak with each of them in turn if we have questions that you cannot answer."

"Mama is not well enough, and Dora..." She did not want him to see Dora. Jealousy made a mockery of the agreement they had just forged, but she felt its bite just the same. "Dora was relieved of her duties last month."

"Why? Was she incompetent?"

"She overstepped her bounds, but in the last few days, we have come to an understanding."

"Perhaps you would consider reinstating her."

"Nay." Her pride could not bear that blow. "People would not obey her. She lost their respect."

"Respect is important." His expression changed subtly. His eyes shimmered with something warm and sensual. Something that made her breath catch and her heart race. She was suddenly aware of how close they stood in the dimly lit corridor, so close she could see the purple flecks in his unusual eyes and smell the soap on his skin. The very air seemed charged with something new and exciting.

Something they dared not explore.

"Let us begin, then." Catlyn whirled away, her legs as shaky as her pulse. Stepping outside into the sunshine and cool air cleared her head. By the time they had negotiated the stairs to the courtyard, she had herself in control. Embarrassing as the discussion had been, she did feel better for having the matter aired and put aside.

They started on the far side of the courtyard with the barracks, then moved on to the smithy and the stables. Ross impressed her with the thoroughness of his inspection and the questions he asked about weapons, mounts and feed.

"Our horses will be a drain on your slim resources," he said as they walked back into the sunshine. "We must decide whether it's best to send men out to cut grass or take the beasts to pasture."

"What of Hakon? Might he attack any we send outside?"

"Not necessarily. There's the threat of the black powder, and he'll be waiting for Seamus to act."

Catlyn shivered despite the warmth of the summer air. "How long will Hakon wait, do you think?"

"Several days. A week. But we will not send anyone out till I've determined it is safe." Obviously he was used to command and took the responsibility seriously.

The weight that had settled on her shoulders eased a bit. When they spoke of mundane matters she could almost forget the thread of tension that ran between them. Almost.

As they walked toward the storage buildings, she noted that the Sutherlands were again engaged in fighting mock battles. A knot of towheaded lads, varying in age from eight to twelve or so, stood off to one side, their eyes wide with admiration.

Catlyn clicked her tongue and called, "Will, are you and the lads done with your chores?"

Will Boyd turned to her while the others hunched their shoulders. "We were just passing by." Will headed toward the keep, shooing the rest of the boys ahead of him.

"I must speak to Eoin about this. He normally saw to such things, but with Papa gone, we are all stretched a bit thin."

"What sort of chores do the lads have?" Ross asked.

"Scrubbing out the tuns, sweeping the settling room."

"Do they get equal time training to bear arms?"

Catlyn shook her head. "Till now it's not been necessary."

"Every man should know how to defend himself and his land."

"We have Adair and the soldiers for that."

"They are your first line of defense, but if something should happen to them…" Ross's jaw flexed. "Beginning tomorrow, every Boyd will take training with my men."

"The women, too?" she asked, arching a brow.

"Aye. And yourself included."

"I could not cut someone. The blood…" Catlyn shuddered.

"You would do it to save yourself or someone you loved."

Catlyn shook her head. "I do not have the time in any case. Let us finish this inspection so I can be about my work."

"The matter is not ended," he warned, blue eyes hard.

She met his stare with icy dignity. "Aye, it is. I will not use a weapon." She punctuated the statement by opening the door to the granary. The effect was ruined by her gasp of shock. "Why has this not been cleaned?" Chaff lay thick on the floors. Dust covered the lids of the bins that lined the two long walls. She gasped again as a pair of rats scuttled across the floor and out a hole in the back. "This is dreadful."

"Vermin are commonplace in a granary."

"Not in ours. The barley is brought for winnowing, then stored till it is made into mash." She advanced into the room and sneezed as the dust motes rose around her. "Cleanliness is vital. We take great pains in making our whiskey. We use only the best barley and pure water from the loch. Which we boil before mixing into the mash."

"Surely the mash is cooked and strained."

"Aye." She shuddered. "But we want no dirt, and especially no vermin droppings, in with it."

"I had not realized it was such an exacting process."

"Well, it is." Hands on hips, she glared at the floating

dust and grimy floors. "I must set Dora on this at—" She broke off and glanced sidelong at Ross. "I will see to this."

Ross nodded. "How soon before the crop is ready to harvest?"

"A week, two at most."

"This is a delicate time," Ross said, stepping aside for her to exit ahead of him. "You want to take the grain when it's at its peak, but you risk having a bad storm flatten it. And lying about in the wet can ruin the whole lot."

"You sound more like a crofter than a warrior."

"My family primarily raises sheep, but we've fields of oats and wheat and even a bit of barley for making the whiskey."

"Your family makes whiskey?"

"A few barrels, but nothing so fine as your Finglas." He grinned, eyes dancing. "I shudder to think what's been cooked up with the mash."

That small bit of shared mirth warmed her. "I thought you didn't care for whiskey," she said as they crossed the bailey.

He sighed. "It was not that. My last night in Stirling I fear I did drink more than I should have."

"Ah, you had a bad head?"

"And a worse belly." The corners of his mouth turned down, his expression grim. "No more than I deserved, though."

"Whiskey is a powerful brew. We are taught to sip in moderation."

"Another of those inflexible Boyd traditions?"

"We are not inflexible, only—"

"I was teasing." He grinned and touched the tip of her nose. "You Boyds are serious folk. All work and no merrymaking."

"Life is serious business."

"True, but it need not be somber. In Edin Valley, the maids lighten their tasks by singing or gossiping."

Catlyn sniffed. But as they entered the kitchen building,

she noted the strain on the servants' faces and the silence, broken only by the clatter of pans. "Robert?"

The cook whirled from the worktable. His fleshy face went as white as the hair frothing about it. "My lady. Sir Ross. Is something wrong? Did someone take sick? Oh, I knew I should not have used that mutton."

"All is well." Ross strolled over to the table. "Lady Catlyn has hired my band to protect you from Hakon, and we are but inspecting the keep to see what needs doing."

"Thanks be to God!" Robert grabbed her hand in his sticky ones and kissed it. "I feared disturbing ye with my wee troubles when ye have such a weighty burden to bear, but we're in a sorry state." He waved a hand toward the shelving at the rear of the kitchen. "We have hardly anything left. Every day it is a struggle to make something edible out of nothing but dried meat and a few beans."

"I—I had not noticed," Catlyn said weakly.

"I know." Robert patted her hand. "Ye're that busy running the stills. But others have. There's been a bit of grumbling."

She had not heard that, either. "I am sorry."

"It is not yer fault." Robert turned away to scold a maid. "Mind those beans don't burn, Mary."

Catlyn looked up and found Ross watching her, his expression patient yet alert. "You knew what we would find."

"Only that things did not run smoothly."

"Why did you not just tell me we were short of food?"

"Because I was not certain if this was the normal way of things at Kennecraig. And my da told me it is often best for a person to learn a thing for himself. Or herself."

Catlyn nodded. It would have been far worse to have him stand up in the hall and shout the news. "Thank you."

"Not at all." He inclined his head in a polite nod, but the fire in his eyes was less tame. Respect burned there. More warming, even was the sensuality that smoldered just below the surface. Tempting, beguiling. His gaze dropped to her mouth, and she knew he wondered what it would be like to kiss.

Her lips parted of their own accord.

"Catlyn?" Robert tugged at her sleeve.

She jerked around, her cheeks hot. "Make a list of what you need most," she said briskly. "I will buy what I can with the whiskey profits while we're in Doune for the fair."

"Salt," Robert said promptly. "And meat. And—"

"Make a list." Ross took hold of Catlyn's arm, hustled her out of the kitchens and back across the courtyard to the dusty granary. Kicking the door closed with his foot, he demanded, "What is this nonsense about going to the fair?"

"We always go to sell the first of the whiskey. It's—"

"Hang tradition. This year you are staying away."

"We need the money for food and to pay you."

"I can wait for my coin."

"Well, we cannot wait for supplies. You heard Robert."

Ross cast a meaningful glance at her neck. "I also heard Seamus's threats," he murmured.

"The fair is a truce day. He'd not dare break the peace."

"Hakon Fergusson has spent his whole cursed life breaking laws and such," Ross grumbled.

"We have to go." Desperate to make him understand, Catlyn laid a hand on his arm. It was like touching stone covered in wool. Hot stone. The feel of his muscles bunching beneath her palm sent tingling heat up her arm. What would it be like to have those strong arms around her? The bottom dropped out of her stomach as she watched his eyes darken.

"It is not safe." He seized her shoulders and shook her once. "God, do you think I could live with myself if something happened to you." His mouth came down on hers, hard, demanding.

Catlyn stiffened, her gasp of shock muffled by the kiss. Instinctively she tried to twist free.

Ross tasted inexperience in her unyielding lips. It tempered his anger as nothing else could have. Instantly he gentled the kiss, apologizing with slow, lingering caresses, his hands running up and down her supple spine.

She trembled. A sigh that was part longing, part surrender slipped between them as her hands went around his neck. Her lips softened, molding to his as she followed his lead.

The sweet purity of her response went to Ross's head as swiftly as a cup of her whiskey. He wanted her. Here and now. The force of his desire shook him, had him groaning her name as he wrenched his mouth from the haven of hers. "Catlyn," he whispered again, his voice harsh with need.

"R—Ross?" The catch in her voice, the slight tremor that passed from her body into his made him look down. Her eyes were so dark they were nearly black, reflecting his own ravenous features. "Why did you do that?"

"I made a mistake." A serious mistake on top of the several he had already made. Ross groaned again, with shame this time. Somehow he found the will to let her go and step back. "Please accept my apology."

She put a hand to her mouth, wet and reddened by his kisses. "You said that if we spoke of it, it would go away."

"So I thought." He managed a wry smile. "Apparently I underestimated my *interest* in you." And his weakness. "Be assured it will not happen again. I will leave you to compose yourself." He walked to the door, then recalled the argument that had led to this insanity and turned back. "But I meant what I said. The Boyds are not going to the Doune Fair."

"You have no say in the matter," she shouted after him.

"But I do. You hired me to protect your clan, and I say it is too dangerous." He closed the door. A heartbeat later, something hard hit it from the other side.

Mathew strolled over, his face sweaty from swordplay. "What was that?"

"My lady's shoe, no doubt," Ross said dryly, starting for the keep.

Mathew walked with him. "You have not won her over?"

Ross groaned. "That depends on your view. The lady and I do not see eye to eye on many things, but the tour of the keep went well." Caught up in showing him about, she had relaxed. Being with her had the opposite effect on him. Everything about her, from the gentle sway of her hips beneath the somber brown gown to the curve of her cheek, entranced him. By the time they'd reached the kitchens, his body had been strung as tight as a lute string. "Unfortunately, I lost what ground I'd gained by losing my temper." *And nearly my self-control.*

"You?"

"Aye." In so doing, Ross had nearly compromised her innocence and his own honor. "She refuses to realize that attending this fair in Doune is dangerous."

Mathew stroked his chin. "Dora says it's important for the Boyds to attend. They use the sale of this first batch of whiskey to set the price they'll ask in Edinburgh."

"Aye, well, they will just have to find another—"

"Robert!" called a clear, sharp voice.

Ross spun on the stairs, eyes narrowing as he watched lady Catlyn bustle toward the kitchens.

"Robert!" she called again, turning heads the length and breadth of the crowded courtyard.

The cook rushed from the kitchen building. "What is it?"

Catlyn stopped, glanced at Ross, then at the cook. "I fear there will not be any supplies fetched from Doune."

"But we'll starve," Robert whined, wringing his hands.

"It is out of my control," she said sadly but loudly. "Sir Ross has decided it is too dangerous for us to go."

Cries of protest rang off the old stone towers enclosing the courtyard. Women wept. Men cast furious glances Ross's way.

Ross groaned.

"What is this?" Mathew hissed.

"A fine bit of playacting, I'd say." Ross shook his head. "Never anger a canny lass, my friend. They are devilish quick at finding a way to pay you back."

"He doesn't have the ordering of us," Roland shouted.

Eoin stepped up beside Catlyn. "I say we dispense with their services. We can protect ourselves."

Catlyn moved away from Eoin, her mocking gaze on Ross. *That will teach you to order me about,* it said.

Witch, Ross replied with a steely gaze of his own, hiding his admiration for her cleverness.

"What are we going to do?" Mathew asked over the growing din. "Will we leave?"

"We cannot afford to do that." He cocked his head and sent Mathew a cheeky smile. "I guess we will just have to find some way to attend the fair without Hakon's knowing we've gone."

"Impossible."

"Nay, only...difficult." Ross grinned, relishing the notion of outwitting the bastard who had blackmailed him and threatened to hurt Catlyn.

Chapter Eight

Catlyn hurried away from the courtyard, driven by equal parts fury at Ross's high-handedness and shame at her wanton behavior. Realizing someone followed her, she stopped and turned. "Do not think you can...oh, Eoin, it is you."

"Aye." He fairly bristled with righteous indignation. Behind him came Roland, Wesley and half a dozen of the distillery workers. "We should get rid of these knights."

"Nothing would please me more." Especially after that disastrous kiss. "But Adair thinks we need them to thwart—"

"A pox on what Adair thinks," Eoin grumbled.

"What we need is to get the Finglas Water to Doune," Roland said sharply. "The fair begins day after tomorrow, and the Boyds have always been there a day ahead."

Catlyn nodded. "We will select some kegs of the four-year-old whiskey and get them ready to take."

"Done." Roland bristled. "Nigh forty years I have in this trade. I ought to know what's done when."

"I did not mean to suggest otherwise," she said carefully. "What of the ten-year-old whiskey?"

Roland sniffed. "Not ready."

"Papa thought it was."

"I disagree. It'll be smoother for another year in the keg." His eyes went hard in his fleshy face.

Catlyn raised her chin. It seemed this day was full of arrogant males. "Or it'll grow too strong. You know that's happened before. I want to take a keg along to be sampled by David Erskine at the Golden Thistle."

Roland's lip curled. "Ye think he's a better judge than I?"

What she thought was that Roland was just being contrary. According to her father's notes, Roland had agreed the ten-year-old would be ready. Another value of the copious records her family kept. "Nay, but David was a good friend to Papa. He will be expecting to taste it for Papa promised." And if David judged it fine enough, she'd be marketing it in Edinburgh this autumn. No matter what the prickly Roland said.

Roland sniffed and brushed past her, opening the doors to the distillery with such force they banged against the wall. He stomped through the portal, his son and workers scurrying along in his wake like frightened mice.

"You should not have upset Roland," Eoin said.

"Everything I say displeases him." Because she was not a man. Still Catlyn's steps dragged as she entered the settling room and headed for her counting chamber. It was hard to carry on without her beloved Papa. She did not need the added weight of Hakon's threats and friction with her own people.

"I only want what is best for you," Eoin said, sticking to her side like a troublesome burr.

Then why do you badger instead of helping? But it would be useless to ask, for they saw things differently. Maybe men and women were not meant to work together. Into her mind leaped this morning's tour. Ross had arranged for her to see for herself the problems at Kennecraig instead of flinging them in her face or, worse, announcing in the hall that she'd been too busy with the distillery to notice her people were like to starve.

Ross's sensitivity surprised her, but then she thought of the kiss and wondered if he had an ulterior motive. Perhaps he, like Eoin, wanted control of the distillery. Only he was more clever than Eoin and thought he could seduce her to gain it.

"Catlyn, let me help you." Eoin put his arm around her shoulder. Any lingering possibility that she might wed him vanished. His touch disgusted her.

"Thank you." Shuddering, she slipped free and unlocked the door to her counting room. "Could you see to readying the wagon and a troop of men to escort me to Doune?"

"I will lead them myself. When do we leave?"

"On the morrow, as planned."

Eoin drew himself up very tall. His eyes glowed with purpose. "I will guard you with the last ounce of breath in my body. When we return triumphant, perhaps you can find it in your heart to forgive me."

"Eoin…"

"Only give me a second chance. That is all I ask. I did not realize how greatly you prized fidelity. I swear I have learned my lesson, dearest Catlyn."

It did not matter, for she had learned something more important. She had tasted passion, and her notions of marriage had altered completely. Before, she might have settled for a loveless marriage for the sake of bearing children to continue the distillery. But now, knowing there was this fire inside her, how could she lie with a man who made her feel nothing?

"Please see to the wagons, Eoin," she said.

He scowled but left her in peace.

Catlyn sank down into the chair behind the table that had been her great-grandfather's. His name was carved into the top, as were the names of all the Boyd lairds who'd gone before her. Catlyn traced the letters with her finger and thought about the old man whose whiskey-sense she had supposedly inherited.

According to family history, old Erik—the fourth of that name—had been a deeply passionate man. He had fallen in love with an unsuitable woman. Five years his senior and put aside by her husband on the grounds she was barren, Adel was living with her parents when she and Erik met at the Doune Fair.

Erik had not cared that she was older or that she could not give him an heir. He had two younger brothers who would have bairns. He would have Adel to wife and none other. The match had been a passionate one, inspiring many a bawdy tale of midnight trysts in all manner of places. 'Twas said they'd been discovered making love on this very table. And nine months to the night, Adel had given birth to twin sons.

Catlyn stood and moved away from the table as though distance from it would cool her blood.

"Do not think about him," she muttered, but her lips tingled with the memory of what it had felt like to be kissed as though she were the most desirable woman in the land.

Why could her passion not have found focus in a worthy man? A man of her clan who might help her run the stills as they had always been. Instead, she had developed an unholy desire for a mercenary knight too handsome to be faithful. Worse, he scoffed at their traditions.

Great-grandfather Erik's story had had a happy ending, but Catlyn could not see the same rosy future for herself and Ross Sutherland. He was too arrogant.

"Catlyn." Eoin rushed into the room. "You'll never guess. Sutherland and some of his men have left the keep."

"He has gone?" She sank down into the chair again, her heart contracting.

"Aye, they look for Hakon's camp."

"Why? Why would he endanger himself?"

"Some fool notion about locating the enemy. But we will fox them both. We will leave now."

"Now?"

"Aye. Roland and his men are already taking the kegs out to the courtyard."

"What of the ten-year? Did he take a keg of that?"

"I do not know. There's no time to see. Run up and get a change of clothes if you want to come."

"I do." The clan leader always went to Doune Fair.

Dickie Fergusson was drowsing at his post in the warm noon sun when the creak of chains echoed down the glen. Sitting bolt upright, he rubbed the grit from his eyes and stared across the narrow ravine to Kennecraig Keep. The portcullis slowly rose, and a troop of men rode out, followed by a rickety cart.

"At last." Dickie scrambled off his rocky perch and hurried down the trail to the Fergusson's camp beneath the pines. Most of the troopers Hakon had left behind to watch the keep were still wrapped in their blankets around the smoldering remnants of last night's campfire. The ground was littered with empty ale kegs and the gnawed bones of a brace of rabbits they'd caught in their snares. Smack in the middle of the mess lay Guthrie, sprawled on his back, snoring fit to rouse Old Cootie himself.

Dickie approached cautiously, nudged the body with one toe and stepped back. Guthrie was a mean drunk and meaner still if awakened before he'd slept it off. "Guthrie?"

"Get away," said a slurred voice. Guthrie lashed out with one booted foot, swearing when he didn't connect.

"I got news, Guthrie."

Guthrie opened one bloodshot eye, winced and closed it again. "It had best be worthwhile or I'll skin ye."

"It is. I spotted riders leaving Kennecraig."

"How many?"

"Less than the fingers on two hands." Dickie had been dropped on his head as a bairn and learning came hard to him.

Guthrie forced his eyes to slit and came up on one elbow. "Could ye tell if it was Ross Sutherland's knights?"

"I—I don't think so. They was wearing tattery clothes."

"Was Seamus with them?"

Dickie frowned. "It was too far to see his face."

"Idiot. Was any of them small enough to be Seamus?"

"Nay. They was tall fellows. And they had a wee cart," he added, proud to have noted that detail.

"Servants going to cut grass or gather wood. Ye waked me for that, ye fool?" Guthrie grumbled. The sound of his own voice made his head throb. He shouldn't have drunk so much, but what else was there to do? He cursed his father for leaving him here to watch a keep that might as well have been empty for all the activity that went on. "We could kill them, I suppose."

"But Hakon said we was not to let on we was here."

"No one would miss a few slaves." But thinking about getting up made his head pound. Guthrie gingerly lay back and put an arm over his eyes. "Find me more ale."

"Aye, Guthrie. Do ye want I should go back up and watch?"

"I dinna give a damn what ye do, so long as ye're quiet." Guthrie listened to Dickie scurry away and thought about going back to Dun-Dubh. A run-down pile of mud and stone, his da called it, but there'd be ale there.

Stripped to the waist, Ross and eight of the nine men who'd left the keep cut grass with their borrowed scythes and piled it into the cart. They looked for all the world like a defenseless work party, but each man had a long knife in his belt and a claymore on the ground at his feet.

"I thought we were supposed to look like grass cutters," Dallas grumbled. "I didn't realize we'd actually have to work."

Ross wiped the sweat from his eyes and grinned. "What better way to fool Hakon if he has someone watching? And we need the fodder for the horses."

"That's true." Dallas cut another handful of grass and laid it in the cart. "Are we still going to make drawings of the Boyds' stills and steal their recipe?"

The answer to that had troubled Ross since last night

when he'd foiled Seamus's plans. "I have got to give Hakon something if I'm to save Stratheas."

Dallas frowned. "But he lied to you about what he wanted in exchange for the note."

"I've no doubt of that, but the fact remains that he has it. And I've no desire to see Hakon in Edin Valley."

"We could say he forged your signature on it."

"My father would recognize it as mine." Ross shook his head and seized a sheaf of grass, severing it with controlled fury. "If I thought he'd be content with drawings and a recipe, I'd make something up and give it to Hakon. But it's clear to me that he is determined to gain control of Kennecraig and make slaves of the Boyds if he can."

Dallas swore and flung down his scythe. "We have to do something. They are decent folk."

"That they are." Ross broke off as he saw High Harry Carmichael wander out of the trees bordering the meadow.

Older than Ross by six years, Harry was lean of build, with the black Carmichael hair and eyes as sharp as a hawk's. He was nearly as fearless as that predator when it came to scaling heights. 'Twas he who had taught Ross how to climb.

"Found 'em, I did." Harry's cinder gray eyes gleamed. "Up on yonder ridge where ye thought they'd be."

Ross nodded. Yesterday and again this morn the sentries had seen a flash of sunlight off metal on the ridge opposite the keep. "How many? How vigilant?"

"A dozen." Harry grinned. "All but one either passed out or still dead drunk. The camp's a filthy, stinking mess."

"You are sure they don't have a patrol out?"

"Nay. Twelve men. Twelve horses."

"Excellent. Was Hakon there?"

"Nay, but Godless Guthrie was, laying in his blankets like a beached fish. If we attack now, they'd not put up a struggle."

A low murmur of approval swept Ross's men.

"It is tempting. If Hakon was there, I'd agree, but capturing Guthrie might not buy us anything. Hakon is not known for his loyalty. He might not be willing to ransom his son back for my note and a guarantee he'd leave the Boyds alone.''

"He'd not keep such a vow," Dallas said.

"My point exactly," said Ross. "And Hakon has a large, vicious band of clansmen on the Borders. If he's pressed, he might send word to them for help."

"Why hasn't he done that already?" asked Harry.

"Greed, I'd guess. Doesn't want to share this rich bounty with his kin. But all that could change if he has reason to start a feud with the Boyds."

"So we have gained nothing," Dallas grumbled.

"Knowledge of our enemy's position and his weakness for drink." Ross ruffled his cousin's hair. "And feed for our horses. Let's fill up the cart." He bent to cut more grass.

"What about the fair?" Harry asked as the men worked. "Unless they are blind drunk, the Fergussons will spot us leaving with the wagons and likely follow."

"Aye, so they would." Ross pondered this for a moment. "Hakon may already be in Doune with most of his men. But that's a chance we'll have to take. There may be a way for us to leave without Guthrie seeing."

"How?" Harry asked warily.

"Oh, just a wee deception."

"Something dangerous by the look in yer eyes."

"Risky, that's sure." Ross grinned. "I was thinking that if we could arrange for Guthrie and his thugs to find a keg or two of whiskey, they'd be blind drunk come morn."

Dallas chuckled. "Aye. That's a good idea."

The cart horse suddenly picked up its head and looked toward the road. In unison, Ross and his men reached for their swords.

"Guthrie?" Ross asked of High Harry.

"Nay. He'd have come through the woods if he followed me."

Ross nodded. The road was little more than a trail through hills winding down from Kennecraig to this spring-fed meadow before taking a sharp bend and climbing up in the opposite direction. The horse stared toward the bend, away from the keep.

"If someone comes, they are not from Kennecraig." Dallas's frown mirrored Ross's concern.

"We'd best get back. Gather your tools and weapons. Lang Gil, drive the cart on ahead while we cover the rear."

The men tossed the scythes into the cart, caught their horses and swung into the saddle. Ross put Dallas in the lead and took the rear with High Harry beside him. Down the road they went at a gallop, eating dust from the cart, glancing over their shoulders as they went. They had just gained the top of the slope when Ross looked back and saw riders rounding the bend on the opposing hill. He thought he saw a tall, fair-headed man in the lead. Hakon Fergusson?

A shout went up, warning the Sutherlands had been spotted.

"Harry, go ahead, tell the men to make a run for it," Ross shouted over thundering hooves. "If it looks like Gil is falling behind, take him up with you and leave the cart."

The race was on in earnest. Ross's men had the advantage. Their mounts were rested and they had reached the top of the long, steep grade that would slow their pursuers. As he followed his men along the lip of the ravine, Ross glimpsed Kennecraig on the other side. Not far now. If he remembered correctly, just beyond this next bend the trail dipped down through a boulder-filled gulch, then climbed again to the plateau on which the keep sat.

Ross looked back just in time to see Hakon Fergusson urge his mount up the hill. Man and beast were both la-boring hard, eyes steaming, mouths open and white with froth.

The sight sent a cramp of fear through Ross's belly. Set-ting his heels into the ribs of his borrowed horse, he lunged down the trail. But as he rounded the bend and plunged into the gulch, he nearly ran over his men. They milled about, shouting and cursing, when they should have been riding on.

"What the hell?" Ross slid to a halt in a hail of loose gravel. Then he looked to the center of the mob, and his heart nearly stopped.

Catlyn was perched on the seat of a small wagon, holding the reins of a shivering horse, her face white with fear. She was flanked by Eoin and a dozen other equally shocked Boyds. The reason for this foray was clear at a glance. Lashed to the wagon was a mound of kegs. The damned whiskey.

Ross had one moment of stark terror before reason returned. "Dallas! Gil! Get everyone up to the keep!" he shouted and made for Catlyn. But when he reached down to pluck her from the wagon, she ducked under his arm.

"I cannot leave the Finglas." She flicked the reins, setting the horse in motion.

Ross's men were already beating a retreat, herding the Boyds before them like sheep. But he knew the laden wagon would never make the grade out of the gulch. Grabbing hold of the cart horse's bridle, he tugged it off the trail, into the tumble of boulders that filled the belly of the gulch. Some were easily ten feet across and twice as tall. When they'd ridden through here earlier, on their way to the meadow, he'd thought a whole army could hide in here. Now he prayed he'd been right.

The track, little more than an animal path, twisted and turned between the mammoth rocks. His arm ached from dragging the reluctant horse behind him. He gritted his teeth and ignored the pain, concentrating on the way ahead. Night was fast falling, draping the trail in deep shadows. The faint hope that this trail would lead out into the open ended when they came face-to-face with a wall of rock.

"This is it, then." Ross leaped from the saddle, tied his

lathered mount to the wagon and ran back to Catlyn. "Get down."

"Why? Where are we—?"

"Shh." Ross dragged her off the seat and clamped a hand over her mouth. "We must leave the horses here, lest they make a sound and betray us. Understand?"

Her eyes were wide, glistening with fear and unshed tears. He felt her lips tremble behind his fingers, but she nodded.

"That's my lass." He released her mouth, drew his sword with his right hand and took her hand with his left. "Stay behind me. Move quickly and quietly. Can you do it?"

She licked her lips. "Who...who is out there?"

"Hakon Fergusson."

She gasped, her eyes going round as serving platters. "Sweet Mary, what if he finds us?"

"Bah, I could hide an army in here. Come." Ross tugged on her hand, pleased when she followed without question. He led her through a maze of boulders, keeping low and out of sight of the trail, but with one ear cocked for trouble.

Catlyn moved stiffly at first, but as the moments passed without incident, her steps became surer, smoother. "Why are we going back?" she whispered.

Because he had no wish to be trapped in that blind canyon. "So we can see when Hakon departs and know the way is clear."

They were nearly to the crossing when Ross heard the sound he'd been dreading. The crunch of hooves on stone.

Catlyn whimpered and looked at him.

Instinctively Ross put an arm around her, his heart contracting as she burrowed into his embrace. "Be still," he whispered into her ear. "They cannot see us."

"Who were they?" asked a coarse voice from beyond the rocks that hid Ross and Catlyn.

"Not Sutherland's men, that's sure," Hakon growled. "They turned tail and ran like frightened sheep."

Ross stiffened and looked at Catlyn. Would she wonder how Hakon knew his surname? Her expression didn't change, and he realized she was too terrified to think.

The clatter of hooves grew louder as the cavalcade passed by. "Must have been Boyds," Hakon added. "Else the keep would not have opened to them so quickly."

Their people had made it to safety. Ross smiled at Catlyn again, and this time she managed a faint smile.

"Where was Guthrie? Why was he not on the road and trailing these folk from the moment they left Kennecraig?"

"Oh, we'll be finding that out quick as we reach his camp," Hakon growled.

Ross released the breath he'd been holding. It was going to be all right. Hakon would seek out Guthrie and they could leave.

As Hakon moved away, one of the Fergusson's horses nickered. From deep in the rocky gulch came an equine answer.

The wagon horse. Ross cursed under his breath.

"Someone's back in the rocks," a Fergusson cried.

"Spread out. See what you can find." The voice was Hakon's. Rocks clattered as he came down the trail. Closer. Closer.

A scream bubbled in Catlyn's throat.

Ross covered her mouth with his hand and pressed her face into his shoulder. "Easy, dearling," he breathed against her ear. "They cannot see us. Just stay quiet."

Catlyn shivered and burrowed further into his embrace. He smelled of sweat and fresh-cut grass and something uniquely Ross. The feel of his strong body wrapped around her settled her panicky nerves. Once before he'd saved her life. He would do it again. Over the thudding of her heart, she heard the Fergusson cavalcade clatter past them.

"They've gone by," Ross whispered.

Catlyn's relief was so great she sagged in his arms.

"Don't faint on me now, sweetheart." He chafed her back, his voice low and urgent. "We cannot stay here."

"Why?"

"When they find two horses, they'll look for riders."

"But where will we go? The keep is so far."

"Aye. It is." He sheathed his sword and drew her to her feet. "We're going to climb a tree."

"What?" Catlyn looked up at the face hovering over hers. The boulders cast shadows over his features, hiding everything except his eyes and the white slash of teeth when he smiled.

"Come. There's no time to waste." He wrapped an arm around her waist and half carried her up the trail toward the crossing. A stand of stalwart pines and giant oaks guarded the upper bank. He threaded his way into their midst, stopping at a pine whose lower branches were only a few feet off the ground. "Up."

"I—I've never climbed a tree before."

"A braw lassie like you won't let that stand in her way. And I will be right behind you. I won't let you fall." His eyes glowed with determination. His grin challenged her.

The distinct clatter of horsemen coming along the ravine decided the matter. Catlyn lifted her foot onto the lowest branch, gasping slightly as two wide hands cupped her bottom and boosted her up onto the limb. Twigs tore at her hair and clothes as she worked her way onto the branch above and the one above that. As she swung onto the fourth limb, Ross hissed her name.

"Stay there and be absolutely still." He whispered from the branch directly below.

Catlyn perched precariously on the branch, her fingers finding purchase in the rough bark. Looking down and out through the fringe of pine needles, she saw dark shapes moving along the rocky trail.

"They must have left the wagon and run off," someone said.

"Aye. Likely long gone," said another. "We should get this whiskey away before they come back with reinforcements." You could practically hear him licking his lips.

Catlyn compressed hers into a thin line as the wagon bearing her whiskey jostled into view. Her shoulders sagged as the wagon crept out of sight. Gone.

"You can come down now," Ross whispered. "They've left."

Catlyn shook herself and slowly worked her way out of the tree. At the last limb, her numb fingers lost their grip, and she started to fall. Ross caught her before she hit the ground. Stunned, she lay still in his arms. His face hovered above hers, a grim mask in the pale half-light. "What is it?"

"Dieu." He pressed his rough, stubbled cheek to hers. "When I think of how close they came to getting you..."

"But they didn't. You saved my life." Strong emotions tumbled inside her: fear, relief, gratitude and something else. Something powerful and needy. "Ross." She turned her head, mouth searching blindly for his.

He growled her name as their lips met and melded. Their first kiss had been gentle, seductive. This one was all heat and hunger. She welcomed it, opening to the spearing edge of his tongue, gasping as he claimed those hidden recesses for his own.

Aye. This was what she'd wanted, needed. This passionate celebration of life to drive out the fear. Sliding her hands into his damp hair, she followed where he led. Heat cascaded through her body, igniting little pulse points in her breasts and the hidden juncture of her thighs.

"Catlyn." Ross lifted his head, his breathing as ragged as her own, his eyes glowing, burning into hers.

"Ross. I...I...". She had no words to describe what he made her feel, made her want to the very marrow of her bones.

"Aye. But we cannot." He shut his eyes, and his big body quivered. "We must be strong," he whispered, his voice as weak and wanting as her own rioting emotions.

"I know," she murmured. It did not change what she felt.

He opened his eyes, looking out toward the trail instead of at her. "We've a long walk ahead of us. Are you up to it?"

If not, he would carry her. She knew that and was tempted to let him. "I can make it."

"I've no doubt of that." He glanced at her then, his eyes reflecting respect and a touch of regret.

Chapter Nine

"What are you going to do now?" Mathew asked.

Ross tossed aside the damp linen towel and reached for a clean tunic. Less than a half hour ago he had walked through Kennecraig's gates with Catlyn in his arms. Her women had taken her off to tend her scratches and the ankle she had twisted during their swift hike up to the plateau. His men, of course, had given him a hero's welcome. From the Boyds he had received a mixed reception. Ironic, he thought, for his purpose here was part protector, part destroyer. "I am not sure."

"Tell that to someone who does not know you as I do," his cousin grumbled. "You've had that look about you since you carried Lady Catlyn into the keep."

"I've found a way to get their whiskey to Doune."

"What?" Mathew yelped.

Ross repeated the statement into the folds of his tunic as he pulled it on. When his head emerged, Mathew was looking at him as though he'd taken leave of his senses. And maybe he had. All he knew was that he had to help them...before betraying them.

"One close call was not enough for you?" Mathew snapped. "Do you not suppose Hakon's devils will be waiting on the road, hoping to intercept another shipment?"

"I gave that considerable thought while walking back to

the keep. I wager Hakon will take the whiskey off to sell. Leaving Guthrie to watch us. Guthrie, being Guthrie, will likely steal a keg or two and be too drunk to see us pass by.''

"Humph." Mathew's scowl eased. "You've a plan, I suppose."

"The beginnings of one." Ross raked back his damp hair, then buckled on his sword. "I'll tell you after we've spoken with the Boyds." He started for the door, conscious that Adair and the others waited in the hall to question him. Ross had made a brief escape to take Catlyn to her chamber and see to himself.

"Once the lads and I got inside Kennecraig, I had another fight keeping the Boyds from going out to fight," said Mathew.

"I feared Adair would try that."

"And Eoin, too. He was beside himself with worry and guilt. Dora, too, begged me to go after her." His features softened. Could it be Mathew was attracted to the lovely Dora? "Some of the others were more concerned about the whiskey."

"Roland."

"Aye. He demanded we get back his precious Finglas."

"That would have made the fiasco complete."

Mathew closed the door to their chamber and frowned. "Well, I was about to defy your orders and go out after you. The lads and I were getting into our mail and gathering our arms when you were spotted carrying the lady up the road."

"She turned her ankle," Ross said defensively. He'd not have touched her otherwise. Even now, nigh an hour later, he could still recall the heady feel of her in his arms and the even more disastrous impact of her eyes gazing up at him. So soft. So trusting. How could he betray her? How could he not?

"It did not appear to be a grave hardship."

It was. He had no right wanting her the way he did. For

when all was said and done, he still had to get back that damned promissory note. Any way he could.

Ross's steps slowed outside Catlyn's door. He was tempted to knock, to inquire after her health. *And catch a glimpse of her. Dieu,* he was a sorry case, mooning after the one woman he could not have. Shaking himself, he hurried along the corridor to the stairwell. He took the steps with callous disregard for their steepness. Halfway down, he realized he was running from something he could not outdistance. His own conscience.

High Harry waited in the lower hallway. "Dallas said ye wanted a word with me."

"I need to know what is going on at Guthrie's camp."

"Do I go out the gate or over the wall?" Harry asked.

"Over the wall?" Ross asked. "Is it possible?"

Harry chuckled. "Aye. We're usually trying to get into a place without being seen, not out. It'd work right well." He went on to describe the land beyond the west wall. The drop was steep, some three stories down a sheer stone face. "But ye canna see that section of wall from yon hills where Guthrie's camped."

"Could you make it there without a horse?" Ross asked.

"In under an hour's time," said Harry, who each year won the footrace at the annual gathering of Clan Sutherland.

Ross looked down the gloomy corridor and leaned closer. "Take Lang Gil with you and a keg of the Boyd's whiskey."

"In case we've a thirst?" Harry asked, arching a brow.

"To leave where Guthrie and his band of merry lads are sure to find it," Ross replied. "Standing guard is boring work."

"Leads a man to drink." Harry winked, laughter deepening his wrinkles. "Ye do not think Hakon will drink what he stole?"

Ross shook his head. "I wager he will sell it as he did the other load." *The one he killed Thomas Boyd to get. The one he used to trap me.* "See if you can find out where he's going."

"Do we try to take it from him?" asked Harry eagerly.

"I'd like nothing better, but we cannot afford to openly oppose Hakon." Yet. Not till he had back that damned note.

"We will return before dawn." Harry turned and melted into the shadowy corridor as was his way.

"What are you planning to do?" Mathew asked again.

Ross shrugged. Best he kept his half-formed plan to himself. Talk of taking twenty men and a like number of whiskey kegs—not to mention horses—over the wall wouldn't ease Mathew's nerves. "We will find some way to help the Boyds get their brew to market." Mind awhirl, he led the way to the great hall.

It was filled with Boyds, all buzzing like a hive of angry bees. They fell silent the moment Ross entered.

Roland leaped up from the table he shared with his son, Eoin and several of the distillers. "What do ye mean, ye're not going to try and get back our whiskey?"

Ross crossed his arms over his chest and stared down the irate little man. "You can go after it if you like. I'll give you directions to their camp."

"Where the fiends are likely swilling our Finglas."

With any luck they were and would be dead drunk come morn. But tempers were too riled to appreciate that. "I warned you against trying to send a shipment to Doune," Ross said.

"You were supposed to protect our whiskey." Eoin rose to stand with Roland, smugness underlying his furious expression.

Adair moved to Ross's side. "And how could he be doing that when you sneaked out of the keep whilst Sir Ross was away and I was locked in the still room?"

Eoin flushed and looked down at his boots. "Catlyn wanted to get the whiskey to the fair, and I—"

"You weren't thinking clearly." Adair advanced and poked a blunt finger into Eoin's chest.

Ross waited. This lecture was best coming from a Boyd.

"It nearly got the lot of you killed, Catlyn included," Adair continued. "If not for Ross's quick thinking—"

"Why didn't ye drive the wagon up to the keep?" Roland demanded. "There was time."

"Nay, there was not." Catlyn entered the room, flanked by Dora and Old Freda.

Ross whirled, his objectivity vanishing the moment their eyes met. How small and vulnerable she looked. Her face was too pale, her eyes dark and haunted. He took a step forward, needing to hold her, to protect her.

"You should be abed," Adair grumbled.

Ross stopped. This, too, was best handled by a Boyd.

"I am fine." Catlyn raised her chin, scanning the room with a quick glance before coming back to Roland. "I am as dismayed as you are over the loss of the shipment."

"Laird Thomas wouldn't have lost it," Roland said.

"Doubtless." Her chin came up another notch, but Ross noticed her hands trembling in the folds of her gown. "But he would not have wanted blood spilled over the whiskey." She hesitated, then added, "You will recall the time one of the tuns burst and threatened to drown everyone in the far still room? Papa ordered the old drainage tunnels opened. A quarter of that year's Finglas washed down them, but the lads were saved."

Adair chuckled. "Aye, but they'd swallowed so much of the whiskey they were drunk for a week."

Laughter rippled through the hall, easing the tension. People nodded and smiled. All except Roland, Wesley and the workers gathered around them.

"Jest if ye will, but how will we get the Finglas to Doune?" Roland grumbled.

She opened her mouth, closed it and looked at Ross, a single glance filled with dashed hopes and mute frustration. "We will not. It is too dangerous," she whispered.

"I think there may be a way," Ross said into the awful silence that followed her announcement.

"Really?" a dozen Boyds cried at once. Their faces glowing with hope, they pelted him with questions.

"There are details to be worked out," Ross replied. "But I know how much you need the coin it will bring, so my lads and I will do our utmost to succeed."

Catlyn drifted over and gifted him with a sweet, dazzling smile. "Oh, Ross, is it safe? Do you really think you can get through without Hakon seeing us?"

"Only if he can sprout wings and fly there," Eoin shouted over the din, quieting the celebration.

Ross felt the weight of a hundred anxious eyes but looked directly into Catlyn's. "My men and I can do it."

"It is a trick," Eoin insisted. "A ploy to turn our whiskey over to Hakon Fergusson."

Ross shivered as Eoin's barb struck closer to home than the man could have dreamed.

"That is ridiculous," Catlyn said.

"Is it?" Eoin glared at Ross. "The Sutherlands got inside Kennecraig because of Hakon's supposed attack. Then their scout turns out to be a Fergusson spy come to remove the black powder from around our stills."

"It was Ross who killed him," Catlyn cried.

"Aye." Eoin's eyes narrowed to suspicious slits. "But what if it was a ploy to gain our trust?"

Ross felt Mathew shift closer, but he kept his gaze locked firmly on Catlyn's. "I had no knowledge of Hakon's plans or Seamus's part in them," Ross said honestly.

"I believe you." Catlyn's quick support was echoed by more than half the folk in the hall.

"He has bewitched you with his handsome face and courtier's tongue," Eoin exclaimed, eyes wild with frustration.

Catlyn eyed Eoin coolly. "Sir Ross has impressed us all with his warrior's skills, a prowess we lack."

"Then why did he not regain our whiskey?" Eoin shouted.

"The loss of the whiskey was my fault." Catlyn's admission rang off the rafters far above. "Had I heeded Sir Ross's warning not to leave Kennecraig, we'd have the kegs still. I am only glad no lives were lost through my stupidity."

"Bravely spoken, my lady," Ross murmured. He knew the admission was a blow to her pride and respected her all the more for making it. Looking away from her shining eyes, he scanned the hall then raised his voice to reach all within. "I know how important it is that your Finglas Water reach Doune. We will do everything in our power to get it there and bring back the supplies you so badly need."

A cheer went up. Men pressed forward to clasp his hand. Women kissed him on the cheek and cried his name.

Ross tried to shrink back, knowing he was unworthy of their gratitude, but Adair clapped him on the back and thrust him into the horde of Boyds. And at his other side, Catlyn held fast to his arm, beaming like a proud parent.

After a few moments, Catlyn raised her hand for silence. "I have one more thing I would do before we go on about our business. And that is to reinstate Dora as housekeeper." Turning, she beckoned the lass forward.

"Nay. I am no longer fit." Dora tried to disappear behind Mathew's tall body.

"Of course you are," Catlyn whispered. "Mathew…"

"Aye." Mathew wrapped an arm around Dora's waist and coaxed her forward.

Dora stood with her head down.

Catlyn's eyes swam with tears. "We need you, Dora."

"I can attest to that," Ross said in a carrying voice. "Lady Catlyn may have her sire's knack for managing the distillery, but if someone else does not take the running of the keep in hand, we are all like to starve."

A moment of awkward silence followed, broken by Catlyn's light, musical laughter.

"I freely admit I have no idea how to do any of this."
Catlyn's expansive gesture took in the whole hall with its
dirty rushes on the floor and scanty fare on the table.

Adair chuckled. "Well said, lass. And welcome back to
you." He patted Dora on the shoulder.

Freda, Ulma and a few other women came forward to
offer words of congratulations. Many folk held back, the
men, especially, casting speculative glances between Dora
and Eoin.

"It will not be easy for her," Catlyn whispered. "Maybe
I should not have forced her to this."

"She has friends who will support her," Ross replied.
"And I think my cousin will see none of the lads bother
her."

Indeed, Mathew still had his arm around Dora's waist,
and she seemed to lean into him as she spoke to Freda.

Catlyn frowned. "Will you walk with me, Sir Ross?"

"Of course." Ross followed her from the hall, grateful
for her formality. Clearly she, too, regretted the kiss they'd
shared in the woods.

"What are his intentions toward Dora?" Catlyn asked as
they walked down the dim corridor.

"Mat's?" Ross hesitated. Any man would have to be
blind or half-dead not to desire Dora, but... "He is an honorable man."

"Related to you, how could he not be," Catlyn said.
"But she has suffered so much already. First the loss of
her husband, then Eoin's selfish seduction and my jealous
rage."

"Your capacity for forgiveness amazes me." Ross wondered if, when all was revealed, she could forgive him.

"There is not as much to forgive as I first thought."
Catlyn fiddled with the ends of her leather belt, then
glanced at him through her lashes. "It was not till recently
that I realized how ill suited Eoin and I were. He came here
as Papa's foster son ten years ago, shortly after my
brother...died."

"I see." Her brother's loss pained her still.

"From the beginning, Papa assumed that Eoin would wed me and together we would run the distillery. I agreed because…because it was my duty." She sighed and wriggled her shoulders, as though shifting the weight she had borne since her brother's passing. "But there was no passion between us." The dimness did not hide the flush in her cheeks.

"Such is the way of arranged marriages," Ross muttered. He did not like the direction this conversation was taking, given the passion that had flared between himself and Catlyn.

"Aye. And I accepted that." She stopped and looked up at him, her expression heart-wrenchingly earnest. "Because I did not know how it could be between a man and a woman."

"Catlyn."

"I am only trying to explain why it was so easy to forgive Dora. And Eoin, too, for that matter. Their betrayal hurt my pride, but not my heart. We would have been miserable together, Eoin and I, because he is like a brother to me, not a…a lover." Her eyes were wide, filled with yearning.

Ross groaned. It was hard to think logically, honorably when she stood so near, the scent of her hair clouding his senses. "You will find another man who, er, appeals to you."

"Oh, I am certain of it." Her smile brimmed with the secrets women had been privy to since Eve.

Ross cleared his throat and tried to ignore the memory of her mouth parting beneath his. Sweet, lush and so tempting. "You have hired me to protect you and yours, my lady," he said stiffly. "I had best be about the task." Mentally he crossed himself and asked for forgiveness for what he must now do. "I need to see the still room."

Her smile faltered momentarily. "It is highly unusual,

but if it is necessary for our defense.'' She lifted her skirt in one dainty hand and started down the corridor.

Ross followed, his soul in a tangle.

"Mathew told Dora that you own a fine keep and lands to the south. That makes you more than a hirling knight.''

Curse Mathew's clacking tongue. "My estate is forfeit to…'' he hesitated "…to the moneylenders.''

She fell into step with him. "Lack of funds does not make you less worthy.''

"There are other thing…things I have done in my life…that do,'' he said curtly. "How many kegs of whiskey were you taking to the fair?''

She sighed, and he could feel her eyes on him, measuring, no doubt, in that serious way she had. "Twenty. Do you think we can get the Finglas to Doune?''

"With a bit of planning.'' And a lot of luck. "I will need plain garments for myself and my men. And ropes.''

"Whatever for?''

Ross debated, then shook his head. "The less said, the better. With your permission, my men will bring up what we need and see to setting plans in motion.''

"You think Hakon has another spy here?''

"I think there are several people at Kennecraig who would like to see me fail.''

"Roland and Eoin. But they would not do anything to harm the distillery.''

"The thirst for power makes men do that which they might not normally.'' Ross had seen too much of that while serving as his uncle Hunter's commander.

She hesitated for only an instant before nodding. "I will see you have access to all parts of the keep and leave to use whatever you need.''

He had what he wanted. But as he followed Catlyn down the steps into the still rooms, Ross's heart felt as cold as the old stone walls surrounding them.

* * *

The moon was just peering up over the jagged mountains when Hakon bade his troop make ready to leave camp.

"The Boyds may try to sneak another load of whiskey past ye, Guthrie, so keep a sharp watch," he commanded.

Guthrie scowled at the wagon full of kegs just getting underway. "Don't see why I cannot come with ye to Doune." There would be drinking and gaming and women.

"Because I need ye to stay here."

"Ye're punishing me because of that wagon," Guthrie whined. "I swear Dickie said it was a hay cart."

"That's true." Dickie nodded his misshapen head.

"Aye, it was a hay cart we chased off the high road," Hakon said. "Doubtless the Boyds had thought to get the whiskey away while ye were watching it. But we fooled them." He grinned wolfishly. "Reckon it'll fetch a fair price at the fair."

A round of coarse laughter followed that.

Guthrie was too furious to join in. "Let me come with ye. The Boyds won't risk losing another load of whiskey. The lads and me'll be wasting our time here."

"I need ye to stay here." Hakon's mouth was set firm.

Guthrie glared at him but knew better than to argue when his pa wore that look.

"We'll bring ye back ale and meat pies," his father promised before wheeling in behind the last Fergusson. "Be back in three or four days' time," he called over his shoulder.

"I am not a wee bairn to be bought off with meat pies." Guthrie spat into the dust they'd kicked up. "Damn, I should have nipped a keg or two like I planned."

Dickie shambled out of the growing gloom. "I found something over yonder."

"Not now, ye witless—"

"It sloshes around when ye shake it, but it don't smell like ale."

"Ale?" Guthrie brightened. "Mayhap we overlooked a cask last night. Show me where it is."

Dickie led the way, out past the perimeter of the camp to the scrub they'd been using as a privy.

When he saw the little keg leaning against a rock, Guthrie bent and sniffed suspiciously at the wooden bung. "It's whiskey!" he cried. "Damned if Pa didn't somehow lose this one off the wagon. Or mayhap left it for us on purpose."

"I found it," Dickie said proudly.

"That ye did." Guthrie straightened and slapped Dickie on the back. "Tote it along to camp, lad. Ye can have a cup to take up with ye while ye stand watch."

"Again?" Dickie whined.

"Aye. If Da's right and the Boyds try to get another shipment through, it'll fall into our laps."

Chapter Ten

Catlyn selected a key from the ring at her waist. Her hand shook as she inserted it into the ancient door guarding the stairwell that led down to the still rooms.

"You need not do this if it troubles you," Ross said.

She looked over her shoulder at him, standing tall and straight behind her. The harsh wash of the torch he held aloft seemed to strip his face bare of pretext, emphasizing the high cheekbones and square jaw, shadowing the sockets but not dimming the brilliance of his eyes. They burned like twin blue flames, so searing and intense a woman could get lost in them. But Catlyn had seen beyond their startling beauty to the rare mix of compassion and intelligence that was Ross Sutherland.

"It is not reluctance that makes me clumsy." She smiled. "I am only excited." *By your nearness, by the things you make me feel.* "And anxious to share this with you."

He blinked, and when his eyes opened, they had lost some of their sheen. "And I am eager to see these famous stills."

"Come along, then." She turned the key and pulled the door open, taking it as a sign of approval when the old hinges did not creak in protest. Though Roland had been vehement in his disapproval, she was certain her father would have agreed that showing Ross the stills was the right thing to do. She wished they could have met, her father and this darkly handsome knight who so fascinated her. She wished she could have asked her sire if it was wrong to desire a man who did not value the stills.

Catching her skirts up in one hand, Catlyn crossed the threshold into a large entryway. The stairwell itself lay in the far corner, a gaping black hole over which two huge winches poised like crouching beasts.

"Ingenious." Ross walked over to inspect the winches.

"It was great-great-grandfather's idea. The distillation is best carried out in the chill of the cellars, but we needed a way to get the kegs up here for the settling."

He bent down and examined the cross members holding the winches to the floor. "I need to move one of these."

"Move? Where?"

"To the top of the west wall."

Catlyn just stared at him.

"Two of my men have gone down that wall and out to scout the Fergussons' camp. But even after they report back, I cannot be certain Hakon is not watching the front gate."

"I do not understand why you want a winch."

"So we can lower ourselves and the whiskey over the wall."

"Ingenious," she murmured, vastly impressed.

"And the horses, too." Her gasp of surprise made him grin. "You cannot expect us to walk all the way to Doune toting twenty casks of whiskey."

"You could use a wagon," she pointed out.

"Now that would be chancy to lower over the wall." His eyes danced with humor.

Catlyn found herself chuckling despite the seriousness of the discussion. That was another part of his charm, she had discovered. His ability to laugh in the face of opposition made an impossible task seem possible.

"This way is better. Each man will carry a keg lashed to the back of his horse and covered by a rolled plaid.

Anyone who sees us on the road will think we are simple soldiers.''

"Not merchants." She nodded. "And if you encounter Hakon, it is unlikely he would recognize you from that skirmish."

Ross made a noncommittal sound and looked at the winch. "As soon as I've seen the stills, I will set my men to moving this."

"Roland may know how to free it." Catlyn cringed, thinking of yet another confrontation with the master distiller.

"Aye, but will he tell me?" Ross asked wryly.

"Of course he…" She smiled. "He will not want to."

"I will ask Adair." Ross rose, towering over her in the gloom, just as he had at the crossing. He stood so close she was enveloped by the unique scent of the man who had saved her only hours ago.

She remembered the kiss they had shared so clearly her lips tingled and her blood heated anew. A single step would obliterate the distance between them. She wanted to take it, longed to have him sweep her up in his arms again and hold her close. Nothing had ever felt so good, so right. Inexperienced she might be in the ways of love, but she knew instinctively that it would feel just as good, just as right to lie naked with him, to have him touch—

"The stills?" he asked softly.

Catlyn jerked free of the images that had danced in her head. "Aye, of course." She turned, stumbling in her haste.

"Easy." His hand was on her arm, steadying her. "Perhaps your ankle is not recovered enough for this."

"My ankle? Oh, it is fine." Her heart, on the other hand, was galloping. The heat of his hand seeped through her sleeve, setting fire to her skin and her imagination. What would it be like to have him peel off her clothes and touch her everywhere? Her whole body seemed to come alive at the thought.

"Good." The simple word meshed so thoroughly with

her thoughts it seemed he'd read her mind. His eyes glittered with the sort of sensual speculation that was driving her wild. He lowered his head.

Catlyn raised her face, lips parting, anticipation spiraling through her like a sip of fiery whiskey.

"This is madness," he whispered, his mouth a hairbreadth from hers.

"Why?"

He blinked, then straightened, his lips drawn into a thin line. "There are reasons. And much work to be done."

Catlyn heaved a sigh of disappointment and picked up her skirts. Why had her stupid question ruined things? She knew why. Because Ross had too much honor. Everything he did proclaimed it, even his refusal to take advantage of her infatuation. And he was right, much as she hated to admit it. There were reasons aplenty why they could not be together. Not the least of which was her duty to her clan. Sighing, she led him down the stairs and into the first room.

There a huge tun, capable of holding five hundred buckets of barley mash, squatted over an empty fire pit like a giant spider on thick metal legs. Thin, hollow tubing made of the same metal used in chain mail sprang from the top of the tun and coiled down into the mouth of a collection vat.

"This is amazing." Ross walked around the tun. "So much larger than anything I've seen used. Is this what makes your Finglas Water so fine?"

"Size is nothing. It is the cleanliness of the array that matters. If you crawled down inside the tun, you'd see it has been scrubbed with ash. And the tubing has likewise been washed. Dirt ruins the liquor, according to Henri the Boyd, who brought home from the Crusades the recipe for distilling spirits."

"Henri was your ancestor?"

"Aye, the son of a Norman knight who won lands in the north of England and wed with a Scots lass from these glens. We still have Henri's notes, along with the scrolls and journals of those who came after him.''

"That is why you can speak French," Ross murmured. "Cleanliness, then is the reason your whiskey is so fine?"

"In part. But there is much more to the distilling." Catlyn launched into a description of the process, from the selection of the ripest barley to boiling it with just the right amount of purified loch water. "Henri's sons and grandsons discovered that the size of the barley kernels affected the sweetness of the whiskey. In years when they are undersized, we add a wee bit of honey to the mash.''

"And that is the secret.''

"In part. Careful records are kept of each year's production. From them, we have learned that if we distill the liquor more than once, it is that much smoother.''

"You put the liquor twice through the still?''

"Or sometimes thrice. It all depends on how the liquor tastes after the first time.''

"Roland decides this?''

"He helps, but the final word is mine.''

"Really?'' Instead of the skepticism she often received, even from her own clansmen, she saw admiration lighting his face. "This is something your sire taught you?''

"It is a gift he passed to me.'' Her voice rang with pride in her ancestors and pride in the skills she had inherited from them. "Though all of the Boyds work in the distillery, only a few in each family seem to have *the taste*, as we call it.''

Ross nodded. "My mother has the second sight. Her gift did not pass to either my brothers or me, but our sister can look into a flame and tell you what the future will bring.''

"We could use her now to tell us what Hakon plans.''

Ross chuckled. "Ella's predictions run more to which lad her friends will wed.''

"Whom did she see for you?'' Catlyn blurted out.

His smile dimmed. "She says I am too wild a beast for any woman to tame.'' He turned away, examining the still as thoroughly as though he expected to build one himself. Lastly he went over to the two casks of black powder in the corner. "Could you really destroy all this if Hakon came?"

"When my father placed them there, he made me swear, on Grandda's soul, that I would do that." She hesitated. "Though I expect Roland and some of the distillers might try to stop me."

He nodded, stroking his chin as he looked about. "It would not be impossible to rebuild the stills."

"Do not even say such a thing." Catlyn shivered. "To think of losing them, and the records. They could not be duplicated, and they are as much a key to our success as the stills."

"An explosion would likely destroy the kegs stored above."

"I know." Catlyn shuddered again. "I lie awake nights thinking what I would do. I can only pray there would be time to move some of the whiskey to safety."

"Have you considered what I said a few days ago, about moving your stills to another place entirely?"

"Leave Kennecraig?" she exclaimed. "Absolutely not. This has been our home for generations. My ancestors survived droughts and disease and famine and—"

"I doubt they faced as grave or as determined a threat as Hakon," Ross said. "He means to have your distillery, and he will not go away."

"The black powder..."

"Has stayed him thus far, but it will not keep him out indefinitely. Hakon will send another Seamus to try and move the powder or open the gates or take a hostage. Whatever he has to do to win, Hakon will do."

Catlyn lifted her chin to meet his challenge. "We will do whatever we have to to survive. Even if it means selling the older whiskey we have put by and hiring an army."

"Older whiskey?"

"Papa believed that the longer the whiskey was kept by,

the smoother it became. Ten years ago, he began setting aside a few barrels to age. It is stored in the far chamber, protected by a stout, banded door and a thick stone wall.''

"Was he right about it aging?"

"Aye. I know you've no fondness for whiskey, but our aged *uisge beatha* is something special. A liquor without peer."

"And it would fetch a higher price?"

"Oh, most assuredly." Catlyn was relieved to put aside the subject of moving from Kennecraig. "Papa planned to take a barrel to David Erskine. He owns the Golden Thistle in Doune, and is nearly as knowledgeable as Papa. Each year Master David tastes the Finglas and helps us set a price. It is through him that we sell to the taverns in Edinburgh."

"I see." Ross left the still room and walked to the bottom of the stairs, his expression thoughtful. "I should take the whiskey directly to Master David, then."

"*We* will take it."

"You are not going."

"I must. I have to hear what Master David has to say about the Finglas, especially the ten-year."

"It is too dangerous. Hakon may well have taken to Doune the whiskey he found this afternoon."

"It is a large town and very crowded during the fair. I can be in, do my business with Master David and be gone in a few hours. But his advice is precious. And too, with all that's happened, he may think you have stolen the whiskey."

"You could give me a note for him."

"Nay, this is something I must discuss with Master David. It was a dream of Papa's to prove an aged whiskey was the finest to be had. He wanted so much to make the Finglas more than just a local brew renowned at the Doune Fair. He thought to secure not only the clan's future prosperity, but our name in history. I must do this. I must fulfill his dream," she added fervently.

"Too risky," Ross said, but she thought he was weakening.

"I will go disguised as a man."

"Oh?" Ross looked her up and down, his eyes glittering. "No one will believe that."

"I have baggy trews and a knee-length tunic."

His gaze switched to her face. "And a sack over your head?"

"If you think I should."

"What you should do is stay safely inside Kennecraig," he said gruffly.

"I will go to Doune," she assured him just as firmly. "Either with you, or on my own."

Ross grunted. "That willfulness will get you into trouble."

"Oh, it frequently does." She smiled up at him. "But I am counting on you to pull me free, as you did this afternoon."

"*Dieu,* let us hope it does not come to that." He motioned for her to precede him up the stairs. "I had best find Adair and see to moving that winch."

"And I to selecting the kegs we will take."

"You are the only Boyd who is going with us," he warned in a hard voice that brooked no arguments. "I will have my hands full guarding you without a horde of innocents to watch."

"Agreed." Catlyn sighed. Another battle with Roland.

Hidden in the shadows of the settling room, Roland, Wesley and Eoin watched Catlyn and the knight exit the distillery. When the door clanked shut behind them, the men stood.

"See the way she looks at him?" Roland hissed. "She's so bewitched by her new lover she cares nothing for my Finglas."

Eoin nodded morosely. He could not imagine Catlyn taking a lover, especially one as raw and virile as Sir Ross.

The only passion she had ever evidenced was for her family and their whiskey. Yet he could not deny there was hunger in the glances she sent Ross Sutherland's way when she thought no one was watching. Had she shown *him* a bit of that fire, he might not have been forced to turn to other women, Eoin thought.

"How can they take the Finglas to Doune without ye, Da?" Wesley asked angrily.

"She will make a hash of things, without me, that's sure," Roland grumbled. "I sat at Thomas's right hand while Old Master David tasted. We shared this, the laird and I, same as we shared the work. But *she* is bent on taking the distillery over."

"I am sure that is not what Catlyn intends," Eoin said.

"It's what she's about, right enough." Roland stomped off toward the shelves that held the new whiskey, last year's nearly raw distillation. "But she'll find I don't easily give over what's mine." He took down a keg and carried it to the table in the center of the room.

Eoin followed him. "What are you doing?"

"Causing her a bit of shame, I'm hoping." Roland turned to his son. "Fetch me ink and the hide we use for labels. Be quick about it, now. Herself will be back to choose the kegs for Doune." He snorted as he ripped off the hide square glued to the keg. "We'll see what Master David makes of what she brings him."

"You are going to switch the kegs?" Eoin exclaimed.

Roland's head snapped up, his eyes narrowed to furious slits in his fleshy face. "I'm doing what's best for the Finglas, and if ye breathe a word of this, I'll tell everyone ye was swiving Crofter Donald's daughter all the while ye was courting Catlyn *and* trying to bed Dora."

Eoin flushed. "I have not seen Megan in months."

"Aye, be that as it may, it's yer bastard she's carrying. If Catlyn finds out, ye'll be wedding the lass. And that'll put an end to yer hopes of winning back our lady."

"That...that is blackmail," Eoin snarled.

"And ye're naught but a common lecher. Give me a hand with these kegs, or they'll all know the truth and ye'll be turned out of Kennecraig as poor as ye were when Thomas took ye in."

Eoin contemplated cracking a keg over Roland's bald head, but the way his luck had been running, the old man would die and he'd be accused of murder. Actually, that was not a bad idea, only if he were going to kill someone, it would be Ross Sutherland.

Ross entered the solar and closed the door behind him with an angry snap. "Damn, damn, damn."

"Trouble?" Mathew asked, turning from the saddle pack. "Did you not get to see the stills?"

"I saw them." Ross crossed to the table, poured a cup of ale and downed it in two swallows. It did not wash the foul taste from his mouth. The taste of betrayal. "She showed me everything, told me about the hundreds of ledgers and scrolls on whiskey making dating back to the first batch of Finglas Water ever made. These Boyds keep better records than Mother Church." He slammed down the cup. "She trusted me. She showed me things no outsider has been allowed to see. And how will I repay her?"

"Ross." Mathew abandoned his packing and joined him. "I understand how you must feel."

"How can you? It is my fault we are here. My—"

"I understand because I have come to admire them, too. They are much like our own families, these Boyds, gentle people wanting only to raise their families and engage in a craft they love. One they have practiced for generations."

"Bogged in tradition, that is what they are." Ross stared out the window at the jagged peaks surrounding the keep. "And it will be the death of them."

"What do you mean? What has happened now?"

"I suggested to Catlyn that they leave."

"Leave? Leave Kennecraig for all time?"

"She said the same, only with more force. Stubborn little

fool. She does not realize the extent of Hakon's ruthlessness, and how can I make her understand without telling her—?''

"The truth. Why not tell her all?''

"You want me to tell her we came here to steal her family's secrets and give them to their sworn enemy?'' Ross laughed, a short, mirthless sound. "They would toss us out, if Eoin did not kill us. Then we would not only be unable to get the note from Hakon, we would leave the Boyds to his mercy.''

"Aye.'' Mathew sighed and raked a hand through his hair. "There is no way we can convince these folk that no matter why we first came here, we now want to help them.''

"The problem is, how to do that and still save our own kin?'' Ross's eyes widened. "What if I were to give Hakon a drawing of the stills and the secret of making the Finglas?''

"Have you gone mad?'' Mathew exclaimed. "Hakon does not really want those things. He wants control of Kennecraig.''

"Aye, but our bargain was for the recipe and drawings.''

Mathew still stared at him openmouthed. "You would betray Catlyn and her people?''

"Nay, save them.'' Ross paced before the solar's window, turning the problem this way and that. "I now know enough about the distilling to fool Hakon. I will prepare false drawings and a recipe to exchange for the note.'' He spun away from the window and went in search of writing materials. "Once I have it, I'll be free to help the Boyds.''

Mathew followed him. "What if Hakon does not stick by the bargain you made? What if he demands you open the gates of Kennecraig for him?''

"That I will not do, no matter what he threatens.'' Ross bent and pawed through his saddle pack till he found a roll of parchment. On the table lay a quill and ink.

"So what are we going to do?''

"Take the whiskey to Doune and bring back supplies.''

"What if Hakon has gone there, too, to sell what he stole?"

"I am hoping he is." Ross sat and began to sketch the huge whiskey still he'd seen in the cellars. It would not matter if it was accurate, since Hakon had no intention of building one. "That will save me from having to find his stronghold."

"I do not like this," Mathew said dolefully.

Ross smiled up into his cousin's worried face, hiding his own misgivings. Hakon was not the sort to play fair, and there was every chance the bastard would not honor their bargain. "I am sending Harry off to Edin Tower to warn Papa what is afoot."

"Ah." Mathew sank down in the other chair, his relief comical. "How many men can he send us, do you think?"

"None. I will advise him to call up the clan to protect Edin Vally in case Hakon goes there to press his claim."

"But…"

"I do not think Papa could muster a force and reach us before Hakon's patience runs out. And too, in this wild, mountainous country, a band such as Hakon's could pick apart an army with bloody raids."

Mathew nodded morosely. "So we go to Doune to beard the lion."

"Indeed." Ross grinned. "Beard him and pull his teeth. While I am finishing these papers, will you go and make certain the winch is moved? I want to be away well before dawn. Oh," he added as Mathew started for the door. "Bade our lads borrow saffron shirts from the Boyds. They are to put them over their chain mail. And we'll be wearing our plaids. We want to blend in as much as possible. It will help if we look like a band of Highlanders come to enjoy the fair."

Chapter Eleven

The town of Doune drowsed in the fading afternoon sun. Behind it soared the rugged peak of Slymaback Mountain. To the south, the blue waters of the Teith River flowed lazily past the ancient stone buildings, while on the opposite bank, Doune Castle stood guard like a silent gray sentinel.

Catlyn, riding at the center of the Sutherland band, heaved a sigh of relief. Doune had never looked more welcome.

"Tired?" Ross leaned over to gently ask.

"Not at all." She was exhausted. First had come the terrifying climb down Kennecraig's walls. In the dark. If not for the knots in the rope and Ross's steadying presence below her, she would have slid the whole way. Then the ride. Eight or maybe nine hours in the saddle took a toll on a lass who had never ridden more than two at a stretch. Surreptitiously she shifted her numbed bottom.

Ross chuckled. "Not much farther now, I'd guess."

"Nay." Catlyn looked past the troopers in their yellow shirts and plaids to the cluster of tents on the outskirts of town. Brightly colored pennants flew from their tops, fluttering in the breeze that carried the scent of roasting meat and the sounds of laughter. "The fair is already underway."

"Aye." Ross followed her gaze. His eyes lost some of the wariness that had filled them every step of the journey. "It has been some time since I've been to a fair."

"I have never been," Catlyn said wistfully.

"Never? But I thought your clan came here every year."

"We do, but Papa was always anxious to sell the Finglas, buy our supplies and return to Kennecraig."

"That does not seem right. You work hard all year. I think an afternoon of entertainment is a small reward for—"

"The Finglas is reward enough," Catlyn said stiffly.

"Hmm." His eyes probed into hers, then he smiled. "Work is satisfying to the pride, but the soul craves more."

Catlyn looked away, feeling as though he had seen clear through to her innermost secrets. Her dreams. And desires. She wanted him still, more with each moment passed in his company. Speaking of this unexpected, unprecedented passion had not dimmed it one wit. Because now she knew he was more than a handsome, virile warrior. He was kind and compassionate, possessed of a razor-sharp intelligence that drew her even more than did his physical appearance.

Though men were not said to be beautiful, Ross Sutherland had beauty of spirit as well as face and form. When she was with him, all else faded. When she gazed into his eyes, she wanted to do something wild and wanton. She wanted to throw herself at him, wrap herself around him and melt into his kisses. She wanted to feel—

"Which way to the Golden Thistle?" he asked.

Catlyn started, felt her cheeks flush with shame and withdrew further into the hood of the cape Ross had insisted she draw up to hide her features. "It...it lies in the center of town, just off the main street."

Ross nodded and scanned the approaching town. His eyes were narrowed, his expression turned hard again. So he must look on the battlefield as he sized up an enemy. "Keep your head down and stay close to me," he muttered. "And if you value your safety, do not speak to anyone."

Normally Catlyn would have bristled at such orders, but her belly was already tight with apprehension. Hakon might lurk somewhere in the crowded fair grounds. Or, more likely, he was in one of Doune's taverns trying to sell the Finglas. What if he went to the Golden Thistle?

Catlyn chewed on her lower lip and glanced at Ross. How straight he sat in the saddle, even after all these hours. His face was in profile to her, its rugged planes as stalwart as Doune Castle's sheltering walls. Safe. That it was he made her feel. Among other things. Aye, Ross would keep her safe. To a lass with a greedy dragon breathing down her neck, the notion that she had a knight protector was heady indeed. Almost as heady as those kisses she craved.

Sighing, Catlyn turned her attention to the street.

Though the fair did not officially start until the morrow, the narrow thoroughfares were thronged with people, most dressed in their feast-day best. No one was in a hurry. Groups of men sauntered down the dusty track, singing and arguing, some already sloppy with drink. Couples strolled along, so wrapped up in each other they barely glanced at the merchandise in the shop windows. The exception was the children, who darted about like crazed things, shrieking, laughing and begging for treats.

Watching them, Catlyn chuckled.

"What is it?" demanded the vigilant Ross.

"Oh, nothing." She turned to peer at him. "I but realized that I had lied to you."

His eyes widened. "You lied?"

"Well, not intentionally. I had forgotten, really, that I did once go to the fair. I was twelve that year, and Mama took me to the cobblers to be fitted for my first pair of boots. While we waited for them to be stitched, we walked about. It was like no other time I remember. We ate meat pies and gundy toffee, listened to a storyteller and watched a dancing bear." She wrinkled her nose. "I felt sorry for the poor creature and cried till Mama took me away. Mama, being Mama, became distracted by the threads displayed in the cloth merchant's stall. By the time Papa found us, he was quite angry.''

''He was doubtless worried.''

''Aye, I'm sure he was, but we were fine. And it was quite the most fun I've ever had.''

''Despite the bear.''

She grinned and nodded. ''I felt so...so carefree.''

''As you should have. You were but a bairn.''

''I had lessons.'' Catlyn's smile dimmed. ''And duties. The next year, my brother died.'' Saddened, she turned her attention to guiding her horse through the street.

Ross studied her profile, so calm and composed despite weariness and worry. But then, she was used to both, his hard-working lass. Never had he met a woman he respected more...unless it was his mother. But even in the dark days when Edin Valley had been threatened by invaders, Lady Laurel had had her grandsire to guide her. And, eventually, Kieran Sutherland's mercenary army to protect her.

Catlyn had only Ross's small band of fighting men to stand between her clan and Hakon Fergusson's murdering thugs. And she could not know that the very man she counted on to protect her was himself Hakon's pawn.

What would he do if he could not get the note from Hakon?

''There...there is the Golden Thistle,'' Catlyn murmured.

Ross halted beside her and studied the tavern.

It was a two-story stone building set back from the dusty, rutted street. Wide alleyways on either side separated it from a house on one side and a bakeshop on the other. In deference to the warm weather, the tavern's door stood open, and the shutters had been loosed on the high, narrow windows. On the whole, it looked better kept than most drinking houses.

Ross dismounted and handed the reins of his horse to Lang Gil. ''See if there is a stable in back or nearby. As soon as we've unloaded the kegs, the horses can be fed and watered, but leave them saddled.''

In case we must leave quickly.

Though he did not speak the words, Catlyn shivered. Neck prickling, she glanced about but saw no familiar fiendish faces among the folk passing by. She gathered herself to step down.

''Wait,'' Ross cautioned. ''Dallas, take a look inside.''

''Surely they cannot know we will come here,'' said Catlyn.

''Nay, but I would know what lies within. Did your father conduct his tasting in the main room of the tavern?''

Catlyn shook her head. ''Master David has a chamber in the back where he keeps his accounts and does his private business.''

''Excellent, and is there a back door, as well?'' At her nod, some of the tension left his face.

''Do you think Hakon may come here?'' she whispered.

''It is possible, and if he does, I do not want any in the tavern to recall having seen us. You especially, Catlyn.''

She was fairly sweltering in the woolen cap that hid her braids and the cape he had insisted she throw on over her male tunic and trews. ''The only thing visible is the tip of my nose.''

''And a bonny nose it is.'' His tone and smile were teasing, but his eyes darted watchfully about, and his right hand rested on the hilt of the claymore at his waist.

My protector, Catlyn thought. Not once during the ride had he left her side. She supposed this was not the time to tell him how handsome he looked in his Highlander garb. The saffron shirt contrasted with his tanned skin, the length of plaid draped across his chest emphasized the width of his shoulders.

Dallas returned. ''I did not recognize anyone, but the tavern is crowded,'' he warned.

Ross nodded. That was evident from the laughter and loud voices drifting out the door. Even had it not been for the danger, he would not have wanted Catlyn in such rough company. Glancing sidelong at Mathew, he murmured, "Take Catlyn around behind the tavern. I will seek out Master David and ask that he let us in by the back way."

"Give him my name," Catlyn said. "He will come at once if—"

"Go along with Mathew," Ross replied, not wanting to upset her further by repeating the need for secrecy. She was afraid but trying bravely to hide it. Just as she tried to hide her fatigue, but her eyes were shadowed, her mouth pinched. *Dieu,* he wished she was safely back at Kennecraig. He glanced again at Mathew. They had agreed that at the first sign of trouble his cousin would rush Catlyn out of Doune and into the hills.

Mathew nodded, took hold of Catlyn's bridle and led the troop down the side alley.

"Should someone not go with Ross?" he heard Catlyn ask.

Mathew snorted. "He can take care of himself, my lady."

Ross scowled as he headed into the tavern. Thus far, he had not proved very adept in that art. Stopping just inside the door, he waited a moment for his eyes to adjust to the gloom. As they did, he saw every seat was indeed taken and several men were standing before the oak plank bar at the far side of the room. Behind the bar, two sturdy lads and an older man were filling pitchers and passing them to a trio of serving maids.

Ross made for the bar and addressed the older man. "Are you Master David Erskine?"

The man straightened, scowling as he looked Ross over. He was tall and thin to the point of gauntness, his bald head rimmed by gray fringe. His eyes were gray, too. They glared at Ross down a beak of mammoth proportions. "Who is asking?"

"A friend of the Finglas," Ross murmured.

If anything, the barkeep's expression grew colder. "I told the other man that I had no coin to buy whiskey."

Had Hakon already been here? Gooseflesh danced across Ross's skin. "I've come on behalf of the lass," he said.

"Lass?" Interest warmed the gray eyes. "What lass is that?"

"One with hair the color of honey and her father's nose for the *uisge beatha*."

"Where?"

"If you are the Master David she bade me seek out, you'll know where such business is usually done."

"I am he." David Erskine's eyes flicked toward a door behind the bar. "Give me a few moments. I will let you in through the back."

Ross nodded, turned and worked his way out of the crowded tavern. Two men took his place at the bar, arguing over whose turn it was to pay for the ale. Once on the street, Ross ambled toward the bakeshop. Unlike the tavern, it was nearly empty.

"We're out of pies," called the baker, his flour-dusted face bent over a worktable. "Come back in a half hour."

"I just may do that." Ross walked through the shop and exited by the side door, which put him in the alleyway. A quick glance at the main street showed no one lurking about. He walked down the alley to the back of the tavern. As he rounded the corner, a large figure blocked his path.

"Oh, it's yerself." Johnnie Sutherland stepped aside.

Ross clapped him on the shoulder. "Keep a sharp eye open." He moved quickly to Catlyn's side.

"What happened? Is he not here?" she cried softly.

"Your Master David will let us in." Ross took hold of her waist and lifted her from the saddle in a gesture he'd not have dared on the main street. What knight treated his squire so? The moment her feet touched the ground, he heard her gasp, felt her collapse against him. "Easy, lass, you've been long hours in the saddle." It was heaven holding her like this, hell knowing he should not. Still he kept his arms around her, savoring the feel of her softness, the scent of her skin, teasing himself with the memory of their kiss. If things were different—

The creak of hinges broke the tableau. The door opened, and David's shiny head poked out.

"Master David," Catlyn whispered, pulling away from Ross.

"Catlyn?" A smile lit David's austere face. "Catlyn." He bounded out the door and swept her into his arms.

Ross felt bereft without her, and more than a little jealous of the old man who had a right to hug her close and drop a kiss on her forehead.

"I've been that worried about you," David said, his voice rough, his face wet with tears.

"We are...fine," Catlyn whispered, sounding anything but.

"Your mother?"

Catlyn's lower lip quivered. "She is much the same."

"Can we go inside?" Ross asked.

David's head jerked up, and his eyes narrowed once more.

"It is all right, Master David," Catlyn said softly. "This is Sir Ross—"

"The lady hired me to protect her," Ross said brusquely. "And I would be remiss in my duty if I did not get her inside before someone chances by and recognizes her."

"Of course." Eyes wide with alarm, Master David took Catlyn's arm and hustled her inside the tavern.

Ross gave orders to have the kegs brought in, then followed the innkeeper. Master David's counting room was half the size of the tavern's main room, but like the settling room at Kennecraig it was a maze of shelving. The open space in the middle of the room was occupied by a large table. A pile of ledger books listed precariously on a nearby stool. The bench set against the adjacent wall held baskets of tally sticks.

"Sit here, lass." David scooped the tally baskets from

the bench and deposited them on the floor. "You look done in."

"It was a long ride." She smiled ruefully. "And I think I'll stand a moment."

Ross chuckled. "We're all a bit numb in the backside."

"Humph," said David, obviously a man of little humor. "Food, then? Or ale?" he asked her solicitously. "I can have a room readied upstairs if you would like to lie down."

"Ale would be most welcome," Catlyn replied. How small and fragile she looked, her flushed face framed by the cap, her shoulders hunched beneath the long cape.

While David bustled into the tavern to fetch the ale, Ross crossed to her and undid the ties on her cape. "I think we can dispense with these while we are in here." He flung back the hot wool, then plucked off the cap.

Catlyn sighed and swayed toward him. Her eyes closed, her lashes lying like fringe on her rosy cheeks.

Poor lamb. Ross splayed one hand on her back to steady her, fighting the urge to lift her into his arms and cradle her. The heat seeping through her tunic alarmed him. "Are you all right?" Gently he brushed the back of his hand over her cheek.

"Just tired and hot."

"You should have told me you were burning up."

She opened her eyes and smiled faintly. "The disguise was warm but needful. You said so when you agreed to bring me. I would not endanger us all for my comfort."

"Duty does not always come before your well-being."

"Aye, it does, but I have taken no permanent hurt."

Ross sighed and leaned his forehead against her warmer one. She felt as precious and fragile as spun glass. For a moment, her nearness erased everything else. The distillery. Hakon. The note. He could stand here with her forever. Just like this, needing nothing else to complete him. Oh, he still wanted her. Desire pulsed through his body, raw and wild, tightening the muscles below his belt, making his blood sizzle. But there were other, more subtle changes. A jumble of needs that made a mockery of his past, easy dealings with women.

There was nothing light or flip about what she made him feel. For her, with her, he could be serious and constant. He should not feel this way about her. He knew that, but knowing didn't change the ache deep inside, the almost driving need for honesty between them. "Catlyn, when our business is concluded, there are things I would tell you. Things I..."

"See here, what are you doing?" David cried, hurrying in with a tray.

Ross stepped back but kept a proprietary hand on Catlyn's waist. He felt her tremble, and his heart quaked. Whatever happened, he had to make certain she was not hurt. Not by Hakon. And most especially not by himself.

"It is all right," Catlyn assured David. "Sir Ross is..." She hesitated, obviously as uncertain as Ross was how to describe what lay between them. "He was concerned for my weariness."

"Humph. Then he should not have dragged you hither." David set the tray on the table with a thump.

"Dragged?" Ross chuckled and released her. "If you say that, you cannot know of the lass's stubbornness."

That drew a smile from David. "Aye, well..."

"I had to come." Catlyn sat on the bench because her legs were suddenly too shaky to support her. It was not weariness, but excitement. Something had changed in that moment when Ross held her. What had he been about to say? Intrigued, she accepted the cup of ale David poured, realized it had been watered and downed it in a few thirsty swallows.

Ross's men entered, bearing kegs on their shoulders.

"You've brought me the Finglas after all?" David exclaimed. At Catlyn's nod, he fairly beamed, and rushed about clearing a space near the table where they might stack the whiskey.

"See the men and horses are tended," Ross said to Mathew.

"Aye." Mathew's expression did not relax. "We will be outside…watching."

"I am counting on it," Ross said grimly.

David hovered over the kegs, rubbing his hands together in anticipation. "Do you want to rest, or shall we begin?"

"Begin," Catlyn said at once. Always before she had enjoyed the ritual of the tasting. Now she was as impatient as David to have it done so she and Ross might leave. And go where?

A bit of Catlyn's excitement faded when she realized that when the tasting was over, they would buy supplies and set out again for Kennecraig. More long hours in the saddle with no chance for private conversation.

The sun was just kissing the top of Slymaback Mountain when Roland, Eoin and Wesley approached Doune.

"I wonder if Catlyn and the Sutherlands arrived safely?" Eoin asked for perhaps the dozenth time since setting out a scant hour behind the troop. "Perhaps I should go to the Golden Thistle and make certain she is all right."

Roland glared at him. "I have told ye we are not going near the Golden Thistle till after we've sold our Finglas."

"But suppose the owner of the Sword and Shield does not want to buy from men he doesn't know?" Eoin asked.

"Coinnech McNab is none too particular about where his whiskey comes from, so long as it's good quality." Roland reached back to pat the keg riding pillion behind him. "When he tastes the ten-year, he'll fall over himself to buy." His smile faded. "Too bad we couldn't have brought a wagonload."

"That would have been insane," Eoin growled. "Bad enough we defied Adair's orders and left Kennecraig."

"What care I for Adair's orders? It's Laird Thomas's wishes I'm thinking of. He dreamed of seeing the distillery get the notice it deserves, and I am going to make that happen.''

''How?''

''When Coinnech tastes the Finglas, he'll be more than willing to advance us money on another shipment. We'll hire our own guards to escort a wagonload. We won't be bringing it here though. We'll go straight to Edinburgh and the king.''

''Catlyn will not like that,'' said Eoin. ''She'll be angry enough when she finds out we took three kegs of the ten-year.''

''We do not need her approval. The distillery belongs to everyone in the clan. With the king's seal on it, the Finglas will get the respect our laird worked so hard for.''

Eoin stared at Roland. All the master distiller said was true, but his zeal made Eoin uncomfortable.

''When can we go to the fair?'' Wesley demanded.

''There won't be time,'' Roland snapped. ''When we've sold this lot, we will return to Kennecraig and make preparations for the shipment to Edinburgh.''

Eoin frowned. ''We cannot start back before the morrow. The horses will need rest.'' And he was determined to make certain Catlyn was all right, even if it meant showing up at the Golden Thistle and facing Ross Sutherland's wrath.

Wesley scowled at his father. ''I rode all this way to see the fair, and I'm going to.''

''Very well,'' Roland grumbled. ''Once the Finglas is sold, we will find a room for the night. Ye can go to the fair for a short while, Wesley. Eoin and I will guard our coin.''

''I may go to the fair myself,'' Eoin said, by way of a ruse.

Ross and Catlyn left the Golden Thistle just as the sun sank behind the mountains, turning the sky a bright red. Master David had tasted just one of the kegs, pronounced it the finest whiskey ever to slide down his pallet and given them notes of credit for all twenty kegs.

"Are you sure you would not rather be resting?" Ross asked.

"I am too excited to rest." Indeed, she fairly skipped along at his side, looking as carefree as a young lass in the clothes borrowed from one of the widowed David's daughters. A white cap hid her hair, but the loosely belted woolen gown showed off her slender waist, rounded hips and high, full breasts. Its mossy color brought out the green in the eyes she raised to him. "I feel guilty leaving the buying of the supplies to Mathew and your men."

"There is no reason why you should. Neither of us is adept at the task, and Mat is so anxious to impress Dora with what he brings back, we'd actually be doing him a favor." Smiling, he extended his arm. "Shall we see the fair, then, lass?"

"Are you certain it is safe?"

Oh, how he hated that dimming of her smile, the wariness that dulled her eyes. "I'd not have suggested we go otherwise. It'll be dark soon, and if Hakon came to Doune, he'll be in the taverns, not enjoying the fair."

"All right, then." Grinning, Catlyn linked her arm with his. That humor set the tone for their adventure.

Eager as two bairns let out of their lessons early, they hurried toward the fairgrounds. The crowd thickened as they neared the field, and they found themselves swept along on a tide of humanity. Ross shifted his grip, putting one arm around Catlyn's waist, pleased by the way she relaxed against him. They passed the first tent and stepped into a world of tempting smells and bedazzling sights.

"Oh," Catlyn exclaimed. "There is so much."

Indeed, there was. A veritable sea of colorful tents and booths selling everything from mundane cloth to exotic spices. Somehow, Ross kept a protective arm between Catlyn and the jostling crowd as she walked slowly past each stall, admiring this, touching that. Somehow, whatever struck her fancy wound up stuck to her. From the toy seller, a tiny wooden doll with woolen hair. A bit of green ribbon to tie the end of her braid, because Ross insisted the color matched her eyes. Catlyn spied the packets of silken thread and thought of her mother. The charming set of bells were for Dora. A peace offering.

At the bakeshop, they bought gingerbread, a delicacy Catlyn had never before tasted, and fed it to each other while they listened to a balladeer sing "Thomas The Rhymer." Some of the verses were so ribald they made Catlyn flush.

Laughing, Ross whirled her away from the singer. "You are beautiful when you are flustered," he whispered in her ear.

"Only then?" she teased with newfound confidence.

"Nay." His gaze grew serious as it caressed her face, feature by feature, coming lastly to her eyes. Gazing deep into them, he said, "Yours is a beauty that shines from within."

"Now that is a compliment I will gladly accept."

"It is the truth." His eyes twinkled again. "But you are the prettiest when you are laughing. Come." He grabbed her hand and tugged. "I hear the pipers warming up for the dancing."

"I do not know how to dance," she said, stumbling along in his wake.

"I'll teach you. I'm very good at it."

He was, and patient, too. He kept them on the fringe of the frantic activity, showing her the steps over and over till he pronounced her ready. "Now." He drew her into the fray, holding her close, guarding her from the press. They leaped and spun till she was dizzy, clinging to him, her anchor in a world gone mad. Insanely, happily mad.

Somehow, her feet followed his, her body swaying with his to the wild cry of the pipes. Catlyn's heart seemed to soar with the music, her blood rushing faster and faster, like water after a spring thaw. Aye, that was how he made her feel, fresh and alive after a long, cold sleep. Delighted, she threw back her head and laughed.

"Pleased with yourself, sweet?" he shouted over the din.

"And with you." She knew it was wrong and wanton to look at him so openly, to let all she felt show, but she couldn't seem to help herself.

"Ach, Catlyn." Suddenly he lifted her high over his head and turned in a circle.

Catlyn looked down and found him staring up at her, his mouth curved into a tender smile, his eyes glittering with emotion. "Aye," she whispered, knowing he felt the same aching need she did, the same overpowering hunger.

He lowered her slowly, letting their bodies brush, the tempered strength of his teasing the softness of hers. She melted against him, pliant yet eager. Her arms slipped around his neck. She felt his heart jolt against hers and smiled at this small sign he was as vulnerable, as needy as she was. His mouth was level with hers, so tempting.

Ross groaned as Catlyn's lips closed over his. She kissed him with a thoroughness that stole reason and will. He had been waiting for this, he dimly thought as their tongues tangled and their bodies strained, not for days, but for his whole life. No matter how far this went, it would not be enough. Never enough.

Shaken, he drew back. "Nay," he whispered. "We cannot."

"Not here." Her eyes were dark, hazy with passion. "Let us go back to the Thistle."

David had given them rooms, one for Catlyn, one for Ross. They would be dark, quiet, private. It was tempting.

Ross shook himself free of the drugging need. "Aye, we will go back." But he must find the strength to resist. Until he had settled things with Hakon, he was not fit to touch her, much less make love with her. Taking her hand, he led her from the swirl of dancers, stopping long enough to pick up the cloth sack with her purchases.

Night had fallen while they were a-fairing, but the streets

were no less crowded than they had been before. If anything, the folk were louder, more rowdy. Craving quiet, Ross changed direction, taking a less traveled side street.

"I enjoyed myself," Catlyn said after a moment. She clung to his hand in a way she would not have before.

"As did I." Remembering her laughter, the joy she had taken in the things they had seen and done lightened his heart. Ross lifted their joined hands and kissed the back of hers. "But..." *But we cannot be lovers.*

Catlyn stopped suddenly. "Look," she whispered, pointing toward a nearby tavern. "That is our wagon." She dropped his hand and ran into the side yard of the inn.

"Wait." Ross hustled after her, sword in hand.

Catlyn leaned close to examine the cart in the light spilling from the tavern's windows. "It is ours." She straightened, expression fierce. "The one Hakon stole. He is likely inside this place selling my whiskey." She glared at the device hanging above the entrance: a sword across a huge shield.

"Shh. Keep your voice down." Ross caught her around the waist and hustled her into the shadows.

"What are we going to do?" she whispered.

"I am taking you to the Thistle, then I will come back and see what I can learn."

Catlyn supposed she had to be satisfied with that, but she was so afraid Hakon would leave that when the Thistle came into view, she begged Ross to return to the Sword and Shield at once.

Ross frowned. "I would place you in Master David's care."

"He said he'd likely be working on his accounts in the back. I will tap on the door, and he can let me in. Where is the danger?" she whispered. "Hakon obviously chose the Sword and Shield, and no one knows we are in Doune." Ross had bade David keep their presence secret, even from his servants.

"Very well." Ross kissed her quick, then trotted back toward the Sword and Shield.

Catlyn immediately headed for the rear of the Thistle. If Mathew was there, she'd send him to the Sword. As she rounded the corner, she heard a sound to her right. She turned, caught a blur of motion, then pain exploded in her head.

The world dipped. Stars exploded.

Catlyn screamed, even as she felt herself slipping, going down. Down.

She heard a shout.

Then heard no more.

Chapter Twelve

In the time it took Ross to deposit Catlyn at the Thistle and return to the Sword and Shield, it seemed that half of Doune had descended on the tavern. The crowd spilled from the open doorway into the street, a shifting mass of dark shapes set out against the light from the tavern's windows. Holding wooden cups sloppily aloft, they shouted a rowdy verse of "The Rover of Loch Finn" into the warm summer night.

Ah, here at least was a bit of cover.

Ross glanced at those closest to him, and though the light was chancy, saw no one who looked familiar. Hunching his shoulders, he made for the tavern. As he plunged into the herd, he caught the unmistakable smell of whiskey. By the time he reached the door, it was a wonder he was not drunk on fumes.

Hakon had obviously found a buyer for the Finglas.

Inside, all was chaos. The tables were full, the spaces between packed. Men shouted out their orders to the barmaids, who bored through the press like weevils. Holding trays precariously over their heads, they tossed cups right and left into the outstretched hands of eager drinkers.

"The drink must be exceptionally fine," Ross said to the man standing, nay, weaving in place, next to him.

"Best damned stuff I've ever tasted." He was a tall fellow, his face flushed nigh as red as his wiry hair. He tipped back his head, drained his cup and toppled like a felled oak.

Ross winced, stepped over him and worked his way along the wall toward the bar. It was the most likely place to find the owner and hopefully learn how long ago Hakon had left. Halfway to his goal, he chanced to spot a familiar face in the throng.

Hakon sat at a corner table with two other men.

Ross withdrew to lurk on the other side of the large hearth that dominated one wall. Partially hidden by the support beams, he slumped against the mantel and feigned drunkenness while watching Hakon and his companions.

The burly one with the scar on his cheek had the look of a soldier. One of Hakon's men? The bald man with his thick arms and stained shirt could easily be the tavern keeper. All three wore satisfied expressions that grated on Ross's temper.

The urge to rush across the room and throttle Hakon rose in Ross's throat, nearly strangling him. He countered it with logic. Among the revelers could be a dozen of Hakon's men. Best to wait and see if he might get the Fergusson alone.

What seemed like an eternity later, but was likely only a quarter hour, Hakon rose and stretched. Surmising he might be visiting the privy, Ross edged along the wall and out the door. He ducked around the corner of the tavern and followed his nose to a low wooden building at the back of the property. It was flanked behind by a trio of pines and on one side by a lush tangle of berry bushes. The stench was enough to make a man gag, and the darkness was alleviated only by the moonlight filtering through the pines.

Not the sort of place where a crowd was likely to linger, Ross thought. Indeed, the only folk about were two men who had passed out on the ground.

Ross flattened himself along the shadow-draped side of the garderobe and waited. A moment later, Hakon sauntered around the tavern and headed for the privy. Noting that the bastard's steps were a mite unsteady made Ross smile grimly. Hakon had gotten him drunk and duped him. Now turnabout was fair play. Ross waited till Hakon had nearly reached the door, then he stepped out of hiding and grabbed the Fergusson's arm.

It was satisfying indeed to see Hakon's crafty brown eyes widen with surprise. "Ye," he whispered.

"Aye." *Your victim. Your tool.*

"Wh-what are ye doing here?" He stank of whiskey and fear.

Brave enough with words and schemes, is Hakon, Ross thought, *especially when he has men to back him. But he is a physical coward.* No wonder he was intimidated. Ross outweighed him by three stone and topped him by a good four inches. His size was an advantage Ross seldom used, except in battle, for he despised bullies. But for Hakon he was willing to make an exception. If force was what it took to win, he'd use it. Anything short of murder. Though the notion of eliminating Hakon permanently was tempting.

"I've come to redeem my note," Ross growled, letting the hatred he felt show in his face. It was a look that had sent more than one hardened soldier into full retreat.

Hakon paled, his lean shoulder trembling in Ross's grasp. "Ye...ye have the Boyd's secret recipe?"

"And the drawings." Ross patted the pouch on his belt.

"How...how did ye get them so quickly?"

"I seduced them from the lady, just as you wanted."

Hakon was quickly losing that dazed look. "That was fast work." He licked his lips. "What of my scout?"

"Seamus stayed behind at Kennecraig."

"Good." Hakon's eyes gleamed in the half light, ripe with anticipation. Doubtless he thought his spy was moving the pesky barrels of black powder. "I'll see him soon enough, then."

Only if you are planning a trip to hell. "I want my note."

"Ah, well…" Hakon's eyes were beginning to lose that glazed look. "I dinna carry it about wi—"

Ross shoved him against the side of the privy and pinned him there with a forearm to the throat. "I do not believe you."

"It…it's the truth," Hakon wheezed.

Ross doubted Hakon would know the truth if it knocked him down. But he also suspected that Hakon was not the sort to leave his valuables lying about for others to steal. "Let us see what is in your sporran."

"Of course." Hakon smiled as he loosened the ties on the hide pouch and offered it to Ross.

Ross was not about to take his eyes, or his hands, from the tricky Borderer. "Take out each item, hold it up where I can see it, then drop it on the ground."

Hakon shrugged and did as he was asked. Where most men carried sentimental bits, like a lucky stone or a hunk of amber, and useful things like cord and a fishing hook, Hakon's treasures ran to dice, gaming cards and thin strips of metal for picking locks. "As ye can see, I've not got it."

A burst of laughter and the crunch of footsteps warned their privacy was about to be breached.

Hakon brightened and looked toward the tavern.

Ross hesitated, thought of all the pain Hakon had inflicted and buried his fist in the man's belly. Hakon folded with a soft, satisfying grunt. Ross drew his dirk and pressed it to Hakon's neck. "Not a sound."

"So, this is the way ye keep a bargain," Hakon gasped.

"If it were, I'd have run you through straight away and searched your body for my note," Ross whispered. "Cry out, and I'll forget I'm an honorable man."

Hakon grunted and kept his head down.

"Told you not to drink so much of the whiskey," Ross said loudly for the benefit of the two strangers who tromped by and entered the garderobe.

A few tense moments later, the two hastened back out,

gagging and rearranging their clothes. Only when they had left did Ross let Hakon straighten.

"What the bloody hell was that for?" Hakon whined.

For Thomas Boyd, Ross thought. But he could not afford to tip his hand just yet and let Hakon know he sided with the Boyds. "For the two of my men who were wounded when you ambushed us outside Kennecraig."

"'Twas needful to get ye inside." Hakon rubbed his belly.

Ross just glared at him. "Give me your boots."

"My what?"

"Boots." Ross's uncle had taught him there were many places a man might hide his valuables, the soles or lining of his boots, the hem of his cape and even a secret flap in his belt.

"Ye've no right to—" Hakon broke off as Ross pressed the edge of his dirk against his throat. "All right." He toed off first one, then the other boot. "There."

"Pick each one up, slowly, and turn it inside out."

Hakon paled, and his mouth thinned, but he did as he was told. As he rolled down the top of the first boot, there came the unmistakable crinkle of parchment. Hakon swore. "Ye're more clever than I gave ye credit for."

"Open it."

Another string of curses accompanied the jerky movements as Hakon parted the seam in the boot's lining to reveal a bit of white. He extracted a parchment square and handed it to Ross.

Keeping the blade to Hakon's throat, Ross worked the folds free with one hand and hastily scanned what was written on it. It was the note, so hastily scrawled some of the words were not recognizable. Even the name at the bottom was shaky.

Ross Lion Sutherland, Laird of Stratheas.

Relief surged through Ross, so heady he felt nearly as giddy as the men singing out in the street. He let none of his joy show as he refolded the parchment and tucked it inside the pouch at his belt. "The drawings of the Boyds' still and the recipe are here." He nudged the sheets lying at their feet. "This settles my debt to you."

"Yer family's been a thorn in the side of mine for years," Hakon said, his voice low, filled with venom. "Take yer note and yer petty victory. Next time we meet, it'll be over crossed swords, not bits of paper."

"I'd welcome that," Ross whispered. "Because then I'd not feel honor-bound to let you live." Ross backed into the darkness and made good his escape, barely able to contain his glee. He had the note. His family was safe. Now he could concentrate on saving Catlyn's clan.

It was all going to work out.

The drawings of the Boyds' still and the recipe are here. This settles my debt to you.

The words rang over and over in Eoin's head as he watched Hakon Fergusson stomp back into the Sword and Shield.

Dod! Eoin sagged against one of the pines behind the privy, his mind spinning. He had been on his way to meet Roland when he'd spotted Ross emerging from the Sword and Shield. Something in the way the man moved had screamed intrigue, so Eoin had surreptitiously followed. It had been worth the wait behind the stinking privy for this bit of news.

Ross Sutherland had sold them out to Hakon.

As the shock receded, satisfaction crept in. Grim satisfaction. When Catlyn heard of this, she would toss the Sutherlands out on their arses.

She would be grateful to him, Eoin thought. Surely this would wipe out his previous sin, and things would be as they had been. As they should be.

A string of pithy curses scattered his thoughts.

Hakon charged around the tavern, a scar-faced man and three others close on his heels.

Eoin retreated behind the pine and peered out.

"Search the streets!" Hakon bellowed. "I want Sutherland found and brought to me...alive, mind ye, Murdo."

The scar-faced man nodded. "Which way did he go?"

"To the right, toward the fair."

"Likely thinks to lose himself in the crowd." Murdo fingered the ugly red line bisecting his left cheek. "Some of our lads went a-fairing. I'll round 'em up for the search."

"Remember, I want him alive." The hatred blazing in Hakon's eyes defied the gloom. "I want to see him pay for what he and his kin have cost me. I want to see him plead for his life."

"He doesn't look the sort to beg," Murdo muttered.

"All the better." Hakon smiled suddenly, a slow, evil grin. "Guthrie likes a challenge."

"Aye." Murdo looked paler. "Come along, lads, best get at it." He headed away from the tavern, and the others followed.

Hakon grabbed the last man. "Come with me. We'll search to the left, toward the main street in case he doubled back."

Eoin straightened and stepped slowly from hiding. It did not matter, he told himself. It did not matter that the thieves had had a falling-out, and Hakon now wished Ross ill. The fact remained, Sutherland had betrayed them to their sworn enemy.

Clinging to that thought, Eoin plunged into the crowd and headed toward the inn at the edge of town where he and Roland had found lodging. It was not a room, mind, just a corner of the stable loft. But with so many in town, they'd been lucky to get that. And luckier still, it lay on the opposite side of town from the fair, where the Fergussons would be searching.

At that moment, Eoin spotted Hakon's blond hair up ahead and slowed his steps. Hakon might not remember him from the few times they'd met, but there was no sense taking chances.

"Eoin! Eoin!" Roland popped out of a side street, bleating like a lost sheep.

"Bloody fool." Eoin grabbed hold of the distiller and hustled him back into the alleyway.

"What are ye doing?" Roland exclaimed, trying to pull free.

"Saving your neck...both our necks, you idiot." Eoin herded his charge through the congested streets, not allowing him to stop till they reached their lodgings.

Roland jerked his arm free. "Ye've no business hauling me about like a sack of flour."

"Then try acting like you've more sense than one," Eoin snapped. *Should he tell Roland what he'd heard?*

"I've sold the whiskey."

"Fine." *Roland liked the Sutherlands no better than he did, but he also chafed under Catlyn's leadership. Roland might somehow twist this to make it seem Catlyn had had a hand in it.*

"'Twas not an easy thing. I'd counted on selling to Master Coinnech, whom I know, but after ye saw our wagon in the yard, ye said it was too dangerous to—"

"I know what I said," Eoin snapped. They had parted company then. Roland and Wesley had gone to visit another prospective buyer. Eoin had headed to the Thistle for news of Catlyn. Only to be told by the barkeep that Master David was away for a few hours and no one from Kennecraig had been there.

"Do ye not want to know who I sold it to?"

"I suppose." What he really wanted was a few quiet minutes to think over what he should do about this plum that had dropped into his lap.

"Master David at the Thistle."

"What?" Eoin's mouth dropped. "You went there, after we agreed not to?"

Roland's eyes narrowed. "None of the other taverns were suitable. They didn't appreciate what they were tasting. 'Twas either David Erskine or Coinnech McNab."

Eoin sighed. "So now Catlyn knows we stole the ten-year."

"We didna steal it!" Roland fairly shouted. "The ten-year is Laird Thomas's, and I mean to see it gets its proper due. Besides," he added defensively, "she was not there."

"Not there?" Eoin's gut knotted. "But—"

"Oh, they got there," Roland growled. "Sold him the whiskey, they did, then went off to buy supplies."

"Where are they now?"

"I did not ask. On their way home, I'd guess. Which is where we'd be if ye hadn't insisted we stay here."

"The horses need rest and so do people. Damn him for dragging her back into the saddle." Eoin ground his teeth in impotent fury. Ross must have sent Catlyn on ahead with his men while he met with Hakon. "She's not used to riding. She must be exhausted."

Roland snorted. "She's stronger than she looks, more's the pity. But she's still no fit master for the Finglas. Laird Thomas should have named me. Course, all that can change." That mad light was back in his eyes again.

"What did Master David say about the Finglas Catlyn sold him? Did he not realize it was the new-made whiskey?"

"Not yet." He scowled darkly. "Cheeky lass. She did not take all the barrels I'd set out, but chose a few of her own. They really were the four-year whiskey. Curse the luck, 'twas one of those David tasted. Raved about it, he did. But he'll get to the others soon enough. Then her reputation'll be in shreds. Then she'll pay for trying to usurp my rightful place."

Eoin was suddenly afraid for Catlyn. "If she and I were to wed, would you accept me as laird? And master of the stills?"

"That's not like to happen."

"It might. What say you?" Eoin asked confidently.

Instead of the expected nod, Roland scowled. "I dunno.

Ye've a way with the grain and the mash, but she's got the better nose, though it pains me to say so.''

"Not better than yours," Eoin said quickly. "If she was wed and busy with the babes I'd give her, the running of the stills would be up to us."

"That's something to think on."

Eoin supposed he had to be satisfied with that, but he was anxious to carry out his own plans. "I've decided that you may have been right after all. We should start back tonight."

"I'm for that, but what of the horses?"

"We may be able to trade for fresh ones."

"We can't leave without Wesley," Roland grumbled. "If only ye'd said something before he went to the fair."

"When did he say he'd be back?"

"Who knows. The lad's developed a wild streak. Takes no interest in the Finglas at all. Why, I'd scarce sat down to taste with Master David and Wesley was whining to be off."

Eoin sighed. There was no help for it. "I'll see what I can do about the horses. Maybe he'll be back by then." If not, Eoin was leaving them to find their own way. He couldn't bear the thought that his Catlyn was in the clutches of that traitor.

Ross did not go directly back to the Thistle. Instead, he took a circuitous route, just in case Hakon had somehow managed to set men on his trail.

As he walked, dodging drunken men and amorous women, he thought about what this might mean. To his clan, to Catlyn's people, and most important of all—to them.

For the first time since meeting her, his conscience was clear. The information he had given to Hakon would not aid the Fergussons in setting up a distillery to rival the Boyds. If that was Hakon's intent, which it was not. So he had not really betrayed her trust.

That good news was offset by the bad.

Hakon still wanted Kennecraig and would do whatever he had to to get it. But now he hated Ross, as well, and had an additional incentive for taking the keep and all within.

Ross toyed briefly with the idea of sending to his father and uncle for troops. But had he any right to involve his clan in a bloody fight over lands that were not theirs? And if he did, would Hakon call up his ruthless Border kin?

The situation and the lay of the land actually favored the aggressors. The Fergussons could hide in the rocks and ambush shipments of supplies and whiskey. They could burn the barley fields and kill the crofters. Then they could besiege Kennecraig and starve out the Boyds.

The Boyds' only weapon was the threat of destroying the stills. If they did that, they also destroyed much of their home, leaving them with no source of income to rebuild.

So why not leave before it was too late? Ross thought as he neared the Thistle. Catlyn would not like the idea, but maybe he could make her see how desperate—

"Ross!" Dallas sprang from the doorway of the apothecary two buildings from The thistle. "Thank God you are back."

"What has happened?"

"Not here." Dallas towed him toward the tavern.

"Is it Catlyn?" Ross whispered.

"Aye, she was attacked—"

Ross did not wait to hear more. Tossing men from his path like sheaves of wheat, he mowed through the few remaining revelers in the street and around to the rear door.

Mathew was waiting on the stoop. "Ross!"

"Where is she?"

"Inside. Upstairs, Master David—"

Ross pushed past him, only to find himself caught and held.

"Wait. She is not badly injured. Only shaken."

"I need to see her." Ross tried to break free.

Mathew pinned him to the door frame. "Aye, you do, but not till you've calmed down. She needs quiet, not some wild-eyed berserker charging in and oversetting—"

"I am calm," Ross said through his teeth.

Mathew smiled ruefully. "I've never seen you less so, cousin." Behind him stood the men they'd gone through hell with. Men who looked at Ross as though he'd gone mad.

"Aye, well…" Ross scrubbed a hand over his face. "What happened? Was it some drunk? God, he did not—"

"Nay." Mathew's grip on his shoulders eased. "She was hit on the head, just outside the back door."

"I knew it wasn't safe. I should have made certain she was inside," Ross cried, the guilt eating at him.

"Master David was working in his counting room, heard a cry and came at once."

"Did he see who did it?"

Mathew shook his head. "A dark shape, leaning over her. That is all. The bastard ran off into the night."

"*Dieu.* What if he had not heard her cry out?" Ross whispered, shaken by the horrible possibilities.

"But he did."

"It could have been one of Hakon's men," Ross muttered. "But a Fergusson would not have been driven off so easily."

"My thought exactly," said Mathew.

"Still, I would feel better knowing what Hakon and his thugs are about. Send a couple of the lads to keep an eye on the Sword and Shield."

Mathew nodded. "Do you still propose to leave at dawn?"

"Earlier if we can. I'd rather be ahead of Hakon than behind, worrying he was waiting around the next bend."

"We will be ready an hour before dawn, then," said Mathew. "Now go and see to your lady."

Your lady. Aye, Catlyn was that, Ross thought as he slipped in through the back door. It amazed him how

quickly he had taken to her, his prickly, independent lass.
A week ago he had known no more than her name. Now
she was the focus of his every waking thought and more
than a few of his dreams.

Chapter Thirteen

A noise jerked Catlyn from an uneasy sleep. Warily she opened her eyes to a shadow-draped room. The candle on the nearby table cast a circle of golden over a surprising sight. Ross slouched in the straight-backed chair beside the bed. As though she'd spoken his name aloud, his eyes suddenly opened.

Instantly alert, they darted about the room before coming to rest on her face. "How do you feel?" he asked.

She took in his rumpled clothes, his darkly stubbled jaw and smiled. "Better than you do, I'd wager."

"I am serious." Indeed, he had never looked so grim, his mouth set in a thin line. "Your head, does it hurt?"

Catlyn gingerly touched the knot on her crown. It was tender. Her left knee throbbed a bit from hitting the ground, but neither injury was unbearable. "I am fine."

"You are not. You were knocked unconscious by—"

"Not entirely unconscious. I heard myself scream, Master David's answering shout and the sounds of the man running."

"I should never have left you." Ross groaned and buried his face in his hands. "God, when I think what might have happened…"

"Shh." Catlyn reached out to ruffle his hair. It was thick and wondrous to the touch, like a mink pelt. She wondered if the hair springing from the neck of his tunic would feel as soft. "It is all right."

"Nay, it is not." He exploded out of the chair and began to pace, both hands thrust into his hair as though to keep his head from flying off. "You could have been killed, or worse."

"But I was not." Nor had she even had time to be afraid. One moment she'd been running to the door, the next she'd been on the ground with Master David leaning over her.

"No thanks to me," he growled. "How could I have been so stupid? Damn my impatience." He continued to pace. Gone was the merry Highlander who'd taken her a-fairing. Dressed now in his black tunic and hose, he was the warrior once more.

Catlyn watched, perplexed by his anger. Then she remembered something Mathew had said. He and the rest of the Sutherlands had returned with the supplies only moments after Master David's shouts had driven off her attacker.

Mathew had sent men searching for the fiend and carried her up to this room himself, asking worriedly for a physician or an herb woman, if memory served. "Ross will never forgive himself," Mathew had repeated over and over again. It seemed he was right.

"I know you take your duties seriously," Catlyn said.

Ross wheeled to face her. "What duties?"

"Well, I did hire you to protect me, and—"

"You think that is what this is about?" He came to her slowly, his expression more anguished than before, filled with hurt and bewilderment. "You think the only reason that I care about this is because you have paid me to?"

"I do not know."

He sank down onto the edge of the bed, his eyes fastened on hers. They were still brilliant and mesmerizing, but unshuttered for the first time, as transparent as the loch in spring. She saw herself reflected in them. And more. She saw tenderness and passion, needs tempered with empathy.

"Ross," she whispered, lifting a hand to his cheek.

"Aye, you feel the pull same as I, but do you truly understand what it means?"

Catlyn's heart swelled till it nearly burst from her chest. "I love you."

"Thank God for that." He turned his head to kiss her palm. When he looked at her again, his eyes shone like precious gems. "For if you did not, I don't know what I'd do."

"Oh, Ross." Catlyn looped her arms around his neck and pulled his head down. Their mouths met, meshed. *So good. So right,* she thought, her lips parting on a sigh of pleasure. An answering growl rumbled through his body seconds before he took control of the kiss, devouring her with all the pent-up fury of a mountain storm. She could hear the thunder echoing in her ears as her pulse began to pound.

Inside her something broke free, something sweet and wild and wonderful. A craving unlike anything she'd ever known. Desire surged through her, making her shake and quake like a leaf in a gale. Clinging to Ross's neck, she followed where he led, trusting him in ways she'd never expected to trust any man. But then, she had never felt about anyone as she did about Ross. Her whole body ached and pulsed to the cadence he set. She strained against him, struggling to get closer, needing to find the heart of this sensual storm and share its secrets with him.

Catlyn's frenzied response tore at Ross's control. He had guessed her calm control hid a passionate nature, but its depths surprised and delighted him. Never had desire built this swiftly or raged this fiercely. Never had he met a woman who matched him so perfectly in wit and in desire. He ran his hands down her supple back, fighting to remember she was new to this. But then, everything about this seemed new and different. Because Catlyn was different, so fragile and so infinitely precious. Yet her passion, unbridled for the first time, nearly drove him wild. He wanted to tear off their clothes and bury himself in her welcoming heat. He wanted to give and take and give till they were both mindless. But he wanted more, so much more. For both of them.

Wrenching his lips from hers, Ross kissed her cheek, her temple, the shell of her ear, dragging in the unique scent of this woman. His woman. "We cannot," he whispered, and sat back to put space between himself and temptation. Or tried to.

She clung to his neck. "Please don't leave me."

"I must." Ross gently disentangled her arms, placing a kiss on each palm. "If I stay, I will do something we will regret."

She wouldn't. "Why do you say that?"

"Because I love you, dammit."

Catlyn smiled. She had received scores of similar declarations and known them for lies, known it was her property that was loved, not herself. But she could not doubt he meant what he said, for the words seemed to have been dragged from him. "You do not want to love me?" she asked cautiously, while her heart hung heavy in her chest.

"Aye, but…" He dragged a hand through his hair, stood and walked to the tiny window, his gait somewhat stiff. Leaning his hands on the sill, he stared out. "It is because I love you that I am doing this," he muttered. "It would be dishonorable for me to, er, to bed you ere we are wed."

Wed. Oh, was there ever a more wonderful word? Catlyn savored it while she watched Ross across the room. He could be arrogant and controlling, but his sense of honor ran deep and pure. He could be a charming rogue, but those teasing smiles hid a sensitive, compassionate nature. She had thought herself immune to handsome men after Eoin's betrayal, but now she very much wanted to spend the rest of her days with this intelligent, complex man. Yet she feared passion might force his hand. "You do not have to wed me to bed me," she said softly.

He turned to face her again. The candlelight did not quite

reach to the window, leaving his face in shadow. "Aye, I do, for I do not think I could live the rest of my life without you."

"Oh." Catlyn leaped from the bed, the slight ache in her head, the stiffness in her knee forgotten as she flew to him.

Ross met her halfway, catching her as she threw herself into his arms. "Catlyn, you should not be out of—"

"Hold me. Just hold me."

He enfolded her in an embrace so satisfying it nearly drove the air from her lungs. "You have been injured."

"Closer. Hold me closer."

He whispered her name and his hands slid down her back, lifting her so their bodies fit together. Hard to soft.

It was wonderful, but it was not enough. "Please do not leave me," she whispered, trying to wriggle closer.

A tremor shook his big body. "I must. If I stay—"

"I need you." And he needed her. She felt the proof of it pressing against her belly, and the wanting intensified, spiraling though her like hot syrup. Desperate, that's how she felt. And determined. She was not letting him go. Not tonight, not ever. "Love me," she whispered, rocking her hips in an instinctive, wordless plea.

His eyes closed. He groaned and clasped her tight, a shudder marking his silent battle against what they both wanted. When his lashes lifted, his eyes were gentle but regretful. "I do, and that is why we must wait." He set her on her feet, leaving her feeling cold and bereft despite the warm hands he kept around her waist. "This must be done correctly. You deserve a lavish ceremony, with your kin nearby to wish you well."

Catlyn thought about those who waited at Kennecraig. "Oh, it would doubtless be memorable," she grumbled. "My mother would not know it was going on. Eoin would hound me to change my mind and try to kill you when he found he could not. And Roland would make both our lives miserable before, during and after."

He sighed. "I suppose you are right, still…"

"I need only you and a priest," she said firmly.

"Are you certain? You Boyds set great store by tradition, and I am sure no Boyd ever wed without careful consideration."

Catlyn did not feel cautious or reasonable. She felt wild, reckless and a little desperate. As though she must seize this moment before the chance was lost. "I was never more certain of a thing in my life." She dragged his head down for a kiss, tasted surprise on his lips, felt a groan shudder through him in the instant before he surrendered and kissed her back. A heady sense of feminine power ran up her spine. Or was it his hand, molding her close? His mouth moved over hers with devastating thoroughness, the kiss wet and deep and as bold as he was. By the time he raised his head, she was clinging to him, her mind awhirl, her senses clogged with passion.

"We must wait," he whispered, gasping. "Wait for the morrow. Find a priest."

Catlyn decided that honor could be a vastly overrated thing. Especially at times like this. "I cannot wait." She punctuated the statement with another kiss, giving all she felt for him free rein.

Ross groaned, a heartbeat away from turning his back on a lifetime of doing what was right. He might have been stronger if he did not recall what it had been like to hear she'd been hurt, to rush into this room and see her lying so still, to realize he could have lost her when he'd scarce found her. He might have resisted if only she hadn't felt so soul-wrenchingly good in his arms. If only…

"Love me," she whispered against his lips, and he was lost.

Sweeping her up, he carried her the few feet to the bed and laid her on the rumpled sheets. Even as he stretched out beside her, she was reaching for him, her arms sliding around his neck, her lips parting at the first touch of his. Her tongue tangled eagerly with his, her heart pounding as fiercely as his own. He felt her nipples peak as she slowly twisted in his embrace.

He dragged his mouth from hers, stringing kisses down her neck and over her collarbone to the valley between her breasts. "I want to touch you, everywhere," he murmured, resting his hand over the vee in her robe. "But especially here." He splayed his fingers, letting them graze the soft curves inside.

"Aye. Oh, aye." She shivered as he parted the robe, baring her to the candlelight and his touch.

"Beautiful." He brushed his knuckles over the upper swell of one high, perfect globe, then cupped it, kneading gently, watching her lashes drift shut on a moan. "So beautiful," he murmured, caressing the soft mounds, drinking the little gasp of surprise from her lips as his thumbs stroked over the nipples, hardening them. He tugged sensuously till the gasp became a throaty purr, then bent to taste her, delighted by the way she shivered as his tongue trailed over her skin from the delicate hollow of her throat to the curve of her breast. She started when he laved her nipple.

"Easy, trust me," he growled.

"I do. It is just so much…" The word ended on a throaty moan as his mouth closed over the sensitive peak and gently drew down. "Ross, oh, Ross." Catlyn clutched his head, holding him there. Her senses came vividly alive, her skin tingled as though brushed by fire, her pulse pounded thunderously. Her head fell back as he transferred his attentions to the other breast, devouring her with satisfying greediness. The rhythm spiraled down through her body, coiling tight in the hidden cleft between her thighs. She whimpered, shifting her legs, seeking to ease the pressure building there.

"What is it, love?" he whispered.

"I cannot wait. I want it all…everything."

"You will have it, everything I have to give." His hands and mouth roamed over her with possessive familiarity, finding every pleasure point and stroking it to life. Lastly his fingers brushed over the curls guarding her layered secrets.

Catlyn gasped when he touched her there, where she needed it most. The gasp became a moan of pure bliss as his long, clever fingers slipped inside and sent her flying.

The feel of Catlyn coming apart in his arms, the sound of his name falling like a litany from her lips, shattered the last of Ross's control. Stripping off his tunic and hose, he rose above her, parting her thighs with hands that shook. He was as eager and awestruck as a green lad with his first lass.

"Open your eyes, love," he murmured.

Catlyn blinked when she saw him poised over her, his face flushed with passion, his eyes soft with tenderness. He loved her. She'd felt it in his touch, now she saw it in his face. Smiling, she opened her arms to him, welcoming his weight and then the slight pain that accompanied his first swift thrust.

"Catlyn." He held himself above her, his body taut, his expression troubled. "Are you all right?"

"More than." He stretched her to the limits, yet there was no sense of fear or invasion. He filled her, enriched her body and soul. "Now we are one," she whispered, awed.

"One. Forever." He lowered his head and kissed her, a slow, erotic mating echoed by the sensuous thrusts of his body.

Catlyn gave herself over to the magic of the moment, stunned by the joy she felt, the sense of completeness as they moved together. She groped for words, but one look into his eyes, shining with a love that went beyond this physical joining, and she knew none were necessary.

"Come with me, love," he murmured. Sliding his hands down to cradle her bottom, he lifted her to meet the deep, swift strokes he'd somehow known she craved.

Her arms wrapped tight around his neck, Catlyn matched

the pace he set, then quickened it as the ache inside her intensified. With each thrust of their hips, she flew higher, burner hotter until her molten core shattered on a wave of ecstasy so pure she cried out. "Ross. Oh, Ross."

Growling her name, Ross buried himself in the heart of the explosion that rocked her. Consumed by the flames, by the sweet tightening of her body around his, he gave her all he had to give, his body, heart and soul.

Dazed and gasping for breath, Ross rolled onto his side to spare her his weight. But he kept her secure in his arms, their bodies still joined. "Are you all right?" he rasped.

Catlyn managed, barely, to lift her lashes and stare at him through a tangle of hair. "I do now see what it was that drove Great-Great Grandfather Erik to make love with my great-great grandmother on the counting room table."

"Indeed." Ross smoothed the hair from her flushed face. "Is that where you came by this unbridled passion of yours?"

"Unbridled?" Catlyn frowned. "Was I too…too wanton?"

Ross chuckled. "Wantonness in a wife is a very good thing. And I did think that we were well matched, in all respects."

"Is it always like that?"

"Nay. Oh, for the man there is always some pleasure. For the woman I've heard it depends on the patience of her lover."

"You must have been much sought after, then, for you are very patient." It hurt to think of him with other women.

"I have not been…till you." He grazed her cheek with the backs of his fingers. "All things are different with you, love. But I was not as patient or tender as I wanted to be. Hot as you make me burn, 'twas all I could do not to devour you like a starving animal."

Catlyn giggled. The sound was as novel and wholly charming as the teasing light in her eyes. "You did devour me, especially certain portions of me."

"And did you like it?" he asked, grinning.

Her cheeks turned a becoming rose. "You know I did." Her voice was low, husky with remembered intimacy.

Ross's body responded instantly and predictably, despite the explosive release that should have sated him for a fortnight. He tamped down the wave of desire. Catlyn was delicately formed and new to this. "We should get some sleep." Impossible as that would be with her temptingly nearby. "I had wanted to leave before dawn. Do you think Master David may know of a priest who would not mind being chased from his bed for a very early wedding?"

Her smile faded and she ducked her head, but not quickly enough to hide the sudden pain and vulnerability. "Do not feel you must wed me because we...we..."

"Are in love and as well matched as two halves of a coin?"

She looked up, the hope in her gaze more touching than the pain had been. "But I am stubborn and bound by traditions you do not respect, and you can be an arrogant beast."

"Aye, it should make for a lively time." He smiled tenderly. "No two people are exactly alike, that will be part of the charm and challenge of learning to live together. There will be arguments aplenty between us, I'd guess, for we are both strong willed and used to having our own way. But they will be tempered by the respect and the love we have for each other."

"Are you certain you are not a poet?" she asked, smiling through the single tear that trickled down her cheek.

"Ah, first I am an arrogant beast, now a poet."

She giggled again. "More beast, I think, than poet. Did your sister not say you were in need of taming?"

"She did. But I do think Ella would agree that I've met my match." Ross kissed the tip of Catlyn's nose and then tucked her head under his chin. "Sleep, love, we must be up and away before first light tomorrow."

While Hakon's men would hopefully be sleeping off a

night of excess. The reminder of the dangers that awaited them kept Ross awake long after Catlyn had relaxed against him, so trusting, even in her sleep.

Pray God he could find a way to keep her and hers safe.

It lacked a few hours till dawn by the time Hakon and his men returned to the Sword and Shield. Empty-handed, they came, unless you counted the two Fergussons they'd found passed out behind the ale tent. Of Ross Sutherland, there had been no sign. It was as though Doune had swallowed him up.

Hakon threw open the door to the tavern and stomped in, stepping over a man as dead drunk as the two Fergussons they had dragged back from the fairing.

"Murdo, see these two idiots are sober and the rest of ye ready to ride at first light." Without waiting for a reply, Hakon seized a torch from beside the hearth, lit it on the banked embers and sought the stairs to the second story. Coinnech had given him a room, and Hakon meant to make use of it for what was left of this wretched night.

Hakon found the third door on the right and pushed it open. As he swung into the room, the light from his torch played over a narrow chamber furnished with a washstand, a chair and a bed.

There was someone in it, a definite shape beneath the tumbled blankets.

Cursing softly, Hakon switched the torch to his left hand and drew his sword with the right. Stealthily he crossed to the bed, raised his sword and brought the flat side down, hard, on whoever had taken his spot. "Up, ye poaching bastard."

"Bloody hell," croaked a young, male voice. The covers erupted into a welter of linen and limbs. From the center popped two heads, ruffled as owl chicks. A lad and a lass. Lovers by the looks of their naked arms twined around each other. "Who...who are ye?" asked the lad, clutching the lass to him.

"I'll be asking the questions. Who are ye and what the hell are ye doing in my bed?"

"Mar-Margot McNab," whispered the girl. "My pa owns the inn. And this is my...my betrothed, Wesley Boyd."

Hakon frowned. She had Coinnech's gray eyes, right enough, so she was likely his get. Pretty, too, with pale red hair and milky skin. Doubtless they'd thought the room vacant and theirs for a night of fun. Tired and angry as he was over the encounter with Ross Sutherland, Hakon was in no mood to be understanding.

"Well, yer pa gave me this room for the night. Ye'll be leaving so as I can get a bit of sleep."

"Will ye tell him ye found us here?" the lad asked.

"Depends." Hakon studied the young girl and her protective lad, wondering how he could profit. Habit, he supposed, for they'd not have anything he'd value. Still he wanted to give them a hard time. "Does yer pa approve of yer betrothal?"

Margot nodded, scattering thin red hair about her shoulders. "Wesley's family owns a distillery, so he's familiar with the trade. It's his family what's the problem."

"They can't keep me tied there," Wesley grumbled.

Boyd. Distillery.

Hakon lowered his sword. "Ye'd not be related to the Boyds of Kennecraig, would ye? Them of the famous Finglas whiskey."

"Aye." The lad smiled, his wariness dissolving. "My pa is the master distiller, there."

"So." Hakon could scarcely believe his good fortune. It was all he could do to keep from pouncing on the lad then and there. But nay, that would not do, not with Coinnech asleep in the room at the far end of the hall. What he needed was a plan, a way to make young Wesley help him. The lass would figure into it, of course. 'Twas just a matter of getting them out of the tavern and away from Doune without causing a ruckus.

"Master Roland doesn't approve of our match or our plans," she said. "This is the first we've seen each other in months."

Hakon shook his head sadly. "And here I come, blundering in and spoiling yer time together. Tell ye what I'll do," he said giving them that disarming smile. "I'll go down and sleep in the common room with my men."

"We cannot take yer bed," said Wesley.

The girl beamed at Hakon. "We'd be ever so grateful. Would we not, Wesley?" She elbowed her love in the ribs.

"Aye, but I do not feel right about—"

A pox on honorable men. "Not at all. I'm always one to smooth the course for true love." His mind was whirling feverishly, searching for the right scheme. He needed both of them, in his power and away from here. But without arousing suspicion. Should he wait, come back with Murdo? Nay, he could not take the chance they'd grow fearful of discovery and leave.

"Thank you again," said Margot. "May we know yer name?"

"Dunbar, Robert Dunbar, wool merchant. I bid ye good night." He started for the door, then turned back. "Oh, I nearly forgot. I left my pack under the bed. Mind if I fetch it?"

"Certainly not," said the lad. No wariness now.

Hakon sauntered over to the bed, hunkered down and peered under it. "Ach, silly thing's on the other side. Could ye reach under and give it a shove, lad?"

"Aye." The ropes holding the straw mattress creaked.

Hakon sprang up like a hungry trout. Catching the lass around the mouth with one hand, he efficiently brought the hilt of his sword down on the back of Wesley's head.

"Hardly sporting at all," Hakon muttered. Smiling down into Margot's fear-widened gray eyes, he gave her a wee crack on the head. She folded without making a sound.

Sometimes, things worked out when you least expected, he mused as he set about securing his prisoners.

Chapter Fourteen

It was still dark when Ross led Catlyn down the stairs and into the tavern's main room. She was surprised and touched to find Ross's men assembled there. Despite the early hour, they wore clean clothes and freshly scrubbed faces.

The room had been cleaned, too, the faint smell of ale the only reminder of last night's revels. Two tables had been pushed together, covered with a cloth and arrayed with bread, cheese and cold meat on which they might break their fast. Flanking the platters were pitchers and cups.

"We should have waited till things could have been done right and proper," Ross grumbled.

"This looks very nice," Catlyn whispered back. "Master David and his servants have gone to some trouble to arrange this. And before dawn, too."

"You deserve finer."

"A smiling groom, perhaps?" she asked archly.

He sighed and managed a faint smile. "I am sorry, but there should be a priest, at least." The one who ministered to Doune had been called away to a neighboring village to officiate at a funeral, and was not expected back for a few days. They could not wait. Nigel had just reported that the Fergussons were still asleep at the Sword and Shield, having staggered back there but a few hours ago, carrying some of their more drunken companions. Ross wanted to be well away before they stirred.

"A handfasting will serve as well, and then we can be wed again before a priest, if you like."

Ross nodded. "I would, with your family and mine in attendance to wish us well."

The mention of his family reminded her how little she knew of him, aside from the name of his home and that he had a sister with the second sight. A niggle of worry prickled down her spine. Judging by his noble bearing and costly trappings, they were likely a wealthy and powerful clan. What if they did not like her? What if they thought her beneath his station?

"Catlyn." David came in from the back room and held out his hands to her. "How lovely you look."

"Thank you, for the compliment and the use of your daughter's gown." It was a trifle tight in the bosom and long in the hem, but Ross had assured her that the pale gold color did compliment her eyes. And she could hardly be wed in her boy's disguise of hose and tunic.

Mathew stepped forward, drew from behind his back a rather wilted bunch of flowers and presented them to her with a graceful bow. "Welcome to our family, fair Catlyn. I am most heartily grateful that my cousin has decided to settle down. I do think you will finally curb his high spirits and his unfortunate penchant for taking unnecessary risks."

Oh, I doubt that, Catlyn thought, her lips twitching as she recalled a risky encounter early this morn involving a chair, three pillows and a crock of honey left over from her supper. "Thank you," she said, solemnly accepting the tribute. As she glanced sidelong at Ross, she saw him struggling to contain his mirth and choked on a spurt of laughter.

"Easy." Ross thumped her on the back, leaned forward and whispered in her ear, "Shall I tell him how *you* led *me* astray?"

"The honey was your idea."

"Oh, and who was it woke me with her marauding fingers?"

"I only wanted to touch the hair on your chest," she whispered. "But things got rather out of hand."

"I thought you had them nicely *in* hand," he drawled.

Catlyn's face went hot as fire.

Master David cleared his throat. "We should begin if you want to leave before it is light."

Ross nodded, took Catlyn's hand in his and turned to face the assembly, men with whom he'd lived and fought for years. "We stand before you, the lady Catlyn and I, to declare we are husband and wife, wed this day of our own free will. And I do solemnly swear to love her and protect her all the days of our lives." He tried to infuse the words with special meaning, for he regretted that she'd been cheated of the glitter and fuss all brides deserved.

If she felt the lack, it did not show in Catlyn's face. She positively glowed, from the burnished gold braids entwined atop her head to her flushed cheeks and shining eyes. Unwavering love shimmered in them as she met his gaze levelly and repeated her vow. "I declare myself to be the true wife of Ross Lion Sutherland, and I do swear to love, honor and obey him all the days of our lives."

Ross's chest tightened, his heart so filled with love he thought it might burst. Though he'd not expected to wed soon, if ever, he could not imagine a life without his Catlyn.

"Kiss her to seal the pledge," Mathew hissed.

"Gladly." Ross leaned down to give her a very quick, very proper kiss of peace. But somehow her arms slid around his neck, and her mouth slanted across his. Last night she'd met his passion with scorching fire. This morn, her kiss held the sweet promise of everlasting love. He basked in it, could have gorged on it had they not had a rapt audience and miles to travel.

Raising his head, he whispered, "Tonight, wife."

"'Tis a long time to wait."

"I will make it worth your while."

A delicate shiver coursed through her, and her eyes darkened. "And I yours."

Ross chuckled. "I think I have created a monster." Still smiling, he turned to accept the congratulations of his men. Then they all sat to eat the hasty meal before departing.

David bustled about, seeing everyone had enough to eat and clucking over Catlyn like a mother hen. But something about his manner seemed a little forced. Anxious, almost. When the innkeeper crossed to fetch more ale from the bar, Ross followed.

"What is wrong?" Ross asked without preamble.

David straightened. "Nothing, I—I am just concerned for Catlyn's welfare. The bump on the head was not serious, but…"

"There is more to it than that."

David sighed, set down the pitcher he'd drawn and looked toward the tables where Lang Gil was telling Catlyn about the time Ross had tried to capture a boar piglet and been chased up a tree by its irate mother.

"It is the whiskey," David said slowly. "The kegs of Finglas Catlyn sold me."

"Someone has stolen them?"

"Nay. Ten of the kegs are not what they should be. They contain raw whiskey, likely last year's distilling. We discovered it late last night when we opened one to serve and the customer spat it on the floor. I immediately tasted it myself, of course, and realized he'd been right to refuse it. Naturally I opened all the others and tasted each."

Ross frowned. "Catlyn selected them herself."

"Aye." David's expression was cool and shuttered.

"There must be some mistake. I do not know whiskey, but she does. She would never cheat you, and she has too much pride in her Finglas to ever sell less than the best."

David relaxed fractionally. "What you say is true. But how could such a thing have happened?"

"The kegs may have been mislabeled."

"I suppose, but Catlyn does all that herself."

"Someone could have switched the labels."

"It was not one of my people."

"Agreed. Likely it was done at Kennecraig, before we left for Doune."

"No Boyd would do such a thing. The distillery is too important for any of them to want to ruin its reputation."

Maybe not as important as discrediting Catlyn. Which made Roland the most logical suspect. "It may have been an honest mistake. Things have been unsettled since Laird Thomas's death. I will check into this when I get back to Kennecraig." Starting with Master Roland and his son.

David cleared his throat. "I—I am sorry to do this, but I must ask that you buy back the ten kegs. If it were not so many, I might stand the loss, but…"

"Nay, it is not fair you should lose by this."

"One of the taverns down by the river might buy them, for a lesser sum, of course," he added. "Their customers are not so particular as mine."

Ross hesitated. Nearly all the money from the sale of the whiskey had gone to buy supplies. They could not be returned, for the folk of Kennecraig needed food. "I have four gold florins. Will that cover the cost of the ten kegs?"

"Indeed, and then some. Oh, I thank you for understanding, Sir Ross." David was so relieved he babbled on about upholding the reputation of the Finglas and not cheating his customers.

"Let us go into the back and conclude the transaction," Ross muttered, not wanting to ruin Catlyn's day with this.

David nodded and led the way into the counting room. "The kegs are there, if you want to take them back."

Ross barely glanced at the stack. "We are burdened enough without." Each man would be carrying back a portion of the supplies wrapped in his plaid. "If you keep them for a few years, they may be smoother and more to your liking."

"Ah, you understand. When you told me you and Catlyn

intended to wed, I did worry because you were not of the trade. But I see you have a feel for the whiskey making."

What he had was a burning need to get back and find out who had tried to ruin Catlyn's reputation.

"There is something else I feel I must tell you." Master David sat behind his worktable, his lean features troubled. "Last night I had a visitor. One who bade me keep his mission a secret. I agreed only after hearing of his noble purpose, but—"

"Who was it, Roland or Eoin?"

David blinked. "It was Roland. Did he confide in you, too?"

Hardly. "What did he want?"

"Why, to have me evaluate some of the ten-year-old and help him see it reaches the finest markets in Edinburgh."

"A noble attempt at lining his pockets."

"Not at all. He is carrying out Laird Thomas's wishes, helping to make the Finglas the finest distillery in the land."

"Is that not up to Thomas's daughter and heir?"

"Aye, certainly, but Roland did tell me that Catlyn's grief is so fresh she cannot think of it just yet. He wanted to surprise her by undertaking this delicate task."

"Oh, she will be surprised." Among other things.

"I did feel odd about keeping this from her," David said. "But now that you are her husband, such tasks will fall to—"

"What tasks?" Catlyn stood in the doorway, her searching glance darting between the two of them.

"Ah, the task of seeing you safely home," Ross said smoothly. But he had forgotten about the gold florins lying in his palm. As he stood, David scooped them up.

Catlyn walked toward them. "For what are you paying David?"

"Oh, our lodging and the ale my men drank."

She glanced at the florins and raised one brow. "That much ale would put half of Doune under the table."

A pox on canny women. "Ah, well."

"Do not rile yourself, lass." Master David rose and rounded the table to pat her arm. "Your husband was but doing you a service. Ten of the kegs of—"

"Were drunk last night." Ross took hold of her other arm, sensing a disaster in the making. "It is time we were going."

"What has happened?" Catlyn asked of David.

Ross looked at the innkeeper over the top of her golden braids and shook his head violently.

David was too busy smiling at Catlyn. "I fear that ten kegs of the whiskey were not as seasoned as they should have been."

"What?" Catlyn jerked free of Ross, spun in a circle till she spotted the kegs, then pounced on them. She ran her hands over them like an anxious parent, sniffing at the bung, checking the label. "They look all right. Wait." She removed the square of smooth hide and brought it nearer the candle. "This is similar to my writing, but it is not quite the same."

"Ross thinks they were wrongly labeled, due to the confusion following your father's death," said David.

"Are you saying I made a mistake?" Catlyn asked slowly.

"Nay." Ross went to her, wanting only to get her away before she found out about the ten-year, as well.

"Someone changed the labels? Why?" She hesitated only an instant before answering her own question. "To discredit me."

"I think it likely." Ross took her arm. "We will settle this when we get back to Kennecraig."

"Aye." She looked at David. "I am sorry for this."

"No harm done," David said generously. "My people will keep quiet about what happened, and Ross had paid me for them."

"Paid?" Catlyn glanced sidelong at him. "How?"

Ross shrugged. "I had some money put by."

"You paid my debt with your own coin?" Catlyn asked.

"Of course," Master David said. "A husband is responsible for his wife's debts."

"I am responsible for myself." She gave Ross a stiff, cold look, one that boded ill for a peaceful ride home, before turning her attention to David. "Thank you for all you did, Master David. I hope to be back with another shipment inside a week. One I will taste personally before bringing hither."

"I look forward to it. Perhaps we can set a price and schedule for shipping to my friends in Edinburgh."

Catlyn nodded and headed for the door.

Ross released the breath he'd been holding and trailed after her, but he relaxed too soon. Halfway to the door she suddenly stopped, turned and knelt beside a trio of kegs.

"This…this is Papa's ten-year whiskey." Her voice climbed with every word. "How did this get here?"

"Er," David looked to Ross for help.

Ross knew there was no easy way out. "Roland brought it last night. He said he was trying to further your father's hopes of making the Finglas a—"

"He dared do this behind my back?" she cried. "How dare he lay this trap to ambush me, to discredit me?"

Her words jarred something in Ross's mind. "When was Roland here?" he asked David.

"What difference does that make?" Catlyn exclaimed.

A great deal if he was the one who hit Catlyn on the head, Ross thought grimly.

"He left not long before you returned, Catlyn. Likely you just missed seeing him."

Ah, but perhaps *he* saw *her*. Ross clenched his teeth so hard his jaw ached. "We will question him when we get home."

"I will strangle him," said his usually calm darling.

"And I will hold him down for you." Ross vowed he'd also have a private talk with Master Roland.

"The ten-year is everything Thomas hoped it would be,"

said David. "I would like to send a keg of it to an acquaintance in Edinburgh. He has contacts at court. If we show the king and his nobles what a superior whiskey the Finglas is, your fortune would be assured."

It occurred to Ross that his family had excellent connections at court. Uncle Hunter had been the king's chief justice and was even now called upon for advice. But Catlyn might take it amiss if he tried to sell her whiskey for her.

Catlyn sighed. "That was Papa's fondest dream, but I do not like the way Roland took matters upon himself."

Nor would she thank *him* if he tried to interfere," Ross thought. Still a word in the right ear... "We will settle with Roland." He held out his hand to her. "Come, we'd best depart."

She nearly took it, then seemed to remember that she was also wroth with him. With a curt nod in David's direction, she swept from the room.

It promised to be a long, tense ride to Kennecraig. And not just because he wanted to stay ahead of Hakon.

But Ross did have one advantage—many years of watching his father match wits with his high-spirited mother. He had learned early that trying to cajole an angry woman out of her ire was like throwing oil on a fire. Best to let her cool of her own accord.

"We cannot just leave Wesley behind," Eoin exclaimed. Though he would have loved dearly to do just that. It was past noon, and he was itching to reach Kennecraig. Every moment they delayed was a moment Catlyn spent with that traitor.

"Well, we've searched everywhere, and there's no sign of him." Roland turned in a slow circle, one hand shading his eyes as he scanned the tents again.

They had gone first to the ale tents. This early in the day there were few people around and none who remembered a lad of Wesley's description amongst the hundreds who been hanging about drinking and flirting with the lasses.

"Maybe he's run off," Eoin said.

"Why? He's got a soft life, he has, and a future any lad would envy. He'll be the master distiller after I'm gone."

"Hmm." Eoin did not think now was a good time to point out what was obvious to everyone except Roland. Wesley did not like whiskey making. Nor did he seem to have the gift for it. "What do you want to do? Shall we go back to the inn and see if he has turned up there?"

Roland frowned, clearly torn between his duty to his son and his obsession with the Finglas. "We cannot wait too much longer. *She* is likely home by now. I do not want her to learn I am taking the ten-year to market. She does not understand that Laird Thomas would have wished me to carry on his work. She must suspect nothing." His eyes held that odd, mad light again.

Eoin shivered and looked away. He did not care if Roland took the ten-year and gave it away. All he wanted was to reach Kennecraig, tell Catlyn what he had learned about her precious knight and see him pay for his betrayal. Traitors were often drawn and quartered, but he supposed Catlyn would be too soft to order so heinous a death. Hanging, then, and when Ross Sutherland was dead, Catlyn would be his again.

"What say we leave money with the innkeeper for Wesley's food and lodging when he does return," Eoin said. "Along with a message saying you will be back in a week or so."

"Aye. I will come back before that if I can. The sooner I can get the Finglas to Edinburgh, the better."

Chapter Fifteen

It was difficult to keep your anger burning bright with the rain dripping off the end of your nose.

Catlyn blew away an offending droplet and tried not to think about how miserable she felt. Inside and out. Four long hours they'd been in the saddle, two, at least, since the sullen gray skies had dissolved into a fitful drizzle that seeped through her hastily donned cape and riding clothes.

When they had first set out, she'd braced herself to resist Ross's explanations and apologies. None had been forthcoming. He rode stalwartly beside her, but he'd spoken no more than a half-dozen words, all concerning the path they would take. Not that she'd have replied if he had tried to apologize.

Still...

Four hours with nothing more interesting to do than stare at the muddy track ahead gave a body too much time for thinking.

She thought about the mislabeled kegs. Not a mistake, surely. Someone had done that purposely to discredit her. Roland was the likely suspect. And he'd compounded the crime by stealing the ten-year and taking it to Master David. After telling *her* it was not yet ready.

When they reached Kennecraig, she would... What could

she do? Roland was someone she had looked up to all her life, a power second only to her father. What would Papa have done? Chided Roland? Fined him? Stripped him of his post? It hardly signified, for Roland would never have done this to her father. The two of them had grown up together, learned the craft of whiskey making side by side.

"Catlyn." Ross's rich baritone interrupted her thoughts. "We'll be stepping down here to water the horses."

She looked around, startled to realize they had left the trail and entered a small copse of trees. The leaves provided protection from the rain; the gurgling burn promised to ease her parched throat. If only she could make her legs work.

Ross reached up and plucked her from the saddle without a by-your-leave, steadying her when her knees gave way and she buckled against him. "'Tis sorry I am to set such a pace, but you've borne up like a seasoned trooper."

"I feel as old as one." She didn't protest his help in reaching a flat rock beside the stream and easing her numbed bottom onto it.

He produced a wooden cup from inside his cape, filled it with water and offered it to her.

Catlyn drank greedily, keeping her gaze carefully away from the man on the adjacent rock. She felt as awkward and uncertain around him as when they'd first met. It angered her still that David had told Ross about the mislabeled whiskey and the two had conspired to keep the problem from her. Because she was a woman. Because Ross was her husband and that gave him power over her and hers. She did not like that or the fact that he had paid her debt out of his own pocket. But the long, dreary ride had cooled her temper. She realized Ross had paid knowing she could not. He had tried to spare her both concern and embarrassment.

So what did she do now? How could she upbraid him on the one hand and thank him on the other?

As she pondered the problem, she was dimly aware of

the horses watering downstream, the men moving efficiently about in the woods, seeing to private needs and posting guards, she supposed. A dirk flashed in the gloom, cutting bread and cheese.

Dallas brought them the first pieces, wrapped in a length of linen napkin. "You are a wonder, my lady. The lads were laying bets you'd not come so far without a rest."

"How much did you win?"

Dallas was an ordinary-looking man, the sort you might meet and not remember, but his smile lit up the gloomy clearing. "Enough to buy a new dirk as fine as Ross's."

Catlyn laughed with him and found some of her weariness falling away. "They are good men," she said when Dallas had walked over to join the others.

"I like to think so."

Why did he not say something? Apologize? Explain? So she could vent her fury. She popped a piece of cheese into her mouth, annihilated it, then risked a sidelong glance at him to see if he was watching her.

He was chewing slowly on a hunk of bread, his eyes on the canopy above. "There is a squirrel up there."

"A squirrel?" The bitter quarrel lay between them, her insides were in shreds, and he was watching a squirrel?

"It looks as though he is caught somehow."

Catlyn tipped her head back and looked. Sure enough, a small, heart-shaped gray face peered at them through the leaves. "Why do you say that?"

"Our presence should have driven it off."

"Maybe it fancies a bit of bread and cheese."

"Nay. Something is wrong with him." Ross stood, unbuckled his sword and leaned it against the rock.

Catlyn stood, too. "What at you going to do?"

"Climb up and have a look." He jumped, grabbed hold of a lower branch and swung onto it with an ease that belied his size. Then he disappeared into the maze of leaves, only a bit of cracking and rustling to mark his progress.

"Ross?" Catlyn called warily.

"At it again, is he?" Mathew and several of the others drifted over, munching on their meal and watching Ross climb.

"He has gone after a squirrel."

"To eat?" asked one man.

"He thinks something is wrong with it." Catlyn searched till she found the squirrel again. "It still hasn't moved."

The branch on which the squirrel sat bobbed up and down. The little animal squeaked in terror and twitched, as though it wanted to run but couldn't. A short scuffle ensued, more squeals interspersed with pithy curses.

"Damn! Hold still! I'm trying to— Ouch!"

"It bit him." Mathew was grinning.

"He was only trying to help," Catlyn said.

"He always is," Mathew said. "Trouble is, when you stick your nose in where it isn't wanted, it ofttimes gets bit."

Things grew ominously quiet overhead. "Ross? Are you all right?" she called.

"Nay, I bloody well am not. Get some bandages ready, I'm coming down."

Not certain who the bandage was for, Catlyn snatched the napkin from beneath their food and raced to the tree trunk just as Ross swung down.

His eyes were bright, his hair full of twigs. He had removed his tunic, exposing the gleaming chain mail shirt beneath, and carried the tunic in his left hand, bundled around the squirming squirrel. Blood dripped from his right thumb.

"You are hurt!" Catlyn cried, rushing to him.

"Just a scratch." He thrust the thumb into his mouth and held out the bundle. "Someone take this," he mumbled.

The trio of hardened warriors backed up. "Not me," someone said. They turned as one and fled.

"Cowards," Ross called after them. "I don't suppose you'd be willing to help me?" he asked Catlyn.

"Of course."

Ross grinned. "That my braw lassie." He knelt and gingerly maneuvered the trapped squirrel. "Someone shot at it. The arrow struck his tail and pinned him to the branch."

"Oh, dear." Catlyn hunkered down beside him. "How long do you think he's been there."

"No telling." He wrapped the bulk of the tunic around the squirrel's head and body, then exposed the bloodied tail. The tip had been completely severed. "It happened when I freed him. Mat!" he yelled over his shoulder. "Fetch me some moneywort powder from the medicine pouch."

Mathew hustled over with the parchment square holding the herb, offered it to Catlyn then beat a hasty retreat.

With Ross holding the squirrel still, Catlyn sprinkled a liberal amount of the pale green powder on the stump. A few moments were all it took for the herb to stanch the bleeding. "A most useful thing to have with you," she commented. "How is it that a man is so versed in healing?"

"Because my mother insisted all her children learn enough of her art to help themselves and others." Ross inspected the injury and nodded. "It will have to do. Let go of him and stand back," he warned, loosening the wrappings.

The squirrel burrowed its way out, shook himself and bounded off into the woods with a flick of his short tail.

"Should we follow to see he is all right?" Catlyn asked.

Ross climbed to his feet and tweaked her nose. "Not even High Harry could keep up with that fellow. He'll be fine. Besides, we've done all we can."

She marveled that he had done anything. Few people would have bothered to help a squirrel. Especially after it bit them. "How is your thumb?"

"Just a scratch."

"Let me see."

"It's bloody." He frowned. "Dammit, I'm sorry I made you help, I forgot the sight of blood sickens you."

"This time it did not. I guess I was so busy helping I had no time to remember the day I found my brother."

Ross put a hand on her shoulder and squeezed gently. The gesture was more comforting than a dozen platitudes. "Maybe that day haunts you because you could not save him."

"Aye. What I see when I think back is the blood. What I feel is helplessness that I cannot push it back in him."

"I've felt so about men I've lost in battle." The gaze that met hers was shadowed with a grief she understood.

The last of Catlyn's anger drifted away, like sand before the winds of reason. She must face the fact that her wedded husband was the sort for whom defending the weak was as natural as breathing. He had done what he thought best to protect her. It was up to her to make him see that she could, and would, look after herself on occasion. But first she'd look after him.

"Let me see your hand." She took it, despite his feeble attempts to deny her. The three sets of teeth marks oozed blood. The sight made her belly roll, but it was concern, not nausea. Picking up the moneywort, she sprinkled some on, then bade him hold still while she ripped the napkin into strips.

"This is not necessary."

"I could not let my husband go about with an untended wound any more than you could let your wife worry over ten kegs of mislabeled whiskey." She tied on the makeshift bandage.

"Ouch," Ross said.

"Did I hurt you?"

"Aye, you've a sharp mind and a sharper tongue. I wager I've got the point.'' His eyes were dancing, his grin disarming.

Oh, how she'd missed that today, the warmth and easy camaraderie. ''I do not like it when we quarrel,'' she whispered.

He stepped closer, his chest brushing hers, warming her through the wool and metal that separated them, though he did not take her in his arms. ''Nor do I. When we get home, I do promise to make it up to you.''

Home. It touched her to have him call Kennecraig that. And it made her think of what Mathew had said about Ross sticking his nose into things. ''All I ask is that you ask if I need help before rendering it.''

''I'll try to remember, my stubborn, independent wife.''

It was late afternoon when they arrived at Kennecraig, having taken the longer way around to avoid being spotted by Guthrie. The sentries on the west wall answered Ross's hail and sent down the rope sling. He sent Catlyn up first then he followed, leaving the retrieval of the supplies to Mathew.

When Ross topped the wall, he found the narrow walkway jammed with smiling Boyds.

Adair clapped him on the back. ''Well done, lad. Catlyn says you've sold the whiskey and brought our supplies.''

''Did everyone come back all right?'' asked Dora.

''Aye.'' Ross climbed out of the rope sling and sent it back down. ''Mathew is below, making certain everything gets lifted up here in good shape.''

''Did he get everything on my list?''

''Aye. You'll find my cousin is a man of his word,'' Ross said. *Unlike Eoin.*

Dora smiled shyly. ''He frets about things not being right.''

Ross just rolled his eyes, making Dora giggle. ''Where did Catlyn go?''

"To see her mother, I'd guess. She hugged me and ran off."

Or she is looking for Roland. "Is Roland back from Doune?"

"Nay, curse their stupidity," Adair growled. "Sneaked off they did, while I was checking on the barley fields. All three of them are likely dead or—"

"Three?" Ross's jaw tightened when he heard Eoin and Wesley had also gone. "Roland reached Doune." Not wanting to air their problems before all and sundry, and worried about Catlyn, Ross drew Adair with him down the stairs and out into the nearly deserted courtyard. As they walked, Ross told the captain what Roland had done.

"Bloody hell! Has he lost his mind? Trying to discredit Catlyn and stealing the ten-year."

"The same notion occurred to me." Ross hesitated. Should he voice his suspicions about the attack on Catlyn? "Do you think Roland is capable of harming her physically?"

"Nay," Adair whispered, eyes wide. "Granted he's been acting queerly since Thomas died, but hurt wee Catlyn?" He shook his head. "Roland's known her from birth."

Catlyn rushed down the steps from the keep. "Have you seen Mama, Adair, she's not in her room."

"She has been out and about more," Adair said. "Seems someone suggested she should read to Ross's poor injured squire. They are usually in the garden this time of day."

Catlyn turned to Ross, eyes tearing. "Did you do that?"

"Ah, well, Callum was wanting to be doing more than he should, so I thought if I assigned him to watch your mother..."

"And my mother to watch over him." Catlyn framed Ross's face with both hands and gave him a blistering kiss. "There are times when your meddling is not such a bad thing."

Ross stared into her shiny face and wondered how long

till bedtime. "I knew you'd eventually appreciate my finer points."

"What is this?" Adair exclaimed, scowling darkly at them.

Ross started and exchanged an uneasy glance with Catlyn. "Well, there is one other thing that happened while we were in Doune. Catlyn and I are wed."

"Wed?" Adair's eyebrows disappeared into his hair.

"Handfasted, really," Catlyn hastily added.

Ross did not like the way she said that. "Only till things are more settled and we can be wed by the priest."

Adair looked at them and chuckled. "Wed...the pair of you." He divided another glance between them and laughed.

"Are you disappointed?" Catlyn asked in a small voice.

"Not in the least." Adair wiped tears from his eyes with the back of his hand. "I'm thinking you two will lead each other a merry chase." He snorted. "It'll be a lively winter."

"It's already been an exciting few days," Ross said, grinning. "Go along and see your mama, love, Adair and I have matters of strategy to discuss."

His love narrowed her eyes. "And afterward, you'll be filling me in on all you two have arranged."

Afterward Ross sincerely hoped they'd be tucked up in a nice, soft bed enjoying their wedding night.

Catlyn walked slowly down the rows of kegs, examining each by lantern light and checking the label against her ledger. She had been at it for hours, her back and legs ached, but she was determined to discover the extent of Roland's mischief.

"Hello there." Ross strolled into the circle of light, a covered tray in his hands, a lazy smile on his lips.

Catlyn straightened, groaning as her muscles cramped. "What are you doing here?"

"Bringing food."

"I have no time to eat. I must check each keg."

"You need food to keep up your strength. We both do, since we missed dinner."

"Where were you?"

"Out checking on Guthrie's camp."

Catlyn gasped. "Ross, you could have been caught."

"Nay. I am very good at sneaking up on things. And besides, the Fergussons were gone," he added, frowning.

"That worries you?"

"Everything they do concerns me."

"Perhaps they prefer life in Doune." She tilted her head. "You never did say what happened when you went back to the Sword and Shield. Was Hakon still there?"

"Come and eat."

She sighed and allowed herself to be herded into her counting room. "I am not hungry," she said as he set the tray on her table. Her stomach grumbled in disagreement.

Ross grinned. "We can talk while we eat. I'd hear what you've found thus far."

The idea of sharing news with him was more tempting than the food. She sat in her chair. He leaned a hip on the worktable and whisked the cover from the tray to reveal cold roasted fowl, oatcakes and stewed apples.

Catlyn selected a chicken leg. Between bites, she told Ross she had found all ten of the kegs that she had originally selected to take to Doune. "I knew them by the mark I'd placed on the label. They were on the floor behind the second row of shelves. I've found nothing else amiss thus far." She threw down the half-eaten leg in disgust. "He wanted to shame me, to make Master David think I was not fit to run the Finglas."

"Well, he did not succeed." He handed her an oatcake. "When Roland returns, I will question him."

"Managing the distillery is my business."

He regarded her levelly. "Have I interfered in the making of your whiskey?"

"Nay, but you constantly stick your nose in—"

"Nor will I tell you how to go about the distilling," he continued. "But matters of defense are my province. As is punishing a traitor who seeks to discredit you and the Finglas."

Catlyn sighed, tempted to give in because she did not want have to confront Roland. "When he returns, we shall see how best to handle this."

Ross smiled and nodded. "Agreed. Now eat. You must keep up your strength. Cook apologized for this plain fare. On the morrow there's to be a feast to celebrate our marriage."

"I hope Eoin is not back by then." She did not want something awful to have happened to him, but his presence was sure to mar any festivities.

"Eoin will cause no trouble." Ross tore off a hunk of chicken and popped it into her mouth when she opened it to ask what he planned to do. "I will not harm him," he said. "But he must understand that you are mine now. Seeing us together might make him see that for himself."

"How?"

"Because a man would have to be blind not to see the passion that sizzles between us."

Catlyn nodded, mesmerized by the flame leaping to life in his eyes. It kindled an answering fire inside her, one that never seemed far from the surface when he was near.

"When you look at me like that, I am lost." Ross drew her to her feet and into his embrace. "I never knew it was possible to want anyone as I want you."

Catlyn felt the proof of his desire pressing against her belly, and her bones melted. How perfectly they fit together, she thought as his mouth touched hers. Her lips parted with delicious ease, welcoming him, drawing his tongue in to taste and tangle. His hands were on her back, stroking lightly. She remembered what those clever fingers could do, and the wanting inside her intensified. By the time he lifted his head, she was dizzy with anticipation. "Lock the door," she whispered.

"Let me take you upstairs, to bed."

"Too far."

Ross knew she was right. He stumbled to the door, barred it, then turned. His gaze moved over his new wife, taking in her flushed face, lingering on the thrust of her breasts against the bodice of her plain brown gown. This was their wedding night, and he meant to see they both remembered it. He pulled off his tunic and walked slowly toward her, liking the way her eyes widened, then heated as they caressed his naked chest.

"Ross." She reached for him, running her hands into the pelt of dark hair, glorying at the growl that rumbled through his chest beneath her palms.

"Now it is your turn." He unlaced the back of her gown and peeled it slowly from one shoulder, kissing each bit of flesh, the swirls of his tongue making her shiver. He uncovered the other shoulder, then drew the fitted sleeves down her arms. Her nipples peaked, hard and sensitive as he bared her to the light and his gaze. "More beautiful than I remembered." He caged her ribs with his hands, then slid them up, filling them with soft flesh. His mouth closed over one waiting peak and suckled.

Catlyn groaned, her head fell back in abandonment, her breath coming in short, choppy gasps. She slid her hands into his hair, urging him on.

Ross needed no encouragement. He was already on fire, so hungry for her it was all he could do to keep from taking her here and now. But he wanted to go slowly, to draw out the pleasure, for both of them. Battling for control, he lifted his head to look at her, transfixed by her flushed beauty.

She whimpered. "Please...please don't leave me."

one, a craving she had not known she possessed. ''I would love that above all things…except you, my husband.''

''Ach, Catlyn.'' He cradled her head against his chest, his heart thundering beneath her ear. ''I never thought it possible to love someone as I do you.'' His voice was rough with emotions. They shimmered in his eyes when he glanced down at her.

Tears.

She had not thought it would affect her so deeply or move her so profoundly to see tears in a man's eyes. They did not make him a weaker man, but stronger one, unafraid to show what he felt and share it with her.

''Take me upstairs,'' she whispered, running her hands up his chest to frame his face. ''Make love with me all night.''

''It would be my pleasure.''

It pleased them both, but they did not reach her room with its canopied bed till much, much later.

Chapter Sixteen

Catlyn drifted slowly back to earth, her pulse still racing, so languorous she could scarcely move. It was night, the room lit only by the gutting flame of the night candle.

"I have created a monster," Ross whispered. The hands that had roused her to such heights after she had kissed him awake now gently stroked her back.

"Hmm," she mumbled, burrowing into his hairy chest, relishing the feel of his rough, muscular legs tangling with her smoother ones. Beneath her ear, his heart beat steadily. Turning her head, she kissed the spot. "Complaints, husband?"

"Nay." He trembled, and his heartbeat quickened. "I never thought to find someone who completes me as you do."

Catlyn smiled, moved that for all his size and strength, he was vulnerable to her. The realization she held such power over him humbled her, made her feel oddly protective. "I love you."

A loud knock shook the chamber door.

"Catlyn?" Eoin called from the other side. "I must speak with you on a matter of some urgency."

Catlyn started, eyes widening as she looked up at Ross.

"I'll handle this." Ross released her, flung off the covers and grabbed his hose from the floor. Cursing under his breath, he pulled them on, then stalked bare chested across the room.

"Be gentle with him," Catlyn whispered, sitting up and clutching the bedcovers to her throat.

"Gentle be damned!"

"Catlyn," Eoin demanded. "I need—"

Ross wrenched open the door. "What do you mean disturbing us at this unholy hour?"

Eoin's eyes bugged out. His mouth opened, but no sound emerged. Judging by his unshaven face and mud-spattered clothes he had just arrived. So he could not know.

"My God, what is going on?" He looked from Ross to Catlyn and gasped again. "Lecherous bastard!" He threw himself at Ross.

Ross grabbed the front of Eoin's tunic, shoved him against the door frame and held him there. "We are wed," he growled.

"Wed!" Eoin seemed to strangle on the word. He turned incredulous, horrified eyes on Catlyn. "You are married to this thief? This…this…"

"Ross and I are wed," Catlyn said as gently as she could.

"He betrayed us!" Eoin cried. "He sold our secrets to Hak—"

"That is enough," Ross snarled.

"I know you are hurt, Eoin," Catlyn said, "but to make up lies about Ross—"

"They are not lies. I saw him give Hakon papers, heard him say they were drawings of the distillery and our secret recipe."

"It cannot be true." Catlyn stared at Ross, waiting for him to deny Eoin's wild charges. When he did not, her heart stopped.

"I will speak with Catlyn alone." Ross shoved Eoin out the door, threatening him with bodily harm if he did not go away.

"I will be out here if you need me, Cat—" Eoin's defiant words were cut off by the slamming door.

Ross set the bar across it, then stood there, his hands braced on the oak planking. The muscles in his back quivered and jumped like those of a man who expected the lash.

In that instant, Catlyn knew it was true. He had betrayed them. Her heart seemed to shrivel. She rose from the bed where they had made love so blissfully during the night. That joy was tainted now. Seizing the bed robe from the chest at the foot of the bed, she pulled it on, her movements jerky. The slight ache in delicate muscles reminded her of all they had done together, all the lush, private things, and she felt sick.

Ross turned. "Catlyn, if you will just listen to me."

Catlyn focused on a spot just over his head, afraid if she looked at him she would burst into tears or throw up. "Tell me."

"I will. I want to." Damn, he had hoped she would never find out what he'd been forced to do. Ross crossed to her and reached out a hand to offer comfort, groaning in despair when she shied from him as though his touch now revolted her. "The tale is long, and I know you must be weary. Will you not sit?"

She shook her head. "That is why you went to the Sword and Shield, is it not? So you could sell him our secrets."

"I did see Hakon there, aye, but—"

"His attack on you outside our gates. It was all part of the scheme to win our trust."

"Hakon planned that, not me. I had no idea he was going to ambush us. My God, two of my men were injured in that—"

"But you did come here for the purpose of gaining entrance to Kennecraig and stealing our secrets for him." Grief ravaged her beautiful features; tears roughened her voice.

Her pain tore at him. What could he say? How could he make her see that he had not planned to harm them? "He blackmailed me into coming here, that is true,'' Ross said. ''But I soon realized that he did not want the drawings, he wanted Kennecraig.''

''We were such fools. Such gullible fools. And I the biggest fool of all,'' she said numbly. Cold. So cold. Catlyn wrapped her arms around her waist and huddled into herself as she had when she had heard her father was dead. Now, as then, she found no comfort. ''How could I have believed your lies?''

''I did not lie to you, except—''

''How could I have lain with you? How could I have loved you?'' The last was said in an agonized whisper, the tears she'd held at bay sliding down her cheeks.

Ross grabbed hold of her shoulders then, goaded beyond respecting her wishes. ''I did not lie about loving you. Think how it is between us. *Dieu,* we nearly burned down the night with our loving. You cannot think that was a lie.''

She trembled in his grasp but did not struggle. Her eyes bright with loathing, her voice cold, she said, ''I think you are a skilled lover and an even more skilled manipulator of people.''

''I love you,'' Ross shouted.

''You used me to try and gain control of Kennecraig and the Finglas,'' she said stonily.

Someone pounded on the door. ''Catlyn! Catlyn, are you all right?'' It was Adair, this time. Alerted, no doubt, by Eoin.

Catlyn hesitated, then lifted her chin, some of the life returning to her eyes. ''I am unharmed,'' she replied.

''Open to me at once,'' Adair demanded. ''And if you have harmed Catlyn, Ross Sutherland, I will hang you myself.''

Ross groaned, knowing he had lost whatever slim chance he had had to convince Catlyn of his innocence. ''Catlyn, if you would only let me tell you the whole story, I—''

''Oh, you are very good at that, at twisting words and things to suit you.'' She stepped back, and he let her go.

''But now I am wise to you, and I do promise you will not succeed, even if I have to lock you in the deepest hole I can find.''

In the end, it was not a dark hole, but the cooperage to which Ross and his men were confined. All the underground rooms were dedicated to the distillery, and Roland had been adamant about not wanting the traitors housed there. So Adair and the Boyds had led them up here, all except Dallas, who had apparently melted into the shadows and not been missed. And Callum. When they had tried to take the boy away, Lady Jeannie had become so upset Eoin had relented and left him in her charge.

''What will we do now?'' Mathew demanded.

Ross sighed and turned from the window, drained by the encounter with Catlyn. His men sat about on upended whiskey kegs or on the floor. Some still wore their chain mail, having been standing watch when this mess had blown up in his face. Others had been roused from sleep and herded here by the angry Boyds. This time their weapons had been confiscated, even their eating knives. Eoin had been for hanging them all on the spot. Adair's cooler head had prevailed.

Ross supposed he should be grateful for that, but with the memory of Catlyn's grief-ravaged face fresh in his mind, it was hard to feel anything but pain. And regret. So many regrets.

''Ross.'' Mathew crossed the room and laid a gentle hand on his shoulder. ''Do not blame yourself.''

''Who else is there to blame?'' he snapped.

''Hakon. It was his greed caused all of this.''

''Nay, the fault is mine. I should have guessed what Hakon was and refused to sign the damned note.''

''You could not have known.''

''Well, then I should have run him through out behind the Sword and Shield when I had the chance.'' Ross leaned back against the wall, his shoulders slumping, his hands clenched into fists at his side. "That, at least, I could have done."

"Killing a man in cold blood is not your way."

"For him, I should have made an exception."

Mathew just grunted. "Perhaps you will have another chance to rectify that. But for now, what do we do?"

"What is there to do?" Defeated and hopeless for the first time in memory, Ross slid down and sat on the floor. "Even if she would speak with me, let me explain that Hakon does not really want the drawings I gave him, it would not change the fact that I did exchange their secrets for my note."

Mathew hunkered down in front of him, his usual pessimism replaced by anger. "That is past and done. We cannot change that. What we must do now is find a way out of this mess."

"I do not think they will kill you lads."

"Damn. That is not what I meant. What if Hakon comes?"

"I had not thought of that." In truth, his mind seemed to have stopped working. All he could see was Catlyn's horrified expression. All he could think about was that he had lost her. "If he does, they will blow up the stills."

"And this room with it," Mathew growled.

Ross nodded. "In a bit, I will ask to speak with Adair." He needed time before he faced the man's disillusion and hatred. "I will ask him to move you. Or perhaps I should speak with Eoin. He wants me dead. He might trade me for your lives."

Mathew seized Ross's shoulders and shook him. Never had he seen this look of utter despair in his cousin's face. No matter how grim things seemed, Ross always had a plan. "What is wrong with you? Why are you talking as though you have given up?"

"Maybe I have," Ross said listlessly, his eyes stark with grief. "It is as though a great piece of me has been torn away." His arms lay limp on his bent knees. Slowly he lowered his forehead to rest on them. "Tired," he murmured. "So tired."

Mathew stared at him, momentarily stunned.

"*Dieu,* what is wrong with him?" whispered Nigel Sutherland.

"He's lost the will to go on," Lang Gil replied. "I've seen it before in others. In battle. When a man's hard pressed and loses hope."

"What happens to them?" Mathew asked.

Lang Gil shook his head. "I've known them to walk straight into an arrow, never seeing it was coming. Not caring."

A moan of despair rose in Mathew's throat. Always Ross had led and he had followed. Without him, Mathew felt adrift on a very dangerous sea. The smell of fear hung heavy in the cooperage's dusty air. What could he do? What would Ross have done? A dozen memories played over in his head. Ross issuing orders before a battle, keeping the men so busy they had no time to fret over what might happen.

Mathew stood and turned to the circle of anxious men. Motioning them to follow, he walked to the other end of the room. "He is tired and heartsick over letting the lady down."

"And losing her," said Lang Gil. "Don't think I've ever seen him so taken with a lass."

"He loves her," Mathew said. "She's the first lass he's felt so about, and we know how hard that hits a man."

The men nodded and exchanged faint, knowing smiles.

"Makes him crazed as a buck in rut," someone said.

"He'll get her back," said Nigel. "There's not a lass alive who could resist our Ross."

Mathew was not so certain about that. Lady Catlyn had been betrayed once before, and Ross's supposed theft affected her whole clan. Glancing over his shoulder at the solitary, desolate figure slumped against the wall, Mathew prayed it would happen. "Meantime, it is up to us to carry out his orders."

"What orders?" Nigel asked.

"We're supposed to be protecting the Boyds," said Mathew.

"From in here?"

Mathew nodded and started issuing orders. Men were set to search the cooperage for anything that might prove useful either as a weapon or a tool. Others were posted in the cooperage's high windows, a vantage point that gave them a clear view over the walls of the land to the east and south.

Mathew worked alongside the men all morning, keeping one eye on Ross. It troubled him that his cousin seemed oblivious to the activity around him. Even the sound of the bar being lifted from the door did not rouse him.

The door opened, and Adair entered. His gaze swept over them, his eyes as censorious as they had been hours before when he had incarcerated them here. But when he spied Ross, his gray brows rose in surprise. "What…?"

Mathew crossed to the captain. "If you've questions, you'd best put them to me. Ross is…resting."

"Resting?" Adair glanced at Ross then at Mathew. "Is this some ploy to gain sympathy?"

Mathew's first instinct was to deny anything was wrong, but behind Adair he spied two servants with trays, and Dora. The pain and bewilderment in her eyes tore at him. This is how it must have been for Ross when Catlyn learned about the note and the drawings. Only that would have been ten times worse because Ross had been the one to make the trade.

"I do not expect you to believe me," Mathew said, staring directly at Adair but pitching his voice so Dora could hear. "But Ross has been like this since we were brought here."

"Pricked by his conscience, is he?" Adair growled.

"Aye, he is as much a victim here as you are. Hakon got him drunk and lured him into betting his estate on a crooked game of chance. When Ross sobered, he naturally looked for a way to get back the lands that had been in our family for generations.''

Adair's lip curled. ''By selling Hakon our secrets?''

''Hakon does not want really want them,'' Mathew said, knowing his time was short. ''He wants control of Kennecraig and the distillery. Not that it matters, for Ross deliberately falsified the drawings and the recipe he handed over to the Fergusson.''

''So, he cheated Hakon, too.'' He was still scowling, but some of the loathing had left his eyes.

Heartened by that, and hoping that a bit of what he said might find its way to Catlyn's ears, Mathew pressed on. ''Aye, he did, because he realized that Hakon had lied to him. He had sent us here for the sole purpose of getting his man inside.''

''Seamus.''

''Ross feared the man was up to no good and was watching him. Luckily he was able to save Lady Catlyn's life.''

''And silence the man so we could not question him.''

''Ross had no choice. Just as he had no choice but to try to get back the promissory note.''

''He could have told us the truth.''

''And found ourselves either tossed out of the keep or locked up as we are now.'' Mathew dragged an exasperated hand through his hair and looked toward Ross, but his cousin had not moved. ''Besides, when we realized what you were up against, we wanted to help.''

''Help.'' Adair grunted and cast a scathing glance at Ross's inert figure. ''By breaking my Catlyn's heart?''

''Ross loves her, he did not mean for her to be hurt.''

''Well, it's happened. She's buried herself in work, same as she did when her sire was killed, but...'' Adair motioned Mathew aside. ''We've brought food and drink. Step back and we'll set it on yon table.''

''Will you not listen to the rest?''

"Nay, I've no stomach to hear more and no time. Eoin was against bringing you anything."

Mathew stood aside as the servants entered. He tried to catch Dora's eye, but she kept her gaze from him as she directed the men in transferring the plates of bread, meat and cheese to the table. Damn. He had not realized how much he cared.

"Wait," Mathew called as the Boyds began to file out.

All eyes swung toward him. He cared only for Dora's. They were red-rimmed and filled with such sorrow.

Instinctively, Mathew lifted a hand, wanting to comfort her. To explain that his attention had not been false.

"Keep away from her," Adair grumbled. "She's suffered enough, too."

Mathew nodded and tore his eyes away from Dora. "I wanted to ask about the lad…Callum."

"He is with Lady Jeannie. She keeps him close by."

"But some may seek to punish him in Ross's stead." Like Eoin.

"We know where to lay the blame." Spinning on his heel, Adair ushered the others out and shut the door.

Mathew bowed his head and prayed that the little seeds he had planted would grow.

It was midafternoon by the time Hakon reached the hills opposite Kennecraig. The horses were spent from the brutal pace he'd set, his men drooping in the saddle. Small enough price to pay for arriving before dark, Hakon thought, glancing sidelong at his prize.

Wesley Boyd rode hunched over, his hands bound to the pommel, his legs tied beneath the horse's belly. His eyes were shut, and pain still twisted his lips.

Ah, but the honorable made easy pawns, Hakon thought, smiling faintly as he relived the moment when young Wesley had realized what it was Hakon wanted in exchange for Margot's life. The lad had refused, initially, weeping and carrying on about not betraying his clansmen. But Hakon had ordered Murdo to break the lass's arm and changed all that. Margot had screamed and fainted. Shaking visibly, the lad had agreed to do whatever he had to to save her, then listened in wide-eyed silence as Hakon once more outlined his plan. And a brilliant plan it was.

As they approached the perimeter of Guthrie's camp without being challenged, Hakon's smile dimmed. Where the hell were the guards? Had Ross Sutherland attacked Guthrie? "Spread out," he growled. "See if ye can—"

"Hakon!" Dull Dickie Fergusson scrambled down the ridge to their left and skidded to a halt before him. "Ye're back."

"Where is Guthrie?" Hakon demanded.

Dickie scratched at his misshapen skull and thought that over. "Hunting."

"When did he leave?"

Another long pause. "When the sun was lower."

That told him little. Hakon sighed and swung down from the saddle, even his hardened body protesting the ride from Doune. "He should have waited. I told him I'd bring back food."

"Didn't go looking for food. Went for more whiskey."

"Where did he get whiskey?"

"I found the whiskey." Dickie licked his lips. "Mighty fine, it was, too. Musta fallen off the wagon ye took."

"Stolen, more like. And the lot of them were too drunk to spot Ross Sutherland when he left the keep."

"I watched."

"No help that is." Hakon gave orders for Wesley and Margot to be hauled off their mounts. "Mind ye keep an eye on him," he muttered, striding through the trees and into camp.

Dickie followed. "No one on the road. I watched good."

"Not good enough ye didn't," Hakon snarled, rounding on the idiot. "Because Sutherland showed up in Doune."

"Oh." Dickie blinked, his struggles to comprehend pitiful.

Hakon snorted and walked away, kicking piles of soiled blankets and discarded ale kegs from his path. "All my care and hard work ruined because my lazy sod of a son cannot go a day without drink to…" He stopped, an awful notion taking root in his mind. Wheeling, he glared at the still-puzzled Dickie. "That fool did not go to Doune for this whiskey, did he?"

"Nay." Dickie shook his head slowly. "Hakon said no go there. Stay here. Guthrie not gone far."

"Where did he go? To the keep?"

"Nay. Too strong. Never get in."

Hakon glanced at the whey-faced pair his men were even now tying to a tree. Wesley and his dear Margot, the lass he'd betrayed his clan to save. "I'll get in, Dickie, but I need Guthrie and the lads." His plan hinged on having every Fergusson ready to rush into Kennecraig when Wesley opened the gates.

"Hmm." Dickie scratched his head, then gave him a toothless grin. "Crofts. Crofters got whiskey."

"The Boyds' farms? Guthrie went to the Boyds' farms?" His voice rose with every word.

"Aye. Got whiskey." His dull eyes glinted in the sunlight. "Got women, too. Guthrie bring me one. He said."

Hakon swore, snatched Dickie up and shook him. "Idiots! I am surrounded by idiots." He threw Dickie to the ground. "The Boyds said they'd burn the farms if we came near."

Murdo sidled up. "What does it matter? We've young Wesley to get into the keep."

"The fire will alert them to trouble, that's why. The crofters will tell them 'twas us. Come, we've got to prevent the farmers from reaching Kennecraig."

Chapter Seventeen

Catlyn bent over the journal and tried to concentrate on the lists of numbers. Instead, her mind kept slipping back, to last night when she and Ross had made love on this very table.

For her, it had been love. For him, just another step in his plans to betray them. Lies. All lies.

Groaning, she squeezed her eyes shut, but she could not block out the image of Ross's face as he had looked down at her. So tender, glowing with love as he slowly made them one.

Lies. All lies.

She stuffed a knuckle in her mouth to keep from crying her pain aloud. How could she have been so blind? So stupid?

Dimly she heard someone scratch at the door.

"Go away, Eoin," she pleaded, unable to bear another round of his tirades against Ross. Or worse, more of Eoin's clumsy attempts to ingratiate himself with her.

"It is me." The door opened a crack, and Dora peeked in.

"Dora. Oh, Dora." Catlyn opened her arms. Her friend rushed to her side and hugged her closely. "I have made such a mess of things," Catlyn choked out. Tears boiled inside her, but she feared if she let any more fall, she would never stop.

"You have done nothing wrong."

"Nothing except give myself to a man who…who…" Catlyn swallowed hard. "Dora, he betrayed us to Hakon."

Dora gave her a last hug, then moved to perch on the desk. "Are you certain of that?"

"He admitted it to me." Sweet Mary, how that had hurt. Her heart still ached. "He gave Hakon the drawings of the stills and the recipe for the Finglas."

"How can that be when there is no recipe? Or at least, not any one thing." Dora turned to look at the rows of journals, ledgers and scrolls. "How could Ross have read all of these so quickly and summarized them into one document?"

Catlyn frowned. That was true. Her father had seen the need for a single ledger that contained the best of their ancestors' advice. He had set her to working on just such a compilation. Three years she had been researching and writing and it was not quite complete. No one, even Roland, knew of its existence, and she had not mentioned it to Ross. Just this morn she had checked to make certain the leather-bound book was still locked in the floor safe concealed by the thick rug her grandfather had brought back from Italy.

"What you say is reasonable, Dora," Catlyn said slowly. "I admit I was too shocked and too hurt to wonder what Ross had turned over to Hakon." The anguish was so great it nearly overwhelmed her. She wanted to curl up in some dark corner and never emerge. Now she understood what had driven her mother to retreat from a world she could no longer tolerate. But Catlyn could not afford such weakness. Kennecraig's safety and the lives of her people were her responsibility. Straightening her shoulders, she sighed. "The fact remains, Eoin saw Ross give Hakon some parchment sheets. And Ross did admit to the deed."

"Hmm. The drawing Hakon might make use of, but I would be most surprised if such a man could read."

Catlyn's heart stilled, then beat quickly. Too quickly. She must not hope, but it was hard to kill the spark. "True."

"And if Ross is Hakon's man, why would he twice save your life?" Dora mused.

He blackmailed me into coming here, Ross had said.

"I—I do not know." Catlyn covered her face with her hands, struggling to sort things out. When she raised her head, she was no closer to understanding. "He admitted it," she whispered. "He told me he had done it and broke my heart."

"I know, and I am sorry for that. I know how badly that hurts, but I wonder..." She tapped a finger on her lips. "What would a ruthless warrior like Hakon want with plans to build a still and a whiskey recipe? It seems far more likely he would try to take our distillery."

Into Catlyn's mind crept the words Ross had uttered. *Hakon does not really want the drawings, he wants Kennecraig.* "I do not know." Restless suddenly, she stood and paced between the bookshelves. "Why would Hakon ask Ross to get the drawings and recipe if he did not want them?"

"Because Hakon is a clever man." Dora cocked her head. "I think that he gained some hold over Ross and forced him to come here. He told Ross that he must get these papers from us. But what Hakon really wanted was to get a man inside Kennecraig."

"Seamus," Catlyn whispered.

"Aye. Perhaps he was to move the black powder from the stills or take you hostage to force our surrender."

Catlyn chewed on that for a moment. "If that is so, then why did Ross not confide in me once Seamus was dead?"

"I do not know." Dora frowned. "It may be that Ross still did not understand Hakon's true purpose. Or—"

"Or it maybe that Ross sent you here to spread his lies," growled Eoin. He stood in the doorway, hands on hips, his hate-filled gaze fastened on Dora.

Dora jumped from the desk, bristling with indignation.

"That is not true. I came here to comfort Catlyn and tell her what I knew."

"What you learned when you visited the prisoners, you mean," Eoin sneered. "Against Catlyn's express orders they were to be left alone, I might add."

Catlyn gasped. "Dora, did you do that?"

"Aye." Dora raised her chin. "I took them food and drink, at your lady mother's insistence."

"Mama did that? But why?"

"Because she, too, sides with them." Eoin took Catlyn's hand. "I am sorry this distresses you, my dear, but you should know who is with you and who is not."

"We are on her side, Eoin," Dora insisted.

"Dora would say anything to please her new lover," Eoin said silkily. "And your mother is being unduly influenced by young Callum Sutherland. Ross was clever in selecting the lad to coerce her, for he reminds Lady Jeannie of her dead son."

Catlyn bit back a sob. It took every last bit of her remaining strength to stand there and listen to Eoin. Because what he said was true. Dora was as much in Mathew's thrall as she herself had been in Ross's. And her mother had become attached to the young squire. Merciful God, Catlyn had even thanked Ross for suggesting the two spend time together, for it had brought her mother back into the land of the living.

"What can I do?" Catlyn whispered.

"Trust me." Eoin put his arm around her. "Let me help."

It felt strange to have him touch her, but she was so tired, so very, very tired. Catlyn leaned against him. "What should we do?"

"We will double our patrols and keep watch for Hakon. If he does try to attack Kennecraig, we will put the Sutherlands up on the wall and use them as shields."

"Nay, Hakon is no friend to them," Dora cried, her eyes wild with fear. "He will shoot them down."

Catlyn stiffened. "I do not want that, Eoin. No matter what Ross has done, I do not want his death on my conscience."

"Hakon will not harm them," Eoin assured her. "Now, let me take you upstairs that you may rest a bit."

"Rest." Catlyn nodded, her limbs so heavy she could scarcely feel them. The numbness was welcome, better that than the unremitting pain she'd suffered since learning what Ross had done. "I will rest, then we can speak of this again."

"Catlyn, wait. If Hakon attacks, we will need the Sutherlands to help fight," Dora cried.

Eoin shoved her from his path. "You would say anything to discredit me, but I am wise to your schemes. And the Sutherlands'. I will keep Catlyn and Kennecraig safe."

"You?" Dora called after them. "Ross and his Sutherlands are the only ones who can save us. Release them, I beg you."

"I cannot," Catlyn muttered as Eoin led her away. Even if what Dora said was true and Ross had been forced to do Hakon's bidding, how could she trust him not to betray them again?

"Dod, what is that!"

The shouted question jerked Ross awake. He lifted his head, wincing as cramped muscles protested. It was either dawn or dusk, judging by the gray light in the windows. For a moment, he could not think why he had been asleep, sitting up on the floor. Nor did he recognize the room filled with saws, piles of lumber and kegs in various stages of completion.

Kegs. The Finglas.

His memory returned in a daunting swirl of images, chief among them, Catlyn's horror-stricken face when she forced him to admit what he'd done. *Dieu,* he had felt her pain, twisting and burning like a knife thrust in his own belly.

Ross groaned and buried his face in his hands. He had

saved his family from Hakon, but he had lost Catlyn. How could he live knowing he had hurt her? How could he live without her?

"Fire!"

The single word brought Ross's head up as Nigel whipped away from the window.

"Fire in the distance."

Mathew leaped up and ran to the window, followed by every man in the room.

Shoving aside his own misery, Ross hurried to join them. Sure enough, a plume of gray smoke rose to the east. "It's the barley fields," he muttered.

The men turned toward him, eyes wide and questioning.

"How do you feel?" Mathew asked cautiously.

"Dead inside," Ross said, still watching the fire.

Mathew nodded. With a jerk of his head, he sent the rest of the men away. "But you are up, about and talking."

Meaning he had not been earlier. "I remember little after Catlyn refused to hear me out."

"Aye, it upset you that you had hurt her."

"Upset? I wanted to die." Ross shuddered, reliving the horrible moment. "It was unbearable to see her suffer after all she has already endured. Knowing I was the cause of her pain made it even worse." He searched in vain for a way to describe what had happened. "I think I went a little mad, as Lady Jeannie did when confronted with the loss of her husband."

"Exhaustion," Mathew said. "And panic. Just when it seemed we had outwitted Hakon, Eoin arrives and deals a killing blow to all your hopes."

"He must have overheard my conversation with Hakon." Ross sighed and dragged a hand across his face. "If only there was some way I could speak with Catlyn, make her understand that the papers were a ruse to retrieve that damned note. They did not harm her clan in any way."

"For what it's worth, I did tell Adair and Dora that when they came with food and drink."

"Did they believe you?" Ross asked eagerly.

Mathew shrugged. "Hard to say. It takes a leap of faith for someone to believe you acted poorly but with good intentions."

"I had hoped Catlyn's love for me was stronger." Perhaps that was what had driven him over the edge, the fact that she had so quickly believed the worst, without giving him a chance to explain his side of things.

"The facts are daunting."

"Aye," Ross said slowly. "And the situation getting worse." He looked out the window again. "What do you make of the smoke?"

"It must be the barley fields."

"Question is, did the crofters burn them because Hakon attacked?" Another of Laird Thomas's measures to hold off the vicious Fergussons. The Boyds, Eoin and Roland in particular, had refused to destroy the precious crops. Ross had persuaded Adair and the farmers it might be necessary. "Or is this a ruse on Hakon's part to draw the garrison from Kennecraig?"

As they watched, Boyds poured out of the barracks and into the courtyard below, some still struggling to buckle on their swords. Dogs barked and raced in circles around the horses being led from the stables, making the beasts shy and caterwaul. Eoin was in the thick of things, shouting orders.

"*Dieu,* they are going to ride out." Ross leaned from the window, his knuckles white on the sill. "Wait! Do not go!"

No one heard him.

Ross swore and threw a leg over the sill.

"Wait yourself." Mathew grabbed hold of his arm. "What are you going to do, fly?"

"Nay. I've traveled this roof before. If I can work my way along the gutter, I can slide down the waterspout and—"

"Do you really think they'd listen to you?" Mathew snapped.

"I have to try." Ross looked down again. "Some of those men they are sending out are just lads."

"You cannot stop them. No man could."

"I have—"

A sharp sound, like the clap of thunder, echoed up from the courtyard. It silenced the crowd in an instant.

Adair stood midway down the steps. Once more he struck his sword against his shield, the sound deafening in the near quiet. "What do you think you are doing?"

A dozen men tried to answer at once, a flood of indecipherable words.

Adair held up a hand and stilled them. "Eoin, what passes here?"

"The barley fields are ablaze. We are going out—"

"You are not!" Adair roared.

Even from two stories up, Ross read the mutiny in Eoin's eyes, the sullen set of his jaw.

"I am in charge of defense," Eoin shouted.

"Oh, and when did you supplant our lady?" asked Adair.

Eoin lifted his chin in silent challenge. "Catlyn is unwell and has asked me to lead in her stead."

"Unwell. Jesu," Ross whispered. "What have I done to her?" He tried to shake off Mathew's hold. "I must go to her."

"She seems fine to me." Adair turned and extended a hand.

Catlyn came into view, dressed in her bed robe, her hair loose and tumbling like liquid gold against the green wool. "I know your intention is good, Eoin," she said, her voice firm. "But it would be suicide to leave Kennecraig when Hakon may be outside, waiting for us."

Ross stared at her, admiring her cool wisdom and her courage in confronting her angry clansmen. He willed her to turn so he might see her face, might know she was all right.

"The barley fields. We must save something," Eoin said.

A man close to him took up the cause. "If the fields are gone, there'll be no whiskey this year."

"I know, and that grieves me." Catlyn shook her head, making her hair ripple. "But not as much as it would grieve me to have you all march out to your deaths."

"We have more men than Hakon," Eoin cried. "And we have the Sutherlands' grand weapons." Indeed, several in the crowd were wearing chain mail, more carried the finely crafted claymores fashioned by the Sutherland smiths.

"The Fergussons are experienced fighters," Adair reminded them. "You've not the skill to win against them, swords or no."

Eoin raised his arm and turned, looking at the assembly. "We cannot just sit here like staked sheep, waiting for the wolf to close in and finish us."

Silence followed. Ross could sense the would-be army was poised on the edge, teetering between listening to Catlyn, the voice of reason, or following their natural urge to protect what was theirs. And maybe to enact revenge.

"Do you know what they call Hakon's son?" Ross shouted, drawing every eye to him. He avoided looking at Catlyn, focusing his attention instead on the Boyds in their borrowed mail, their belts dragged down by the unfamiliar weight of swords they had not the muscle to heft. "Godless Guthrie, he's called. Because he fights like Old Cootie himself."

"Do not listen to him," Eoin shouted. "He is Hakon's man."

But they were listening. They gazed up at Ross with the horrified fascination of bairns hearing a ghostly tale.

"Godless Guthrie." Ross stared into the fear-widened eyes of the women, the mothers, wives and sisters of these untried warriors. "Because he knows no honor and shows no mercy. Torture is his favorite sport, and he does excel in it. Along the Borders, 'tis common knowledge Godless Guthrie cuts the hearts from his victims while they still live.''

A gasp rose from the crowd. More than one man—and his woman—crossed themselves.

"What of the folk at the crofts?" Eoin cried, sensing he was losing his army. "Would you leave them to die?"

"Would you join them in death, with no hope of saving either the farmers or yourself?" Ross countered.

"He is right," Adair shouted. "If the fields are burning, Hakon has already attacked. We can only hope that some of our kin were able to get away and hide in the woods."

Mumbles of agreement greeted Adair's speech. Men looked down and shuffled their feet. Even Eoin dropped his gaze.

Ross let go the breath he'd been holding and allowed himself to glance at Catlyn. As though sensing his regard, she turned. Their eyes met, locked.

Such anguish. Such pain. His. Hers.

He looked as wretched as she felt, Catlyn thought. His pale face contrasted sharply with the stubble of his beard, his eyes red rimmed, burning in their shadowed sockets. The sight of him made more tears well.

His mouth formed words that reached her despite the distance and growing gloom. *I love you.*

Liar. Betrayer. But the accusations she had hurled at him in the middle of the night were now clouded by the seeds of doubt Dora had planted. And by the drama just enacted. If not for his grisly tales of Guthrie Fergusson, her people would have ridden out to their doom. Had he spoken to save them? Or Hakon?

I love you, he said again.

Her heart longed to believe. Her mind remained wary, the sting of his treachery too fresh, mingling with old doubts. Shivering, she wrenched her gaze from his and looked to Adair.

''What can we do? Is there no hope for the farms?''

''I wish I knew, lass.''

She thought a minute. ''Could we send a scout down the west wall, as Ross did his men?''

''Aye, but we've none so skillful as his lads.''

''And we'd not dare trust one of his men?'' she asked.

''I dunno, lass. I truly do not know what to make of—''

''Why do ye stand here?'' Roland screamed, stumbled down the stairs. ''The barley! My barley is burning.''

Adair caught him as he tripped and steadied him. ''It is likely Hakon has attacked the fields,'' he said gently. ''If we go out, we risk losing many lives.''

''What does that matter? We must have the grain for this year's whiskey.'' He tore at Adair's confining hands.

Adair adjusted his grip on Roland but did not release him. ''It is too dangerous.''

''Who says so?'' Roland wailed.

''I do.'' Catlyn stepped from behind Adair. ''Roland—''

''Watch him!'' shouted a voice from above. Ross's voice.

''Traitor!'' Roland cried, lunging at her.

Adair moved to block the grasping hands. ''Stay back, lass,'' he whispered. ''Roland, the decision to stay here was mine. Likely Farmer Brandon fired the fields because Hakon attacked them. If we go out, we risk—''

''It is her fault,'' Roland screamed.

''Get him away from her,'' Ross bellowed. ''I think he attacked her in Doune, and he'll do it again.''

Catlyn glanced up and saw Ross hanging out the window while three or four Sutherlands fought to restrain him. There was no mistaking his fear for her safety. Was it true? Did Roland hate her so much he had struck her down?

''Move back, lass,'' Adair murmured.

Even as she sidled down a step, Roland shook his fist at her. ''She does not care if the Finglas fails. She is no fit heir. It should have been me.'' Bits of foam flecked his lips. "I will keep the Finglas safe. I alone can make it prosper."

Catlyn cringed, his every word a blow to her confidence. Was it true? Had her inexperience contributed to this fiasco?

"No one wants the distillery to fail," Adair said.

Roland glared at her. "I swore to Thomas I would carry on."

"Aye, and so you have." Adair motioned two men forward. "You've exhausted yourself with labor and worry. Sim and Alf will take you to your room and see you rest."

"Rest? How can I rest when I've got to save the fields?" He cast about, eyes wild. "Eoin! Eoin, ye understand. Help me."

Eoin shook his head, his expression sad. "I think you do need that rest, Roland. Later, we can speak."

"Nay." Roland began to struggle in earnest, swearing and blaming Catlyn for all manner of things. He kicked at the two guards, so they were forced to bind him with their belts.

She turned away, sickened more by the loss of this once brilliant distiller than by the abuses he heaped on her. The sound of his voice gradually faded away.

Adair laid a hand on her shoulder. "I am sorry, lass."

"I, too," Eoin said. "He was wrong in what he said."

Catlyn nodded, but she was aware of other faces, some closed and thoughtful. Mad though he might be, Roland had made them doubt her abilities. "Adair, perhaps I am not—"

"Dust on the high road," called the sentry on the guard tower. "Someone comes." His cry of alarm sent everyone rushing up the steps to the wall walk.

What now? Catlyn thought as she ran with them. Instinct made her look up, to the window where Ross still stood, watching over her, it seemed. Who was he? Protector? Or destroyer?

There was no time to think of that, for when she reached

the top of the guard tower, she spied a party of people approaching the keep. Judging by the amount of dust, they were many, and they came quickly.

"Is it Hakon?" Catlyn clutched Adair's sleeve.

"I do not know."

They waited in a fever of apprehension as the cloud of dust resolved itself into people, some riding in carts, others walking. A horse leaped out of the pack and raced for the keep.

"Open! Open to us!" the man shouted.

Eoin leaned in next to her. "It is Farmer Brandon." Over his shoulder, he gave the order to raise the portcullis.

"Wait!" Catlyn cried. "It could be a trap."

"It is Farmer Brandon," Eoin insisted.

"Aye, but Hakon has already proved he is not above using others to get his men inside."

Eoin nodded, looking at her with new respect. "I know everyone at the farms. I will go down and inspect each person as they enter."

"Quickly, man," said Adair. "Another group comes."

Catlyn gazed with sinking heart as a second cloud of dust appeared on the high road. These riders seemed to be moving at a swifter pace than the refugees from the crofts. She leaned out through the crenel, silently urging her folk on, her hands gripping the rough stone so tightly they ached.

Having alerted the keep, Farmer Brandon went back for his flock. All around her, she heard prayers interspersed with the creak of the iron grate going up.

The first carts crested the steep trail from the crossing and lumbered across the plateau. As they neared the keep, some folk abandoned their carts and ran up the slope. A cheer went up along the wall as the first of them clattered across the short drawbridge and under the portcullis's teeth.

They were going to make it, Catlyn thought as the last of her people struggled up onto the plateau. They were midway to the keep when a terrible apparition burst onto the plateau.

Hakon Fergusson.

Sword aloft, his pale hair streaming in the wind, his mouth a red angry slash, he urged his lathered mount on. Behind him came another Fergusson and another.

"Oh, Sweet Mary, save them," Catlyn whispered.

"Archers!" Adair cried. "Where are the archers?"

"Here! Here!" Along the wall, men who had been caught up in the unfolding drama reached for bow and arrow.

The first volley arched out, over the screaming, fleeing Boyds and landed harmlessly in the dirt before the advancing Fergussons. But it checked their advance. Perhaps remembering the last time, they slackened their pace. The second volley drove them back, giving the Boyds the precious moments needed to reach the gate.

The sound of the portcullis crashing back down to earth was the sweetest sound Catlyn had ever heard. "Praise be to God for their deliverance," she murmured, slumping against the wall.

"Aye," Adair growled, his eyes on the Fergussons massed just out of bow range. "But now the wolf is at our door. How will we keep him out?"

Dora's words rang in Catlyn's mind. *Ross and his Sutherlands are the only ones who can save us.*

But could she trust him? Catlyn closed her eyes and prayed for guidance, some sign that would tell her which path to take.

Chapter Eighteen

Ross paced the length of the cooperage, trying to work off some of his nervous energy. An hour had passed since the Boyds had taken their frightened, wounded crofters inside. An hour since he had last seen Catlyn. If only there was some way he could make certain she was all right. That had become almost more important than convincing her of his innocence.

"I am certain the Boyds were careful who they let in," Mathew said for the tenth time. "I saw Eoin and Adair speaking with each person as they entered."

Ross turned on him. "Aye, and doubtless they are in the hall celebrating their escape when they should be planning to leave while Hakon is still resting his men and his mounts."

"Tired horses, that is all that saved the crofters."

"They'll not be so lucky next time." Ross dragged an exasperated hand through his hair and stared out the window. The night was dark and moonless, perfect for sending people over the west wall and away to safety. But no such exodus was taking place. The courtyard was quiet and had been except for the moment a half hour past when the sally port had been opened a crack to admit a single man. A straggler. Or perhaps a scout.

Ross had been amazed that the man had made it through,

given the fact that the Fergussons must be watching the keep.

"You are planning something," Mathew said tightly.

"Aye. When the keep settles down for the night, I'm going out. I want to find Dallas, see what he knows. And speak with Catlyn." The yearning to see her clawed at him. Was she all right? Had she recovered from Roland's attack? God, she must be frightened, beset as she was with problems. Burdens she must shoulder alone. A shudder of longing ripped though him. He needed to be with her, to help if he could. But overriding that was the gut-wrenching urge to get her away from here.

The sound of voices penetrated the cooperage door, one of the guards grumbling about something. They were Eoin's men and had already turned away a servant with the evening meal. But this time the bar was lifted.

The burly guard with the nasty temper stomped in and checked behind the door. "Get on with it, then."

A stooped man clad in filthy rags shuffled in, a wooden bucket in each hand.

"He's come to empty the slop buckets. Mind ye stand clear and don't try to rush us." The guard took up a post in the doorway, a long sword held menacingly in front of him.

Ross sighed, about to turn away when the honey man lifted his head and winked.

It was Dallas, his narrow face smeared with dirt, his eyes twinkling with a conspiratorial light. Ducking his head again, Dallas shambled toward the far corner and the screen that concealed the cooperage's privy holes.

Ross glanced at Mathew, then jerked his head toward the guard.

With a quick nod, Mathew crossed to the lout. "What we really need is food," he said loudly, approaching from the right side, forcing the man to turn from the privy. "And ale."

"Eoin said ye weren't to have anything."

"What about water?" Mathew whined, and fell to describing the horrors that overtook men deprived of drink.

Ross sidled toward the privy and rounded the screen to find Dallas waiting. "How fare things below?" he whispered.

"Not as bad as they could have been. Three were lost getting here, cut down by Fergusson spears. A few others suffered scrapes and minor wounds. 'Twas Guthrie who came calling at the crofts, looking for liquor and women. Lookouts saw him. The Boyds escaped into the woods, where they'd hidden the barley carts, as you suggested. They set out for here, except for a few men who stayed behind and burned the fields."

"The diversion kept Guthrie too busy to follow," Ross muttered. "Lucky, that. Luckier still that Hakon's men and mounts were exhausted after the hurried journey from Doune."

"Aye, lucky." Dallas's expression hardened. "But Hakon is still hanging about. We can see his campfires at the far edge of the plateau. Blocking the road, he is."

"And watching the keep." Ross cursed softly. It was no more than he'd expected. "What of Catlyn? Have you seen her?"

Dallas shook his head. "She's been closed up in her solar with Eoin, Adair and some of the others."

"Poor lass. Even a battle-toughened commander would quail at finding himself trapped like this."

"Aye, the fear's running so high in the hall you can fair smell it. Folk are worried that the threat of the black powder will not be enough to prevent Hakon from attacking."

"It is just a matter of time till he figures a way to get inside," Ross said grimly. "Is there talk of leaving?"

"Not with Hakon sitting outside like a hungry cat. But there's lots of praying." Dallas scratched his head. "Do you think High Harry has reached Edin Valley by now?"

"Likely, but the message I sent was a warning to my father, not a request for help." Impotent rage filled Ross.

He clenched his hands till they ached. "Even if Papa decided to come, it might take a week to raise an army and march so far."

Dallas grunted. "We're on our own, then."

"Aye." Ross considered their options. Not many and not good. "Is the winch still on the west wall?" Dallas's nod gave him some hope. "I'm thinking we'd best try to get out that way. Tonight, while Hakon is resting his men and plotting."

"Might work. Do even better if we had a wee diversion to keep Hakon so busy he'd not have time to follow us."

"A fire, say?" Ross asked archly. "Keen as he is to have the distillery, Hakon would forget all about us if he entered and found his new tower ablaze."

Dallas started. "If we burn the keep, the Boyds'll have nothing to come home to."

"If Hakon gets inside, this will no longer be their home."

"Aye." Dallas looked as grimly resigned to this as Ross. "It'll be hard enough convincing the Boyds to leave," Dallas muttered. "If they know you plan to burn the keep…"

"Some would refuse to leave, or tarry too long packing their belongings. But it's the only way to save them."

"What of the whiskey?"

Ross shook his head. It would be impossible to take the thousands of heavy, bulky kegs with them. "The people must be our first concern." But even as he said the words, he shivered, thinking of the agony Catlyn would suffer over this latest loss.

"How can we mount this escape with you and the lads in here?" Dallas asked in an urgent whisper.

"We cannot. I will have to convince Lady Catlyn to release us and go along with this plan."

"A tall order, given she does not trust you."

Nay, she did not, and that hurt. "I am not giving up." Somehow he had to win back her trust. And her love.

"Hey," called the guard. "What's taking so long?"

"There was a spill," Dallas growled.

"Leave it."

Dallas shrugged, smiled faintly at Ross and picked up the two noxious buckets. "What do you want me to do?"

"Meet me behind the stables in two hours." That should give him enough time to go over the roof and speak with Catlyn. Ross stayed behind the screen so as to not rouse the guard's suspicions further.

Barely had Dallas left when the guard called out, "My lady, ye cannot go in there."

Hope soaring, Ross rounded the screen in a single bound, but it was Lady Jeannie who stood on the threshold, not Catlyn.

The lady fixed the guard with a puzzled frown. "Am I not chatelaine here?"

"Of course, my lady, but these men are dangerous traitors. Lord Eoin said no one was—"

"I am not no one." The lady sailed into the room. "Come along, my dears, the food grows cold." In her wake trailed a young girl and a lad, both bearing covered trays.

The boy was Callum.

Ross came forward to meet them, relieved to know the lad was unharmed. "This is an unexpected honor, my lady."

"Indeed?" Lady Jeannie cocked her head, her eyes so alert she scarce resembled the dazed woman he'd met a week ago. "I would say a meal is no more than we owe you." A glance from her had Mathew and Nigel scrambling to clear tools and wood shavings from one worktable.

All three guards stood in the doorway, scowling. Clearly they could not contradict their lord's widow, but the surly-faced one was not giving up. "Go and fetch Lord Eoin," he muttered, shoving one of his fellows toward the stairs.

Ross dusted off a bench and gestured for the lady to sit. "I thank you for coming," he murmured.

"It is not Christian to withhold food and drink." She

perched on the bench. "Especially from men wrongly imprisoned."

Ross sank down beside her. "You believe me?"

"I do." She stared deep into his eyes. "Dora has told me what she knows of the tale. I trust that the papers you gave Hakon did not betray any of our secrets."

"And Catlyn?" he asked.

Lady Jeannie sighed and looked down at her hands. "She is proud and stubborn, as my Thomas was. And she has been hurt too often in the past, deserted by those she looked to for support. Her brother. Her father. Even me."

"You have accepted Laird Thomas's loss."

"I must," she said softly. "Hard as it is, even now, I've come to see the living need me." She looked over at Callum, his head bent as he cut meat for the waiting Sutherlands. "Helping him to heal eased the pain of not being able to aid Thomas."

"Catlyn needs you, too," Ross said.

"I have tried to help, but she is weighed down by the threat we face. Thomas was wrong. Hakon will not go away."

"Nay, I do not think he will." Ross weighed his words, then plunged in. "Escape may be our only hope."

"Escape? How? He is camped outside."

"There may be a way."

Lady Jeannie's eyes widened. "Then we must go."

"Do you think the rest of the clan will agree so readily?" Ross asked eagerly, hope soaring.

"Nay, many will refuse to go, Catlyn among them. She takes her vow to carry on the distillery very seriously."

"You are right, and she has little reason to trust me."

"I will speak with her this evening. Perhaps I can persuade her to listen, at least, to what you say."

Ross sighed. "Our time is short, I think. I—"

"Ross?" Callum held out a hunk of bread topped with roast mutton. "I must tell you something, something important."

"Later, lad," Ross said absently.

"That may be too late," said the lass who peered anxiously over his shoulder. "It's Wesley. My brother."

Ross frowned, then placed her. Brita, the maid who'd tended Callum. Roland's daughter. "I am sorry Wesley was left in Doune." Yet it was possible he might be the only one to survive.

"That is just it," Brita whispered. "He is back."

"Back? How? When?" Ross asked.

"Scarce an hour ago."

The straggler. "How did he get past Hakon?"

"He would not say." Brita choked on a sob, steadying when Callum took her hand. "We've been close all our lives. Now he will not speak with me. He does not even look like my brother. His eyes are wild and darting. He stinks of ale and looks as though he'd not slept in days. He asked for Pa and grew even more upset upon hearing he was locked up."

"That is only natural."

"Wesley did not care that Pa had attacked Lady Catlyn. Over and over he says Pa must help him save Margot."

"Who is Margot?"

"Margot McNab. Her father owns the Sword and Shield."

Ross sat up, his gut tightening with apprehension. "Would Wesley have gone to that tavern?"

"Aye. It was all he talked about for weeks. Seeing Margot again. They met last year at fair time and have passed messages since. She's Coinnech's only bairn, and the tavern will come to her. Of late Wesley has said he'd rather run an alehouse than be stuck in the stills all his life."

"Where is Wesley now?"

"In his room, brooding and whispering Margot's name." Brita sighed. "Likely he came to tell Pa he was leaving to wed her. I fear he will try to go to her, and Hakon will catch him."

Ross nodded. It was possible, but there were other, more

sinister ones. He did not like the ease with which Wesley had passed through Hakon's lines. "I want you two to go down and sit with Wesley. Do whatever you have to to keep him in his room."

She had never felt more miserable or more frightened and alone, Catlyn thought as she huddled beneath the covers in her solitary bed. The pillow still carried Ross's scent. It conjured all manner of memories, tormenting her with images of their brief time together. Perversely, it was the good she remembered most vividly, the strength of his arms as they'd held her close, the wry humor in his eyes as he laughed with her. Most of all, she missed the sharing, the caring.

Stop. You have to stop thinking of him.

Huffing, Catlyn turned on her side, facing the wall, and tried to sleep. But now her thoughts ran back to the council of war the Boyds had held an hour ago.

War, hah! None of them except Adair had any experience in fighting, and he'd not fought in years. Adair proposed sending to Doune for help, even if it meant pledging every keg of whiskey they had. Eoin wanted to go out and raid Hakon's camp.

"Suicide," Adair had growled.

The despair that had gripped her all evening came again in sharp waves. Tears filled her eyes, tears of hopelessness and pain. She had to save her clan, but how?

"Ach, lass. Do not cry," whispered a deep, familiar voice.

Catlyn gasped and rolled over. A wide hand covered her mouth, an achingly handsome face filled her vision.

"Promise you'll not scream," he commanded, his eyes glittering with determination.

Catlyn nodded. When his hand lifted, she licked her lips and tasted him. The longing swept through her, sharp and poignant. She fought to remain logical. "How did you get in?"

"The window." The bed dipped as he sat beside her. "I needed to talk with you."

She stiffened instinctively. "If you've come to try and convince me you did not sell our secrets to Hakon—"

"There is not time for that. I told you I did not give him anything he could use. The drawings were fakes. The recipe a jumble of words that meant nothing. I had to give them over to redeem the promissory note he duped me into signing. Either you believe me, or you do not."

Catlyn tried to hang on to her hatred for Ross, but she kept remembering the good he had done. Charging to her rescue, twice. Forcing her to take the reins of her household and reinstate Dora. Coaxing her mother back from the edge of madness. He was arrogant and managing, but always he strove to do the right thing, to help instead of hurt. "I think you have told the truth about that, but things cannot be as they were before. You sought to harm my clan, and that I can never forgive."

"I see." His jaw flexed as he clenched his teeth, and his eyes glittered with emotions too painful to explore. "That does not change my reasons for coming. You must leave Kennecraig tonight." He held up his hand to forestall her objections, then stood and walked to the window. "Hakon will not go away. He is ruthless and determined to have your distillery."

Alarmed by the tone in his voice, Catlyn left the bed and joined him. "You know what he is planning?"

"Not for certain, but..." He looked down at her, his face taut, his expression guarded.

"Tell me. It is better knowing."

Ross nodded. Lifting a hand, he gently stroked her hair. "You are so small and fair I forget how brave you are."

As she listened to him explain about Wesley's unexpected arrival and what it might mean, Catlyn did not feel brave. She felt frightened. "Why would Wesley open the keep to him?"

"For the same reason I came here. Because Hakon has

some hold over him, something Wesley would do anything to protect.''

"The girl, Margot."

"So I think, too. I must question the lad and get him to tell me how much time Hakon has given him. Meanwhile, we must get your people on their way out of Kennecraig.''

"How?'' she asked, then remembered. "Over the wall.''

Approval briefly eased his tense expression. "Aye. There will be no time to pack anything. Woman and bairns first, with an escort. Whom would you choose to lead them into hiding?''

We cannot leave. We cannot. Kennecraig has been our home for generations. The distillery is our life.

But the memory of the crofters' horrible tales were fresh in her mind. Three stragglers, two old men, one woman, had been killed without mercy by the Fergussons. She could still see the anguish and remorse on Farmer Brandon's face as he told how he had been forced to choose between saving the many or going back and trying to rescue the few who could not keep up.

Catlyn did not want to lose another Boyd to such a violent death. "Adair knows the hills the best." She hesitated a moment before asking what was next closest to her heart. "The whiskey?''

Ross shook his head, the hard line of his mouth at odds with the gentle regret in his eyes. "It would take too long to transfer the kegs, and they would weigh you down as you fled.''

She winced, absorbing the shock and the pain of losing everything her family stood for. "Would there be time to dump some of it out?'' she asked in a choked voice. "The ten-year at least. I would hate to think of Hakon and his thugs celebrating their victory with Papa's finest.''

"I will see what can be done.''

"There are drains in the floors of the still rooms.''

He nodded, his expression mirroring her own anguish. "I am sorrier than you can know that it has come to this.''

She managed a faint smile, though she ached to the depths of her soul. "Thank you. It helps to know you understand."

"Oh, Catlyn." He swept her into his hard embrace. His warmth, his strength, the steady thud of his heart drove every thought from her head save one.

This was right. And good. Sobbing his name, she clung to him, raising her face for a kiss that chased out some of the terrible cold in her belly.

"Can you forgive me?" he whispered into her hair.

She closed her eyes, wishing she did not have to utter these next words, but without honesty between them, whatever future they might have was doomed. "I do not know," she murmured, her heart and mind at war. "I just do not know."

He trembled and hugged her tighter. "I understand." Releasing her, he stepped back. "Get dressed. I would free my men and speak with Wesley. Then we must assemble your people in the hall and explain what has to be."

"It will not be easy getting them to agree." She drew a panicky breath, thinking of the strife to come. "Roland is not the only one who blames me for not saving the barley. They may refuse to leave."

"Any who stay behind are doomed. They must be made to realize that." He glanced out the window, started and leaned closer. "Bloody hell, is that Wesley skulking about the gate?"

"Aye, it is!" Catlyn exclaimed, but she spoke to empty air, for Ross had gone out the window.

"Cannot let anyone out," said the guard at the gate.

"I dropped something on my way in," Wesley said. "My...my mother's cross. I think it is just outside, if I could go—"

"Nope." The guard hawked and spat. "Adair said the gates stay locked." He shut the door to the gatehouse.

Wesley sobbed, his hand reaching for the door latch. "I have to go out, ye don't understand, I—"

"Explain it to me," Ross whispered, having heard enough to know Wesley was uncommonly desperate to leave Kennecraig.

The lad whirled. "Ye-ye're supposed to be locked up."

"Things change." Ross grabbed hold of Wesley's arm and hustled him back toward the keep.

"Please...please, I have to go out." Wesley tried to twist free, but he could not break Ross's hold.

Halfway up the steps, they met Eoin charging down. "How did you get out?" he bellowed, reaching for his sword.

Ross lashed out with his right foot, caught Eoin's wrist and sent the weapon clattering down the stairs.

"Ouch, damn you." Eoin clutched his arm, eyes blazing.

"Catlyn freed me," Ross told him with a calm that belied his raging emotions. "We are going to question Wesley. If you want to be there, leave the sword and come with me."

Eoin started. "Wesley, but what has he done?"

"That is what I mean to find out." Ross headed up, the weeping Wesley in tow. "Easy, lad, we don't mean to kill you."

"Ye won't have to," the lad whispered.

Catlyn and Adair were waiting for them in the entryway. Her eyes anguished, she lifted a hand toward the boy, then dropped it, as though too heartsick to carry on.

"She told me," Adair said. "We agreed the solar was best for this."

"My men?" Ross asked.

"Ach, well, as it happens, Dallas was lurking about outside Catlyn's room when she came to find me. We sent him to release them. What of Eoin?"

"Right behind me."

Eoin stomped into the entryway. He wore a mutinous

expression. The sword he'd retrieved hung from his belt. "Catlyn, what in God's name are you thinking of?"

"Saving our lives." She turned and led the way to her solar, her back straight.

Wesley sat where Ross put him, his arms on the table, his head bent over them in a pose of utter defeat.

"Where did you meet Hakon?" Ross asked.

"Hakon?" Eoin gasped.

Wesley raised his head and blinked. "How'd ye know?"

"The pieces fit," said Ross. "What bit of blackmail did he use to force your cooperation?"

"Margot." Wesley's voice shook. "My...the lass I love."

"He has her?" At Wesley's miserable nod, Ross sighed. Turning away, he began to pace. "What are you supposed to do in exchange for her release?"

"Open the gate." Wesley lowered his head again, tears falling onto the polished wooden table. "I—I said I would not, but he...he broke her arm."

Catlyn went to him and laid a hand on his shoulder.

"I thought...I thought if I could get inside, I might be able to figure a way out of this, but..." He swallowed hard.

"What about the powder?" Ross asked. "Surely Hakon fears we'd blow the stills if he attacked."

Wesley raised eloquent eyes to him. "There is no powder."

"What?" cried Eoin.

"Impossible," Adair said. "I put it there myself."

"Who moved it?" Ross asked.

Wesley licked his lips. "My pa. He did it a bit at a time, 'cause the barrels were too heavy to lift."

"Dear God," Catlyn whispered. "Where is the powder now?"

"Gone, scattered. He threw some of it from the walls when he took his walks. The rest he dumped down the drains."

Eoin groaned and buried his face in his hands. "Our last hope of defending ourselves, gone."

Catlyn was shivering so hard that Ross longed to go to her, but knew he had to press on. "Does Hakon know?"

Wesley bit back a sob and nodded. "I—I tried to lie, tried to make him think it was still there, but... He knew I lied."

"Hakon would, for he is a master at lying," Ross said.

"If I don't open the gate, he'll kill Margot."

"What are we going to do?" Catlyn whispered, looking to Ross. Slowly all eyes turned toward him.

"Assemble your clansmen in the hall, Catlyn. We will explain to them that they must leave Kennecraig tonight."

"We cannot abandon the keep!" Eoin cried. "We must fight."

"If you stay, you will die a horrible death. And still you will be unable to keep Hakon from taking the distillery. I offer you a chance to save yourselves." Ross's words echoed ominously in the narrow room. A half hour later, he repeated them in the great hall. The effect was as stunning, silencing even the most vocal protesters in the crowd.

Catlyn shivered and leaned against him. "What is to prevent Hakon from discovering we are leaving?" she whispered.

"My men and I will keep him diverted."

Eyes widening, she clutched at his sleeve. "But Ross, what if he captures you?"

"Oh, I've every incentive to see that does not happen," Ross replied, kissing her lightly. He gave her his most reassuring smile, but deep inside he knew that he would do anything—even sacrifice himself—to make certain she was safe.

Chapter Nineteen

The walls of Kennecraig Keep stood out black against the night sky, solid and seemingly impregnable. Hunkered down in the rocks a league away, Hakon looked up at them and grinned. It was a false image, for soon he would be inside. Any moment now, Wesley would open the sally port and let them in.

Hakon had not slept in two days, but his mind was so abuzz with plans he scarcely felt the lack. His men, however, were nodding at their posts. Soft, he thought, lip curling as he studied them. Even Guthrie. Especially Guthrie.

"Idiot!" Hakon drove an elbow into his drowsing son's ribs.

Guthrie yelped. "No call for that. Ye've already beat me bloody." Indeed, he had a black eye and a split lip.

"Wanted to make sure ye remembered what I said."

"Patience and forbearance," Guthrie repeated wearily.

"Yer lack of both might have ruined things if I hadn't stumbled onto the Boyd lad and his lass."

Guthrie's undamaged eye glinted avidly as it fell on the girl huddled in the lee of a boulder. "Still don't see why I couldn't have her once he left for the keep."

"Because I said not."

"But she's pretty and young. Don't get many like that."

As though sensing the precariousness of her situation,

the lass pulled the blanket up over her head and burrowed deeper into the covers. The arm Hakon had been forced to snap in order to break young Wesley doubtless pained her, but she had not said or done anything to draw attention to herself.

Smart lass, Hakon thought. And bonny. It had been a long time since he'd had anything as fine as her in his bed. "Ye disobeyed me, Guthrie, and must be punished. The lass's mine."

The bundle of blankets trembled.

Guthrie's bruised face darkened. "That's not fair."

"'Tis if I say so."

"Then I want first choice of the women in the keep." He stuck out his mangled lip. "Two. Catlyn Boyd and another."

Hakon scratched at his whiskered chin. "Two it is, but ye'll not touch them till after Kennecraig's ours. And ye'll be leaving the lady alone. We need her to keep the others in line."

"An hour with me and she'll be begging to help us."

"Bah. Ye'd kill her or torture her witless."

"Would not." Guthrie glared at him, the militant light in his eyes a bit worrisome. He was getting harder to control.

"Hakon," Georas called. "I think the sally port opened."

Hakon scrambled to his feet and began kicking men awake. "Up. Up and arm," he growled. "But mind ye're quiet about it."

"What if they try to trap us?" Guthrie grumbled.

"They won't. The lass is going in first." Hakon snatched her from her little nest, smothering her cry of pain behind a filthy gag. No need to tie her arms. He seized her good wrist and dragged her with him as they crept toward the keep.

* * *

Wesley Boyd stood just outside the sally port door, in plain view, as Hakon had instructed.

Ross stayed back inside, watching through the partially opened door as the Fergussons moved along the edge of the trail. Like vermin, they were, he thought, a pestilence spreading across the darkened landscape, bringing death and destruction.

Pray God his plans worked.

Looking back over his shoulder, Ross scanned the courtyard. A long line of men snaked across it, working feverishly under Eoin's direction to transfer as many kegs of whiskey as they could from the distillery to the stone granaries. The ten-year first, then what they could of the other vintages. Eoin's offer to help with this had surprised Ross.

"I know what you're planning," Eoin had said. "You mean to burn the keep and maybe the distillery, too."

Ross had nodded warily. "We need to keep the Fergussons busy, else they'll follow us."

"I understand, but what does Catlyn think of this?"

"She does not know. I feared she'd not leave if she did." And if he survived this, she'd hate him forever. "Getting her away from here is the most important thing in the world to me."

Eoin had grunted in agreement. "She's the last of her line. The last who knows how the Finglas is made. But that is not why you are doing this. You love her, don't you."

"With all my heart and soul," Ross had replied.

"And she loves you, I think," his rival had murmured. "Despite what you did. Adair and Lady Jeannie are convinced you did not play us false, but I'm not so sure." Still he had lent his expertise to the transfer, and for that Ross was grateful.

Turning his attention to the matter at hand, Ross called softly, "Nigel, go below and tell Dallas he must leave now, whether the fuse is set or no. Gil, have Eoin and the rest of the lads take those last kegs to the granary, then go, too. I want everyone over the wall when Hakon enters. If he catches sight of anyone on that walkway, he's sure to investigate.''

His men nodded and trotted off to do his bidding. Everyone of them deserved high praise for the work they'd done these past few hours. After their initial cries of outrage, the Boyds, too, had labored like demons to try and save what they could. Ross had told them there was no guarantee his mad scheme would succeed, but to a man, they'd wanted to try.

Mathew, calm and capable, was in charge of getting the folk down the wall. Adair waited below in the rocks to lead them to the relative safety of the woods beyond. Ten Sutherlands stood guard there, but they'd be no match for Hakon's men if he discovered what they were about.

"He...he has Margot with him," Wesley whispered.

Ross spotted the lass with Hakon, and his lips tightened. An unforeseen complication, another innocent to protect. "Do not look at me. Just listen. He's doing it to assure this isn't a trap. When he comes close, you must make no suspicious moves."

Wesley nodded, but he was trembling visibly.

"Hakon has no reason to harm you or Margot unless he thinks you mean to betray him. When he approaches, tell him everyone is asleep and you've killed the only guard." In reality, the crumpled body just inside the gate was that of a farmer killed during the escape from the crofts. "Shiver, sob, whatever you can to appear cowed and broken."

"It'll not take much playacting."

"I know you are frightened, lad, and I'd spare you this if I could, but as long as he has Margot..."

"I am all right, my lord."

Ross grinned. "Aye, you are. Point Hakon in the direction of the distillery. Avoid going with him if you can. Weep and clutch at Margot. That, too, should seem natural enough. I wager Hakon will be so eager to take the tower while all still sleep that he'll leave you be. I'll be as close by as I can.''

''Ye are not leaving with the rest?'' The lad's relief was plain in his voice.

''Not without you and Margot.'' And even after he had gotten them safely away, Ross had to climb onto the roof and light the fuse. It ran down the chimney and into the last still room. The distillers had opened the spigots on the mash tuns, flooding the floor with raw whiskey. It would make quite a blaze.

''That's the last of them,'' Mathew murmured. ''You are next, Catlyn, though Ross will have my head when he learns I let you wait this long when he wanted you to be first down the wall.''

''I could not go till I knew my clan was safe.'' Catlyn turned on the wall walk and scanned the courtyard with its neat dependency buildings, the kitchen where she'd filched many an apple tart and the barracks to its left. She had once spent an entire night in the nearby stables, waiting for her favorite cat to have kittens. The keep, a stark gray sentinel standing out against the night sky, was the only home she had ever known.

Finally she looked at the distillery tower rising sharply behind the keep, a silent testimony to the men and women who had come before her. The only things she had managed to bring away were the tasting chalice and the journal she had been working on. She knew it was wisest to leave yet felt like a failure for not staying and fighting with the last breath in her body.

''I will be back,'' she whispered, her words carried away by the freshening breeze. It might take months or years, but she would return and wrest her family lands away from Hakon.

A line of men hustled around the side of the keep and headed for the stairs. She recognized Nigel Sutherland in the lead, with the last of her distillery workers following along.

"What has happened?" she asked when they mounted the walk.

"Hakon comes," said Nigel. "Ross bid us leave at once."

"Where is he?" Catlyn anxiously glanced about.

"He stayed to make certain Wesley and Margot got away."

How like Ross, Catlyn thought.

Mathew looked away from helping Sim Boyd onto one of the climbing ropes. "Is Ross going out the gate with them?"

Nigel frowned. "He did not say."

"Bloody hell." Mathew stood. "I'm going down to find him."

"Dallas and Eoin are with him."

Mathew snorted. "Small comfort, that is. Ross will send them away then he'll be lighting the fuse himself. Doubtless at the last minute. Damn if I want him going up in flames, too."

"What do you mean?" Catlyn asked. No one answered. The Sutherlands watched her with troubled eyes. The Boyds were busy making good their escape down the half-dozen ropes. Like rats fleeing a floundering ship. Or a burning one. "He is going to set a fire to divert Hakon?"

Mathew nodded. "He'd not be doing it if it weren't necessary."

"I...I know," Catlyn said numbly. She looked back over the buildings again. The stable, with its hay-filled loft, would make a fine blaze, and the greasy rafters of the kitchen would go up like a torch. "Still it hurts."

"Aye." Mathew took her hand and squeezed it gently. "But if Hakon is not busy saving his prize, he will follow us."

"What are ye saying?" demanded a high querulous voice.

Catlyn turned in time to see Roland creep out from the shadows at the corner guard tower. "Roland?"

"What are you doing here?" Mathew growled, advancing on him. "I put you on a rope myself a half hour ago."

"Didn't go. Can't leave the Finglas," Roland mumbled. His eyes were fixed on Catlyn's face. "What's this about a fire?"

Catlyn just shook her head. "Nothing."

"Yer cursed knight means to burn my stills," Roland said.

"You are wrong," Catlyn said. "'Tis true we may lose the stables, kitchens and the like, but Ross would never harm the keep or the distillery. They will be here... waiting."

Mathew cleared his throat. "Roland, it is time to leave."

"I'm not going." Roland backed up a step.

"You must. Hakon is here," Mathew said. "He and his men will be inside soon." He grabbed hold of Roland's arm. "We have to be off these walls before he enters."

"We cannot leave now, when we're needed most." Roland shoved Mathew into the men who stood behind and rushed down the stairs.

"Roland," Catlyn gasped. She started after him. Behind her, she heard Mathew hiss her name, heard cursing and scrambling as the Sutherlands tried to sort themselves out. If she waited for them, Roland would have too great a lead. As it was, by the time she reached the bottom step, he was just disappearing into the thick shadows around the granaries. She ran faster, glad she had put on her male garb. He stayed ahead of her, down the side of the building, across the open bailey and into the stables.

Catlyn plunged in after him. The stalls were empty. The horses had been winched over the wall to carry the old and the very young. In the pack of her mother's mount were the chalice and journal. They must be safe in the woods by now, but all would be lost if Roland alerted the Fergussons. Straw muffled the sound of her footfalls, and she guessed

Roland did not realize he was being pursued, either that or he was winded, for his steps seemed to slow.

At the far end of the stables, he stopped, lifted the latch and pushed one half of the double door open. There he paused, his stout body silhouetted against the gray light from the courtyard. As she drew closer, Catlyn could hear his raspy breathing and see why he hesitated.

The sally port was open.

Catlyn froze. Sweet Mary, what if Hakon spotted them?

A figure brushed by Catlyn, tackled Roland and carried him to the ground. Dust and straw flew into the air, mingling with Roland's grunt of pain and another's whispered curses.

"Bloody idiot!" Dallas crawled off his gasping victim, grabbed him by the heel and dragged him inside. "Get the door, lass," he hissed. "Quiet as you can."

"Who the hell was that?" Ross growled under his breath as the stable door closed. He quickly looked to the gate just as Hakon stepped in, holding Margot before him like a shield. Likely his view of the stables was obstructed by the barracks in whose shadows Ross was lurking. And by the darkness. Ross had extinguished the torches that usually burned in the courtyard.

Ross glanced at the stables again. If Mathew had defied his orders and come to help he'd— He felt something move behind. Dirk in hand, braced to fight, he whirled.

"Easy." Eoin edged along the building.

"What are you doing here?"

"It seemed to me you could use some help and it should come from a Boyd."

Ross nodded in grudging respect. "Once Wesley and Margot have gotten away, I will go up on the roof to light the fuse."

"How long will it take to burn down?"

"A quarter hour at least, Dallas figures." It was long,

fashioned from the ones in the stills' useless powder barrels.

"Where do you think the Fergussons will be by then?"

Ross shrugged. "I hope Hakon does not have time to realize the keep is deserted and send men searching for our people."

"I hope he is inside when it burns," Eoin said fiercely. "He deserves to die, and it is fitting he meet his end in the tower he murdered and schemed to wrest from us."

"It would, indeed, but I do not care if justice is served, so long as Catlyn and the rest are free and unharmed."

"Amen to that. What can I do?" Eoin asked.

"Work your way back to the stables and make certain whoever was there a moment ago leaves."

Eoin nodded and melted away into the shadows.

Ross turned his attention back to the gatehouse. More of Hakon's men had entered and were fanning out across the courtyard. The darkness worked against him, too, for he could see only shapes and naked swords glinting in the gloom. Hakon was identifiable by his light hair and the girl he held before him. The slight figure on her other side must be Wesley. As they came closer, Ross heard one or both of them sobbing softly.

"Do we take the barracks?" a Fergusson muttered.

"Nay. We do not want to risk rousing the keep." Hakon's teeth shone as he grinned. "Ye were right, lad, they are stupid as sheep, with no fighting sense at all."

"Please, let us sit down," Wesley whined. "Margot's fair fainting from the pain and the fear."

Hakon scowled. "Not yet." To his men, he gave orders to post guards outside the barracks. "Guthrie, take the stables."

"But Pa," Guthrie grumbled.

Hakon backhanded him. "Do it...and quietly, else there'll be no women and no whiskey."

Ross sent up a silent prayer that Eoin and whoever had been in the stables were safely away.

Wesley went another few steps, then whimpered. "I've gotten ye in, I've told ye where the distillery is, please…"

"Sniveling coward," Hakon grumbled. "Go back and sit by the gatehouse, then."

Ross breathed a sigh of relief as he watched the young couple totter across the courtyard. It was short-lived.

"Go after them," Hakon ordered. "Make certain they do not betray us."

Ross hesitated only an instant, weighing the risks, then he drew his sword and stepped from hiding. Dressed all in black, the nasal of his helmet concealing his features, he should look no different from the Fergussons skulking about. Despite the urgency clawing at him, Ross walked slowly after the assassin. He reached the gate just as Wesley opened the sally port.

"Ach, Hakon was right not to trust ye," the Fergusson growled, lifting his sword.

Wesley turned and shoved Margot behind him, one hand thrown up to ward off the blow.

It never fell.

Ross's sword cut swift and true, piercing leather armor and bone. With a soft gurgle, the man pitched sideways.

"Oh, my lord," Wesley gasped. "I was never so glad—"

"Get out of here," Ross whispered. He watched till they were through the gate, then slipped into the dense shadows cast by the wall. One goal accomplished, one more and he could leave.

Across the courtyard, he saw the Fergussons mount the steps to the keep. One by one, the dark shapes disappeared inside. It was time.

Ross began working his way toward the rear of the distillery. He'd left a rope dangling from the gutter two stories up, ready for his climb to the roof. He was a few steps from the tower when the stable door opened and a stout figure burst out.

"Bastards! Foul devils!" It was Roland's voice, high and keening in the stillness.

The Fergussons on guard outside the stable converged on him as Ross watched helplessly. The flash of steel was followed by a cry of pain. Then all was silent again.

"Oh, God." Catlyn buried her face in Eoin's tunic. "How did Roland get away?"

"I do not know." He sounded as heartsick as she felt.

"Quick, out the back," Dallas whispered. He sprinted the length of the stables and eased the door open a crack.

Catlyn forced herself to follow, grateful for the arm Eoin kept around her. The shock of seeing Roland murdered had robbed her limbs of what little strength they'd had.

Behind them, the hinges of the door creaked.

"Search inside," a coarse voice hissed. "Where there's one, there may be more."

"Run, Catlyn," Eoin whispered. He gave her a little shove as he spun around to face this new challenge. "Come get me, you bastards," he cried.

"Dod, silence him or he'll rouse the keep."

Catlyn stumbled toward the rear door, expecting at any moment to feel the bite of cold steel in her back. Instead, she heard the grating of swords, the rasp of heavy breathing.

She reached the door safely but could not resist turning around to see how Eoin fared.

Three, or was it four men writhed and danced, their swords flashing even in the dimness. Sweet Mary, how could Eoin hope to prevail against so many?

Shivering, she pushed the door open. "Dallas? Eoin is—"

Hard hands grabbed her from behind, pulling her against a chest as solid as rock. Her captor stank of ale and sweat.

Catlyn instinctively fought. She drove her heels into his legs and clawed at the hands that bound her.

"Why, it's a lass. And a feisty one at that." He loosened his hold long enough to deal a stinging blow to the cheek.

Pain exploded in her head. Catlyn whimpered and went limp in his grasp, unable to protest when he spun her about. Dazed, she glanced up at the man who held her and nearly fainted.

There was no mistaking Guthrie Fergusson's evil leer. "Da said I was to leave ye alone, Catlyn Boyd, but how can I?" He took her mouth in a kiss so vile, so brutal it made her gag.

It was a prelude of the horror to come, that she knew, and everything inside her revolted. With her last bit of strength, she bit down on his marauding tongue.

Guthrie howled and lifted his head. Blood flowed from his mouth. Terrible vengeance contorted his face. "Damn, ye'll pay—"

A roar of outrage cut him off. Strong hands tore Catlyn from Guthrie's grasp and shoved her to safety.

Ross. He had come. Somehow he had known to come.

A length of steel shimmered in the half-light then disappeared into Guthrie's midsection. A guttural groan rose from his chest. Hands clutching at the haft of the dirk, he bent double then toppled over. The ground shuddered as he landed.

"Sweet Mary." Catlyn threw herself at Ross.

"What the hell are you doing here?" he growled, hugging her so tightly she could barely reply.

"Are you all right?" asked the hovering Dallas.

Catlyn shivered. "Aye, Guthrie…"

"Is dead or like to die soon," Ross muttered.

"Who are the men fighting yonder?" asked Dallas.

Dimly Catlyn heard the clash of steel and remembered. "Eoin," she managed to say. "Hurry."

Ross nodded, gave her a hard kiss then pushed her toward Dallas. "Get her out of here. Use the west wall. The bastards have not gotten that far." He sprinted into the darkened stable.

Dallas tried to draw Catlyn away, but she would not budge till she had seen Ross dispatch the two men Eoin had been struggling to keep at bay. His agility with the sword and economy of motion were breathtaking. She carried the memory of his skill with her to the west wall and down, certain that Ross and Eoin would follow directly.

She and Dallas joined the other refugees huddling in the woods. Still there was no sign of Ross. The fear that he had stayed behind to save the distillery haunted her. If some harm came to him over this, she would blame herself.

"Where is everyone?" Hakon murmured.

Murdo raised the torch he held, letting the light play over the empty hall. "I begin to think that lad played ye false."

"Aye. He must have warned his clan." Hakon felt better about having Wesley and the lass killed.

"They could not have got past us," Murdo said. "If that lad is any example, we'll find the lot cowering under their beds."

"I cannot imagine Ross Sutherland hiding. More likely, he has organized an ambush. If they be in the stables, Guthrie will get them when they come out. Take ten men and see what ye can find upstairs while I look for the stills."

Hakon smelled the whiskey before he found the double doors Wesley had described. Motioning Dull Dickie to precede him, Hakon cautiously entered. A door to the left stood open. He sent Georas to see what lay beyond.

"Well, look here," Dickie exclaimed from the next chamber.

Hakon hurried through the doorway, lifted his torch and gaped. Row and row of whiskey kegs.

"There's more here than all of us have fingers and toes." Dickie walked off between the rows, goggle-eyed as a bairn in a bakeshop. "Wait'll Guthrie sees this."

"It's not for drinking," Hakon warned. "This whiskey'll fetch us a fortune in Doune or Stirling. Might even get more for it in Edinburgh.'' His palms fairly itched at the thought.

Georas hastened in, skidded to a halt and turned in a slow circle. The air whistled through what was left of his teeth. ''Tis like we died and went to heaven.''

''It's not for drinking. What did ye find below.''

Georas collected himself enough to report the stills were down there. ''Four rooms. Biggest mash tuns ye've ever seen. But these Boyds are wasteful folk. The floor's awash with whiskey.''

''Never mind that. What of the black powder?''

''Twas a ruse. There's two casks beside each still right enough, but they are full of dirt.''

Hakon spat a long string of curses. ''To think I could have taken this place anytime I wanted.''

''Aye, but it's ours now.'' Georas sighed. ''All that lovely whiskey. Can we split a wee keg to celebrate taking the keep?''

''Not till we know where the Boyds and Sutherlands are.'' The queasiness in Hakon's gut returned. ''This was too damned easy.''

Dickie bobbed his head. ''Easy's good.''

''Not always.'' Hakon stroked his chin and stared at the beautiful kegs. His now. He wanted to line them up and count them, see what he had. ''The place is too quiet.'' The knowledge that an ambush could await him just beyond the light of his torch sent a chill down Hakon's spine. ''Georas, get some men and search these rooms. Bid them bring a great many torches. I want this place lit up so there's nary a dark corner to hide in.''

Georas glanced fearfully about, then dashed off.

''Ye've sharp eyes, Dickie,'' Hakon said. ''Go up and walk the outer walls. See if ye find any sign they escaped that way.''

''Why do we need 'em if we've got the whiskey?''

''We need them to make more whiskey, ye daft fool.

Now get along. And while ye're at it, tell Murdo to search the barracks and Guthrie the stable. I mistrust this—''

"Hakon!" Georas streaked into the chamber, his eyes wild. "Guthrie's been attacked."

"Dod." Hakon's knees went weak. "He's not dead?"

"Nay, but he's sore hurt. They've put him in the hall. He's...he's asking for ye."

Hakon was already on his way, their quarrel of yesterday weighing heavy on his soul.

The slamming of a door echoed up the chimney, cutting off Hakon's voice as he asked after Guthrie. Damn, why had Guthrie survived when so many others were dead?

Ross groaned and leaned against the cool stone. He had just extinguished the wee lantern he'd used to light the fuse. A quarter hour, maybe longer, before the fuse burned down to the stills. And who knew how long it would take the whiskey to catch and the fire to spread. Until it did, there would be nothing to divert the man sent to explore the wall walks.

Ross's gut clenched. He tried not to fear for Catlyn, out there somewhere fleeing for her life. Dallas would get her to the woods. But if Hakon discovered where they'd gone and—

Ross killed the thought aborning. Traveling that path would drive him mad. He had to believe she was safe for the moment and concentrate on keeping the Fergussons busy.

His jaw tight, Ross slid down the rope and hurried to where he'd left Eoin. He eased open the door to the smoke-house and was met by the point of a dirk. "Not dead yet?" he whispered.

"Nay." Eoin's chuckle was tight and agonized.

"Let me get you away," Ross said again.

"It would take valuable time, and I can't go far on this leg." He had taken a vicious blow to the thigh and lost considerable blood. "The fuse?"

"Lit." Ross felt his way around the pitch-black hut and hunkered down to tell his unexpected ally what he'd heard. "I need to start a fire now. The rushes on the floor in the great hall should burn quickly if I can get close enough."

"A pot of grease from the kitchen would burn hot and spread the fire," said Eoin. "You could stand in the doorway, fling the grease and throw a torch after it. Let me go."

"Nay." Ross fumbled in the dark, found Eoin's hand and clasped it. "Your suggestion is a good one, but you'd never get away with that leg of yours. Bide here. I'll be back."

"Ross," Eoin whispered, stopping him at the door. "I was wrong about you. Wrong to question your honor and your devotion to our cause."

"And I was wrong about you, too, my friend. When this is over, we will lift a cup to our pigheadedness."

Eoin's wry chuckle followed Ross out into the cool air. The soft glow over the eastern mountains warned dawn drew nigh and with it the end of the concealing dark.

The kitchen was only a few yards from the smokehouse. Warily Ross entered the low building. Foraging Fergussons had been here, tossing things about in their search for food, but the grease pots were untouched by the oven. He took one that had a cover and a torch from beside the huge hearth. As he slipped back outside, he heard men searching the stables across the bailey for hideaways.

The knowledge that time was fast running out sent Ross scurrying along the wall toward the keep, careful to stay in the shadows. At the steps he paused, hunched his shoulders and mounted them with a confident stride. Mercifully, he encountered no one, and the entryway was likewise empty. All the Fergussons must be in the hall. He could hear their angry voices drifting down the short corridor that led to the central chamber.

Ross traversed the corridor in a few quick strides, flattened himself along the wall and peered inside.

Burning torches rimmed the room, flickering over Hakon's furious, frightened face and the anguished one of the man lying on the floor before the empty hearth.

Guthrie still lived, but he writhed in pain, clutching at his father's arm and begging for relief.

Ross wondered if it was unchristian to feel no remorse, no pity. Instead, it seemed to him fitting that Guthrie should suffer a measure of the hell he had inflicted on others.

"Find him!" Hakon cried. "Find Ross Sutherland! Find them all and bring them to me. But I want him alive!" He bellowed that final word, his grim features promising retribution.

The Fergussons moved to obey.

Ross stepped into the doorway. "I am here, but you will not take me or mine." He flung the pot of grease into the rushes, seized the lighted torch from beside the door and tossed it into the room. The grease caught and flared up with a great roar. Spreading quicker than lightning, the flames filled the doorway and drove Ross back. Through the rolling plumes of smoke, he saw a red-orange river flow across the floor of the hall, devouring benches and tables and sending men fleeing for their lives.

"Put it out!" someone called, the voice nearly drowned by the song of the hungry fire.

Ross backed away from the conflagration, then fled down the corridor to the entryway. He could feel the heat on his back, following him. Just as he reached the top of the stairs, there was a new sound, a mighty rumble that seemed to come from the bowels of the earth. The stone steps shook beneath his feet.

The fuse had ignited the whiskey.

Ross vaulted down the stairs, gut tight with dread. Any moment he expected fire to shoot out from the windows. Instead, a tremendous explosion shattered the night.

Black powder, was his first thought, his only thought, before the wave of hot, ash-filled air picked up and hurtled him across the courtyard.

Ross hit hard, and the world went dark.

When Ross regained his senses, it was light, he hurt all over and rain fell on his face. Moaning, he moistened his parched lips and tasted salt.

"Ross?" Catlyn leaned over him, her eyes frightened, tears running down her sooty face. "You are alive."

"I must be. I hurt too badly to be dead." He raised his hand to touch her face, and white-hot pain lanced up the arm.

"Lie still. You have burns on your arm and a gash on your shoulder from a falling rock."

"The keep?" He tried to lift his head, but the pain forced him to lay it back down.

"Gone." Her face was a mask of anguish, the starkness of her eyes underscored by mauve shadows. "The distillery, too."

"It cannot be." Ross did raise his head then, teeth clenched against the pain. It was true. The once-mighty keep had been reduced to a pile of smoldering rubble. Where the distillery tower had stood there was nothing. Moaning softly, he slumped back and reached for her hand. It was icy cold and limp, unresponsive to the pressure of his. "I am so sorry."

"It does not matter. Our people are safe, except for Roland and Eoin is likely to live. That is what is important."

Nay, there were other things, too. "Hakon?" he asked.

"Dead, and Guthrie along with him. Only the few Fergussons who were in the bailey survived, and they have fled." Her eyes did not meet his, and her voice was stiff, impersonal, as though relating events that had happened to someone else.

He knew Kennecraig did matter, and he died a little inside, for her. For them. "I am sorry," he said again. "I did not mean for this to happen."

"But you planned this, didn't you?" she asked coolly.

"A fire was what I planned, not this...this—"

"It does not matter."

Ross wanted to shake her. He wanted to pull her into his arms and comfort her. But he feared she would not accept even that from him. *Dieu,* had he won the battle and lost her love? "Will you find Mat? We must make plans to go home to Stratheas."

"This was my home," she whispered. "But I will fetch him."

Chapter Twenty

Stratheas Tower

Michaelmas, the twenty-ninth of September, dawned clear and cool. Settlement Day, the time when folk came to pay their rent and debtors to clear their accounts.

Ross had a large debt to settle and no idea whether or not his tribute would be accepted. Sighing, he crossed the drawbridge and walked toward the solitary figure sitting beside the loch that surrounded the fortress's thick walls.

How forlorn Catlyn looked, perched on a rock, idly tossing stones into the water. How remote and lifeless she had been in the weeks since the fall of Kennecraig. Ross had gotten her away from the smoldering ruin as quickly as possible, thinking to spare her more grief. For five days their sad little cavalcade had straggled through the Highlands. A scant league from Edin Valley, they had been met by his father and half of Clan Sutherland marching out to rescue them. Their help would likely have come too late to save Kennecraig, but Ross had been touched by his father's support. And his forgiveness.

Equally heartwarming had been the swiftness with which his family had rallied around the weary, battered Boyds. Ross knew Catlyn was as grateful as her clansmen for this outpouring of support but while they were carving out new lives for themselves, she had seemed to retreat into herself.

Ross's heart quailed. What if his gift did not lift her spirits? What if she never regained that vitality, that zeal that had drawn him to her? He would still love her, but it was hard to be wed to a woman who only responded to him in bed. Grateful as he was that she still desired him, Ross wanted more for both of them. He wanted his Catlyn back, dammit, and in these few weeks since their return, he had worked like a man possessed to create what he hoped would please her.

"I thought I'd find you here," he murmured.

She looked up and smiled vaguely. "It's a pleasant spot."

"Aye." Ross surveyed his domain, wondering, as he had often since returning, how he could have turned his back on all this.

Set high in the narrow glen between two craggy mountains, the ancient stone fortress guarded the north end of Edin Valley even more securely than did the rocky pass at the south. Surrounded by high walls, the keep's twin towers were unassailable. Sheer cliffs guarded their backs, and only a wee path wound up to the drawbridge from the floor of the verdant valley. The magnificent fort was dwarfed by the mighty waterfall to its left. The great gush of water plunged some one hundred fifty feet from the mountain peaks that fostered it to the loch at Stratheas's base. "Is it the mountains you like?"

"I suppose," Catlyn said. "They remind me of home."

This is your home now. But he began to despair of making her see that. His mother and Lady Jeannie had both said it would take time for her to adjust. He had been patient and gentle and understanding, but every day he feared a bit more of her slipped away. Hunkering down beside her, he asked the question he had avoided for weeks. "Do you want to go back to Kennecraig?"

Her eyes widened. Hope flickered and a longing that tore

at him. Then the light went out. She shook her head. "There is nothing to go back to and seeing would only make me feel worse."

Ross wondered if that was possible. "The sentries have spotted my family coming up the road." They would be celebrating Michaelmas at Stratheas because Ross's tribute to Catlyn could not be moved elsewhere.

"So soon?" She stood. "I must see if all is ready—"

"Dora will have done that. There is nothing you must do but look beautiful." He rose, letting his eyes travel appreciatively over the gown her mother had made. The crimson velvet brought out the gold in her hair and turned her skin the color of new cream. "Which for you is easy."

"I do want to look nice for them. They have been kind to us. It was good of your father to see Wesley and Margot to Doune himself. Your mother has been a friend to mine, and your sister is…" A ghost of a smile crossed her face. Ella alone seemed able to pierce Catlyn's sadness. Perhaps because she refused to be shut out. "She is so lively and full of life."

"Pesky, you mean."

Catlyn's smile grew. "I like Ella."

"And she likes you. They all do. But I—" Ross dipped his head and kissed her "—love you."

"I love you, too. Please never doubt that." Catlyn wrapped her arms around his neck and kissed him with all the longing pent up inside her. The hungry growl that rumbled through his chest as he matched her urgency set her blood afire. It seemed the only time she felt alive was when they were together like this. Needing more, she twisted against him.

"Catlyn." Ross lifted his head and stared down at her, breath raspy, eyes glittering with suppressed passion. "Easy, love. I'd not start something we must finish in haste. Tonight we will have all the time we want to savor each other." He let the promise hang temptingly in the air.

She smiled, arching her hips into the proof of his desire.

"Aye, tonight will be special." More so than he realized, she thought, hugging the secret in her heart.

"What do you mean?"

"Oh, nothing." She ducked her head to hide her eyes, for he was uncannily adept at reading her thoughts.

"Have we come too early?" asked a merry voice.

"Ella!" Catlyn turned in Ross's embrace, grateful for the interruption. "You are always well come."

"And sometimes more so than others," said the perceptive lass. Beside Ross's red-haired imp of a sister rode her parents. Lady Laurel had the bright hair and irrepressible temperament she had passed on to Ella, along with a reputed gift for seeing into the future. Lord Kieran looked more like Ross's older brother than his sire, only the few lines in his face and the silver hair at his temples to mark the passage of years.

"I hope you are ready for the invasion, my dears," Laurel said. "Behind us ride a host of Sutherlands, MacLellans and Boyds that will fill even Stratheas's great hall to bursting."

Catlyn nodded. "Which is why my wise mother did suggest we set the trestle tables in the courtyard."

"Excellent. If the guests become too rowdy, you can always lock them out of the keep," said Kieran the warrior.

"Lift Catlyn up so she can ride up with me," Ella said. "I've something to tell her before the festivities start." She waited till they were out of earshot to ask, "Does he suspect?"

"I do not think so." Catlyn shivered, excitement mingling with anxiety.

"You will never guess what I saw in the candle flame last night," Ella said.

"Your latest true love?" Catlyn teased.

"You will not laugh when you hear."

Indeed, Catlyn did not. Her eyes rounded, and she gasped in surprise. How would Ross take this news? was her first worry.

* * *

"Does she suspect?" Kieran asked as they followed the ladies up the path to the keep.

"Nay, she is oblivious to much of what goes on at Stratheas," Ross replied with brutal honesty.

"Oh, my dear, I am so sorry," his mother said.

"I, too." Ross walked beside his father, leading his mother's mare. "If only I'd found a way to save Kennecraig."

"It is not only the loss of the keep. She has had one tragedy after another. Such wounds take time to heal."

Kieran put an arm around him. "Your mother has the right of it, as usual. I have seen this in men who have been too long at war. Losing your comrades one by one bruises the spirit."

Ross nodded, grateful for their support and understanding. "I think her spirit is adrift, without purpose."

"Then your gift to her should provide a cure."

"I pray God it will."

"And what of you. Are you content to bide here?" his father asked. "Or will you ride off at the first hint of adventure?"

"Nay, I've had my fill of such." He told them of the message he'd received from his uncle. "Another plot to overthrow the king. I resisted temptation and sent Dallas in my place. I've challenges enough here. And I am content beyond measure. Or I would be if Catlyn were happy, too."

"Ella is right then, Kieran. Our Lion is finally tamed."

"I hope I am not so dull as that, Mama. Only well matched."

"Ross! Good morrow." Eoin approached with Laurel's aunt, Nesta and Rhys ap Owain, her Welsh-born husband. Many of the Boyds had been boarded with Sutherland families till homes could be built for them. Eoin had been placed in her care because his wounds were so severe. Behind them came what looked like every man, woman and bairn in Edin Valley.

"Eoin, 'tis good to see you sitting a horse," Ross said.

"Indeed. Praise be to God for sparing my life and my leg."

Ross thought Nesta's healing skills had actually saved Eoin's leg. But his brush with death had brought Eoin closer to God. His hours of convalescence had been spent in meditation and discussion of spiritual matters with Father Micheil.

Ross was just grateful Eoin had given up on courting his wife. As they rode into the courtyard, he looked for Catlyn and found her deep in whispered discussion with Ella. Whatever had his sister said to make Catlyn look so pale? He dismounted and headed for her, but was cut off by Adair's hale greeting. Then Lady Jeannie needed to speak with him and so it went.

Impatience clawing at him, Ross played the dutiful host. He introduced Catlyn to the few relatives of his she had not met, and he greeted the Boyds who had been boarding with his kin. Finally he could stand it no longer. "Let us begin, Papa."

Kieran nodded and shouted for silence. When he had it, he raised his cup. "I bid you good Michaelmas. May every debt that is outstanding be satisfactorily met this day."

A cheer went up; the cups were drained.

Father Micheil took his place at one of the tables, his ledger book open and ready. Each debtor approached him in turn, rendered payment and made his mark in the book.

When the last man in line had done his duty, Ross turned to Catlyn. "Catlyn, I—"

"A moment." Eoin hobbled through the crowd and came to stand before Catlyn. "There is a debt I owe."

"What?" Catlyn asked warily, shrinking back against Ross.

"In as much as I do owe Almighty God for my life, I would dedicate what remains of it to his service. By your leave, and with Father Micheil's blessing, I go tomorrow to Melrose Abbey."

Cries of amazement drifted through the assembly.

"Eoin, a priest? I—I cannot believe it," whispered Dora.

Chuckling, Mathew cuddled her close. "The Lord does truly work in mysterious ways, my new-made wife." Three weeks handfasted and they still walked about as though joined at the hip.

Ross hid a smile. "We wish you well in your new calling."

Eoin looked at Catlyn, his expression serene for the first time in memory. "Though I did rail against fate when I lost you, things turned out for the best. For both of us. You have found a man who loves you as you deserve. I have found my true path."

"I am so glad for you, my friend," Catlyn said. For he was that. Her friend. "We will miss you." She felt Ross's hand on her back, offering silent support. *It is time,* she thought. *Time to try and heal this breach I have caused between us.* "Ross..."

"Catlyn," he said. "There is a debt I must pay to you."

"You? But I—" Catlyn looked to where her mother stood with Adair, Ross's parents and sister.

"Do as Ross asks, my dear," her mother said gently. "It is fitting we do this first."

"What?" Catlyn asked. No one answered, but it was plain they shared some secret.

"Will you not trust me a little?" Ross asked.

"Aye." Catlyn gave him her hand, surprised to find his cold and slick. He is afraid? Of what? His apprehension fed hers as he led her around the side of the keep to a double door made of wood and banded with metal. "What is this place?"

"It was once the old byre. When my ancestors first came here, they kept their cattle in here." Ross took a deep breath and flung open the doors. "Come." He led her into a long, low room. A lantern burned on the table in its center, sending licks of light over row after row of empty shelves. "Just through here." He pulled open another door and drew her with him.

As Catlyn stepped over the threshold, she was struck by something so unexpected it stopped her in her tracks.

The smell of whiskey. So slight a thing, yet it made her heart ache and tears well in her eyes. She looked up at Ross and found him watching her, his eyes shimmering with emotion: anxiety, love and desperation. "What is it? Did your ancestors also make whiskey here?"

"Nay, but I have hopes my descendants will." He put an arm around her shoulders and gently turned her. "What do you see?"

More shelves. Filled with kegs. The kegs bore small, square labels. Swept by a sense of déjà vu, she swayed against Ross. "It is a dream. I will wake and find I've been dreaming again."

"Nay, love." His voice was thick. "Reach out…touch them."

She did, her fingers trembling as they traced the familiar black letters. Her father's handwriting. "It…it is the ten-year. But how?"

"Later. Later I'll tell you how it came here, but there is more I'd have you see." He herded her past the shelves, through a massive door and down six stone steps to fling open yet another door. In the center of the room a great iron pot crouched over an empty fire pit. Coils of metal tubing sprouted from its top and coiled down into a collection jar. "It is but the first of many, I intend to—"

"What is it?" she asked, scarcely able to believe her eyes.

"A mash tun, or so I'd hope." He sounded worried. "I followed the drawings in your journal and Eoin and the lads from the distillery made some suggestions. I thought you might make the Finglas here, but—"

"Oh, Ross." Deep inside her, something tight and painful cracked open. Catlyn buried her face in his chest and let the tears come. She cried as she had not been able to in months, in years. She cried for her brother, gone before his time, for her father, who had not lived to see his dream come true. She cried for the loss of Kennecraig and the Finglas Distillery.

Dimly she was aware of Ross supporting her, as he had from the beginning, his hands strong yet gentle. His words of love were soft but earnest. "If it takes our whole lives, we will make the Finglas the finest distillery in Scotland. Please do not give up. I know nothing can bring back Kennecraig, but I will do anything to make reparation for what I had to destroy. Please try at least. Please let it be enough."

The suffering in his voice pierced her own sorrow as nothing else could have. He was right. They could begin again. It would be hard work, but he was giving her both the means and the support to carry on her family heritage.

She sniffed and raised her head. His face was blurred by her tears, but his dedication was still plain. "Oh, Ross, this is the most wonderful thing you have done. I—"

"Ross, is she all right?" her mother called.

Catlyn peered around him and saw the doorway was filled with anxious faces. Her mother. Ross's parents. Beyond them were Mathew and Dora, Ella, Adair, Eoin and Father Micheil.

Father Micheil. Her own Michaelmas plans.

Catlyn peered up at Ross through spiky wet lashes. Later, when they were private she would tell him how much his deed meant. Now... "There is one thing you could do for me."

"Name it," he said fervently.

"Marry me."

"What? But we are—"

"Handfasted. I would be wed." It was the only way she had been able to think of to prove her love had not dwindled. "Father Micheil has agreed to marry us today, if you are willing to take a wife with red-rimmed eyes and tear-stained cheeks."

"Willing?" His eyes glowed and his smile lit every corner of the new still room. "I would be honored to wed you, my lady."

And so they were joined, the lord of Stratheas and his lady, not in the chapel attached to the keep. Or in the courtyard as Catlyn had planned. At Ross's insistence, Father Micheil conducted the ceremony in the settling room. Afterward, they returned to the tables in the grassy bailey to eat the Michaelmas feast Dora and Lady Jeannie had prepared. Toast after toast was drunk to the happiness of the newly wedded couple.

Ross began to fear the celebrations would last into the night. And he had other plans. "Make a pretext of visiting the privy and meet me in the distillery," he whispered in her ear.

"The distillery?" Catlyn was disappointed they were not bound for their bedchamber, but did as he asked. She arrived to find him already waiting at the entrance.

"Come in quick before they see us." He shut the door, hustled her through the settling room and into a tiny chamber. Its walls were lined with wooden shelves; a thick carpet covered the floor. The only other furnishings were a sturdy table and two chairs. "I thought you might use this as a counting room. This table is not as old as the one at Kennecraig, but it has been in my family for generations."

On the mellow oak surface lay her journal and the tasting chalice. Catlyn reverently touched each in turn. "I thought these were all I had left of the Finglas. You restored so much to me." Not just the kegs of whiskey but her hope for the future. "You have worked so hard."

"I did not do it alone. Everyone had a part. High Harry and some of the lads went back for the Finglas." At dinner, he had told her about the heroic efforts to transfer the whiskey from the cellars to the granary. "If anything is not done right or not to your liking, you've only to say."

She shook her head. "I am still trying to take it all in."

"And I am dazed by our wedding." He stepped closer,

so his boots brushed the hem of her gown. "When did you decide?"

"The idea came to me a week ago." And in light of Ella's news, she was very glad it had. "I—I know you have been castigating yourself for the destruction of Kennecraig. I wanted to do something to prove I love you and do not blame you."

"Sweetheart." He drew her into his arms and kissed her tenderly. "I was so afraid I was losing you."

"And that is why you built the distillery?"

"I hoped, I prayed, it would bring you back to life."

Catlyn nodded. "As I prayed when we heard the explosion and I feared you had died. When we were searching for you, I did not care that Kennecraig was gone, so long as you lived. And even after you brought us here, I was grateful we all had been spared. Yet my life seemed empty. Mama and Dora were busy setting with the keep. Adair was off seeing about homes for our people. But I had nothing to fill my hours or occupy my mind."

"You missed the distillery."

"More than I'd thought possible. But you knew."

"I hoped I had guessed correctly." He sighed and leaned his forehead against hers. "Welcome back, love, I have missed you."

"I have missed me, too." She wondered how to put into words all that he meant to her. Then their gazes locked, and she knew that once again, none were necessary. The intensity of her love was mirrored in his brilliant blue eyes.

He grinned suddenly. "Come upstairs with me."

"In time. There is something else I would do first." She laced her fingers behind his neck and stood on tiptoe to reach his mouth. The kiss was long, deep and rousing. They were both breathless by the time he lifted his head.

"Come upstairs while I can still walk," he murmured, nipping at her ear, her neck.

"What of the table?" she teased. "We could see if it is as, er, accommodating as my ancestor's table."

His smiled dimmed. "I do regret the loss of that table. I had hopes we might carry on the grand tradition started by your great-great-grandparents and conceive our babes where they had."

"Do not give up hope just yet."

"The table is gone."

"Aye, but it seems it served its purpose right well." She took his hand and laid it on her still-flat belly. "If Ella is right about what she saw in her vision last night, our bairns will be born in May, nine months after we…"

"Catlyn." The most beautiful smile spread across his face. "Oh, my love, I am so…" She marked the moment when her words sank in, for his eyes suddenly widened. "Babes?"

"Twin lads, or so Ella claims she saw. With your black hair and devilishly handsome blue eyes."

"I need to sit down." And so he did, pulling her onto his lap as he sank into the chair. "Twins, conceived that night."

"You did promise we'd make a babe, as I recall." She smiled tenderly. "And I have learned that you are ever a man whose deeds exceed his promises, Ross Lion Sutherland."

"I will try never to let you down again."

Catlyn knew of what he spoke. "You did not set out to destroy Kennecraig. Adair reasons it was the black powder Roland had dumped down the drains that caused the explosion."

"So he told me, too, but—"

"Shh. There has been too much sorrow and regret. Let us look forward not back." Her heart felt lighter than it had in years.

"Forward." He took her hand and linked their fingers together. "We will succeed. We will make the Finglas the finest whiskey in all of Scotland. And we will pass the knowledge of its making on to our children."

"Spoken like a Boyd." With her free hand, she cradled

his cheek and kissed him ardently. When he let her up for air, she added, "All I ask is that we be allowed to live here together and raise our children in peace."

Ross nodded but vowed to do everything in his power to see the distillery succeeded. Her happiness was his main concern. Which is why when she kissed him again and began to unlace his tunic, he let her have her way. If she preferred the table to their bed upstairs, so be it. He suspected it would always be so, for she was his mate. The other half of his soul, and what pleased her, pleased him.

In the sweet aftermath of their loving, while their hearts were just settling back to earth, he cradled her on his lap and whispered, "I do love you, Catlyn. You make me happier than I had ever dreamed possible."

"And I love you. More even than the Finglas."

Ross chuckled. "Now there is a declaration only a master distiller's husband could understand."

"But you do…and that is why I love you so."

Epilogue

Doune, ten years later

David Erskine hobbled out of his tavern and nailed the notice up beside the front door. When he had finished, he stood back, smoothed the parchment and read it again.

Hear ye! Hear ye!
Be it known to all and sundry that the Golden Thistle is proud to serve the finest whiskey in all of Scotland.
The Finglas Water
Distilled in Edin Valley by Clan Boyd, master distillers to His Majesty, King James I of Scotland.

Reverently David lifted a cup of the ten-year whiskey and sipped. He sighed as the mellow *uisge beatha* slid down his throat. It truly was the best he had ever tasted.

"Well, Thomas my old friend, they've done it. Catlyn and her canny husband have made yer dream come true. I always knew ye were right to have faith in her."

* * * * *

Harlequin is proud to introduce:

HEART OF THE WEST

...Where Every Man Has His Price!

Lost Springs Ranch was famous for turning young
mavericks into good men. Word that the ranch was in
financial trouble sent a herd of loyal bachelors
stampeding back to Wyoming to put themselves on the
auction block.

This is a brand-new 12-book continuity,
which includes some of Harlequin's
most talented authors.

Don't miss the first book,
Husband for Hire by Susan Wiggs.
It will be at your favorite retail outlet in July 1999.

HARLEQUIN®
Makes any time special ™

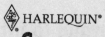

SUPERROMANCE

Due to popular reader demand,
Harlequin Superromance® is expanding
from 4 to 6 titles per month!

Starting May 1999, you can have more
of the kind of stories that you love!

- Longer,
  more complex
  plots
- Popular themes
- Lots of
  characters
- A great
  romance!

*Available May 1999
at your favorite retail outlet.*

Look us up on-line at: http://www.romance.net   HSR4T06